P9-DFR-271

The Building of Jalna

BOOKS BY

Mazo de la Roche

❋

THE BUILDING OF JALNA

YOUNG RENNY (JALNA—1906)

WHITEOAK HERITAGE

JALNA

WHITEOAKS OF JALNA

FINCH'S FORTUNE

THE MASTER OF JALNA

WHITEOAK HARVEST

WAKEFIELD'S COURSE

❋

LOW LIFE AND OTHER PLAYS

PORTRAIT OF A DOG

LARK ASCENDING

BESIDE A NORMAN TOWER

THE VERY HOUSE

GROWTH OF A MAN

THE SACRED BULLOCK AND OTHER STORIES

MAZO DE LA ROCHE

The Building of Jalna

BOSTON

Little, Brown and Company

1944

PRINTED IN THE UNITED STATES OF AMERICA

To

ST. JOHN AND LEONORA ERVINE

and

RACHE LOVAT DICKSON

In friendship
and remembering their
inscription in my copy of

SOPHIA

Contents

The Building of Jalna

I

In England

ADELINE thought that never, never in her life had she seen anything so beautiful as *The Bohemian Girl.* The romance of it transfigured her mind, as moonlight a stained-glass window. And the music! Words and tune possessed her, making her feel like one in a dream. As she hung on Philip's arm on the way out of Drury Lane the ground seemed unsubstantial beneath her feet, the crowd about her to be floating like herself.

She looked into his face to discover what was its expression. She had glimpsed her own, in one of the great gilt-framed mirrors, and had been well-pleased by its rapt expression. She half-expected to see Philip wearing the same look. But in truth he looked just as he had when they had entered the opera house. Pleased to be there, well-satisfied with himself and with her, glad to be back in London once more. She pressed his arm and his lips parted in a smile. Surely no man in all that throng had so fine, so manly a profile as Philip! Surely there was no other man with such well-set shoulders, such a flat back! He turned his head and looked at her. As he looked, his bright blue eyes widened a little in pride. He glanced about to see if others were noticing her beauty. They were, no doubt about that. Two gentlemen on her other side were noticing it more than was compatible with good taste. They were openly staring at her. She was aware of this, as was shown by her heightened color and the daring half-glance she bestowed on them, but she continued to smile at Philip. They were now near the outer door and it took all his skill to pilot her successfully through it, billowing as she was in a flounced taffeta crinoline. Small wonder those fellows stared, thought Philip. It was not often one saw a face so arresting as Adeline's. Was there another anywhere to equal it, he wondered. Her coloring alone made people turn their heads to look after her: the hair thick and waving, of the deepest auburn that could, in sunlight, flame to red; the skin of marble and roses, the changeful brown eyes with black lashes. But, if her coloring had been undistinguished, her proud and daring features, her arched brows, aquiline nose and mobile, laughing mouth would have warranted his fine favor.

There was a clatter of horses' hoofs on the cobbles. Private carriages were drawn up in a glittering row. Adeline looked longingly at these but she and Philip must wait for a cab. They pressed forward to the curb, his mind still occupied in guarding her crinoline. A street musician rose, as out of the gutter. He was gaunt and in rags but he could play. He humped his shoulder against the fiddle and his arm that wielded the bow moved violently, as though in desperation. No one but Adeline noticed him. Yet he was playing in desperation.

"Look, Philip!" she said, eagerly. "The poor man!" He looked and, frowning a little at the waste of time, resumed his scanning of the vehicles. She stiffened herself.

"Give him something!" she demanded.

Philip had found a four-wheeler. Now he determinedly pushed Adeline toward it. The driver scrambled down from his perch and threw open the door. Between the pushing of the crowd and the urging of Philip's hand she found herself forced inside. But the beggar had seen her look of compassion and now his gaunt figure appeared at the door. His eyes were imploring. Philip put his hand in his pocket and produced a shilling.

"God bless you, sir! God bless you, my lady!" The man kept reiterating his thanks. His face was ghastly in the light of the gas lamps.

The horses' feet clattered on the wet cobbles. Philip and Adeline turned to look triumphantly at each other. Both thought they had had their own way.

The crowded streets, the bright lights, were intoxicating to them after their years in India. She indeed had never known London, for

County Meath had been her home and Dublin the great city of her girlhood. She had danced her way through several seasons there but, in spite of her grace and beauty, she had not made the match her parents had hoped for. Her admirers had been well-born and all too attractive, but without sufficient means to set up an establishment. She had wasted good time in flirtations with them. Then her sister Judith, married to an officer stationed at Jalna, a garrison town in India, had invited Adeline to visit her and Adeline had gladly gone. She felt cramped in Ireland and she had quarreled with her father, who was even more high-tempered and domineering than herself. The cause of their quarrel was a legacy left her by a great-aunt. Her father had always been a favorite of this aunt and he had confidently looked forward to inheriting her fortune. It was not large, but in his present circumstances seemed munificent. Now he bitterly regretted that he had named a daughter after his aunt. That had been the mischief. That, and Adeline's blandishments!

In Judith's house she met Philip Whiteoak, an officer in the Hussars. He came of a family long established in Warwickshire. Indeed the Whiteoaks had lived on their estate for several centuries. They had looked up to no man, being of the opinion that they were as good as any and of more ancient lineage than most of the peers of the county. At one time they had possessed considerable fortune which had been handed down intact from father to son. They had been a family of few children but those of fine physique. Their affairs had prospered till the time of Philip's grandfather, who had become addicted to the vice of gambling, so prevalent in his day. He had heavily mortgaged the family estate and had at last been obliged to sell it. It was owing to the sound sense of Philip's father, his sober life as an unpretentious country gentleman, that Philip had been able to enter the Army and to have sufficient means for maintaining his position as an officer.

Philip and Adeline were fascinated by each other. After a few meetings they were passionately in love. Yet, beyond the fire and passion of their love, there was true metal. In the not infrequent dissensions of their married life they always knew they were made for each other, that no one else could possibly fill the other's place—or even approach that place. To Philip other women seemed simple, even shallow, as compared to Adeline. For him there was significance in her every gesture. The intimacy of their companionship never failed to exhilarate him. There was excitement in the thought that he could eventually control her, no matter what her defiance.

Adeline delighted in Philip's stalwart good looks, the clear freshness of his complexion which years in India had not succeeded in damaging, the ardent expression of his daring blue eyes, the boyish curve of his lips. Was there ever a better figure than his, she often wondered, so broad in the shoulders, yet hips narrow! She disliked hair on a man's face and allowed him no more than a finger's breadth of golden whisker in front of each ear. If he had more, she would refuse to kiss him. But, far above his looks, she rejoiced in his power over her, his English reliability, the mystery of his silences, when she in her Celtic suppleness must reach out and draw him back to her.

Their wedding had never been equaled in the Indian military station. She had been twenty-two, he ten years older. He got along well with his men, who would do anything for him, but often there was a feeling of tension between him and his colonel. Philip was not the man to knuckle under with a good grace. He had an indestructible feeling that he was always in the right, and the fact that he generally was only made matters worse. When he opposed others Adeline was always on his side. When he opposed her she could see how wrong-headed and stubborn he could be.

Her sister Judith, two years older than herself, had advised her to order as magnificent a trousseau as possible from Dublin because, as she said, it would certainly be the last thing she would ever get out of her father. So the two had spent happy days in preparing lists for the guidance of Adeline's mother in shopping. The good-natured lady never had been able to deny her children anything and now she, in her turn, had spent happy weeks creating a bustle in the Dublin shops. What her daughter had not thought of, she did, and it took a formidable array of boxes to contain the trousseau. That trousseau created a sensation in Jalna. Dresses, with voluminous flounced skirts and wide pagoda sleeves, came billowing out of the boxes; a green velvet cape with bonnet and muff to match, all embroidered with a creamy foam of lace; a Scottish tartan cloak, lined with blue silk; ball dresses cut very low with tiny waists and trains ruffling like the wake of a ship; shawls with long golden fringe and lace mittens decorated in the same fashion. Adeline floated to the altar in a wedding gown like a silver cloud. Tissue paper strewed the bedrooms of Judith's bungalow when the boxes were opened and the treasures disclosed. For the time even Philip was unimportant.

The young pair settled down to lead as glittering an existence as the military station afforded. No entertainment was complete without them. They were so gay; their wine was the best; their horses and their clothes the handsomest in the station.

It had been a shock to them when they discovered that Adeline was going to have a child. They did not want children. They were sufficient to themselves, and not only that—children born in India were often delicate and always had to be sent home for their education. These partings with children were a melancholy side to Anglo-Indian life. Adeline was horrified at what she would have to go through. She felt as though she were the first woman in the world to face that ordeal. And it had been a great ordeal—a difficult birth and an aftermath of weakness and dejection. The infant did not thrive and filled the house with its wailing. What a change from their happy, carefree years!

A stay in the hills had done Adeline little good. It had seemed that she would sink into invalidism. All this anxiety affected Philip's temper. He had a violent quarrel with his colonel. He began to feel that the hand of fate was against him. He began also to feel a longing for a more open, less restricted life. His thoughts turned toward the New World. He began to be irked by the conventionalities of Army life. If he stayed in India he must get a transfer to another regiment, for the quarrel with his colonel was not of the sort to be patched up. He had an uncle, an officer stationed in Quebec who had written him letters overflowing with praise of the life there. Philip wondered if the Canadian climate would suit Adeline. He asked the opinion of the doctor, who declared that nowhere on earth would she find more bracing air or a climate better suited to her condition. When Philip spoke of this to Adeline he quite expected her to be repelled by the thought of such a change. To leave a life so full of color for the simplicity of the New World would surely be more than she could face. But Adeline surprised him by delighting in the prospect of the adventure. She threw her bare arms above her head (she was wearing one of the silk peignoirs she almost always wore now) and declared there was nothing on earth she would so much love to do as to go to Canada. She was tired of everything connected with India—tired of the gossip of the station, tired of the heat and the dust, tired of swarming natives and, most of all, tired of having less than her accustomed eager strength.

Even with Adeline's consent Philip hesitated to make the plunge. But while he hesitated his uncle died in Quebec, leaving him a considerable property there.

"Now it's all settled!" Adeline had cried. "Nothing can hinder us!"

So Philip sold his commission, his horses and polo ponies, and Adeline sold the furniture of the bungalow, keeping only certain things precious to her to remind her of India—the beautiful painted leather furniture of her bedroom, a brass-bound cabinet and chest, some silken embroidery, carved jade and ivory ornaments. With these she would make a show in Quebec. They set sail from Bombay with their infant daughter Augusta and the ayah who had cared for her since her birth. The ayah was terrified at the thought of crossing the great seas to the other side of the world but she so loved little Augusta that she was willing to go anywhere with her. The most important of the party, in his own opinion, was Adeline's parrot, an intelligent and healthy young bird, a fluent talker and brilliant of plumage. He was a contradiction to the belief that gray parrots are the best talkers for he enunciated clearly and had an ample though sometimes profane vocabulary. He loved only Adeline and permitted only her to caress him. She had named him Bonaparte. She had a sly admiration for the Little Corporal. She had an admiration for the French and she was married for many years to Philip before, under his influence, she became really loyal to the English Crown. Philip had nothing but scorn and dislike for Napoleon. His own father had been killed in the Battle of Waterloo and he himself born a few months later. He had no respect and little liking for the French. He called the parrot Boney for short and that in a tone of good-humored derision.

The journey from India to England had seemed endless. Yet on the whole it was not unpleasant. They were setting out toward a new life. There were a number of congenial people on board and among these the Whiteoaks were the most sought after. The weather was fair and Adeline's health improved during the voyage. But by the time they reached the Bay of Biscay, which was gray and wild, they yearned toward the shores of England. They had landed in Liverpool the week before Christmas.

With their child, the ayah, and a mountain of luggage they had made the long journey by stagecoach from Liverpool to the cathedral town of Penchester, in a southwestern county where Philip's only sister, Augusta, was anxiously awaiting them. For her the baby had been named. She was married to the Dean of the Cathedral, a man considerably older than herself, a bookworm and hater of change and confusion. They were a happy couple for Augusta spent her days in devotion to him and he gave her her own way in everything. She looked like Philip but was softer and less handsome. She had a happy nature and her one sorrow was her childlessness. She had looked forward eagerly to the coming of her little namesake but disappointment lay in store for her. Baby Augusta was so shy that she could hardly bear to go beyond her ayah's arms. And the ayah selfishly encouraged her in this. She wanted her charge to love no one but her. And she clung to the child with a fierce possessive love.

This was bitterly disappointing to Philip's sister. Still she hoped to overcome the little one's shrinking as the days went on. What she really had in mind was to keep the child with her when its parents went on to Quebec. She knew that she could persuade the Dean to let her do this. She had always wanted a little girl to love. To her, the baby's black hair and eyes, her sallow skin, were romantic and alluring.

"How do you suppose they came by her?" she asked her husband. "Philip, with his pink cheeks—Adeline, with her auburn hair and creamy complexion!"

"Better ask that Rajah she's always raving about," observed the Dean. "He might be able to tell you."

His wife looked at him in horror. In all their married life he had never before made such a ribald remark. And that about her own brother's wife!

"Well," said the Dean, in self-defense, "look at the magnificent ruby ring he gave her!"

"Frederick!" she cried, still more horrified. "You are not in earnest, are you?"

"Of course not," he answered, in a mollifying tone. "Can't you take a joke?" But he added—"Then why did the Rajah give her the ring? I can see that Philip didn't like it."

"The Rajah gave her the ring because she saved the life of his son. They were riding together when the boy's horse bolted. It was a spirited Arab steed and it became unmanageable."

The Dean gave what was nearer to a grin than a smile. "And Adeline was a beautiful Irish hussy and she caught the Arab steed and saved the Rajah's heir," he said.

"Yes." Augusta looked at him coldly.

"Was Philip there? Did he assist in the rescue?"

"No, I don't think he was there. Why?"

"Well, the Rajah might not have rewarded an upstanding British officer so handsomely."

"Frederick, I think you're horrid!" she exclaimed, and left him to his own sinister musings.

It was Adeline's idea to have their portraits painted while they were in England. They might never have another such opportunity. Certainly they would never be handsomer than they were at this time. Above all, she must have a real portrait—no mere daguerreotype would do—of Philip in all the glory of his uniform of an officer of Hussars. To the Hussars and to the Buffs the Whiteoak family had, in times past, supplied many a fine officer but never, in Adeline's mind, one so dashing, so noble-looking, as Philip.

The idea was agreeable to Philip too, though the amount he had to hand over to the artist was rather staggering. But his portraits were fashionable, especially among the military class. Not only could he make a uniform look as though it would step out of the frame; he could impart a commanding look to the most insignificant and dyspeptic officer. Where lady sitters were concerned he was at his best with flesh tints, ringlets, and shimmering fabrics. Probably his portraits of Philip and Adeline were the most successful of his career. It was a heartbreak to him that they were to be taken out of England before they could be exhibited at the Academy. He did, however, give a large party to show them in his studio, at which the young couple were present. This had been the night before they had seen *The Bohemian Girl.*

The idea of owning portraits of themselves in their prime had not been all that was in Adeline's mind when she suggested this extravagance. She knew that it would entail many weeks in London for the sittings and she was determined to have as pleasureful a time as possible while in England. There had been three visits to London. This was their last. To-morrow they were to return to the quiet cathedral town. Adeline threw herself into a stuffed velvet chair in the hotel bedroom and exclaimed dramatically:—

"I'm so transported I could die!"

"You feel too much," returned Philip. "It would be better if you took things coolly, as I do." He looked at her anxiously, then added: "You are quite pale. I shall ring for a glass of stout and some biscuits for you."

"No. Not stout! Champagne! Nothing so prosaic as stout after that divine opera. Oh, never shall I forget this night! Oh, the heavenly voice of Thaddeus! Oh, how sweet Arline was! Philip, can you remember any of the songs? We must buy the music! Try if you can sing 'I Dreamt That I Dwelt in Marble Halls'!"

"I couldn't possibly."

"Try 'Then You'll Remember Me.'"

"I couldn't," he returned doggedly.

"Then—'The Light of Other Days!' Do try that!"

"I couldn't—not to save my life."

She sprang up, letting her fur-trimmed evening wrap fall to the floor, and began to pace up and down the room. She had a passionate but not very musical voice and little idea of tune, but she managed to get the first bars of her favorite song from the opera.

"I dreamt that I dwelt in marble halls,
With vassals and serfs at my side—"

As she sang she raised her chin, showing the beauty of her long milk-white neck. She smiled triumphantly at Philip. Her voluminous light-blue taffeta crinoline swayed about her, in all its ruchings and narrow velvet edgings. Above her tiny waist her round breasts rose, supporting a mass of lace, caught by turquoise pins and little velvet flowers. Her shoulders glistened in lovely pallor in the candlelight. Just touching her neck her auburn curls descended from her heavy chignon. Philip saw her beauty but he saw also the thinness of her arms, the too vivid redness of her lips and brightness of her eyes. He rose and pulled the bell cord and, when a servant appeared, ordered the stout.

She had given up the song. Now the tune had quite eluded her but she found it hard to settle down. She drew back the dark red curtains and looked down into the street where the gas lamps made pools of light on the wet pavement and the cab horses clip-clopped past with draggled manes and rain-soaked harness. The mysterious lives of the people in the cabs filled her with a strange longing. She turned to Philip.

"We shall sometimes come back, shan't we?" she asked.

"Of course we shall. I'll engage to bring you back every second or third year. We are not going to bury ourselves in the wilds. And don't forget New York. We will visit it too."

She threw her arms about his neck and gave him a swift kiss.

"My angel," she said. "If I had to go to bed to-night with anyone but you, I'd throw myself out of that window."

"And quite properly," he observed.

They drew apart and stood in decorous attitudes as the manservant reappeared with the refreshments. He laid a snowy cloth on an oval, marble-topped table and then set out several bottles of stout, biscuits and cheese, a cold pigeon pie for Philip and a small bowl of hot beef extract for Adeline.

"How good it looks!" she exclaimed, when they were alone. "Do you know, I'm getting my appetite again! D'ye think I dare eat some of that cheddar cheese? I do love cheese!"

"What expressions you use! You love *me* and you love *cheese!* I suppose there's no difference in your affection."

She laughed. "You old silly!" Then she pressed her hands to her sides. "But really, Philip, you will have to unlace me before I attempt to eat or I shall have room for nothing but a biscuit."

As he helped her with the intricate fastenings of her dress, he said seriously—"I cannot help thinking that this tight lacing is all wrong. In fact the doctor on shipboard told me that it is responsible for many of the difficult births."

"Very well," she declared, "when we are in Canada I shall leave off my stays and go about like a sack tied in the middle. Picture me in the wilds! I am on a hunting expedition. I have just trapped or shot a deer, a beaver, or something of the sort. I am on my way home with my quarry slung over my shoulder. Suddenly I am conscious of some slight discomfort. I recall the fact that I am *enceinte*. Possibly my hour has come. I find a convenient spot beneath an olive tree—"

"They don't have 'em there."

"Very well. Any tree will do. I make myself comfortable. I give birth to the child, with scarcely a moan. I place it in my petticoat. I resume the burden of the deer or beaver on my back. I return home. I cast my quarry at your feet and my infant on your knee. 'By the way,' I remark, 'here's a son and heir for you!' "

"Egad! That's the way to do it." He struggled with the hooks and eyes. "There—my angel. Out you step!"

The blue taffeta fell in bright cascades to the floor but the crinoline still stood out about her lower half, above which her tiny waist appeared as a fragile support for bust and shoulders. Somehow he got her out of the crinoline, the petticoat, and the many-gored corset cover but he had a time of it with the corset lace, which had tied itself in a tight knot. His fair face was flushed and he had given vent to an oath or two before she stood released and graceful in her shift. He gave her an abrupt little push instead of the kiss she expected, and said:—

"Now, put on your peignoir and let's have something to eat."

He stood watching her with an air half-possessive, half-coaxing, while she drew on a violet velvet dressing gown and divested her wrists of her bracelets. As she seated herself at the table she gave a little laugh of complete satisfaction. Her eyes swept across the viands.

"How hungry I am!" she declared. "And how good everything looks! I must have some of that cheese. I adore it!"

"There you go again!" he said, cutting a wedge from the cheese for her. "You adore *food!* You adore *me!* What's the difference?"

"I said nothing whatever about adoring *you,*" she returned, putting her teeth into the cheese. She laughed like a greedy young girl. It was part of her charm, he thought, that she could sit there eating greedily and still look alluring. She appeared unself-conscious but her passionate love for him, her desire to express it, to put her nature beneath him, even while, in her femininity, she triumphed over him, made her slightest gesture, her half-glance, symbolic. He sat watching her, feeling that in some strange way the fact that she was eating greedily, that her arms were too thin, that her stays had been too tight, only increased her desirability.

At last she rose and came to him. My God, he thought, did ever a woman move as she moves! She can never grow old!

She came to him and sank into his arms. She lay along his body as though her will were to obliterate herself in him, willfully to become no more than a creature he had created by his passion. She tried to time her breathing with his, so that their two hearts should do even this in unison. He bent his face to hers, and their lips met. She turned her face swiftly away. Then, turning it again, with closed eyes, toward him, she kissed him in rapture.

But the next morning she felt a sadness in her. They were leaving London. When might she see it again? Perhaps never, with all the dangers of travel between. What would happen to them in the New World? What strange distant place lay awaiting them?

It was a journey of many hours from London to the cathedral town of Penchester. When Adeline alighted from the train she was very tired. Dark shadows made her eyes sombre. She looked ill. But the Dean's carriage was waiting to meet them, with its comfortable cushioned seats and its lamps shining bright in the dusk. The streets were quiet, so they bowled along easily. Soon the towering shape of the Cathedral rose against the luminous west. Its windows still held a glimmer from the sunken sun. It looked ethereal, yet as though it would last forever. Adeline leant forward to gaze at it through the carriage window. She wanted to imprint its image on her mind, to take with her to Quebec. She felt that not even the Dean understood and loved the Cathedral as she did. And the sweet little streets that clustered about it—so dim, so orderly, so melting into the tradition of the past!

And the Dean's house itself! Adeline wished she owned it as she descended from the carriage. It looked so sedate, so warm-colored, so welcoming. She might indeed have been the mistress, to judge by her luggage that cumbered the hall, her husband's voice that rapped out orders to the servants, her infant that made the echoes ring with its crying, her parrot which rent the air with erotic endearments when it heard her voice. Augusta and the Dean seemed mere nobodies in their own house. Adeline flew to the parrot, chained to its perch in the drawing-room.

"Boney, my sweet, I'm back!" she cried, advancing her lovely aquiline face to the bird's beak.

"Ah, Pearl of the Harem!" he screamed, in Hindu. "Dilkhoosa! Nur Mahal! Mera lal!" He nibbled her nostril. His dark tongue quivered against her lips.

"Where did he learn all that?" asked the Dean.

Adeline turned her bold gaze on him. "From the Rajah," she returned. "The Rajah who gave him to me."

"It hardly seems nice," said Augusta.

"It isn't," answered Adeline. "It's beautiful—and wicked and fascinating."

Philip broke in, "I say, Augusta, has our infant been howling ever since we left?"

His sister's face clouded. The Dean answered for her.

"She has indeed. As a matter of fact I could not find a single spot where I could write my sermons in peace—between baby and parrot." Then he added genially—"But it doesn't matter. It doesn't matter."

But it did matter. Philip knew very well that a dean requires more quiet than does a Hussar, and he was annoyed with his daughter. She was now almost a year old and ought surely to have a little sense. The first time he had her to himself he took her to task. Holding her in his strong hands, so that her sallow little face was on a level with his fresh-colored one, he said:—

"You young minx, don't you know which side your bread is buttered on? Here are your uncle and auntie, childless. Here are you—a baby girl—just what they want! You could stay here with them, at any rate till your mother and I are settled in Canada. If you behaved yourself they'd make you their heir. Now what I mean is, I want you to stop this howling every time your aunt looks at you. You are *not to cry*. Do you understand?"

What Gussie understood most clearly was her discomfort. She suffered from constant colic induced by injudicious feeding and still more injudicious dosing with medicine when the food was not digested. Yet the ayah thought that no one but herself was capable of caring for the child. Certainly she poured out love and selfless devotion on her.

Gussie was precocious, partly because of remarkable intelligence, partly because of the constant changes of scene which had been her lot. She understood that the powerful being who held her high up between his two hands and spoke in such a resonant voice was ordering her not to cry, to keep her miseries of pain and shyness to herself. The next time her aunt on a sudden impulse of affection snatched her up and dandled her, the little creature made what was to her a stupendous effort and controlled her desire to burst into tears. She fixed her mournful gaze on Augusta's face, her mouth turned down at the corners; her eyes grew enormous but she kept back the tears that welled up in them.

Augusta was really shocked to see such an expression on the little face.

"Why," she said, aghast, "Baby hates the sight of me! I can see that she does!"

"Nonsense," said Philip. "It's just shyness. She'll get over it." He snapped his fingers at Gussie.

"No she won't. I've tried and I've tried to make friends with her. And just now she gave me *such a desperate look!* As though she were controlling herself with all her might, when what she really wanted to do was to *scream* at me. Here, take her, Adeline."

Adeline took her child and gave her a not very gentle pat on the back. It was more than Gussie could bear. She stiffened herself and shrieked. The Dean came into the hall, putting on his cloak.

"I think I shall go to the Vestry," he said. "Perhaps I can have peace there."

Then Adeline and Philip became aware that the parrot was screaming too. It was a mercy the Dean could not understand Hindu, for the words Boney was screaming were the worst in his vocabulary, he having picked them up on board ship.

Adeline and Philip began to feel that the time had come for their visit to end. He was impatient to begin the new life but she would have been willing to linger a little longer in the quiet of Penchester, enlivened by visits to London. She loved the sunny walled garden behind the Dean's house where crocuses were in bloom and daffodils swelling into bud, though it was still only February.

One morning Augusta took her brother into the privacy of her own sitting room, and said:—

"I do not think, Philip, that you have had your proper share of our parents' belongings."

Philip's blue eyes widened in pleasurable anticipation. "Were you thinking of giving me something, Augusta?" he asked.

"Yes, if you feel you can safely take fine furniture with you. I should hate to think that precious possessions which our family long cherished might be handled roughly."

"They won't," he eagerly assured her. "They will be strongly crated and I'll personally oversee the loading on to the ship and off it. We are sailing by fast clipper which, I am told, is almost as quick and much cleaner and more comfortable than by steamship."

She sighed. "Oh, I do wish you weren't going! It seems so hard to have you return from India, only to lose you again. And I do so dread the voyage for the dear baby."

"Augusta," he said, earnestly, "if you'd like to keep the baby for a time—"

"No, no. It would never do. Baby Augusta does not take to me. She cries too much. It upsets Frederick. She shall come to visit me when she is older . . ."

"She is a spoilt little creature," said Philip. He frowned, then brightened. "The house Uncle Nicholas left me is well-built, in the French style, I am told. I want to furnish it well," he said. "We brought some things from India, as you know. Adeline has a really picturesque bedstead and inlaid cabinets. We have some fine rugs. Oh, we shall get on! Don't worry."

"But I do worry. I want you to take your place in Quebec as people of consequence and you cannot do that in a sparsely furnished house."

"Oh, we shall get on. I fancy that there aren't many officers of Hussars in the town and Adeline is the granddaughter of a marquis, as you know."

"Yes. She is distinguished-looking, too. Did she show you the pearl brooch and bracelet I gave her?"

"She did indeed and I'm delighted."

"Now I am going to give you the furniture I had from our home. It is mostly real Chippendale and would grace any drawing-room. But I do not need it. This house was filled with furniture when Frederick brought me to it. I have no children to save it for. Will you like to have it, Philip dear?"

"I shall like it tremendously," Philip exclaimed. "It's very handsome of you, Augusta."

Adeline was charmed by Augusta's generosity. Her spirits were high. Her talk, her laughter, the sound of her eager footsteps, filled the house. Philip did not know what it was to desire peace and quiet. But how earnestly the Dean and Augusta wished for it! By the time the visitors had departed with their mountain of luggage (the noise of the furniture being crated had nearly driven the Dean mad), their crying child and its ayah who kept the kitchen in a ferment with her demands for strange food, and their noisy and often blasphemous parrot, the sedate couple were exhausted. Their sincerest wish was to see the last of their relatives and never again to have a prolonged visit from them.

Philip and Adeline, on their part, had felt a cooling in the atmosphere and resented it. They were setting out to visit Adeline's people in Ireland.

"There you will find," she exclaimed, throwing herself back against the cushions of the carriage, "Irish hospitality, generous hearts, and true affection!"

II

In Ireland

Not in all the long voyage from India had Adeline suffered as she suffered in crossing the Irish Sea. The waves were short, choppy, violent. Never were they satisfied to torment the ship from one quarter alone. They raged on her from the northeast, veered and harried her from the southeast, then with a roar sprang on her from the west. Sometimes, it seemed to Adeline, the ship did not move at all, would never move again but just wallow in the gray misery of those ragged waters till the day of doom. The ayah's face was enough to frighten one, it was so green. Gussie, who had not been seasick on her first voyage, now was deadly so. It was maddening to see Philip, pink and white as ever, his firm cheeks moist from spray, actually enjoying the tumult of the sea. Still he was able to look after her and that was a comfort. In fact he gave a sense of support to all who were near him.

The Irish train was dirty, smoky, and its roadbed rough, but it seemed heaven after the Irish Sea. One after the other the sufferers raised their heads and looked about them with renewed interest in life. Gussie took a biscuit in her tiny hand and made a feeble attempt at gnawing it. But more crumbs were strewn down the front of the ayah's robe than found their way into Gussie's stomach.

At the railway station they were met by a jaunting car drawn by a fine pair of grays and driven by Patsy O'Flynn who had been nearly all his life in the service of the Courts. He was a great hand with the reins. A light wind was blowing across the hills which were turning into a tender green, and the leaf buds on the trees were opening almost as you watched them. There was a mistiness on the scene as though a fine veil hung between it and the sun. The cackle of geese, the bray of a donkey, the shouts of young children at play, brought tears to Adeline's eyes. "Oh, 't is good to be home!" she exclaimed.

"Aye, and it's good to see your honor, Miss," said Patsy. "And it's a queer shame to you that you should be thinkin' of lavin' us agin so soon."

"Oh, I shall make a good visit. There is so much to show my husband. And all the family to see. I expected my father to meet me at the station. Is he not well?"

"He's well enough and him off to lodge a complaint against Sir John Lafferty for the overflow of wather from his land makin' a bog out of ours and his cattle runnin' wild as wolves."

"And is my mother well?"

"She is, and at her wit's end to get the house ready for you and your black servant and parrots and all, the poor lady!"

"Are any of my brothers at home?"

"There's the two young lads your mother sent to the English school to get the new accent on them but they attacked one of the masthers and gave him a beatin'. So they were expelled and 't is at home they are till himself decides what to do with them. And, of course, there's Masther Tim. He's a grand lad entirely."

Adeline and Patsy chattered on, to Philip's wonder and amusement. He saw her in a new light against the advancing background of her early life. The road was so muddy after rain and flood that the wheels were sunk almost to their axles but Patsy did not appear to mind. He cracked his whip about the well-groomed flanks of the horses and encouraged them with a stream of picturesque abuse. Several times women appeared in the doorways of low thatched cabins at the roadside and, when they saw Adeline, held up their babies for her inspection, while fowls scratched and pecked in and out of the cabins. There was an air of careless well-being about the place and the children were chubby, though far from clean. Adeline seemed delighted to see both mothers and babies. She called out to them and promised to come to visit them later. Apparently Patsy did not approve of this, for he whipped up his horses and hurried them past.

The fields about were bluish-green like the sea and the grass moved gently in the breeze. Cattle stood knee-deep in the grass. Swallows darted overhead. Adeline was looking beyond the fields. The roof of her home showed above the trees of a park where deer grazed. She cried:—

"There is the house, Philip! Lord, to think it is nearly five years since I've seen it! It's more splendid than anything I've set my eyes on since! Look at it! Isn't it grand, Philip?"

"It's fallin' to pieces," said Patsy, over his shoulder, "and divil a one to spend a five-pound note on it."

It was indeed a fine old house, though not so fine as Philip had expected, judging by Adeline's description of it. Though he was no judge of architecture he could see that several styles had, at different periods, been added to the original. All were now blended into a sufficiently mellow whole. But it was not the noble pile she had described and at a glance he could see signs of dilapidations. Not even its rich cloak of ivy concealed the crumbling stonework.

Adeline craned her neck in delight to see every bit of it.

"Oh, Philip," she cried, "isn't it a lovely house?"

"It is indeed."

"Your sister's little house is nothing, compared to it."

"Augusta's house was built in the time of Queen Anne."

"Who cares for Queen Anne!" laughed Adeline. "Queen Anne is dead and so is that stuffy cathedral town. Oh, give me the country! Give me Ireland! Give me my old home!" Tears rained down her cheeks.

"I'll give you a smack," said Philip, "if you don't control yourself. No wonder you're thin."

"Oh, why did I marry a phlegmatic Englishman!" she exclaimed. "I expected you to go into raptures over the place."

"Then you expected me to behave like a fool which I am not."

They had now stopped before the door and a half-dozen tame deer had sauntered up to see them alight from the carriage. Adeline declared that she could recognize each one and that they remembered her.

The footman who opened the door was in handsome livery though rather too tight for him. He greeted Adeline enthusiastically.

"Ah, God bless you, Miss Adeline! It's grand to see ye back. My, 't is yourself has got thin in the body! What have they been doing to you out yonder? And is this lovely gentleman your husband? Welcome, sir, y'r honor. Come right in. Patsy, look after the luggage o' thim and be quick about it." He turned then and shouted at three dogs which had begun to bark loudly.

Philip felt suddenly self-conscious. He did not quite know how to meet his wife's family. All she had told him of them made them seem less, rather than more, real. He was prepared not to like them, to find them critical of him, yet the tall gentleman who now came quickly down the stairway held out his hand with a genial smile.

"How d' ye do, Captain Whiteoak," he said, taking Philip's fingers in a thin muscular grasp. "Welcome to Ireland. I'm very glad to see you, sir. I apologize for not going to the station myself but I had a wearisome business at the Courthouse that must be attended to. . . . And now, my girl, let's have a look at you!"

He took Adeline in his arms and kissed her. Philip then had a good look at him.

Adeline had spoken of her father, Renny Court, as a fine figure of a man, but to Philip's mind his back was too thin and certainly not flat enough at the shoulders, and his legs were not quite straight. It was amusing to see how Adeline's lovely features had been modeled on this man's bony aquiline face. And his hair must once have been auburn too, for there was a rusty tinge across the gray of his head. Certainly his eyes were hers.

Philip became conscious that others had come into the hall, a woman somewhat beyond middle age, and three youths.

"Oh, Mother, here I am!" Adeline turned from her father and flung her arms about her mother.

Lady Honoria Court still retained beauty of a Spanish type which had been handed down in her family since the days of the Armada when a Spanish don had remained to marry an ancestress. Honoria was a daughter of the old Marquis of Killiekeggan, who, with the famous Marquis of Waterford, had raised the sport of steeplechasing from a not very respectable one to its present eminence.

One of the dogs, an Irish staghound, raised itself on its hind legs against the ayah, in order to look into Gussie's face. Both nurse and child shrieked in terror. Renny Court ran across the hall, caught the hound by its heavily studded collar and, dragging it away, cuffed it.

"Did you ever see such a dog!" cried Lady Honoria. "He does so love children! What a sweet baby! We have a man in the town who takes the loveliest daguerreotypes. You must have one made of her while you are here, Adeline."

Lady Honoria laughed a good deal. Unfortunately she had lost a front tooth and each time she laughed she hastily put a forefinger across her lips to hide the gap. She had beautiful hands which Adeline had inherited, and her laughter rang out with contagious mirth. Philip, before he had been two days in the house, decided that she feared her husband's temper but that she circumvented and thwarted him many a time. She had an air of triumph when she achieved this and he a wary look, as though waiting his turn to retaliate. Often they did not speak to each other for days at a time but each had a keen sense of humor, each found the other an amusing person and their sulks were often broken in upon by sudden laughter from which they recovered themselves with chagrin. Lady Honoria had had eleven children of whom four had died in early infancy, but she was still quick and graceful in her movements and looked capable of adding to her family.

Adeline was embracing each of her three young brothers in turn. She led them to Philip, her face flushed, her eyes brilliant in her excitement at being home again. Her bonnet had fallen back and her auburn hair rose in curls above her forehead.

"Here they are," she cried, "the three boys! Conway, Sholto, and Timothy—come and shake hands with your new brother!"

The three offered their hands to Philip, the first two sheepishly, the third with an air almost too bright. Philip decided that there was something queer about him. There was a remarkable resemblance among the three. Their hair was a pale red, their eyes were greenish, their faces long and pointed, their noses remarkably well-shaped with slender, supercilious nostrils. The eldest, Conway, tormented Philip by his resemblance to someone he had met, till he discovered that he was the image of the Knave of Diamonds, in his favorite pack of playing cards.

"Look at them!" exclaimed Renny Court, wtih a scornful flourish of his hand toward the two elder boys. " 'T is a shameful pair they are, I can tell you. They've disgraced me by being sent home from their English school for attacking one of the masters. I knocked their heads together for it but here they are on my hands and God knows what I shall do with them! Put them to work in the stables—or in the fields—'t is all they're fit for! I must tell you that I have two other sons, and fine fellows, too. But my wife would have done well to halt before she had these!"

Conway and Sholto grinned with a hangdog air but young Timothy threw his arms about Adeline and hugged her again.

"Oh, it's grand to have you home again," he said. "I've been saving up things to tell you but now they've gone right out of my head and I can only be glad."

"You have nothing to tell but mischief," said his father, "and devilment and slyness from morning to night. You have one child, Captain Whiteoak. Stop there and have no more! For it's children that are bringing my red hairs in sorrow to the grave."

Lady Honoria interrupted him with solicitude for the travelers. She herself led them to the rooms which had been prepared for them. They bathed and changed their travel-worn garments and descended to the drawing-room.

A married son who lived at some distance arrived in time for dinner. He was a dark, handsome young man and rode a horse he had purchased that very day and intended entering for the Dublin Races. They all crowded out to see the new horse and were delighted by his appearance. This son was evidently Renny Court's favorite of the moment. He could not make enough of him and praised his skill as a rider and his perspicacity as a buyer.

There was a certain grandeur in the dining room and dinner was served by two footmen in livery. The food and the wine were good and, as the meal progressed, Philip felt more at ease with his new relatives. They talked and laughed a great deal. Even the two youths forgot their position of disgrace and raised their voices excitedly. But when their father would cast a piercing look on them they would instantly subside and for a few moments be silent. An old gentleman named Mr. O'Regan appeared at table, spoke little but drank a good deal. Adeline told Philip afterward that he was an old friend of the family who had once lent a large sum of money to them and, as it was impossible to collect the debt, had come to live with them. Mr. O'Regan wore a glum, yet rather calculating expression, as though he watched with morbid interest the decrease

year by year of Renny Court's debt to him. Renny Court, on his part, treated his guest with a kind of grim jocularity, pressed him to eat and drink more and inquired solicitously after his health. Mr. O'Regan seemed to resent this and would give no more definite answer than—"Oh, I'm well enough. I think I'll last—" Though till what, he did not explain.

Renny Court was no absentee landlord, living in England on the rents from a neglected tenantry. He employed no callous bailiff, but himself attended to the business of his estate and knew every man, woman, and child on it.

The Whiteoaks' visit there passed amiably with the exception of a few fiery encounters between Adeline and her father. In truth they could not be together for long without their wills opposing. She was the only one of his children who did not fear him. Yet she loved him less than did the others. It was to her mother she clung and from whom she dreaded to part. Lady Honoria could not talk of the departure for Canada without weeping. As for Renny Court, he poured out his full contempt of the project.

"What a life for a gentleman!" he would exclaim. "What will you find out there? Nothing but privation and discomfort! What a place for a fine girl like Adeline!"

"I'm willing to go," she interrupted. "I think it will be glorious."

"What do you know about it?"

"More than you, I'll be bound," she retorted. "Philip has had letters from his uncle describing the life in Quebec and he knows a Colonel Vaughan who lives in Ontario and loves it!"

"Lives in Ontario and loves it!" repeated her father, fixing her with his intense gaze. "And has Colonel Vaughan of Ontario told Philip what the roads are like there? Has he told him of the snakes and mosquitoes and the wild animals thirsting for your blood? Why, I know a man who stopped in one of the best hotels there and there was a mud puddle in it, and a frog croaking all the night through by a corner of the bed. And this man's wife was so frightened that the next child she had had a face like a frog on it! Now what do you think of that, Adeline?" He grinned triumphantly at her.

"I think if it's Mr. McCready you're quoting," she retorted, "his wife has no need to go all the way to Ontario to have a frog-faced child. Sure, Mr. McCready himself—"

"Was as fine a figure of a man as there was in all County Meath!"

"Father, I say he had the face of a frog!"

Philip put in—"Adeline and I are bound for the New World, sir, and no argument will talk us out of it. As you know, my uncle left me a very nice property in Quebec. I must go out there to look after it and, if what he said was true, there is a very respectable society in the town. And, in the country about, the finest shooting and fishing you can imagine."

"You will be back within the year," declared Renny Court.

"We shall see," answered Philip stubbornly. His blue eyes became more prominent as he flashed a somewhat truculent look at his father-in-law.

The two boys, Conway and Sholto, were fired by a desire to accompany the Whiteoaks to Canada. The thought of a wild life in a new country, far from parental authority, elated them. They could talk of little else. They would cling to Adeline on her either side and beg her to let them throw in their lot with hers. On her part she liked the idea. Canada would not seem so remote if she had two of her brothers with her. Their mother surprisingly did not oppose the idea. She had borne so much dissension because of these two that the thought of parting with them did not distress her greatly. They promised to return home within the year. Renny Court was willing enough to be rid of the nuisance of them. Philip did not relish the idea of such a responsibility but to please Adeline he agreed. He felt himself capable of controlling Conway and Sholto much more efficiently than their parents could. He thought, with a certain grim pleasure, of the discipline that would make men of them.

Even little Timothy talked of emigrating to the New World but this could not be considered. Timothy spoke with a strong Irish accent, from being so much with his old nurse who had brought him up from delicate babyhood. He had a beautiful yet strange face and was demonstratively affectionate to an extent that embarrassed Philip. A stern word from his father would apparently terrify him, yet the very next moment he would be laughing. His hair was sandy—he was freckled and had beautiful hands which Philip discovered were decidedly light-fingered. He missed his gold studs, he missed his best silk cravats, his pistols inlaid with mother-of-pearl,

his gold penknife. Each of these articles was in turn retrieved from Timothy's bedroom by Adeline. She made light of it. She declared that Tim could not help it but it made Philip angry and uncomfortable.

In truth the longer he stayed with Adeline's family the less congenial they were to him, with the one exception of Lady Honoria. He felt that Renny Court, for all his devotion to his land and his tenantry, mismanaged them both. Far too much money and time were spent on steeplechasing. As for politics, they hardly dared broach the subject, so violently were their views opposed. But Renny Court would encourage Mr. O'Regan to hold forth on the theme of British injustice to Ireland. Philip was unable to defend his country because the old gentleman was too arrogant and also too deaf to listen to any views but his own. He would sit close to the blazing fire, his florid face rising above his high black stock like an angry sun above a thundercloud, while words poured forth in a torrent.

What with one thing and another the atmosphere became too tense to be borne. Philip and Adeline accepted an invitation to pay a short visit to Corrigan Court, a cousin who lived ten miles away. They rode over there one fine spring morning, leaving Augusta, her ayah, and Bonaparte, in the care of Lady Honoria. Renny Court accompanied them on a skittish gray mare who danced her way over the muddy roads and did her best to induce misbehavior in the other horses.

A long drive flanked by a double row of linden trees led to the cousin's house, rather an imposing place with an ivy-covered turret at either end. Its many windows glittered in the spring sunshine. Corrigan Court and his wife were waiting on the terrace to greet them. The pair were cousins but bore no resemblance to each other, he being dark with arched brows and a languid supercilious air; she ruddy, fair, and full of energy. They had been married some years but still were childless. They hoped for a son. Bridget Court embraced Adeline warmly when she alighted from her horse.

"Bless you, dear Adeline, how glad I am to see you!" she exclaimed. "And your husband! What a perfectly matched pair you are! Welcome—many times welcome."

"Ah, Biddy Court, 't is good to see you." Adeline warmly returned the embrace but Philip had a feeling that no love was lost between them.

A thousand questions were asked about their voyage and their plans for going to Canada. Renny Court took the opportunity to disparage the enterprise.

At dinner that night another guest appeared—old Lord Killiekeggan, Adeline's grandfather. He was a handsome old man and it amused Philip to see Adeline standing between him and her father, bearing a likeness to each, but she had chosen all their best points. How lovely she was, Philip thought, in her yellow satin dinner gown. No other woman could compare to her.

The conversation hinged on steeplechasing, on which subject the old Marquis and his son-in-law were in perfect accord. Neither of them took any interest in the Army, nor did Corrigan Court, who held himself somewhat aloof, as though he existed on a more intellectual plane. The gentlemen remained in the dining room and drank a good deal, for the port was excellent. On the way to the drawing-room with her hostess, Adeline stopped in amazement before a picture that hung against the dark paneling of the hall. The other paintings were of men in hunting clothes, velvet court dress, or in armor. But this portrait was of a little girl of eight, her flowerlike face set off by a wreath of auburn hair. Adeline exclaimed, in a loud voice:—

"Why, it's me! And what am I doing here, I should like to know, Biddy Court!"

Biddy Court hesitated, looking uncomfortable. Then she said:—

"It's Corry's. Your father owed him money and he gave him the portrait in payment. Not that it covered the debt—far from it! Come along, Adeline, do! It's dreadfully draughty here."

But Adeline stood transfixed. She snatched up a lighted candle that stood on the top of a chest and held it so that its beams lighted the little face.

"How beautiful I was!" she cried. "Oh, the beautiful face of me! Oh, the shame to my father that he should have given such a treasure to Corry Court! It's enough to make me cry my eyes out!" She turned furiously to her cousin. "What was the debt?"

"I don't know," returned Bridget, "except that it was double what the portrait is worth."

"Then it must be a fortune, indeed, for the portrait was painted by one of the greatest artists living!"

"You are welcome to the picture," said Bridget, "if only you will pay the debt."

"I'll pay no debts but my own! But, oh, I do so want this picture. 'T will be a lovely thing to take out to Canada and hang beside my new portrait—the one I've told you of."

"I suppose you'll go on having portraits of yourself painted till you're a hundred! Ah, I wish I could see that *last* one! It's a raving beauty you'll be *then,* Adeline."

"I shall be on the face of the earth, which is more than you will be!"

Still carrying the lighted candle, she flew back along the hall and flung open the door of the dining room. The four men were talking in quiet tones, the firelight throwing a peaceful glow upon them, the candles burning low. The decanter of port in the hand of Lord Killiekeggan trembled a little, as he replenished his glass.

"Oh, but it's a queer father you are!" cried Adeline, fixing her eyes on Renny Court. "To give away the portrait of your own child for a paltry debt, not worth the gilt frame on it! There I was, walking down the hall in my innocence, when suddenly I spied it hanging on the wall and it all but cried out in its shame at being there. The candle all but fell out of my hand in my shame. Oh, well do I remember when my mother took me to Dublin to have it painted and the way the great artist gave me flowers and sweets to amuse me and the sweet little necklace on me that my grandmother gave me! Oh, Grandpapa, did you know that my father had done such a thing?"

"Is the girl mad?" asked Killiekeggan, turning to his son-in-law.

"No, no—just in a temper." He spoke sternly to Adeline. "Come now—enough of this! The picture is not worth this to-do."

"Not worth it!" she cried. "'T is little you know of its value! Why, when I told the London artist the name of the great man who had painted me in childhood, he said he would gladly journey all the way to County Meath to gaze on the portrait!"

Corrigan Court asked abruptly—"And what was the name of the great artist, Adeline?"

Her lips fell apart. She stared at him, dumbfounded for a moment. She pressed her fingers to her brow and thought and then said sadly—"You've knocked it right out of my head, Corry. It was there just a moment ago." Her face lighted and she turned to Philip. "I've said his name to you many a time, haven't I, Philip?"

"You have," said Philip, stoutly, "many a time."

"And you've forgotten it too?" said Corrigan.

"Yes. It has just slipped my memory." He had been drinking a good deal. His fair face was flushed.

"One glance at the portrait," said Adeline, "even from a distance, and the name will come to me." She turned back into the hall. The four men rose and followed her, the old Marquis carrying his glass in his hand. At about ten paces from the picture she halted and strained her eyes toward its lower corner. She had wonderful eyesight. "I could not possibly read the name from here, could I?" she asked.

"No," returned Corrigan. "And if you put your very nose against the picture you won't see any signature, for either the artist did not consider it worth the trouble of signing or he was ashamed of his name."

She all but threw the candlestick at his head. "You've painted the name out yourself, Corry Court," she cried, "you've painted it out so as to conceal its great worth! You knew that if some connoisseur saw it he would tell my father of the evil bargain you made!"

Renny Court threw a suspicious look at his cousin Corrigan. He then took the candle from Adeline's hand and, holding it close to the portrait, scrutinized the two lower corners. "It's a queer little blob there is here," he said.

"Yes," cried Adeline, "that's just where the signature was! It was signed with a sweet little flourish. Oh, the name will come back to me in a moment!"

"It was never signed," said Corry Court. "And you know it was never signed. It's a pretty picture and I've always liked it and, when your father offered it to me, I took it. I well knew it was all I was likely to get for the debt."

"Oh, Father, how could you?" said Adeline, tears shining in her eyes. "There's nothing I want so much as this picture. And I was going to beg it from you as another wee wedding present for you acknowledged yourself, in a letter you wrote me to India, that it was not much you'd been able to give me in the way of a present."

"Not much!" cried Renny Court. "Why, I'm still in debt for your trousseau! If you want this picture so badly—you have the money your great-aunt left you—buy it!"

"I'll not part with it," said Corry.

Adeline turned to him with a charming smile.

"You still love me, Corry dear, don't you?"

They exchanged a look. Corrigan flushed red. Adeline gazed at him with affectionate pity.

"You may keep the picture, Corry dear," she said. "I shall love to think of it here—reminding you and Biddy of me."

"I am not likely to forget you," said Bridget grimly. "Wherever you are, you make trouble."

"Tut, tut, girls," put in Lord Killiekeggan. "Don't quarrel. Don't spoil your pretty faces with frowns."

Bridget knew she was not pretty but his words pleased her. She arched her neck and looked challengingly at Adeline. "Well," she said, "shall we go into the drawing-room?"

Adeline caught her grandfather by the arm.

"Don't leave me alone with Bridget!" she implored. "I'm afraid of her."

"Behave yourself," he said, and gave her hand a little slap, but he allowed himself to be led into the drawing-room.

Corry was not loath to save his old port, of which quite enough had been already drunk. He was a little downcast at the prospect of the quarrel which he knew he would have later with his wife.

Philip was in a state of bland serenity. He seated himself in a comfortable chair and accepted a pinch of snuff from the jeweled box which the old Marquis proffered him. Adeline spread out the glimmering flounces of her crinoline and eyed her grandfather beguilingly.

"What a sweet box!" she said.

Well, she was his loveliest granddaughter and she was going far away. He put the snuffbox into her hand.

"Take it," he said, "and when an Indian chief offers you the pipe of peace you can give him a pinch of snuff in exchange."

No one could have been more charming and self-forgetful than Adeline during the rest of the visit. But there was tension between her and Bridget. They were quite ready to part when the last morning came. The wagonette waited at the door for Adeline's trunks, for she went nowhere without a quantity of luggage. She stood in the hall, tall and slender, in a dark green riding habit, her hair plaited neatly beneath the small hat from which a dark feather drooped against the creamy whiteness of her cheek. Her red lips were parted in a blandishing smile.

"Ah, the beautiful visit I've had!" she cried, embracing Bridget. "Ah, thank you, dear cousin, for all you've done! When Philip and I are settled in our new home you and Corry must come and spend a year with us, for indeed 't would take a year to repay you for all you've done for us!"

Bridget was shorter than Adeline. Her eyes could barely look over the top of Adeline's shoulder as they embraced. Her eyes, protruding a little because of the fervent embrace she was receiving, stared at the paneling on which a vacant space by degrees claimed her attention. Her eyes widened still more as her brain took in the fact that the childish portrait of Adeline was missing from the wall. It seemed too bad to be true! With a cry that was almost a scream, Bridget struggled in that strong embrace. Adeline held her close. In fact, feeling the tempest that was surging through Bridget, Adeline held her closer.

"Let me go," screamed Bridget in a fury. "Let me go!"

The men stared at the two in consternation. With Bridget's great crinoline vibrating about them, their bosoms pressed together, their arms clutching each other, they were a troubling sight.

"What in God's name is the matter?" demanded Renny Court.

"He has given her the picture!" cried Bridget.

"What picture?"

"The portrait of Adeline! Corry has given it her. It's gone!"

Everyone now looked at the wall. Corrigan turned pale. "I have done no such thing," he declared. "If it's gone, she took it."

Adeline was driven to release Bridget, who now faced her in fierce accusation.

"You have taken it," she said. "It is in one of your boxes. Peter!" she called out to a manservant. "Unload the boxes from the wagonette."

"Let them be," said Adeline. She turned calmly to her cousins.

"I did take the picture," she said, "but I only took what was my own, so let's have no more fuss about it."

Peter stood, holding a trunk in his arms, not knowing whether to put it down or put it up. His sandy side-whiskers bristled in excitement.

"Now, look here," said Philip, "I'm willing to buy the picture if Adeline wants it so badly."

"And I'm willing to sell," said Corrigan.

"But I am not!" cried his wife. "I demand to have those boxes unpacked and the picture back on the wall!" She ran down the steps and took one end of the trunk which Peter was still holding, and tugged at the strap that bound it.

Adeline flew after her. They struggled over the trunk. Adeline was the stronger but Bridget was in an abandon of rage. She stretched out her hand and, taking hold of one of Adeline's smooth plaits, pulled it loose.

"Now, now, don't do that!" exclaimed Philip, in his turn running down the steps. "I won't have it." Never in his life had he been involved in such a scene as this. He caught Bridget's wrist and held it while, with the other hand, he tried to make Adeline let go of the trunk.

Renny Court looked on, laughing.

"Kindly restrain your wife," said Philip to Corrigan.

"Don't you lay a finger on me, Corry Court!" cried Bridget. He moved warily between her and Adeline.

Philip spoke sternly to Adeline. "We'll have no more of this. Tell me which box the picture is in."

With a trembling finger she pointed to the box which Peter held.

"Put it down," said Philip to the man. He did so. Philip opened it and there on the top lay the picture! He took it out and handed it to Corrigan. The child face looked out of the frame in innocent surprise. Corrigan looked from it to Adeline and back again. His expression was one of profound gloom.

Renny Court directed a piercing glance into the trunk.

"Did you ever see such extravagance!" he exclaimed. "Is it any wonder she left me bankrupt? Look at the gold toilet articles—the sable cloak! And there is my father-in-law's snuffbox! By the Lord Harry, she's got that too!"

"He gave it her," said Philip tersely. With a set face he put down the lid of the trunk and buckled the strap. He turned to Adeline who stood like a statue looking on, one hand grasping her riding crop.

"Come," he said. "Make your good-byes. You did wrong to take the picture but I must say that I think Mrs. Court has treated you very badly."

"Good-bye, Corry," said Adeline, tears running out of her eyes, "and God comfort you in your marriage, for your wife is a vixen—if ever there was one!" With a graceful movement she turned to her horse. Philip lifted her to her saddle. Her father sprang to his. Embarrassed good-byes were exchanged. Then Adeline turned for a last look at Bridget.

"Good-bye, Biddy Court!" she called out. "And may you live to be sorry for the way you've used me! Bad luck to you, Biddy! May the north wind blow you south, and the east wind blow you west till you come at last to the place where you belong!" She gave a flourish of her crop and galloped off, one long auburn plait flying over her shoulder.

Old Peter, rattling behind them with the luggage, exclaimed:—

"Ah, 't was a quare dirty trick to do to her, and she as innocent as she was the day the pictur' was painted!"

That was not the last of their visits. They went to the house of Adeline's married brother. They stayed with the old Marquis himself but nothing they saw or did weakened their desire for the New World. There was in them both an adventurous pioneer spirit that laughed at discouragement, that reached out toward a freer life.

The day came when all preparations were complete for their sailings westward.

Philip had taken passage on a sailing vessel because he believed it would be quicker and cleaner than the steamship. Adeline's parents and little Timothy were to come to the port to see them off.

Patsy O'Flynn, the coachman, had made up his mind to accompany Adeline to Canada. He was unmarried. He had spent his life in one small spot. Now he was out for adventure. Also something chivalrous in him urged him to add another protector to her train, though he scarcely looked on her two young brothers as protectors. But he was convinced that they were going to an uncivilized country where wild animals and Indians prowled close to every settlement.

Patsy made an extraordinary figure as he stood waiting on the dock. Though the morning was mild and fair he wore a heavy topcoat for he thought that was the best way to carry it. Other bundles, from a huge one sewn up in canvas to a small one tied in a red handkerchief, were mounded upon his shoulders. His small humorous face peered out with a pleased and knowing expression, as though he alone, of all the passengers, knew just what difficulties lay ahead and how to deal with them.

In one hand he carried a heavy blackthorn stick, polished and formidable-looking. From the other hung the parrot's cage, in which the bright-colored occupant disported himself from perch to perch, or hung head downward from the ceiling and flapped his wings in a transport of excitement. Boney had not forgotten the voyage from India. The sight of the sea and the ship exhilarated him almost beyond bearing. At times he poured forth a stream of Hindu. At others he uttered a succession of piercing cries. Never was he still. He attracted a crowd of ragged, dirty children who screamed when he screamed, and jumped up and down in their excitement. When these pressed too close, Patsy would flourish his blackthorn at them and drive them off, shouting at them in Gaelic.

The ayah had taken a fancy to Patsy. To her he seemed a macabre being but somehow benevolent. She stood close beside him, her draperies blowing gracefully in the breeze, her infant charge in her arms. The stay in Ireland had done little Augusta good. Her cheeks had filled out and she was less pale. Her hair had grown long enough to make a silky black curl on her forehead, beneath the brim of her lace bonnet. She sat on the ayah's arm, gazing in wonder at the scene, but when her eyes rested on Patsy she would show her four milk-white teeth in a smile of delight. She had had the milk from one goat during her stay in Ireland and the goat had been given to her to take to Canada, so that no change of milk might upset her digestion. The goat, held on a halter by a shock-headed boy, stood immobile, regarding with equanimity, even with cynicism, what was going on. It had been named Maggie and Lady Honoria had tied a small bell to its neck, and the vicissitudes of the voyage were accented by its silvery tinkle.

Augusta's young uncles had been carefully outfitted for the new life by their mother. But to Philip's mind their clothes looked too picturesque, their hair too long, their hands too white. Conway especially—he was the one who reminded Philip of the Knave of Diamonds—looked too exquisite. They were here, there, and everywhere—giving facetious orders to the sailors who were carrying aboard the crates of hens, geese, and ducks, prodding forward the pigs, dragging the sheep and the cows.

A group of poor emigrants were guarding their luggage, clinging tearfully to those last moments with their kinsfolk who had come to see them off. A priest was among them, doing his best to keep up their spirits, sweeping the heavens with his large gray eyes and prophesying a fair voyage. He was there to put two young nieces aboard who were going out to a brother, and he could not look at them without his eyes running over.

Adeline wore a long green cloak with wide sleeves edged by fur. She stood facing the sea, drinking in the joyful breeze that struck the white sails of the ship as a dancer might strike a tambourine. The shimmering sea lay before her, and beyond—that young continent where she and Philip were to make their home. She wished they two were going on the ship alone. She drew away from the weeping people about her and, slipping her hand into Philip's, pressed his fingers. He looked into her eyes.

"Sure you haven't left anything behind?" he asked.

"Nothing. Not even my heart!"

"Well, that's sensible of you. For, if you had, I should have been forced to go back for it."

The priest shortly came up to her.

"Pardon me, my lady," he said. He had heard Adeline's mother so addressed and thought it proper to use the title to her.

"Yes?" she answered, not ill-pleased.

"I am going to ask you a favor," he said. "I have two young nieces sailing on the ship, and a terrible long and risky voyage it is for thim. Would you be so kind as to give thim a word of encouragement if they are ill or in throuble? If I could carry such a message to their poor mother, sure 't would dry the sorrowing eyes of her! D'ye think you could?"

"Indeed I will," said Adeline. "And, if you will give me your address, I'll write and tell you about the voyage and how your nieces fare."

The priest wrote his address on a somewhat crumpled bit of paper and, full of gratitude, returned to the admonishing of the two rosy-cheeked, black-haired girls whose young bosoms seemed swelling with exuberance.

The confusion was apparently hopeless. The cries of the animals and fowls, the shoutings, bangings, and thumpings as the sailors carried the luggage aboard, the orders of their officers which no one seemed to obey, the wailing and circling of sea gulls, the screams of excited urchins, the flutterings and flappings of the great sails of the ship, were woven into a fantastic tapestry of farewell which would hang forever on the walls of memory.

The moment came. Adeline had dreaded it but now that it had arrived she was almost past feeling. She wished her mother's face was not wet with tears. It was a pity to remember her that way. "Oh, Mother dear, I'll be back! So shall we all! I'll take good care of the boys. Good-bye! Good-bye, Father! Be sure to write. Good-bye . . . Good-bye . . ." She was enfolded in their embraces. Her body pressed against the body that had carried her before birth, against the body that had made that birth possible. She felt as though she were being physically torn; then Philip put his arm about her and led her weeping to the ship.

III

The First Voyage

THE bark *Alanna* had formerly been an East Indiaman. She was bound for Quebec and would return laden with white pine. The Captain was a thick-set Yorkshireman, named Bradley; the first officer a tall lean Scot, with an enormous mouth, named Grigg. There were few cabin passengers and the Whiteoaks held themselves a little aloof, for the voyage would be long and there was the possibility of being thrown too intimately into uncongenial company. Indeed Philip and Adeline had been so surrounded by relatives since their arrival from India that they longed to be alone together. They made themselves as comfortable as possible in the cramped space of their cabin. Philip arranged their possessions in the most shipshape order. Adeline, wrapped in rugs, settled herself in a sheltered corner on deck to read *The History of Pendennis*. Augusta and her ayah were established near by, the tiny girl clasping her first doll, an elegantly dressed wax creature, extremely corseted and wearing a dress and bonnet of plaid taffeta. Conway and Sholto were exploring the ship and Patsy and the goat making themselves as comfortable as they could in their far-from-comfortable quarters. Ireland lay, a hazy blue hump, on the pale horizon. There was a head wind and the ship made but slow progress, though her great sails strained at the masts and a living soul seemed demonstrating its will to move westward. The gulls followed the ship a long way out from Ireland. They lingered with her, as though waiting for messages to carry home.

Besides the Whiteoaks' party there were fewer than a dozen

passengers in the Cabin Class. Of these they became friendly with only five. There were two Irish gentlemen, educated well but with a rich brogue, named D'Arcy and Brent. They were traveling for pleasure and were to make an extensive tour of the United States. There was a Mrs. Cameron from Montreal who had with her a delicate daughter of fifteen. The two had journeyed all the way to China to join the child's father who had previously been sent there to take an important post concerned with the trade between the two countries. But, when they had arrived, they had found that a plague of cholera had carried him off. Now they were retracing the long weary way to Montreal. Mrs. Cameron and little Mary would sit huddled together wrapped in one shawl, gazing into the distant horizon, as though in their hearts they held no hope that their journeyings would ever end but felt that they would go on from ship to ship, from sea to sea, till the Day of Judgment. The young girl had indeed acquired a strange seaborn look, as Adeline described it. Her cloak and hat were faded to the grayness of winter waves; her hair hung like lank yellowish seaweed about her shoulders; her wide-open light eyes had an unseeing look; her face and hands were deeply tanned. Only her mouth had color and between her lips, which were always parted, her small pearl-like teeth showed. Her mother had degenerated, by sorrow and exhaustion, into little more than an element for the protection of Mary.

"Why doesn't she do something to make the child happy, instead of brooding over her like a distracted hen!" exclaimed Adeline, on the second day out. "Really, Philip, I am excessively annoyed at that woman! I shall tell my brothers to make friends with Mary. It's unnatural for a young girl to look like that!"

She did so. However days passed before the boys were able to persuade Mary to leave her mother's side. Mrs. Cameron indeed was unwilling to let her child out of her sight. She looked worried rather than pleased when finally Mary went for a promenade along the sloping deck, supported on either side by Conway and Sholto. They made an extraordinary trio, the boys in their elegant new clothes, the girl travel-stained; the boys bright-eyed, alert to everything that passed about them, the girl seeming in a kind of dream; the boys continually chaffing each other, she looking from one face to the other, scarcely seeming to take in what they said.

The remaining passenger with whom the Whiteoaks became friendly was an Englishman, a Mr. Wilmott who, like themselves, was going out to settle in Canada. He was a tall thin man with sharp but well-cut features and short brown whiskers. He was reserved concerning himself but a fluent talker when politics were under discussion. He and the two Irishmen soon provided entertainment for the rest, for they argued without open rancor. Mr. Wilmott was ironic, with flashes of wit, the Irishmen humorous and ever ready with the most violent exaggerations. Philip had been so long out of England that he felt unequal to political discussion. Also, in any such argument concerning their two countries, he would have had Adeline as his opponent, and the thought of this was distasteful to him.

Adeline's mind was occupied by her desire to bring Mr. Wilmott and Mrs. Cameron together. Here they were, two lonely people (Mr. Wilmott certainly wore a sombre look at times) who would do well to link their lives together. And what a protector, what a father he would make for little Mary! She felt that Mrs. Cameron was melancholy, rather than heartbroken, over the loss of her husband. She was wrapped up in her child. How could a woman be mother before mate, Adeline wondered, as her eyes drank in Philip's strength and beauty. Not she—not she! Her man would always come first. She despised the too maternal woman.

So a new world was created on board the *Alanna,* very different from the world on board the ship that had brought them from India. This was a much smaller, closer world, more cut off from the old life. The last voyage had been a voyage homeward. This was one into what was new and unknown. The last had been a linking up; this was a cutting off. Adeline was conscious of an odd detachment, an exhilaration, as though she were adventuring into a spiritual as well as a material distance.

For a week they pressed forward in fair weather. Then the head wind increased in strength and the ship struggled on against it and against the rising green waves that crashed on her bow, enveloping her in spray. It was no longer possible to stay on deck. They must spend the long hours below where there was not only the close air but the smells and noises from the steerage to be endured. The ayah became seasick and Adeline had the care of the baby on her hands.

Mrs. Cameron and Mary adored little Augusta and took a large share of her care. But at night she was restless and Adeline and Philip did not get their proper sleep.

They were going to their berths early one stormy night when there was a thumping on the door and Conway's voice called out:—

"Philip! There's a leak sprung!"

"What?" shouted Philip, staying the unbuttoning of his waistcoat.

"She has sprung a plank! She's leaking!"

Then there came the heavy tramping of feet overhead and the shouts of officers.

Adeline turned pale. She had the quietly whimpering baby in her arms.

"Will the ship sink?" she asked.

"Certainly not. Don't be alarmed," said Philip. He threw open the door.

Conway stood there supporting himself by the brass railing which ran along the passage. He wore a bright-colored dressing gown and, even in the excitement of the moment, Philip noticed how it heightened his resemblance to the Knave of Diamonds. With the door open, the noise of tramping feet and vehement shoutings, the roar of the steadily rising squall, the thunder and rattle of canvas and tackle, were increased. The sails were being lowered.

"They're lowering the sails!" shouted Conway, but his voice came as no more than a whisper. "It's blowing a terrible gale."

His brother stood close behind him, clinging to the railing. He looked green with seasickness. Adeline said to him:—

"Come in and lie down in my berth, Sholto. You must keep the baby while we go to see the Captain."

The boy obediently stumbled into the cabin and threw himself on to the berth.

"Oh, I'm so ill!" he moaned.

Adeline placed the baby beside him.

"You are not to come, Adeline," Philip shouted.

Her eyes flashed rebellion. She gripped his arm in her hands. "I will come!" she shouted back.

The vessel gave a heave that sent them all staggering into one corner of the cabin. Mrs. Cameron now appeared in the doorway. She had a shawl wrapped about her head and she was holding Mary closely to her, as though determined not to be parted from her at the moment of sinking. But she spoke calmly.

"What is wrong?" she asked.

"Nothing but a leak, ma'am. We are going to see the Captain." Philip's tone, his very presence, were reassuring.

"We will go too." They saw the words on her lips though they could not hear them.

Clinging to the rail and to each other Philip and Adeline gained the companionway. They found the Captain and the first officer supervising the lowering of the sails. The great canvas thundered deckward as in terrifying capitulation. The stark masts looked suddenly fragile and the ship vulnerable. The wind blew with terrific force and green walls of water reared themselves, then came crashing against the side of the rolling ship. The heaving wash of the waters was palely illumined by a cloud-bound moon, that only now and again really showed herself. Adeline had seen storms at sea before this and they were tropic storms, but the ship had been larger, the company more numerous. There was a loneliness about this storm. The little group of people seemed helpless, the wind was piercingly cold. However the Captain spoke with equanimity.

"It's nothing but a squall," he said in his hearty, Yorkshire accent. "I've been round the Cape many times myself and this is naught but a puff of wind. So you'd best go back to your berths, ladies, and not worry."

Above the noise of the storm came confused shoutings and tramping from the companionway. The steerage passengers were pouring up from below. They looked wild-eyed, rough and terrified.

Captain Bradley strode over to them.

"What does this mean?" he demanded.

The second mate shouted back—"I couldn't keep them down there, sir! The water's pouring in below."

The Captain looked grim. He pressed his way through the crowd, ordering them to descend with him, which they did in great confusion.

Adeline heard him shout—"All hands to the pumps!"

Philip was patting her on the back. He was smiling at her. She smiled bravely back. He raised his voice and said—"The squall is passing. Everything will be all right."

"Take Mrs. Cameron's arm," she said. "She looks ready to drop."

Mary Cameron had left her mother's side. Conway Court had his arm about her. Neither of them looked frightened but they both wore expressions of pale hilarity. Philip helped Mrs. Cameron back to her cabin. The wind was falling. Yet the sea was still heavy with great thundering waves and the wind still fierce enough to fill the storm sails, to which the ship had been stripped, to bursting point. In the welter of the waves the *Alanna* lay almost on her beam ends. Now a rainstorm advanced like a wall, seeming to join with the waves in the effort to drown those aboard.

But Captain Bradley was not downcast. He went about, ruddy-faced and cheerfully shouting his orders. The swinging lanterns illumined but little the wild scene. Sailors were thrumming sails together and drawing them under the ship's bow in what seemed a hopeless effort to stop the leak. Adeline felt that, if she went below, she would be desperate with fear. Here in the midst of the activity she felt herself equal to Philip in courage. She drew Mary Cameron and Conway to her side and the three linked themselves, waiting Philip's return.

"I gave her some brandy," he said as he came up. "She needed it, poor lady, for she is half-dead with cold." He turned to the girl. "Shall I take you down to your mother, Mary?"

"Did she ask for me?" Mary's voice was slightly sulky.

"No. I think she'll sleep. Perhaps you are better with us."

Conway Court gave a shout of laughter. "Mary, Mary, quite contrary—" he sang. "Sailed away to the Port of Canary!"

Philip frowned at him but Adeline laughed too and Mary gave him an adoring look. He was a wild figure in his bright-hued dressing gown with his tawny hair blowing in the wind.

Mr. Wilmott came up to them.

"The officers are not alarmed," he said, "but the leak appears to be a bad one. The four pumps are working like the devil. Mr. D'Arcy and Mr. Brent are helping to man them and I'm ready to give a hand when I'm needed."

When morning came there were five feet of water in the hold. The pumps were working hard and the Captain said he had the situation under control. A stewardess brought breakfast to Adeline in her cabin. She had changed into dry things but had not slept.

The tiny room was in a state of disorder, her wet clothing, the belongings of Philip and the baby, scattered promiscuously and depressingly. She felt herself being sucked down into a vortex of confusion, rather than of fear. But the hot tea, the bread and bacon, put life into her. She sat on the edge of the berth and combed out her hair. A pale sunlight filtered in at the porthole. She noticed the lively beauty of her hair. "It would look like this, even if I were drowning," she thought, half resentfully.

In the silver mirror of her dressing case, she saw how pale her face was. She bit her lips to bring some color into them.

"When do you think we shall get to Newfoundland?" she asked the Scotch stewardess.

"Oh, we'll get there right enough."

"How far are we from Ireland?"

"Perhaps six hundred miles."

"How is Mrs. Cameron this morning?"

"Ah, she's fell waur o' the wear."

"And her daughter?"

"Fast asleep. Like your own bairn, poor wee lamb!" She cast an accusing look at Adeline.

"My brother looked after my baby very well last night," said Adeline haughtily, for little Augusta had not been in her thoughts all night. "You say she is fast asleep? Is she with her ayah?"

"Aye. She's with what's left of the ayah—for the woman is more dead than alive." The stewardess stood balancing the tray against the reeling of the ship.

"Merciful heaven," cried Adeline, "what a miserable company we are!"

She crossed the passage to the ayah's cabin and looked in. In the pale sunlight nurse and infant looked equally fragile and remote. But they were sleeping peacefully. Adeline summoned the stewardess.

"Take that basin away," she said in a low but furious tone. "Make the place decent with as little noise as you can."

Adeline went to Mrs. Cameron's cabin. All was neat there but the poor woman lay on her berth exhausted after her last bout of seasickness. The air was heavy with the scent of Eau de Cologne. It was as though someone had emptied a bottle of it there. Mary was seated in front of the tiny dressing table gazing at herself in the glass with a fascinated look. She was unaware of the opening of the door but continued to give her large-eyed reflection stare for stare, while the ship heaved and a cupboard door flew open, then banged shut, with each roll. Adeline laughed.

"Well, what do you think of yourself?" she asked.

"Oh, Mrs. Whiteoak," answered Mary. "I'm pretty—pretty! I have traveled right round the world and never found it out till now."

"Well," said Adeline, "it is a queer time to have discovered it. But if it's a comfort to you, I'm glad you think so."

Still gazing at her reflection the girl answered:—

"Don't you?"

Adeline laughed again. "I'm in no state to judge but I shall take a good look at you later on. Can I do anything for your mother?"

"She feels a little better, she says. She just wants to be quiet."

"Have you had any sleep?"

"A little. I'm not tired."

"You're a better traveler than I am. Have they brought you breakfast?"

"Oh, yes. The stewardess is very kind. So is your brother. He's so brave too."

"Well, I'm glad of that. I'm going now to see how the boys are getting on."

"May I come with you?"

"No. Stay with your mother."

Adeline found Sholto recovering from his seasickness. He was sipping coffee and eating a hard biscuit but he was very pale. Conway was changing into dry clothes. Adeline noticed the milky whiteness of his skin and how his chest and neck were fuller than one would judge from his face.

"Oh, Adeline," exclaimed Sholto, "I wish I'd never come on this voyage! We shall quite likely go down. Oh, I do wish I were back in Ireland with Mamma and Papa and Timothy and all!"

"Nonsense," said Adeline, sitting down on the side of the berth. "In a few days you'll be laughing at this. Here, eat your biscuit."

She took it from his hand and broke off a morsel of it and put it in his mouth. He relaxed and she fed him the rest of the biscuit in this way as though he were a baby.

She turned to Conway. "Go and find Philip and tell him I want him. Just say I must see him and that it is important."

"What do you want him for?"

She flashed a look of command at him. "Do as I say, Con."

"Very well. But he probably won't come." He tied his cravat with as much care as though he were about to make a call.

"Oh, what a little fop you are!" she cried. "To think of you fiddling with your tie and soon we may all be at the bottom!"

Sholto hurled himself back on the pillow.

"You said everything was all right. You said we'd be laughing about this!" he sobbed.

"Now you've done it!" exclaimed Conway. He opened the door and went into the passage but it was a struggle to close the door after him against the rolling of the ship. Adeline had to go and put her weight against it.

She returned to Sholto. "You know I was only joking," she comforted him. "If I thought we were going to the bottom should I be looking so pleasant?"

"You're not looking pleasant! You're looking queer and wild."

She laid her head beside his on the pillow.

"I am looking queer," she said, "because I suspect Con of making up to that little Cameron girl. That's why I sent him away—so I could ask you. Sholto, tell me, has he been telling her she's pretty? Has he been making up to her?"

Sholto's green eyes were bright. "Indeed he has! We are never alone but he is up to his tricks. 'Oh, but you're the pretty thing!' he says. 'Oh, the lovely little neck on you!' he says. 'Oh, the long fair eyelashes! Come close and touch my cheek with them!' "

"And did she?"

"She did. And he laid his hand on her breast."

"And did she mind?"

"Not she. She arched her neck like a filly you are stroking. And she made her eyes large at him like a filly. But she's innocent and Conway is not. He could tell those boys at the English school a thing or two."

Adeline bent her brows into a sombre line. "I shall tell Mary's mother," she said, "to keep her away from that rascal."

"Well, if the ship is going down, Adeline, they might as well be enjoying themselves."

"The ship is not going down!"

The door opened and Conway, clinging to it, looked in. He said:—

"Philip has gone to your cabin. He's as wet as a rat."

"Con—come in and shut that door!" He did and stood pale and smiling before her.

"Now," she said, "no more hanky-panky with Mary Cameron! If I hear of it I shall tell Philip and he'll give you a shaking to make your teeth rattle. Oh, you ought to be ashamed of yourself—making love to a child!"

"What has that little twister been telling you?" he demanded, his cold eyes on his brother.

Sholto began to shiver as fear produced a fresh wave of sea-sickness.

"I did not need to hear it from him," said Adeline. "She told me herself that she'd just discovered she was pretty and I've been watching you. Now, I say no more of it!"

He tried to open the door and bow her out with a grand supercilious air but a sudden roll of the ship flung them staggering together. They clung so a moment and then she said, holding him close:—

"You will be good, won't you, Con, dear?"

"Yes—I promise you."

He saw her out, then, bending over his brother, he gave him half a dozen thumps, each one harder than the one before. Miraculously those, instead of bringing his sickness back, seemed to do him good for in half an hour they were on deck together, watching the sailors raising what canvas they dared, and feeling new hope as the sun came out brightly and the foam-crowned waves harassed the ship less cruelly. When they saw Mary they looked the other way. She, on her part, seemed occupied by her own thoughts. Her mother kept her at her side. Mrs. Cameron's intense spirit went out in a fierce strengthening of the ship so that, made inviolate by her spiritual aid, it might reach land and set Mary's feet in safety there.

Adeline found Philip standing in the middle of their cabin waiting for her. His clothes were wet and crumpled, his fair hair plastered in a fringe on his forehead. He looked so ridiculous that she would have laughed but she saw the frown on his face. He asked curtly:—

"Why did you send for me?"

"I was anxious about you."

"I've been standing here waiting for you."

"Only a few moments! I have been with Sholto. He's sick."

"So is everyone. I brought up my own breakfast. What do you want of me?"

"I want you to change into dry things."

He turned toward the door. "If that is all—"

She caught his arm. "Philip, you are not to go! You'll get your death!"

"I should make a poor soldier if this would kill me."

"But what can you do?"

"For one thing, I can put some courage and order into the steerage passengers. They are on the verge of panic. As for you, you might tidy up this cabin. It's vile!"

"What do you expect!" she cried. "I have a sick baby! I have an ayah who is half-dead! I have Mrs. Cameron to visit! I have my young brother to look after! I worry myself ill about you. The stewardess is useless except to gossip. The ship is leaking! And you ask me to tidy up the cabin!"

In a fury she began to snatch up garments and to thrust them into boxes or on pegs.

"I didn't ask you to get in a temper," he said.

"Oh, no, I'm not to get in a temper! I'm to keep perfectly calm! And as neat as a pin!"

"Then why don't you?"

Before she could answer, the parrot, which had been sitting muffled on the top of his swaying cage, uttered a scream of the purest excitement as he became conscious of Adeline's agitation, and flew violently about the cabin. The disturbance caused by his wings was startling to nerves already tense. He came to rest on a brass bracket, turned himself over so that he hung head down and, in that posture, sent out a torrent of curses in Hindu:—

"Haramzada!" he screamed. "Haramzada! Chore! Iflatoon! Iflatoon!"

"I sometimes wish," said Philip, "that we had never brought that bird."

"I dare say you do," retorted Adeline. "I dare say you wish you had never brought me. Then you might have had your old shipwreck in the most perfect order! You might—"

Philip's face relaxed. "Adeline," he said, "you make any situation ridiculous. Come, my pet, don't let us quarrel." He put his arms about her and his lips to her hair. "Do find me a pair of gloves for I've blistered my palms at the pump."

She was instantly solicitous for him. First she kissed the blistered palms, then she bathed them, applied a soothing ointment, a bandage, and found a pair of loose gloves for him. So administered to he became quite meek and changed into dry clothes and brushed his hair. All this while Boney regarded them quizzically, hanging for the greater part of the time head down.

"Philip," she asked as she coiled her hair, "is everything as simple as the Captain says? Are we in danger? Will the ship carry us safely to Newfoundland? He says he will stop there for repairs, doesn't he?"

"We can cope with the leak," he answered gravely. "And if only this damned head wind would fall and a favorable wind spring up we should do very well."

They did keep the leak under control, the sun came out fitfully; a kind of order was created on the ship, the wind promised to fall. Regular shifts at the pumps were arranged and, when the time of changing came, the cry of "Spell ho!" rang out from Grigg's enormous mouth. The Captain looked determinedly cheerful. The *Alanna* pushed on through the buffeting of the waves. She seemed running straight into the ruddy sunset. A sailor came bounding up to the Captain who was talking with Philip and Mr. Wilmott.

"The cargo has shifted!" he said, out of breath.

Philip went to where Adeline and her brothers had found a sheltered corner on the deck. The boys were tired and had stretched themselves in complete abandon on either side of her. Conway's head lay against her shoulder, Sholto's on her lap. Upon my word, thought Philip, they look no better than the emigrants. Adeline raised her eyes from the pages of *Pendennis*.

His stern expression startled her.

She sat upright. "What is it now?" she demanded.

Conway woke and sprang to his feet. He looked dazed. He stammered:—

"Why—Philip—why? Adeline—the deck! Look at the deck!"

"Yes," said Philip. "The ballast has shifted. She's listing badly. The Captain says there's nothing for it but to go back to Galway for repairs."

"Back to Galway for repairs!" repeated Adeline and Conway in one voice. Then he laughed. "What a joke on us!" He shook his brother by the shoulder. "Wake up, Sholto! You're going to see dear old Ireland again!"

"How long will it take?" asked Adeline.

"With this wind behind us we'll do it in a few days."

"We must not let my mother know we are there. It would upset her so. She'd be bound to come all the way to Galway to see us, and the good-byes to say all over again!"

"I quite agree," said Philip. He felt that he could very well do without seeing his parents-in-law again.

Sholto wore a strange look of joy.

The next morning the wind had fallen enough to allow the first officer to be lowered over the side in the Captain's cutter to examine the leak. The sea was a bright hard blue and the waves were crinkling under the wild west wind. His movements were watched with fascination by those on deck. He opened his mouth and shouted cryptic remarks to the Captain leaning over the side. He put out his hand and felt the injured part like a surgeon concentrating on an operation. Then he was hauled up again. Everyone crowded round him. He was loath to relieve their anxiety and only the presence of the cheerful Captain made him say:—

"Ah, I dare say she'll do. That is if there are no squalls. The leak will be four feet out of the water if the sea gets no worse. She may do—but we'll hae to keep at the pumps."

The *Alanna* had turned back with the sound of thunder in her sails as she veered. Now, to the wind she had struggled against for so many days, she surrendered herself, let it drive her back toward Ireland and strained every inch of canvas to be there with the least loss of time. But the shifting of the ballast made her awkward. No one could forget the way she listed. It was as though all on board had suddenly become lame, leaning to one side when they walked.

And there were the pumps always to be kept going, forcing out the briny water that stretched in monstrous fathoms waiting to force its way in again. Aching backs, hands blistered, then callused, monotonous hours that wove the day and night into one chain of weariness and boredom. Every now and again the boredom changing to apprehension at the sight of a ragged cloud that looked the possible mother of a squall. Of all those on board, Adeline was the most buoyant. In her handsome clothes, that were so unsuitable to the situation, she carried assurance and gaiety wherever she went. She would, for all Philip's remonstrances, take her turn at the pumps. She learned sea chanteys from the sailors, though she never could keep on the tune.

A strange intimacy sprang up among the passengers. They seemed to have known each other for years. Their faces, their gestures, their peculiarities, were etched on each other's minds. Then, on the eighth day, the dim shape of Ireland became visible on the horizon.

IV

Repairs

Galway bay lay blue and tranquil, church bells were ringing as the bark, at a melancholy angle, moved slowly into the port. Then, for the first time in ten days, the pound of the pumps ceased. The eardrums of those on board were freed to take in the sound of the bells and the singing of birds.

Adeline stood in the bow facing the light breeze that carried warm scents of the land. Her nostrils quivered and she gave a little laugh. Mr. Wilmott came up just in time to hear it.

"You are fortunate to be able to laugh, Mrs. Whiteoak," he said. "To me this is a most depressing return."

She looked at him over her shoulder, her white teeth gleaming between her parted lips.

"Why," she exclaimed, "aren't you glad to smell the land again —and hear the bells?"

"Not the Old Land," he answered bitterly. "Not *these* bells. I never expected to be here again. I want the New World."

"Well, you'll get it, if only you have patience. You might be at the bottom of the sea. I'm thankful to be alive!"

"You are different. You are young and full of hope."

"But you aren't old! And you have told me of interesting plans you have. This is just a mood. It will pass."

He smiled too. "Of course it will. I certainly cannot feel downcast when I am near you."

The ayah stood near by with the baby in her arms, her pale-colored robe fluttering about her emaciated figure. It was the first time she had been on deck since her bout of seasickness and she looked scarcely able to stand, let alone carry the child. But her heavy-lidded eyes shone with joy at the sight of the green land and little Augusta held out her hands toward the gulls that came circling about the ship.

Philip strode down the deck.

"I have the luggage ready!" he exclaimed. "I'm not leaving any of our valuables on board."

"The Captain says they will be safe."

"Humph! Anyhow we shall need our things. This leak isn't to be mended in a jiffy."

"Have you seen my brothers?" she asked. "Have they got their things together?"

"Here is Sholto to answer for himself." Philip eyed the boy sternly. He was laden with his belongings, gathered together in promiscuous fashion. His pale face was alight with exhilaration.

"I can scarcely wait," he exclaimed in an exaggerated brogue, "to plant me feet on the ould sod! Praise be to God, I shall sleep in a dacent bed and put me teeth in some dacent food before long!"

As he advanced he let fall one article after another on the deck but he appeared unconscious of this.

"Where is Conway?" demanded Adeline.

"I can't make him stir. He's still in bed. Mary Cameron is with him."

"Merciful heavens!" cried Adeline.

Philip threw them both a warning look. Mr. Wilmott considerately moved away, out of hearing.

"She is packing his things for him," went on Sholto. "He says he is too tired and the silly girl believes him! She believes whatever he says and does everything he tells her."

"I shall attend to him," said Adeline.

With her eager step she went swiftly along the slanting deck. She hastened down the companionway and through the narrow passage where most of the cabins were separated from public view by only a curtain. The smell of this passage she felt she never would forget. All the smells of the ship below deck seemed concentrated here—the smell of stale cooking, the smell rising from the livestock, the smell of the lavatory! What discomfort she had endured! The sweet land breeze made it suddenly almost tangible—discomfort and fear.

She stood outside Conway's door listening but there was so much noise of movement and shouting she could hear nothing. She opened the door.

Conway lay stretched on the berth, a happy smile on his face, his pale hair falling about his cheeks. His long greenish eyes followed every movement of Mary Cameron who was bent over a portmanteau carefully packing his toilet articles, under his direction.

"Well, this is a pretty sight!" cried Adeline. "Oh, you lazy pig, Con! Get up out of that and do your own work! Mary, you ought to be ashamed of yourself. Why aren't you helping your mother?"

Mary raised a flushed face. She said, with a touch of defiance:—

"Everything is done for my mother. She is resting till we disembark."

"Then go and sit by her. Don't you know better than to be alone with a young man in his cabin? Have you traveled halfway round the world and learnt nothing?"

"My mamma has told me," answered Mary, "to be afraid of Indians and to be afraid of Chinamen and Frenchmen but she has not told me to be afraid of Irishmen."

Adeline found it hard not to laugh but she said sternly—"Then she did wrong, for they are the worst of all. Now, run off. If Con needs help I'll give it him." She pushed Mary out of the room.

She came to her brother and took him by the ear. She bent down and put her face close to his.

"Con," she said, "have you ever laid a bad hand on that girl?"

With the shamelessness of a child he distorted his face against the pain of his ear.

"Let me be!" he said. "I shan't tell you."

"You will or I'll tell Philip to question you. You'll not like that."

He twisted his head so he could kiss her forearm.

"Sweet Sis," he said.

"Answer me, Con!"

"I swear I've said nothing to Mary you might not have heard—or her mother."

She let him go. "Thank God for that! Now, get up and pack your bags."

But she was soft enough to help him. The beautiful harbor lay spread before them; the gray stone town rising beyond it, and beyond that the dark mountains of Clare. An ancient feudal castle stood on one of the hills. The townsfolk were gathering to see the ship for it was rarely that one of her size entered the harbor.

Now there came all the confusion of disembarking—they who had thought not to leave the ship till they landed at Quebec! Off they came, carrying their belongings, looking paler than when they had set out, some excited, some forlorn, a few in tears. The poor livestock were led or harried off—some so weak in the leg they could hardly walk. They were dirty, they were dazed, though the poultry bore the adventure best. Maggie, the little goat which had been sent for Augusta's nourishment, was the one exception. She seemed not to have suffered at all from the experience but trotted off on her little hoofs, her bell tinkling. One of the sailors had taken a fancy to her and had combed her long silvery hair. As she was led from the pier she saw a small patch of green and hastened to tear off a mouthful and munch it.

Boney, too, had borne the voyage well. The rolling of the ship had been but a pleasure to him. To hang head downward was one of his diversions. He left the ship, sitting on Adeline's shoulder. His beak was parted in what looked like a smile of triumph. His dark tongue was a wonder to the crowd who soon collected about her.

"You had better have carried him in his cage," said Philip.

"Indeed I had," she agreed, "and I'd put him in it now but it's far behind with the stewardess, and it's a heavy thing to carry."

The truth was she enjoyed the sensation they were making. She smiled and nodded at the crowd in a way that delighted them.

"Och, see the fine lady with the bird!" someone cried. "Come quick! 'T is a sight to beat all!"

Others came running. "Bad cess to ye," cried one, giving his fellow a clout, " 't is yourself that do be hidin' the view of her. Sure, I can't see her at all."

The crowd increased. If the sight of Adeline with the parrot was enthralling, the sight of the ayah in her robes with the white-clad child in her arms and, in the child's arms, the beautiful wax doll increased the excitement to screaming point. The two Irishmen, D'Arcy and Brent, shouldered the crowd aside. Patsy had heard of a carriage that could be hired and presently it came rattling over the cobbles, drawn by a decrepit-looking gray horse who still could move with a strange devil-may-care alacrity.

Adeline found the priest's young nieces and asked them where they would stay while repairs were being made. They were weighed down by bundles and looked scarcely so bright and rosy as when they had set out. They had a friend in the town with whom they would leave their possessions. Then they would walk the ten miles to their uncle's house, spend the night with him, then go home for a sight of their parents. They looked more troubled than happy at the prospect.

"Faith, the last good-bye near killed our mother," said the older girl, "and the next one will be worse but she'd think it quare and cruel of us if we didn't go back to see her."

"I can hardly wait," said the other, "to see her and my da and all the young ones agin. Sure we'll have things to tell thim to frighten the life out of thim."

"Don't you do it," said Adeline. "Tell her the sea was as smooth as a pewter plate and the wind no more than a baby's breath. Tell her that only a wee board came loose on the ship but the Captain was so particular he brought us all the way back to Galway to have it set right. Tell her that I have my eye on you and mean to keep it there till we land in Canada."

"Yes, my lady," they agreed, showing their fine teeth, "we'll tell her what you say. We'll niver say a word to scare her."

Adeline watched them trudge off with their bundles. She could see the snowy whiteness of their napes beneath their curling dark hair. Now she thought of Mrs. Cameron and Mary. She gave a sigh, feeling suddenly the weight of responsibility for all these weaker creatures.

She saw Philip putting mother and daughter into the carriage. The ayah and Gussie were already in. He called out:—

"Make haste, my dear! Let's get away from here." An impatient frown dented his fair forehead.

Up the cobbled street the carriage rattled, followed by part of the crowd. Many of them were boys and girls who jumped up and down screaming in their excitement. Philip and the young Courts walked. Philip disliked being a part of such a procession but his brothers-in-law played up to it with gestures and chaff.

Later, looking down from her bedroom window, Adeline saw that a fight had started in the street. Errand boys, butchers, beggars, anyone and everyone were shouting and fighting with fists and clubs. Dogs were barking and howling. Then suddenly a squad of peelers appeared. The fighting ceased. The crowd melted into lanes and cellarways. A Sabbath calm soothed the street.

Philip had watched the scene over Adeline's shoulder with an amused smile.

"A funny lot, your people are!" he said, when it was over.

"They are as God made them," she replied, a little defensively.

"And are you sure it was God, my darling?"

"Well, He may have had a little help from outside."

He kissed her. "I scarcely have seen you alone," he said, "since we sailed. There was always the baby or your brothers or Mary. Egad, I shall be thankful when all this is over and we are established in Quebec."

"So shall I. You'd never guess what Mr. Wilmott said when we stepped off the ship."

"What?"

"He said—'Do you know I never expected to set foot on these islands again? I hoped never to set foot on them again.' 'Never come home to visit again!' I exclaimed. 'Never,' he answered. And he looked sombre—like the hero of a romantic novel. I've done my best to encourage an attachment between him and Mrs. Cameron but it seems hopeless."

"A seasick widow is not alluring," said Philip. "And, to judge by the looks he gives, he is more likely to form an attachment to you. He'd better be careful."

"That old sobersides," laughed Adeline. "He's not at all my sort. But I do like him as an acquaintance and I hope he'll settle in Quebec near us."

"I think we ought to let your parents know we are here," said Philip, abruptly changing the subject. "It will take quite a week for repairs and, if they find out from other sources, it might give them a bit of a shock."

"No, no," cried Adeline, "I can't bear another good-bye! It would be unlucky."

"We could tell them not to come."

"Nothing would keep my mother away. And my father too—he'd come and create some sort of disturbance. He'd probably abuse the Captain for not having a stauncher ship."

"They may see it in a newspaper."

"I'm willing to risk that. Next week they go on a visit to my grandfather. They'll have no time for newspapers."

So she had her way and they settled down to the strange interlude in their voyage. They explored the streets of the gray old town. Philip and Mr. Wilmott went on fishing excursions. Adeline wandered with her brothers and Mary Cameron along the mountain paths of Clare or on the shore of the bay and brought home pocketfuls of shells for little Augusta. Every day there was the visit to the ship to watch the carpenters at work. Every day people thronged from the country about to see the wonders of the ship. It was grand to see them dancing on the deck in the spring evenings—their lithe bodies bounding and leaping to the whistled tune, clear as a pipe. They snapped their fingers and whirled and bounded in the dance. They had shapely limbs and Spanish faces and there had never been so much merriment on that ship before.

One evening they were dancing by moonlight and the moon went under a cloud so that no one could say who was who. But a handsome fellow in a blue coat had had his eye on Adeline. He pushed his partner from him and, dancing past Adeline, touched her with his hand. She was standing between her brothers with Mary Cameron hanging as usual on Conway's arm. Adeline gave a little laugh as the man's hand touched her shoulder and he could see the white flash of her teeth in the dimness. He danced round the deck and in a moment was at her side again. His arm slid about her. She sprang into the dance. Wildly they danced to the sound of the whistling and the pair of them moved in such beautiful accord that it was a pity the whole world could not see—but it was well for her that Philip did not. She was transported by the joy of movement but she kept her eyes on the cloud that hid the moon and, when its edge was silvered, she struck her partner on the breast and whispered—"Let me go, ye divil!"

As the moon cast its radiance on the deck she stood tall and slim by Sholto's side. She saw then that Conway and Mary had been dancing.

He grinned and said—"Now I've something to hold over your head, Sis. Don't you go telling tales of me."

A bell sounded and all had to leave the ship.

The next day a period of fog and drizzle set in. There was no more dancing on the deck. The days moved heavily. The Captain had promised that repairs should be complete in ten days but it was two weeks before they were ready to sail. There was a strange and rather sombre excitement in this second setting forth. The passengers were now so well aware of the evils which might befall them. Their faith in the worthiness of the ship had been shaken. Of course any ship might spring a leak and Captain Bradley declared that the *Alanna* was now as sound as a nut.

They went to church on the Sunday before sailing. Adeline, Philip, Mr. Wilmott, and Mrs. Cameron to the Gothic Abbey church where the beautiful groined arches of the roof, the sculptured bosses, were obliterated under coat after coat of whitewash, and where the congregation was scattered. The Irishmen, D'Arcy and Brent, returned from the Catholic Chapel and told how they were not able to get inside the building for the Mass but had to kneel in the churchyard with the overflowing crowd. Conway, Sholto, and Mary wandered along the shore. They had begged to be excused from church and Mrs. Cameron would deny her daughter nothing. Also she had heard of an epidemic of fever going about in the town and surely Mary would be safer on the shore with the two boys to look after her.

The hour of sailing came and down the cobbled street moved all the conglomeration of objects that had been removed from the ship. The luggage came bumping and rattling over the stones. The livestock was harried, driven, and prodded toward its quarters—all but the little goat, Maggie, who trotted on as gaily as she had trotted off. The ayah looked less fragile after her weeks on land but she wore an expression of foreboding as she glided on to the ship holding the baby close. Gussie, in her turn, clutched her wax doll in its silk crinoline and bonnet. The doll was large, a load for Gussie's tiny arms, so, as the ayah stood with her in the stern and gazed at the churning of the water as the ship moved away from the pier, Gussie leaned forward and let the doll fall overboard. She looked around slyly into the ayah's face. "Gone," she remarked, and it was the first word she had spoken.

For an instant the pink face smirked up at them out of the foam, the crinoline was inflated, then there was nothing. The ayah broke into a storm of Hindu reproaches. She hissed these at Gussie in a terrifying way and shook her but Gussie knew the ayah was her slave.

The sun came out brilliantly, gilding these last moments of departure. The hurry and scurry were over. All was neat and shining. The decks were clean. The brass of the railings and the officers' buttons gleamed. The sails took in a little of the breeze as though testing its quality, then received it in its fullness and spread themselves white and rounded before the masts. Now there was no dreadful listing of the deck, only a tremulous, happy quiver ran across it as the *Alanna* rose and dipped on the small waves.

Philip and Adeline stood with fingers locked looking back at the land. The town, the mountains of Clare, the movement of figures in the foreground, were still so clear—like a painted picture before them. They could see a tall dark woman driving a pig into the sea. She had tied a string to its hind leg. She had tucked up her skirts and waded in after it. She began to scrub it with all her might while it squealed in a manner to split the heavens. Then they saw her drive it out, white as a pearl, all its filth left behind it, a very angel of a pig to look at.

"Oh, the lovely pig!" cried Adeline, laughing in delight. "I do wish my brothers had been here to see that! Why don't they come up from below? Do you know, Philip, that little Mary is wonderfully improved. You should have seen her settling her mother in and fetching her a cup of tea to drink. Why—look! The post chaise and horses! Merciful heaven, Philip, 't is my father and mother and the wee Timothy with them and the four horses all in a lather!" Her voice broke into a scream. "Philip, stop the ship!"

For a moment he stood stock-still in consternation. He saw his father-in-law leap from the box, throw the reins to the coachman, and assist his wife to alight. He saw him take off his hat and wave it, motioning the ship to stop. The space between them was steadily widening. Philip ran along the deck for a few strides, then halted.

"The Captain will never do it," he said.

"He must," she declared, and flew toward the wheelhouse where the first mate had the wheel in his hands.

"Oh, Mr. Grigg!" she cried. "You must turn back! There are my father and my mother on the pier—come to get just one more glimpse of me! I can't leave them like this."

"It's impossible," he declared. "I would na turn back for the Queen of England. It's against all rules."

"I'll take the responsibility."

"I canna let ye!"

"I'll take the wheel from you!"

"I canna let ye do that."

She put her hands on the wheel and strove to turn it. She was strong and she actually was changing the course of the ship. He cried in a panic:

"How daur ye? Ye'll have us on the rocks, wumman! Let the helm loose!"

The passengers were crowding about.

Philip came and took her by the wrists.

"Come away," he said. "I've spoken to the Captain. He cannot turn back. Come and wave to your parents or it will be too late."

She burst into tears and, breaking away from him, ran weeping down the deck. The tears blinded her and at first she saw only a distorted image of her parents on the pier. As their figures became clearer she was horrified to see how they had lessened. Why, they looked no more than dolls! There was her formidable father looking no more than a doll—a doll that shook its fist at the receding ship. Or perhaps at her! She might never know which. Her last earthly vision of him might be of him shaking his fist at her and the ship. She put her palms to her quivering mouth and threw kisses to the fast-diminishing figures of her parents and her young brother.

She saw James Wilmott standing at her side. There was a strange expression on his sombre face. He spoke in a new voice:—

"Darling girl," he said. "Don't cry. I can't bear it. Please don't cry."

At that moment Philip reached her other side. To take her mind off her disappointment, he said:—

"Where are Conway and Sholto? They should come and wave good-bye."

"It is too late! Too late!"

"Shall I bring them?"

"If you like."

He strode off.

On the dock near her people she could see a little group of the relatives of the steerage passengers. They were huddled mournfully together as though for comfort.

The ship was now caught by a fresh wind. She mounted an on-rushing green billow. There was a straining of cordage, a great bulging of white sails. She leant, as though joyfully, she came about, the land was hidden and, when once more it was visible, it was far away and no more had any relation to the ship.

Mr. Wilmott offered his arm to Adeline.

"May I take you to your cabin?" he asked.

"Thank you." She leant on him gratefully.

"I hope you will forgive and forget the way I spoke a moment ago," he said. "I am a lonely man and your friendship is very precious to me. I was moved by your tears. But—I had no right to say—what I did."

"You are kind," she said. "You are a friend. That is all that matters." From beneath her wet lashes her eyes looked gently into his.

With Adeline still leaning on his arm they went slowly down the deck. Sea gulls swung and circled above them. One even alighted on the top of a mast and sat tranquil as a ship's figurehead.

V

The Second Voyage

WHEN Adeline entered her cabin and saw her hand luggage heaped there and realized that another voyage in this cubbyhole lay before her, she had a moment's feeling of desperation. What experiences might she and Philip have to face! They were leaving behind all they knew and loved, setting out for the unknown. She realized this much more than on the first voyage. The thought of her mother standing weeping on the dock came back to torment her. Even her father seemed pathetic for the moment.

She could not bear to begin unpacking yet. She would first see how the ayah and Gussie were faring. She crossed the passage and looked in on them. The ayah was stretched on the berth. Her wrist, on which she wore a number of silver bangles, lay across her forehead. From this shelter her languid dark eyes looked up at Adeline.

Adeline was fluent in the dialect used by the ayah. She asked:—

"Are you feeling ill already?"

"No, Mem Sahib—but I rest a little. The beloved child is very well and quite happy."

"Yes, I see. Still I think you would be better on deck. Baby could play with her shells there."

At the word, Gussie held up one in each hand, then laughed aloud and put them to her ears. Her face became rapt as she listened to their murmur.

"I shall take her to the deck at once, Mem Sahib," said the ayah, raising herself on her elbow with a look of patient resignation, then sinking back on the pillow.

"The smells down here are bad for both of you," said Adeline firmly. She looked about the cabin.

"Where is the doll?" she asked. "I don't see it."

The bangles rattled on the ayah's forehead.

"I put the doll away for safety, Mem Sahib."

"Where?"

"In the box with Baby's diapers, Mem Sahib."

"That was well done. She is too young to appreciate it now. We'll keep it for her."

"Gone," said Gussie.

"Did she say something?" asked Adeline.

"No, Mem Sahib. She cannot yet say one word."

As Adeline went back along the passage she met Mrs. Cameron. Still wearing her dolman and bonnet she turned a face heavy with mingled self-pity and reproach toward Adeline.

"I suppose Mary is off somewhere with those brothers of yours," she said. "I've never seen such a change come over a girl. I used to know exactly where she was. She almost never left my side. But now, half the time, I have no notion of her whereabouts."

Adeline's sympathy, which had been focused on the mother, now veered suddenly to the daughter.

"Well, after all," she said, "Mary is very young. She must have a little fun."

"Fun!" repeated Mrs. Cameron bitterly. "Fun! If she can bear to have fun—after what we've been through!"

"You cannot expect a child to go on mourning forever." Adeline spoke rather curtly. She was tired and Mrs. Cameron was altogether too mournful an object, planted there in her black bonnet and dolman. No wonder the girl wanted to be off with other young people.

"She is nearly sixteen. She'll soon be a woman. She doesn't seem to realize it. That's what I tell her. She's a regular featherbrain."

"I saw her carrying a cup of tea very nicely to you, not so long ago."

Mrs. Cameron flared up. "I hope you are not insinuating that I do not appreciate my own child, Mrs. Whiteoak! She is all I have in the world! My mind is always on her! I'd die a thousand deaths rather than a hair of her head should be harmed!"

"You'd do well to get your mind off her for a bit," returned Adeline. She was growing tired of Mrs. Cameron.

The vessel gave a sudden heave. She seemed to have glided down a steep slope and to be now laboriously mounting another. Adeline's stomach felt suddenly squeamish. Was she going to be sick? She must lie down in her berth for a little.

Mrs. Cameron had burst into tears.

Adeline exclaimed—"Oh, I didn't mean that you are not a perfect mother! I'll go and find Mary for you this minute. I'll tell my young brothers to keep away from her. Pray go and lie you down and I'll send her to you in a jiffy."

Mrs. Cameron stumbled back to her cabin. Adeline listened outside the one occupied by Conway and Sholto. There was silence within. She entered.

There were two portmanteaux standing in the middle of the tiny room. There were odds and ends of things thrown on the lower berth. But what was that on the pillow? She leant over it to see. For some reason her heart quickened its beat.

It was an envelope pinned to the pillow and addressed to her in Sholto's best schoolboy handwriting. She was trembling as she opened it, though she did not know what she expected to read. She tore it open. She read:—

My own dearest Sis,

Conway is making me write this as he says he is the man of action and I am the man of letters. Be that as it may I feel pretty sick at what I have to disclose. I am writing this in the hotel the night before the ship sails. We shall go with our luggage on board and then, while everything is confused, we shall return to the dock and conceal ourselves in the town till you are gone. Dear Adeline, forgive us for not going with you to Quebec. During the voyage we wished ourselves back in Ireland a thousand times. It seemed too good to be true when the ship turned her bow homeward again, we were that homesick.

Now this is the part Conway himself should have written but you know what a lazy dog he is. Mary has decided not to go to Canada either. She has decided to remain in Ireland and marry Con. I should hate to be in his shoes when he faces Father with

Mary on his arm. Mary tried to write but she cried and messed up the paper outrageously. So, dearest Sis, will you please break the news with great tact and sympathy to Mrs. Cameron. Mary says this will be quite a blow to her but, as Mary's happiness was always her first consideration, she will be reconciled to it once she thinks it over.

When you arrive in Quebec will you please put all *our belongings (that is of course including Mary's) on the next east-bound ship and address them very clearly. We don't want to lose anything, especially as after all the outlay for Con and me, Dad will be an old skinflint for years to come.*

Mary will write a long letter to her mother and send it by the next ship. Conway also will write.

We all three join in wishing you bon voyage*—no storms—no leaks—and a glorious time in Quebec.*

Ever your loving brother,
Sholto Court

Adeline stood transfixed when she had finished reading the letter. She had a sense of panic. She felt that she wanted to run to her own berth, get under the covers, draw them over her head and remain so till Quebec was reached. Then disbelief and relief swept over her. It was all a joke! Her brothers were always up to pranks. It could not be true. She would find Patsy O'Flynn and perhaps he would know all about it, know where the three were hiding.

She sped along the passage and down the steep stairs that led to the steerage. Here in the common room people were settling themselves for the voyage, untying canvas-covered bundles, opening packets of food, drinking out of tin cups which a couple of barefooted cabin boys were filling with tea. In one corner a decent-looking Scotchwoman had gathered her brood of children about her and was putting large buns into their hands. A nursing babe still clung to her breast as she moved among the others.

Adeline asked her—"Do you know the whereabouts of my man, Patsy O'Flynn, the one with all the clothes on him and eyebrows that stick out?"

The woman pointed with the bun she held. "Aye, he's yonder, whaur the hens are. Shall I fetch him to you, ma'am?"

"No, no, thank you. I'll go to him."

She found Patsy stretched at ease on his greatcoat which he had spread out on the poultry coops. To the accompaniment of crowings and cacklings he munched a slab of bread and cheese. "Heave ho, the winds do blow," he was singing like a seasoned tar, between mouthfuls, for he wanted to make his bread and cheese last as long as possible. Maggie, the little goat, had somehow loosed her tether and stood at his feet nibbling one of his dangling bootlaces. The pair were a picture of devil-may-care contentment.

"Oh, Patsy-Joe!" cried Adeline. "Do you know where my brothers are? I can't find them anywhere on the ship."

He leapt to his feet and bolted a large mouthful of bread and cheese.

"I do not thin, your honor, Miss," he answered, jerking his head forward for the cheese was still in his throat. "But I'll set out to look for them this instant moment."

"Patsy-Joe, I've had a letter from Master Sholto and he says they've gone back to the town and little Miss Cameron with them. Oh, I dare not let myself think it's so, for it would kill her poor mother and my brothers would be to blame. Have they said aught to you about running away home?"

"Aye, many was the time they said divil take the ship and they hoped they never set eyes on her again."

"But you should have told me what they were saying."

"Ah, wisha, I thought it was just their way o' spakin'. And did ye say the young geerl was off with them?"

"Yes."

His little eyes twinkled. "Sure, I'm not at all surprised for I saw her with thim on the shore last Sunday marnin', and I said to mesilf she was too free with Mr. Conway and himself with time heavy on his hands. And did ye say they've left the ship entirely?"

She was only wasting her time talking to Patsy. She hurried back up the stairway and at the top met Philip. Each saw the concern on the face of the other.

"What have you heard?" she demanded.

"A sailor tells me that he saw your brothers and Mary Cameron walking separately back to the town just before we left."

"My God, why didn't he tell us?"

"He thought we knew. When he saw the carriage drive up he thought it had come to meet them. How did you hear?"

"I had this letter." She took it from her pocket and put it in his hand.

"Those boys ought to be flogged," he said, when he had read the letter.

"Oh, if only they hadn't taken Mary! Oh, how can we break the news to her mother?"

"You did wrong, Adeline, to encourage that friendship. It's led to a pretty kettle of fish."

She took hold of the railing and two tears rolled down her cheeks.

"I know—now that it's too late," she said, in a trembling voice. Then, after a moment, she broke out—"We must go back for them! I'll pay the cost from my own pocket!"

"We cannot. It's impossible."

"What do a few hours more matter—in such a case?"

"Listen to reason, Adeline. If those three scallywags were waiting on the dock eager to be picked up we might do it—at a pretty cost to you. But they don't want to come back to the ship. Doubtless, by this time, they are well on their way in quite another direction."

"Oh, whatever shall I do?" she groaned.

"You'll just have to go and tell Mrs. Cameron what her daughter has done. After all—it's her fault. If the girl had been properly brought up she'd not have dreamed of doing such a thing."

"Philip, darling, would you go and break the news to the mother?"

He looked aghast at the idea.

"I couldn't possibly," he said. "You'll have to do that."

"Well, will you stand beside me, in case—" She hesitated.

"In case what?" he asked distantly.

"She will be terribly upset. She will probably faint."

"I shall stand at a little distance—within reach but out of sight."

"That will do . . . Do you think I might write her a letter, as Sholto did me?"

"By gad, if I had my hand on those boys! Yes—write her a letter, if you prefer that way."

"Perhaps you would write the letter. I believe she would take it better from you."

"I am no letter writer," he answered testily. "Your family excels at that." He took her by the arm. "Come into the salon and I'll get a glass of sherry for you. That will put heart into you."

In the little room, graced by so high-flown a name, Adeline sipped the sherry and thought miserably of what she had to do. At one moment she would ejaculate—"Oh, the young villains!" And at the next—"Oh, the poor mother!"—or—"It were better the ship had gone down with all of us!" But the sherry did her good and finally she sprang up exclaiming—"I'll do it now and have it over."

"That's a good girl," he said.

She scowled. "Don't you 'good girl' me! After all, you should be breaking the news to her. You're a man and 't is your own brother-in-law has done the mischief!"

"Adeline, I cannot."

He followed her down to the door of Mrs. Cameron's cabin. She rapped, trembling in every limb.

"Yes?" came the voice from within.

"Mrs. Cameron, I have something to tell you."

"Come in."

She found Mrs. Cameron putting things in order and still wearing a hurt air. But there was something touching about her. She was small and neat and you could see she had been through a great deal. Adeline spoke gently.

"A while ago you said you supposed Mary was off somewhere with those brothers of mine. You were right. She is."

Mary's mother only stared.

"She is off with them," went on Adeline. "Right off the ship and away home!"

"Are you mad?" said Mrs. Cameron. "What nonsense are you telling me?"

"It is the truth. They left the ship—Mary and my two little brothers—but they've gone home. She'll be quite safe."

Mrs. Cameron had turned ghastly pale. She put her hand to her throat and demanded:—

"Who told you this?"

"I had a letter from Sholto. And my husband was told by one of the sailors who saw them."

Mrs. Cameron spoke in a hoarse whisper.

"Show me the letter."

Adeline handed it to her. She riveted her eyes on it as though she would tear the written words from the page. At the end she reeled across the cabin but she recovered herself. She faced Adeline in a fury, her hands clenched at her sides.

"It's your fault!" she cried. "It's all your fault! You encouraged them. You begged me to allow Mary to go about with that wicked boy. Oh—" As she was struck by the possibilities of the situation her voice rose to a scream—"Oh, what has he done to her! My little ewe lamb! She was as pure as the driven snow till we came on board this accursed ship! Oh, can't something be done? Where is the Captain?"

She pushed her way past Adeline, thrust aside Philip's restraining hand, and bounded up the companionway. So flimsy were the partitions that a general consternation was caused by her outbreak. People came running from all directions (some thought a fresh disaster had befallen the ship) while Adeline and Philip followed after, miserably conscious of what had really happened.

"What's this—what's this, madam?" asked Captain Bradley, coming to meet Mrs. Cameron.

She flung herself against his shoulder.

"Oh, save her! Save my little girl!" she cried hysterically.

"Where is she?" he asked, in his resonant voice.

"There!" She pointed landward. "She left the ship with those horrible Irish boys! I call everyone to witness that she was as pure as the driven snow! Oh, what shall I do?"

"What's all this about?" Captain Bradley demanded of Philip.

"The girl has eloped with my young brother-in-law, a lad of eighteen," he replied, gruffly. "But from what was said in the letter they've gone straight to his father's house."

"If you'd like to go back for them, Captain dear," put in Adeline, "I'll pay for the cost of it."

It was to the Captain's shame that he looked more tenderly on Adeline than on Mrs. Cameron, whom he regarded as a complaining woman of depressing appearance.

"Do you think the young gentleman will marry her?" he asked Philip, in a low voice.

"I'm sure he intends to," said Philip, with rather more certainty than he felt.

"Come, come, it may not be so bad as you think," the Captain comforted Mrs. Cameron. To Adeline he said—"Look backward, Mrs. Whiteoak! The ship's been flying away like a bird. You must understand that it's impossible for us to return for a young runaway couple."

"It's all her fault!" shrieked Mrs. Cameron. "She's as wicked as her brothers. We don't want their kind in our beautiful young country! They're evil!"

Mrs. Cameron became hysterical and it was with difficulty that the Captain and the steward got her back to her cabin. For the remainder of the voyage she never left it. Fortunately there had joined the ship at Galway two new passengers with whom she made friends. They were a married couple from Newfoundland. The husband was in the fisheries business; the wife, deeply religious, was a great comfort to Mrs. Cameron.

The other passengers, and particularly those in the steerage, chose to regard the elopement as a youthful romance and poor Mrs. Cameron as a tyrannical parent. Conway Court had been a favorite on board and it was the general opinion that the plain young girl had done extremely well for herself—for it was taken for granted that he would marry her.

The winds were fair and the ship sped on. The livestock became fewer. A poor woman from Liverpool gave birth to a child with a terrible lack of privacy. In the salon Captain Whiteoak and Messrs. D'Arcy, Brent, and Wilmott played at bezique each evening, while they sipped Franch brandy out of small green glasses that were filled from a wicker-clad bottle. Adeline would sit watching them, her wide skirts spread gracefully about her, her chin in her palm while her eyes moved contemplatively from one face to the other of the players.

Then one night a frightening thing happened. James Wilmott had just carried a small glass of the liqueur to Adeline's side, for she looked pale and rather languid. There came a shuffling sound on the companionway, a growling sound of voices. Adeline half-rose in her chair. The four men turned their heads toward the door. Crowding into it they saw a mob of rough, fierce-looking men. They were carrying clubs, sticks, any weapon they could lay their hands on. The whites of their eyes glistened in the light of the swaying hanging-lamp. One of them raised a hairy arm and pointed to Wilmott.

"Yon's him!" he exclaimed.

With a threatening growl the others moved in a body toward Wilmott, who faced them coolly.

"I don't know what you mean," he said.

"You are Thomas D'Arcy, Esquire, ain't ye?"

"No, my name is Wilmott."

D'Arcy rose to his feet. "I am Thomas D'Arcy," he said, smiling a little.

"Yes—that's him—the blackguard! The bloody villain! The cold-hearted brute!"

They came forward with cursings, most of them unintelligible from the brogue.

"What's all this about?" shouted Philip, putting his stalwart figure in opposition to the mob.

Their spokesman shouted—"Get out o' the way, yer honor! That villain, D'Arcy, is the man we want. We're not going to leave two whole bones in his body, and may hell-fire blast it when we've done with it!"

"I've done no harm to any of you," said D'Arcy, pale but contemptuous.

"Haven't ye, thin? And didn't ye evict Tom Mulligan's ould parents into the winter night, and the rint for the tumble-down hovel that was their home only three months behind? And didn't his poor ould father die of the cold and the wet and his poor ould mother of a broken heart? And here's Tom to give ye the first blow himsilf!"

A thickset man waving long arms and a club detached himself from the rest and, with a black scowl, shrieked:—

"Take that, ye black-sowled murderer!" D'Arcy's skull would have been opened by the blow if he had not snatched up his chair and defended himself with it.

In an instant Adeline found herself the spectator of a terrifying scene. Philip, Brent, and Wilmott also snatched up their chairs and met the attackers shoulder to shoulder with D'Arcy.

Philip shouted to her—"Run, Adeline! Out through the other door!"

Instead, she ran forward and flung herself on the raised arm of the spokesman, who brandished a hammer. She uttered a shriek that was heard even above the tumult. And at the same instant Captain Bradley and the mate appeared from the companionway carrying pistols.

"Now, men, do ye want a bullet in you?" shouted Captain Bradley. "Lay down those cudgels!"

Like a sudden squall, the fury of the peasants passed. They stood quiet, relaxed, like the sails from which the gale has receded. They stared in silence at the Captain.

"These men," explained D'Arcy, "seem to think I evicted the parents of one of them and caused their death, but I did nothing of the sort."

"It was yer agent done it!" retorted the spokesman. "It was that twister, McClarty—the murderer—and yoursilf off to the races at Dublin or Liverpool and niver knowing how yer tenantry is trated! Ye didn't care, if you could lay hands on the rints."

"Aye, that's true," added Mulligan. "And my poor ould parents getting their death out of it!"

"It's a shame to him!" cried Adeline. "And if I had known it I should have been fighting on your side, Mulligan, instead of against you!" She was beside herself with excitement and exhilaration. She could hear the whistle of the wind, the clash of the waves. The wild scene had stirred something savage in her. The peasants crowded about her.

"Thank you, me lady! God save you."

"May the Saints bless you! May yer children grow up to comfort you."

D'Arcy spoke calmly to the men. "Why did you attack me," he asked, "after all these weeks?"

"Sure, we'd just found out who you are, divil take you!"

A movement passed through them and it seemed for a moment that Adeline might be put to the test. But Captain Bradley's authoritative voice ordered them below and like a troubled wave they receded, though with mutterings.

Philip had been embarrassed by Adeline's outbreak against

D'Arcy. He foresaw that their relations would not be so pleasant for the rest of the voyage. D'Arcy was watching her sulkily as she paced up and down the salon declaiming against the cruelties of absentee landlords, telling of how her own father never left his estate and knew the personal history of every man, woman, and child on it.

"Your father may be a paragon, in all truth, Mrs. Whiteoak," returned D'Arcy, "but you cannot blame me for all the wrongs of Ireland."

"You've no love for the people nor for the land," she answered. "Your heart is not there! So what can you bring to the place but misfortune?"

"Well," put in Brent, "I've sold every acre I owned in Ireland, and I'm glad of it!"

"I'd be better off if I had done the same," declared D'Arcy.

Adeline flashed a look of scorn on them both. "And have ye no pity in your hearts," she cried, "for the suffering of those poor people?"

"Come, come, Adeline," interrupted Philip. "It's late. You should go to your bed." He turned to D'Arcy. "She is overwrought and tired."

"I'll lay my head on no pillow to-night. I've seen too much. I'll stay here with Mr. D'Arcy and Mr. Brent and argue the matter out with them till sunrise."

"I'm sorry," said D'Arcy, "but I think I shall have to rest for a bit." He put his hand to his forehead and she saw a discolored swelling near his temple.

She went close to look at it. "Ah, well and did a blow really land on you!" she exclaimed. "Ah, I am sorry for that!"

Her anger was gone. She had a basin of hot water brought and herself bathed his head. Their friendship was restored.

But the next day she was not well. She could not leave the cabin. The weather became stormy. She suffered from nausea. Philip, coming into the cabin, found her sitting on the side of her berth, very pale, her eyes wet with tears. But there was nothing tearful in her voice as she turned its vibrant tones on him.

"Well," she demanded, "and what do ye think has happened to me?"

"Are you worse?"

"Aye, I'm worse." She stared moodily for a space at the heaving floor of the cabin, then raised her eyes accusingly to his. She said:—

"Aye, I'm worse and shall be worse still before I'm finished with it. I'm going to have a baby!"

"My God!" The glass of sherry he had brought her dropped from his hand.

"Well," she cried, "you are a ninny! To think that you'd let fall a glass at the news, when it's I who ought to be throwing things about."

"I didn't throw it! I dropped it."

" 'T is one and the same—at a moment like this—and I needing the sherry!"

"Are you positive?" he asked.

"That I need the sherry?"

"That you are going to have a baby?"

"I wish I were as positive that this ship would arrive in port."

He could not help exclaiming—"I wish to God you'd waited till we were settled in Quebec!"

She retorted, the color returning to her cheeks—"And I wish *you* had waited. But no—would such a thought ever enter your head? No—my lord, you must have your pleasure, let come what may! And now you say you wish *I* had waited! Oh, it's well that the good Lord made women patient and mild with all they have to go through from the unreasonableness and selfishness of men! Yes—I wish we'd both waited before ever we took the way to the altar."

"You took good care not to let me see you in one of your tempers before I married you."

She looked him in the eyes. "And did you ever give me such cause for temper before you married me?" she demanded.

He burst out laughing. "Now you are just ridiculous," he said.

He brought her another glass of sherry.

As he saw her sitting on the side of the berth wrapped in a great shawl with red stripes on it, and her fingers playing with the fringe of the shawl, a pang of pity went through him. For all her fine proportions she looked like a forlorn child. He sat down beside her and held the glass to her lips.

"My only reason," he said, "for wishing this had not happened till later is because of the discomfort of traveling when you're *enceinte.*"

She gripped his fingers and managed to smile a little.

"Oh, I shall be all right," she said.

He gave her another sip of the sherry. Then he exclaimed—"If it's a boy we'll call him Nicholas, after my uncle!"

"I'd have liked Philip."

"No. I don't want any Philip but myself in your life."

"Very well. He shall be Nicholas. But never Nick or Nicky for short."

"Never."

A knock came on the door. It was the overworked stewardess to tell them that the ayah was once more very seasick and quite unable to look after the baby. The ship was now wallowing in a trough of the waves. She herself seemed to be suffering also, for her timbers gave forth the most melancholy creakings and groanings. Those on board could not help remembering her former betrayal of them and were prepared at any moment to hear that she had sprung another leak.

"Bring the child here," said Philip.

The stewardess brought Augusta who came smiling, a shell held to each ear.

"Would it be possible for you to look after her?" Philip asked the woman. "My wife is not well. I shall make it worth your while."

"I'll do what I can for the poor bairn but I'm nearly run off my feet as it is. Half the passengers are sick again."

When she had gone Adeline exclaimed:—

"I do dislike that woman! She never speaks of Gussie without calling her 'the poor bairn'—as though we neglected or ill-treated her!"

Philip set his daughter on his knee. "If only she had taken to my sister," he said, "as she should have done, she might be enjoying herself in England now, instead of adding to our problem here!"

Gussie threw her shells to the floor and reached out for his watch chain. He took out his large gold watch and allowed her to listen to its tick, which enraptured her so that she bounced on his knee.

The weather grew stormier. There was no forgetting it. Day and night the struggle between it and the ship went on. Wind, waves, and teeming rain hammered, tossed, and drenched the ship. Sailors scrambled to the most precarious and dizzy heights up the masts as she struggled on, hour by hour making the way a little shorter. Oh, that the land would appear! Adeline had never felt so ill in her life. She could scarcely stand, yet she had to drag herself into the ayah's cabin and do what she could do for her, which was little enough. She had to tend her child who still cried a great deal and, when the child was quiet and Adeline might have slept a little, Boney would take it into his head to shout of his pleasure which seemed unbounded.

Suddenly the condition of the ayah became alarming. Her small form grew shrunken, her face almost green. Only her great burning eyes, with the dark shadows under them, looked alive. Her fevered mouth babbled of far-off days in India. Adeline was distraught to see her so. She gathered together all her strength to care for her. She supported her in her arms and every few moments wiped the sweat from the sunken face with a handkerchief.

The silver bangles on the small brown wrists tinkled ceaselessly as the restless hands moved upon her breast. Then suddenly her eyes opened wide. It was on the third day of her terrible illness. She looked up mournfully into Adeline's face as though in question.

"What do you want, Huneefa?" Adeline asked.

She seemed not to hear but began to arrange her heavy dark hair on her forehead. She took it lock by lock in her thin fingers and arranged it as though for a festival.

Adeline laid her back on the pillow. She tottered out into the passage and called hoarsely for Philip. He was not near but James Wilmott heard her and came, his face full of anxiety.

"Come quick," she said. "Huneefa is dying!"

He came into the dark, sour-smelling cabin.

"I must fetch the doctor," he said.

As though to add to their miseries the doctor had, two days before, slipped on the deck and injured his hip. He could scarcely move for the pain but he came supported on Wilmott's shoulder. He was a young man of little experience but one glance at the ayah told him that her hour had come. He told Wilmott to take Adeline back to her cabin but she refused to leave. In a short while Huneefa died.

Her death came as a shock to Adeline and, in a lesser degree, to Philip. All their married life she had been an intimate shadow, first as a maid to Adeline, later as ayah to Augusta. They had taken her devotion for granted. As she was never really well, her illnesses caused them no alarm. Even the jaundice which had complicated her seasickness had not brought real apprehension. Now it seemed that she had willfully deserted them—Huneefa who had been so unquestioningly faithful! They discovered what a strong prop her frail body had been in the edifice of their life.

Even the ayah's death did not cause Mrs. Cameron to relent. She remained remote in her cabin, her new friend at her side.

Adeline herself prepared Huneefa for burial, arranging her best robe about her, crossing her hands on her breast. For the last time the silver bangles tinkled on the thin wrists. Then Adeline carried Augusta to her side, for a last look. Augusta was pleased and leant down from Adeline's arms with a little laugh.

"Kiss her then," said Adeline. "Kiss her good-bye."

Gussie planted a moist kiss on the bronze cheek and held the shell she carried to Huneefa's ear.

"Oh, dear—oh, dear—why did she go!" groaned Adeline. She would have given anything she owned to have brought back life to Huneefa. She drew the yashmak over the still face and turned away.

Gussie did not give another glance at the one who had been her slave. She held the shell to her mother's ear and, clutching her neck, leant down to peer into her face. She was surprised to find that Adeline was not laughing but that tears were on her cheeks.

It was a cold gray day when they gathered on deck to commit the ayah's body to the sea. The sea was not so rough as it had been but the waves still surged in sullen aimlessness about the ship. The deck had been cleaned. The sailors were drawn up in order, looking neat and clean, their bare feet planted on the moist deck. The steerage passengers were also collected, their children grouped about them. The women wore shawls over their heads. Those among them who were Irish, and they were by far the greater part, had the keening ready on their lips but held it back.

Patsy O'Flynn was there, wearing his greatcoat and a strange woolly cap that came down to his shaggy eyebrows. He had brought with him a bundle containing his most cherished possessions, from which he would not be parted for an instant, and this lay on the deck beside him. He had asked to be allowed to hold Augusta in his arms during the ceremony. She had on her white coat and little lace bonnet. Patsy was so proud of her, and of the importance of his position in carrying her, that he could not keep his mind on the ceremony but cast self-conscious looks at his fellow passengers to make sure that they were noticing him.

It was strange to see D'Arcy, who not many days before had been the object of these men's fury, standing face to face with them with apparent forgetfulness, on both sides, of what had passed.

Adeline stood between Philip and Wilmott. The nervous tension seemed to have given her strength for the occasion but the flush on her cheeks looked fevered to Philip and he frequently turned his anxious eyes on her. Wilmott stood austere and motionless as a statue.

At the Captain's feet lay the body of Huneefa, sewn securely in canvas. He read the Burial Service in a clear, resonant voice. It was odd to see him on deck not wearing his gold-braided cap. He was getting a little bald and the lock of fair brown hair on the top of his head continually rose and fell in the gusty wind. Adeline noticed the uncovered heads of all the men and that Patsy alone wore his cap. She motioned him to take it off but it was some time before he could understand what she meant. He made a number of comical attempts at obeying the message he did not grasp, shifting the baby from one arm to another, hiding his bundle behind his feet, assuming a more funereal expression. Then suddenly he discovered what she wanted him to do and, with a happy smile, pulled off his cap and stood with his unkempt thatch uncovered.

Deliberately Captain Bradley read the service for the dead, ending with the appropriate words: "We therefore commit her body to the deep, to be returned into corruption, looking for the resurrection of the body (when the Sea shall give up her dead) and the life of the world to come, through our Lord Jesus Christ; who at his coming shall change our vile body, that it may be like his glorious body, according to the mighty working, whereby he is able to subdue all things to himself."

There was a movement among the sailors. The ropes that controlled the body tautened. It was raised above the deck over the railing, then slowly, gently, with a kind of meek majesty, lowered into the sea. It seemed to Adeline, looking over the side, that the waves parted to receive it, then without a sound slid across it, enfolded it, and so it was lost to view. A fresh gust of wind caught the sails. A lively thunder passed through them and the ship moved forward as though eager to be at her journey's end and have done with these delays.

Gussie, from the security of Patsy's arm, watched the body of Huneefa sink out of sight. She turned to look into Patsy's eyes.

"Gone," she said.

"God bless the child!" he exclaimed to those about him. "She understands everything. Och, the cliver brain she has and a way of talkin' to beat all!"

A hymn now rose from the throats of those assembled. "Eternal Father! strong to save, Whose arm hath bound the restless wave," they sang, and the sound of their own voices, the act of singing which expanded their breasts, the confidence in the words they uttered, made them happier. The meek figure that had been lowered into the waves became less dominating, was at last left far behind. The steerage passengers returned to the accustomed evil smells of their quarters; Gussie was once more in her mother's arms.

Adeline, feeling suddenly exhausted, carried her to a sheltered corner on the deck and gave her the bag containing her sea shells, and a biscuit to eat. Wilmott sat down with his pipe and a copy of the *Quarterly Review*, beside Augusta. They were strange companions but there was a kind of understanding between them. Adeline then went to lie down in her berth.

The days that followed were afterward looked back on by Philip as a kind of nightmare. Adeline developed a fever which, before many hours, threw her into delirium. She talked wildly and incoherently, now fancying herself back in India, now a young girl in County Meath, now in terror of red Indians in Canada. Sometimes it took all Philip's strength to keep her from springing out of the berth. The young doctor, still suffering cruelly from his injured hip, scarcely left her side. Boncy perched at the head of the berth and it was a curious thing that, when her delirium was at its height, his cries had a soothing effect on her. He would listen to her babblings, his head on one side, then as her voice rose louder and louder he would raise his own in shrill shouts, as though to show how he could outdo her.

The dreadful lack of privacy was abhorrent to Philip. The partitions were so thin that all their miseries were audible. It was said that Mrs. Cameron was ill too. Certainly she made neither sign nor offer of help. She and the Newfoundlanders kept quite to themselves. The stewardess kept Augusta with her as much as she could but there was much sickness on board to claim her. Wilmott would carry Gussie up and down the deck by the hour, singing to her. But often she was on Philip's hands and he was at his wit's end to know how to cope with the intricacies of her diet and her toilet. She was left for a good deal of time alone in the cabin where the ayah had died. The stewardess provided her with a tin plate and a large spoon with which she enlivened what might have been many dreary hours. She was pinned to the bedding of the berth with large safety pins so that the rolling of the ship might not hurl her to the floor. Her attitude toward Philip was one of curiosity mixed with suspicion. When he did things for her she looked on patronizingly as though she were thinking how much better Huneefa would have done them.

On the third day Adeline's delirium left her. She had been babbling and Boney had startled, then silenced her, by his cries. She lay quite still, looking about her with large mournful eyes, then she spoke in a natural voice.

"I'm tired of listening to that bird," she said.

Philip bent over her, his face solicitous.

"Shall I take him away?"

"No, no. But give him a fig. That will quiet him. They are in the tin box in the cupboard." She stared at him as he obeyed her. Then she laughed weakly. "How funny you look! As though you hadn't shaved for days!"

"Neither I have."

"Have I been very ill?"

"Pretty bad."

"I'm better now."

"Thank God for that!"

The parrot sidled along the perch to meet the fig. He accepted it with a humorous expression, then began tearing small pieces from it and spitting them out. But it kept him quiet.

Philip sat down on the edge of the berth and Adeline took one of his strong brown hands in her thin white hands and stroked it. She pressed her teeth against her quivering underlip.

"I was just remembering Huneefa," she said.

He kissed her. "You must not think of anything unhappy," he said. "Just think of getting well."

"We shouldn't have brought her from India."

"She wanted to come. She would have been brokenhearted if we'd left her."

"I know."

She was undoubtedly better. She drank some broth and would have slept but Augusta was beating on her tin. The noise excited Boney. He began to scream. Adeline tossed on her lumpy pillow and filled her hands with her long hair.

"Is there no peace on this ship!" she cried. "Whatever is that noise?"

Philip went to Gussie and took the plate and spoon from her and gave her the bag of shells in their stead, but she threw these to the floor one by one and then set up a lugubrious crying.

Philip decided he would take her to Wilmott and ask him to amuse her for an hour. He strode back to where she sat with streaming eyes tight shut, mouth square, and everything within reach hurled as far as her tiny strength would allow. He picked her up not very gently. He discovered by the dampness of her underthings that a change was imperative. He rang the bell furiously for the stewardess. There was no answer. From the confused heap that now constituted her wardrobe he extricated two garments. Laying her across his knees he managed to put the diaper on her but the white flannel petticoat which had been washed by the stewardess and extraordinarily shrunken baffled him. Tired of lying with her head hanging downward, Gussie had begun to squirm. She had ceased to cry on being taken up but now she began again. Sooner would he have set out to subdue a rebellious hill tribe than this squalling little creature. He saw that her legs were red and chafed and he swore.

At the next instant he pricked her with the safety pin—why the devil had it been named *safety* pin!—and at the sight of blood trickling from the tiny wound, sweat started on his forehead.

"I didn't mean to! Upon my soul I didn't mean to!" he stammered, but she didn't believe him. As he set her upright on his knee she drew back her chin and looked at him with apprehension, wondering what he would next do to her. What he did was to carry her through the passages and down the companionway to where the emigrants were sitting in their common room. Here he almost threw her on to the lap of the respectable Scotswoman, mother of five, and commanded her to care for his daughter as best she could. It turned out that she cared for Gussie very capably, neglecting her own hardy bairns to do it, and he paid her well for her trouble.

As though the *Alanna* had not had enough to contend with, she next had a narrow escape from collision with an iceberg. As it was early for these, there was perhaps not such a strict watch kept as should have been. Terrifyingly at dawn the monstrous, pale, cathedral-like form gathered itself together out of the mists. Some unusually hot weather had freed it from the mass. It loomed, rising out of the Gulf Stream, like cold malice made palpable. Yet it was shaped as a sacred edifice.

Shouts, warnings filled the air. Grigg was at the helm and doubled himself over it to force the ship from calamity. She just escaped but the chill air from the iceberg plunged those on board into sudden winter. Philip ran down to the cabin. Now Adeline had been convalescent for five days. She was beginning to draw on her clothes, frightened by the running footsteps, the shouts. She had not heard Philip leave her side.

"Are we taking to the boats?" she asked, in agitation.

"No. Nothing to worry about. But you must come on deck and see the iceberg. It's stupendous, Adeline. You have your shoes and stockings on. Just put your cloak over your nightdress. You must not miss this sight."

He half-carried her to the deck. Now the iceberg was farther off. It had lost its terror and gained in beauty, for the sun, just showing a rim above the horizon, had touched a thousand facets into fire.

It rose out of the green waves in majesty, ethereal as a dream, unsubstantial as hope. Yet deep down in the sea its icy foundation was greater than its visible part.

After the Gulf Stream there was cold again and tall green seas arose. As the *Alanna* dived into them a snowstorm whistled out on the wind from land, obscuring all but the nearest waves from sight. If more icebergs were around, the ship was at their mercy. The lookouts posted high in the shrouds could see nothing but the myriad white flakes that swarmed over them, turning them into figures of snow, whipping their skin to rawness, blinding their eyes. It became so cold that the spray froze on the bulwarks, forming long sharp icicles like teeth shown in a grin.

The cabin passengers with the exception of Mrs. Cameron and her friends gathered in the salon, a little sad, yet resigned that their long intimacy was drawing to a close. But they would write to each other. They would not forget. They sat wrapped in their traveling rugs trying to keep warm. Philip had got a large soapstone heated and this was at Adeline's feet. The men sipped rum and water but she had a glass of port. Wrapped in her fur cloak, as well as her traveling rug, she was quite comfortable. She felt that she had returned from an individual voyage that had carried her near to death. When she thought of Huneefa, it was as of someone lost long ago.

D'Arcy and Brent brought out their guidebooks and maps and talked eagerly of their prospective travels in Canada and, more especially, in the States. The portholes were as though covered by cotton wool. All sounds on the ship were muffled, except that the cordage rang with the onslaught of the wind.

Out of all this they came at sundown into a navy-blue sea and a red sun glowing on its rim. The waves were streaked by foam, the icicles were diamond bright and then, wonder of wonders, they heard the whimpering of a gull and its shadow sped across the deck!

It was the first but others followed, circling and crying out to the ship, as though they carried a new message to her from a new world. A tall spout of water from a whale's mouth rose bright out of the sea. He swam close to the ship, amazed at the size of this great bird, then leapt clear of the water and, with a glorious violent movement, disported himself in the air, smooth as silk, dripping and muscular. All from the cabin were now on deck and the monster seemingly was trying to show them his strength.

Captain Bradley was beaming his satisfaction. He said, his brown hands resting on the rail:—

"We shall land in Quebec before many days! I never arrive after a voyage like this without being struck afresh by God's mercy in bringing us safely through. When you think of all that has passed since we first left Ireland—and here we are with land nearly in sight!"

"You might add that a large part of the credit is due to your own good seamanship," said Philip.

"But God's mercy is at the bottom of it," said the Captain.

The next morning land was in sight. The weary travelers in the steerage crowded together to peer out at it. The air was crisp but kindly. Little crinkles ran across the surface of the long waves. The icicles dripped, then dropped into the Gulf of St. Lawrence. The *Alanna* entered the mighty river. Green banks rose above the river and unfolded into dark forests. Tiny white villages came into view mothered by white churches with bright crosses on their steeples. Long narrow farms stretched close for comfort. Cattle stood near the river's edge and the sweet smells of the land came out to meet the voyagers. Was it possible that only a few days before they had been in a snowstorm—that icicles had been hanging from the ship?

It was Sunday morning and Captain Bradley read the church service with the note of satisfaction and the thanksgiving still in his voice. There was a tiny organ in the salon on which Wilmott played the accompaniment to the hymn. The voices rose robustly, as though fear never had been their companion. The words were enunciated with satisfaction.

"Fierce was the wild billow,
Dark was the night;
Oars laboured heavily,
Foam glimmered white.
Trembled the mariners;
Peril was nigh:
Then said the God of Gods,
'Peace: It is I.'

"Ridge of the mountain wave,
Lower thy crest;
Wail of the tempest wind,
Be thou at rest.
Sorrow can never be,
Darkness must fly,
Where saith the Light of light,
'Peace: It is I.'"

Now Philip and Adeline were packing their belongings. Though some articles had been lost or worn-out during the voyage, they found the greatest difficulty in squeezing the remainder into their portmanteaux. Some fresh article always was turning up. Philip was irritated by the fact that he still had to be very careful of Adeline's feelings. He would have liked to blame her for some of the disorder. Surely she was to blame for heaping traveling rugs and her own shoes and a dressing case on top of his best coat. When at last the packing was done, though badly enough, they suddenly remembered the ayah's cabin and all that lay heaped and strewn in it.

Boney was furious at being put into his cage. He screamed and fretted there, flapping his green wings and throwing about seeds and gravel. Adeline's voice came back to her, loud and strong in the stress of the moment.

"I can't do any more!" she cried.

"Nobody's asking you to," snapped Philip and he added as he went out—"You've done too much already in the way of disorder."

"What's that you say?" she cried.

He did not answer.

She was weak but there was no need for her to totter as she entered the ayah's cabin, or for her to sink panting on the side of the berth with her hand to her side. Her voice was now a fierce whisper.

"What was it you said?" she asked.

"I said, Goddamme, I never saw such a mess! I should have brought a valet from England."

"What you really said was that this disorder was my fault."

"You're talking nonsense." He grasped a handful of Gussie's small garments. "What about these? Hadn't we better leave them on board and buy her new things?"

"Leave them!" she almost screamed. "And they of the finest Irish linen and hand-embroidered! I will not leave one of them! Open that black box. There will be room in it."

With flushed face he opened the box. She peered into it. "Where is the doll?" she asked.

"What doll?"

"The beautiful doll your sister gave to Gussie. Huneefa kept it in that box."

"It isn't here."

"It must be. You must find it."

He sat back on his heels and glared at her out of angry blue eyes. He exclaimed:—

"Have I come to this—that I must search for a *doll* at the moment of landing? It's not enough that I should pack diapers but I must crawl about on my hands and knees searching for a *doll!* Egad, Adeline—"

"Never mind," she interrupted, frightened by the sight of his face. "Don't search for it. It must be in the other cabin."

Somehow they got their things together. Somehow a couple of stewards carried them toward the gangway, to the accompaniment of Boney's screams. Philip carried the cage and kept his other arm firmly about Adeline. He said:—

"I sometimes wish we had never brought this bird."

"Leave him behind," she cried, "if he's a trouble! Leave him behind, and me too! You can get another woman and another bird in Quebec."

He pinched her arm. "Behave yourself. People will hear you."

"I don't care! You were hurting me."

"Well, I care, and I *wasn't* hurting you."

Wilmott came to meet them. "What a pity you have not been on deck! We have had a grand view of Quebec. You should have done your packing earlier. Can I help in any way?"

Philip put the bird cage into his hand.

There was a great bustle and confusion. The air was full of shouts and the whimpering of gulls. The great white sails of the ship were drooping like weary wings. Barefoot sailors clung in the shrouds gazing down on the crowded pier. Adeline turned a smiling face on Wilmott. "What should we do without you?" she said.

"You know it is my pleasure to be of service to you," he replied, somewhat stiffly, but a flush had risen in his sallow cheek. "You are feeling much better, aren't you?" he added.

"I should be dead if I weren't."

"It is a good thing you found someone who could look after your child."

"Merciful heaven!" cried Adeline. "Where is Gussie? Oh, Philip, where is Gussie? That terrible Scotchwoman has probably landed and gone off with her!"

"The ship has not docked yet," said Philip, calmly. "The Scotswoman is an excellent creature and has no need of another child. I have arranged everything with her and paid her as well. Here comes Patsy now with Augusta."

He watched his approaching daughter a little grimly. She was perched on Patsy's shoulder, grasping him around the head. Her clothes were crumpled and stained, her face and hands had a strange grayish cleanliness. The cloth that had washed them had seen so much service! However she looked distinctly less ailing than when Philip had transferred her to the steerage and she greeted her mother with a faint smile of recognition.

"Oh, the darling!" cried Adeline, and kissed her. "Oh, Gussie, you do smell sour," she added under her breath.

Boney decided to leave the ship head downward as he had come aboard. Clinging by his dark claws to the ceiling of his cage, he saw recognizable bodies moving about him. He felt the crisp May breeze in his face that had a very different flavor from the air below decks to which he had become accustomed. He turned it over on his tongue, not quite sure whether or no he liked it. Over the shoulders of those about he glimpsed the dark fortress with white clouds banked behind it—for Wilmott was a tall man and held his cage high.

Adeline felt strangely weak as she moved toward the gangway. She turned pale. Suddenly D'Arcy and Brent presented themselves and, gripping each other by the wrists, made a chair for her on which they implored her to seat herself. She looked questioningly at Philip. Would he allow it?

"A good idea," he declared. "Thank you very much. Adeline will be delighted."

So Boney saw his mistress carried off and screamed his approval. He heard the shouts of French porters, saw the carioles drawn by their horses, in line by the side of the pier. Some passengers were met by friends or relatives. Others had no one to meet them but stood disconsolate and confused beside their little mounds of luggage. The two young Irish girls were there, looking not quite so buxom as when they had first sailed. Adeline gave them her address and told them to come and see her the next day. Before D'Arcy and Brent set her on her feet, she gave each a kiss on his cheek.

Brent exclaimed—"Is there anywhere else we can carry you?"

"Faith," added D'Arcy, "it would be no trouble at all to carry you to the top of the Citadel!"

The Scotswoman darted from her brood to plant a last kiss on Gussie's little mouth.

"Eh, the poor wee bairn!" she cried.

Her own children, thinking she had deserted them, came howling after her. She turned to them and was lost to view.

How many priests there were about, thought Adeline, and how foreign everything looked! She felt better now, really exhilarated and eager to see her new home. Philip had got a carriage for her. Their three friends were going to a hotel. She had a fleeting glimpse of Mrs. Cameron being met by relatives. Fascinated, she saw their astonished questionings, Mrs. Cameron's tragic gestures. She saw her raise a black gloved hand and point to Philip and herself. She stood motionless a moment, then threw the group a smile. "I may as well let them think I don't care," she said to herself, "for they hate me and my brothers and nothing can change that!"

Philip lifted her into the carriage and took Gussie on his own knee. The wheels rattled over the cobbles and up the steep narrow streets.

Adeline began to laugh rather hysterically. Philip turned his head to look at her.

"I was just thinking of the way Mrs. Cameron looked at me," she said. "You'd think an elopement was a monstrous thing and that I had engineered it. For my part, I think that little Mary did extremely well for herself."

VI

The House in the Rue St. Louis

IT STOOD before them, tall and a little severe, with a many-windowed façade. The knocker on the heavy door was a frowning gargoyle head. Philip's firm knock echoed through the house. Adeline stood gazing at the small-paned windows, the frames of which were painted black with a narrow gilt rim. She exclaimed:—

"I can picture the old days here—satin breeches, powdered heads and all that!"

"Nice to think it is ours," said Philip.

"Isn't it!"

Gussie, from her father's arm, reached out and thrust her tiny fingers into the gargoyle's mouth.

"The street looks quare and foreign," put in Patsy, waiting on the pavement with the bird cage and his bundles. "Haven't we any land with it at all?"

Philip could not get used to Patsy's way of joining in their conversation. He frowned a little and knocked again. The door opened. A short stout woman in a black dress stood before them. Obviously she was French but mercifully spoke English. She explained that she had been engaged as cook for them by the solicitor who had charge of Mr. Nicholas Whiteoak's affairs. Doubtless Captain Whiteoak had communicated with him. For herself she was eager to serve them. Her name was Marie.

Her appearance was reassuring. Philip ordered tea for Adeline. He looked about the large drawing-room with satisfaction. Marie gave a cry of delight and pounced on Gussie.

"Ah, *la pauvre petite!*" she cried.

Patsy had been standing in the dimness of the hall with the tiny silent girl on his shoulder. He showed his large teeth between his straggling whiskers in an ingratiating grin at Marie, who now took possession of Gussie.

"Ah, Madame, may I have the pleasure of feeding her? She looks so fatigued, so pale."

Adeline thankfully agreed.

When they were alone Philip said again:—

"It's nice to think this is ours. It looks like a well-built house and there will be plenty of room for the things we brought."

Adeline flung open the solid dark red shutters and the May sunshine flooded the room which obviously had been but casually cleaned and dusted for their reception. Adeline's bright gaze flashed about it. She saw the black and gilt furniture, the ornate chandelier with its four cylindrical red glass shades hung by crimson velvet cords. She cried:—

"It's hideous!"

"Do you think so?"

"Don't you?"

"Well, I don't like everything in it. But it has possibilities."

"Was this your uncle's taste?"

"He bought it furnished—just as it stands."

She came and threw her arms about him.

"Oh, Philip, I shall have great fun doing it over! I declare I've never so looked forward to anything. Let's explore the whole house."

"Not till you have had some refreshment. Remember your condition."

"Merciful heavens," she cried, "why are you always throwing that up to me! I can't wink an eyelid but you say, 'Remember your condition!' "

Marie came in with a tray on which there were a pot of tea and some small iced cakes. She gave them a beaming smile.

"*La pauvre petite* is ravenous!" she exclaimed. "She has already eaten three cakes and drunk a small cup of *café au lait*. It is much, much better for her than tea. Ah, her intelligence—her *savoir-faire*—her beauty! That person who carried her tells me she has made the journey from India and that the native nurse died. But never fear, I will of a certainty guard her—better than she has ever been guarded before!"

Marie's devotion to little Augusta was not passing. Indeed it grew day by day. She had the child continually with her. The suggestion that a nurse should be engaged filled her with horror. There were no good nurses in Quebec. She herself was the only person capable of giving Gussie the proper care. All she needed was a young boy to do the rough work and she knew the very boy—a nephew in fact of her own—and a capable girl to act as housemaid —a niece of hers would exactly fill the requirements. Much could be found for Patsy to do in a house of this size. For example, the goat had to be cared for, the steps cleaned, and the garden kept in order. The goat was free to graze in a small near-by orchard, which property also belonged to Philip.

He spent happy days becoming acquainted with the details of his inheritance. He had long talks with his uncle's solicitor, Mr. Prime. The deeds were in perfect order. There was nothing to worry about. He and the two Irishmen, D'Arcy and Brent, who were staying at a near-by hotel, accompanied by Wilmott who had less expensive accommodation in a pension just down the street, explored the old town, climbed the hill to the Citadel, dined with the officers at the Fort. Every fine afternoon Philip hired a carriage and took Adeline and one of the gentlemen for a drive into the country. The scenery was delightful, the late Canadian spring flowering into a plenitude of spreading leaf and bloom. They looked down at the majestic river and talked of their past voyage which was beginning to seem like a troubled dream. The invigorating air, Marie's good cooking, soon brought color to Adeline's cheeks and strength to take the place of weakness.

Their furniture arrived in excellent condition. The uglier of the pieces belonging to Uncle Nicholas were banished and the elegancies of Chippendale took their place. The rugs they had brought from India were laid with fine effect on the polished floors. The red-shaded chandelier was replaced by one of cut crystal. Uncle Nicholas would have found it difficult to recognize his house.

They speculated a good deal about him but could find little in the house by which they could reconstruct his life there. There was not a single picture of him but a portrait of the Duke of Kent, under whose command he had come to Quebec, hung in the drawing-room. Mr. Prime, the solicitor, described Colonel Whiteoak as fine in appearance, a little hasty in temper, hospitable in habit, a connoisseur of good wine. But though Philip searched every inch of the cellar he did not find a single bottle to reward him. It was strange, for his uncle must have had a good supply at the time of his death. Among his papers there was little to reveal him. He had kept no journal as a receptacle for his thoughts. There were however a few letters of an amorous nature from a French lady in Montreal. These were tied together with a piece of tape and on the last one was written, in the Colonel's small legible hand—"Marguerite died January 30th, 1840."

As it was difficult for either Philip or Adeline to read French handwriting, they made out little from the letters except that Marguerite had a husband whom she detested, and that she adored Nicholas Whiteoak. What a blessing it was that she had not been free to marry him! So simply might this pleasant property have been lost!

Letters from Philip's sister and the Dean had been preserved also. Philip and Adeline read these with interest and sometimes chagrin, for there were several references to the extravagances of their life in India.

Within two months Philip and Adeline had become happily domiciled in the French-Canadian town and knew everyone who was worth knowing. Her health was vastly improved and her condition hampered her activities but little. She was hospitable and liked to entertain her friends and be entertained by them. She found more interesting people here than she had dared hope for. She wrote long letters home enlarging on the elegance and liveliness of the *soirées* given by the socially distinguished. She wanted her father to know that she was not living in the barbarously primitive community he had pictured. She had had, as a girl, a French governess and, though she could read little French, she could speak it after a fashion and now set to work to improve herself in the language. By her vivacity and gaiety she drew to herself the French as well as the English society of Quebec. She became intimate with the next-door neighbors on either side of her.

The Balestriers, on the left, were a lively married pair with a half-dozen children. Madame Balestrier was congenial to Adeline and the two spent many hours together, she imparting to Adeline the intimate gossip of the place. They drove together; shopped together; the two families had picnics on the banks of the river, the scenery now in its summertime glory. The one disadvantage in the society of the Balestriers was the behavior of their children. Adeline's own young brothers had been spoilt by their mother and Adeline had always vowed she would never spoil a child of her own. But it was not that the young Balestriers were so greatly humored as that they were always in evidence. Life was one prolonged struggle between them and their parents. They did everything under protest. Their manners were exemplary toward the Whiteoaks but they never addressed their parents except in a high complaining voice. Even the eldest boy, who was fourteen, used this same voice when talking to his mother and father.

Their neighbors on the other side were the de Granvilles, who were natives of France. They were an elderly brother and sister whose parents had been executed by the revolutionists, and who had been brought out to Canada by distant relations. Mademoiselle de Granville was in the middle sixties, a clever talker, kindhearted, full of vitality. Her life was given to the care of her brother's comfort. She had been little more than a baby at the time of the Revolution but Monsieur de Granville had seen horrors which had made an impression on him never to be erased. He was subject to spells of melancholy which came upon him at the most unexpected times, perhaps in the middle of a dinner party. Then he would sit staring straight ahead of him with a dazed expression, hearing nothing, seeing nothing, frozen in some terrible, though dimly remembered happening of childhood. At those times his sister would take a masterly lead in the conversation, holding the attention of all till Monsieur de Granville had regained possession of himself. Then he would be quick of wit, gay and charming. He had a beautiful and distinguished face, in contrast to his sister's plainness of feature.

Adeline felt a relief which she never acknowledged to Philip, in the fact that her brothers had returned to Ireland. Conway and Sholto might well have been a handful in Quebec. What might not their pastimes have been, with endless time on their hands! Certainly they would have had clashes with Philip. Her mother wrote telling of their return home with Mary Cameron and of the scene that ensued. She covered a dozen pages describing the tirade of mingled anger and derision which Renny Court had poured out on the three. She said she had never seen a girl so completely absorbed by love as the fifteen-year-old Mary. It made her impervious to all else. It was in truth rather disgraceful at her age, especially as Conway was little more than a schoolboy. The only thing to do was to keep a strict watch on the pair, though to guard them now, after all the freedom they had been allowed on board ship and in Galway, was little more than a farce and it did seem rather hard that, just when she had looked forward to a period of peace, this should have happened and her husband as usual blaming her for everything. She also had had a long letter from Mrs. Cameron who declared that Adeline had been aware of all that went on and who demanded that Mary should be put on the next ship bound for Montreal, under suitable chaperonage, as though the girl needed a chaperon now!

Renny Court wrote briefly to Adeline saying what a pity it was that she should have traveled all the way from India to bring such trouble on the family. It would be well, he wrote, if, instead of returning the luggage the two boys had left on the ship, she would send him a check for it as the contents would be of no use to them in Ireland and would doubtless be of great value in the wilds.

"Oh, the meanness of him!" Adeline cried. "Oh, he'd take the coppers from a dead man's eyes! He'd skin a flea for its hide and tallow! Of what use are my brothers' things to me or to anyone here? I'll not send him a copper for them! Oh, I don't forget the time when I broke off my engagement to Edward O'Donnel! Edward refused to take back his ring. He said I was to do as I liked with it. My father said it would be a disgrace for me to wear the ring and he gave me twenty pounds for it. Later I found that he had sold it for four times as much and, when I upbraided him for it, he said he had needed the money to pay off a debt of my brother, Esmond's. He's my favorite brother so what could I do? But, oh, what a bold brazen face my father has! He can look you in the eye and say anything."

"He can," agreed Philip. "Just the same I think I shall send him the check for your brothers' things. The trunks and portmanteaux are better than one can buy here. The guns and fishing tackle can always be used. As for the clothes, I dare say we can find someone who will be glad of them."

The next letter Adeline had from Lady Honoria told of the marriage of the youthful pair in the Chapel at Killiekeggan Castle. After careful consideration, she wrote, they had decided that Conway must make honorable amends to the girl he had wronged. Mary herself had declared that she was the possessor of a tidy fortune and investigation had proved this was true. Therefore honor and foresight would each be satisfied. Mary was a sweet, gentle girl and already the family were becoming attached to her. It would look well on the part of Philip and Adeline if they would send a handsome wedding present.

Between one thing and another the summer passed. It rolled past swiftly and pleasantly like the St. Lawrence in its summer mood. Sometimes the heat was great but the house in the Rue St. Louis was comparatively cool. How lovely the walks on the terrace in the evening, when one gossiped with one's friends, while far below the lamps of the Lower Town twinkled and the lights of ships came out like jewels on the breast of the river. Sometimes Adeline gave a mourning thought to the ayah whose slender bones must by this time be bare of her dusky flesh. The mystery of Gussie's doll was never cleared. Gussie herself did not repeat the word "gone." Now she was learning to chatter in French and when she was addressed in English she would turn away her little head with an offended air. She could toddle, holding fast to Marie's hand, and she had an enchanting way of lifting her feet high as though she were mounting a flight of stairs. Patsy O'Flynn was her slave. She loved the smell of his strong pipe and the feel of his coarse grizzled hair in her hands. Pull as she would she could not pull it out.

James Wilmott came to the house every day. Philip supplied him with the London papers which came regularly. They talked politics by the hour, disagreeing just enough to make the discussions stimulating. If they grew a little heated, Wilmott invariably made his departure, as though he could not trust himself to quarrel.

"He's a gloomy dog!" Philip would exclaim. "And I sometimes wonder why I like him about, but I do."

"You like him because he has brains," returned Adeline. "He has a very good mind. I wonder that he hasn't done more with his life."

"He tells me he is hard up. He can't go on living here. He is going to take up land and farm."

"Heaven help him!"

"It's what I should like to do."

"Aren't you happy here, Philip?"

"Yes, but it is more Frenchified than I had expected and there is so much in the way of parties and gossip that we might almost as well have stayed in India. There's something in me that isn't satisfied." He thrust his hands into his pockets and strode up and down the room.

"Still, you have a very good time with the officers in the Fort. You have had some splendid fishing. You are going duck shooting and deer shooting in the autumn."

Philip frowned and pushed out his lips.

"Deer *shooting!*" he exclaimed. "*Shooting* deer! For a man who has chased the stag on horseback! It's barbarous!"

"Then don't do it."

He glared at her. "Well, I've got to do *something*, haven't I? A chap can't sit twiddling his thumbs all day."

Adeline suspended her needle and glared back at him. She was making a petticoat for the coming baby. It was of fine white flannel with a design of grapes and their leaves embroidered above its scalloped hem. She was an accomplished needlewoman and nothing in the way of ornament was too much trouble for her. Indeed a simple garment did not seem to her worth the making and it was a blessing her eyes were strong, for she bent over the finest stitching by the hour in candlelight. Now she suspended her needle and remarked:—

"The trouble with you is you're too well. If you were miserable and ill, as I am, you would be glad to sit still."

"You are not miserable and ill," he returned, "or you wouldn't be, if you did not lace yourself so disgracefully."

"Then you'd like to take me out looking like a bale of hay?"

"I'll wager your mother never laced so, when she was in the family way."

"She did! No one ever knew when she was going to have a baby."

"No wonder she buried four!"

Adeline hurled the infant's petticoat to the floor and sprang up. She looked magnificent.

At that moment Marie ushered Wilmott into the room. He threw Adeline an admiring look, took her hand, bent over it and kissed it.

"Upon my word," exclaimed Philip, "you are getting Frenchified!"

"The fashion becomes this room and becomes Mrs. Whiteoak," Wilmott returned, without embarrassment.

"It's namby-pamby," answered Philip.

"Namby-pamby!" repeated Wilmott, flushing.

"Yes," said Philip, sulkily.

Wilmott gave a short laugh. He looked at Adeline.

"I like it," she declared. "Manners can't be too elegant for me."

"Each country has its own," said Philip. "I am satisfied to leave it at that."

"It is much pleasanter," she said, "to have your hand kissed than to be given a handshake that presses your rings into your fingers till you feel like screaming, as Mr. Brent does."

She picked up her sewing and again seated herself. Wilmott took a stiff-backed chair in a corner. Philip opened the red shutters and put up the window. He looked into the street. The milk cart, drawn by a donkey, appeared. The brass can flashed in the hot sunshine. Six nuns passed close to the window, their black robes billowing, their grave faces as though carved from wax.

Philip went for his duck shooting and returned in high spirits. The sport had been excellent, the weather perfect. The St. Lawrence, now of a hyacinth blue, swept between its gorgeous banks that were tapestried in brilliant hues by the sharp night frosts of October. Adeline felt extraordinarily well as compared to the period before Augusta's birth. She walked, she drove, she went to parties and gave parties. The friendship between her and Wilmott strengthened. He had a fine baritone voice and could accompany himself on the piano. Sometimes they sang together and, with him for support, Adeline managed to keep the tune. They would sing the songs she loved, from *The Bohemian Girl.* She would lean against the piano, looking down into his face while they sang, "I Dreamt That I Dwelt in Marble Halls" or "Then You'll Remember Me," and wonder what his past had been. He was always reticent concerning it. He often spoke of the necessity of his finding congenial work but made no move to do so. He left the lodgings he had taken and moved to still cheaper ones. Philip and Adeline had a suspicion that his meals were all too slight, yet he preserved his almost disdainful attitude toward food at their abundant board. He talked of purchasing land.

The sudden sharp cold, the squalls of snow that came in November, were a surprise. If November were like this, what would winter be! Philip bought Adeline a handsome sealskin sacque, richly shaded from golden brown to darkest, and of a rare fineness. A great muff accompanied it and, at the French milliner's, she had a little toque made of the same fur. Philip declared he had never seen her handsomer. Against the background of the sealskin, the colors of her hair and eyes were brightly accented, the scarlet of her lips declared.

For himself Philip ordered to be made a greatcoat lined with mink and with a collar of mink. A wedge-shaped mink cap was worn at a jaunty angle on his fair head. Adeline could not behold him, thus clothed, without delighted laughter.

"Philip, you do look sweet! " she would exclaim and kiss him on both cheeks in the French manner she had acquired.

They both were proud of Gussie's appearance. She stepped forth firmly in fur-trimmed boots of diminutive size, a white lamb coat and muff and a bonnet of royal-blue velvet. Marie then would place her in a snow-white sleigh with upward-sweeping runners and push her triumphantly along the steep and slippery streets. They chattered in French when Marie paused to rest.

Wilmott provided himself with no adequate protection against the cold. He must save his capital, he declared. He said he never felt the cold, though he looked half-frozen when he appeared at the Whiteoaks' door and always went straight to the fire. Sometimes he would bring a newspaper printed in Ontario and read aloud advertisements of land for sale in that province, or accounts of its social and political life.

Philip had engaged the best English doctor in town for Adeline's confinement but willfully, it seemed to him, she was confined a fortnight before the expected time. The doctor had driven in his sleigh to a village twenty miles down the river to attend another accouchement when Adeline's pains came on. She was sitting with Philip in the drawing-room playing a game of backgammon. It was late afternoon, the curtains were drawn and a fire blazed on the hearth. Boney, on his perch, was conducting a low-toned conversation with himself in Hindu. His breast was pouted, his neck sunk into his shoulders, he kept opening and closing one claw on the perch like sensitive fingers. Adeline gave a cry and put her hand to her side.

"A pain!" she cried. "A terrible pain!"

She doubled herself over the backgammon board, sending the men in all directions. Philip sprang up.

"I'll fetch you some brandy," he said.

He strode to the dining room and returned with a small glass of brandy. She still had her hand to her side but she was calm.

"Are you better?" he asked.

"Yes. But give me the brandy." She sipped a little.

"It must be something you ate," he said, eyeing her anxiously.

"Yes . . . those nuts . . . I shouldn't touch Brazil nuts." She took another sip.

"Come to the sofa and lie down."

He raised her to her feet. She took a step, then gave another cry. Boney echoed it and peered inquisitively into her face.

"My God!" said Philip.

"Send for the doctor! Quick! Quick! Quick!" she cried. "The child's coming!"

"It can't! The doctor's out of town."

"Then fetch another!" She tore herself from him, ran to the sofa and lay down, gripping her body in her hands. "Get Berthe Balestrier's doctor! Call Marie!"

In half an hour a short, burly French doctor with a pointed black mustache stepped out of the December dark into the brightly lighted bedroom to which Marie had supported Adeline. Philip walked the floor below, filled with apprehension and distrust.

Inside of another hour a son was born to the Whiteoaks.

The celerity of this birth as compared to Gussie's, and Adeline's speedy recovery from it, were a miracle to her. She gave all the credit to Dr. St. Charles. She sang his praises to everyone who came to see her. She even gave him credit for the vigor of the lusty babe.

Though Philip did not much like the idea, she added St. Charles to the chosen name, and, though Christmas was three weeks off, the name Noel. She was truly happy. Adeline was able to nurse Nicholas, which she had not been fitted to do for Gussie. She found an English nurse who, with the arrogance of her class, took almost complete possession of the babe. Marie however would not give up Gussie. She and the nurse established two hostile camps in the domestic quarters. The nurse had the advantage of knowing she was almost indispensable to Adeline. Marie knew that Philip reveled in her *soufflés* and meringues. When it came to having words, she had all the advantage of being able to pour forth a flood of mingled English and French, unintelligible as she grew angrier, unanswerable except by glares and head tossings. The nurse extolled her charge's beauty. He was the handsomest infant in Quebec. He looked like the Christ Child. Marie could see no such resemblance and she, being a good Catholic, ought at least to know something of the appearance of the Blessed Infant. She told how people stopped her in the street to admire *la petite* Augusta, in her white lamb coat and blue velvet bonnet.

There was no disagreement between the parents as to the relative beauty of their children. Nicholas was indeed a fine child and, in the months that followed, he grew more attractive each week. His skin was like a milk-white flower petal. His brown eyes had golden lights in them and early sparkled with mischief and vitality. He was not bald at his birth but had a pretty coating of brown down which grew so fast that, by the time he was five months old, his nurse could coax it into a fine Thames tunnel, the very pride of her life. Adeline could see in him a strong resemblance to her mother but there was a promise of Whiteoak stalwartness in his infant frame. Philip said he was the image of Adeline without the red hair. Adeline thanked God he had not inherited that. She hoped none of her children would for she looked on red hair as a blemish. She had her wish. Not one of her four children had an auburn hair in his head. It remained for her eldest grandson to inherit, even in a more pronounced degree, her coloring.

The christening was an event in Quebec. The robe worn by Adeline and her brothers, somewhat the worse for wear, was sent out from Ireland to adorn him. The ceremony was at the Garrison

Church, the guests being entertained afterwards at the Whiteoaks' house where short but effective speeches were made and much champagne was drunk to the health and future happiness of Nicholas Noel St. Charles.

The Whiteoaks gave a still larger party at mid-Lent. The guests were asked to wear the costume of the reign of Louis XVI. How they were transformed by powdered hair and patches, by the elegance of their costumes! Philip and Adeline were charming hosts. They were in their element. The house in the Rue St. Louis echoed laughter and the music of the dance, as it had not since the days of the Duke of Kent. During the supper a cageful of artificial singing birds which Adeline had been given by Philip as a Christmas present broke into song to the delight of the company. Monsieur Balestrier drank a little too much champagne. Adeline danced rather too often with Wilmott, though it was small wonder for he danced perfectly and his satin breeches and silk stockings displayed the shapeliest of legs. He was wrong in having spent so much money on a costume whose usefulness was for no more than a night, but such was Adeline's ill influence on him, he told her, smiling somewhat grimly down into her eyes.

The elderly brother and sister, Monsieur and Mademoiselle de Granville, wore authentic costumes of the period brought from France in the early days. He wore the costume with melancholy distinction which, as the night wore on, changed to a strange gaiety. He was Adeline's partner in a quadrille when suddenly he stopped dancing, fixing his eyes on her with a look of terror.

"What is the matter?" she asked anxiously.

"*Maman!*" he said, in a choking voice. "*Maman!* Don't leave me!"

He stood transfixed, his fine face frozen into a mask of fear. His sister came hurriedly and led him away. Those who noticed the incident remarked only that poor Monsieur de Granville had had another of his attacks of nerves but his sister perceived something more serious and early next morning sent for Dr. St. Charles. He could do little to stem the violence of the fever and delirium that followed. All the haunting horror which had darkened Monsieur de Granville's life burst upon him like an electric storm that throws a vivid light into the darkest shadow. He recalled everything. The dimly remembered horrors of his childhood were as though they had happened yesterday.

For almost a week he was in this state, then the fever left him. He became calm. He had no recollection of what had happened. He spoke regretfully of his having to leave the charming party of the Whiteoaks and begged his sister to see to it that his costume was carefully folded and laid away. That night he died in his sleep.

The death of Monsieur de Granville was a shock to Adeline. Birth and death had visited the adjacent houses in so short a time! If only she had not given the fancy-dress party, poor Mademoiselle de Granville would not now be going to Mass weighed down by black, with black rings under her eyes! A bronchial cough kept Adeline indoors. The weather was bitterly cold. It had been a severe winter and surely it was time for spring. But day by day it grew colder. Great snowfalls made the streets impassable; snow weighed upon the roofs till, having formed a mass too great for the slope, it slid off with a crash into the street. All day long men in mufflers and ear muffs shoveled the snow, building high walls of it on either side of the roads so that to see anyone on the opposite side was impossible. Milk was delivered in frozen blocks. Meat was frozen. One morning Pat O'Flynn found a dog frozen stiff on the doorstep. Philip had his ears frozen when returning from dinner at the Fort. The thermometer sank to thirty degrees below zero. The lights of the Lower Town twinkled palely at night like little cold stars. The sun, aloof all day, blazed at its setting into crimson grandeur across the ice-bound St. Lawrence. Like ice made manifest the metallic clangor of church bells sounded in early morning across the town. Adeline could hear the closing of the door and Marie's footsteps crunching on the snow as she hastened to Mass. Gussie made herself a little shrine in a corner of the kitchen out of a white table napkin laid over a box on which stood a picture of the Sacred Heart and, in front of it, a candle in a tin candlestick. She genuflected when she passed this. She knelt before it crossing herself and moving her lips as in prayer. And she scarcely two! Marie's eyes filled with tears as she watched her. Was the little one perhaps too good to live? Nicholas's nurse exclaimed to Adeline:—

"The child is turning into a papist, ma'am. Right here, under our eyes."

"She might do worse, Matilda. If it pleases her to make a little shrine, I shan't interfere."

A new member of the household and one who took up a good deal of room was Nero, a huge black Newfoundland dog. Though he was young he was burly and possessive. He behaved as though he were master of the house and his coat was so thick that he was puzzled to know whether a beating was in correction or play. He usually rolled in the snow before coming into the house. Once inside he gave himself a tremendous shake, creating a fair snowstorm, then took his place on the best rug, at Philip's feet, and set about licking his great snowy paws.

He was the centre of the Whiteoaks' first "family group." The photographer arranged Adeline on a Louis Quinze chair which her billowing garments quite concealed, with Nicholas on her lap. She wore her sealskin sacque and little cap beneath which her hair escaped in thick curls. The infant on her lap was clothed in white rabbit skin with the exception of his dimpled feet, which were bare. Gussie stood at her mother's knee, looking almost as broad as long in her white lamb coat and velvet bonnet. Philip, in his fur-lined coat, stood proudly beside his family and at their feet lay Nero, also manifestly impervious to twenty-below-zero weather. Behind the group was a somewhat Grecian landscape but this was offset by the impressive snowstorm that enveloped all.

The Whiteoaks and their friends gazed long at this picture. Philip bought a magnifying glass, the better to discover its details. Two dozen photographs were ordered, twenty-three of which were carefully wrapped by him and posted to friends and relations in England, Ireland, and India, from which countries came in return letters admiring, jocular, and commiserating as regards the climate of Quebec. The twenty-fourth picture was framed in maroon velvet and stood on a marble-topped table in the drawing-room, along with an alabaster casket and ivory and jade figures from the East.

The cold was indeed trying. It was still winter when April came. Wilmott had definitely made up his mind to go to Ontario. He did his best to persuade the Whiteoaks to do the same. Philip already had a friend, a retired Anglo-Indian Colonel, who had settled on the fertile shore of Lake Ontario. Colonel Vaughan was an older man than Philip. The Colonel had known him in India, and his attitude toward him in this new land was almost fatherly. He urged him to remove to Ontario where they might be neighbors. "Here," he wrote, "the winters are mild, we have little snow, and in the long fruitful summer the land yields grain and fruit in abundance. An agreeable little settlement of *respectable* families is being formed. You and your talented lady, my dear Whiteoak, would receive the welcome here that people of your consequence *merit*. If you come, our home shall be yours till you have built a suitable residence. My wife joins me in this offer in the most whole-hearted manner. Our house is comparatively large and, though we live simply, I think we could make you comfortable."

The transplanting to Canada had stimulated Adeline's venturous nature. She was ready to move on, from province to province if need be, till the ideal situation was found. She had made friends in Quebec but she could go back to visit them. Her health had not been what she had hoped for there. She dreaded another winter in that cold draughty house. The death of Monsieur de Granville had affected her deeply. She felt in a small degree responsible for it. And the crêpe-clad figure of Mademoiselle de Granville was a sad reminder. More than any of these, her desire to retain Wilmott as a friend influenced her. His friendship meant more to her than that of anyone in Quebec. If he went to Ontario this would be lost to her. She consented to the migration.

Once Philip and Wilmott had won Adeline over, they threw themselves heart and soul into the preparation for the journey. The property in Quebec was disposed of, though for a lesser sum than Philip had hoped for. The packing of the furniture, the innumerable small preparations, took time and energy. Only a year had passed since they had thrown themselves with enthusiasm into turning the house in the Rue St. Louis into an abode to their liking, and now it was dismantled! It resumed its air of melancholy. They had made no impression on it.

All the Balestriers wept at parting from them. From Monsieur Balestrier downward, they wept with less and less restraint till, when it came to Lou-lou, the youngest, he clung to Adeline's neck screaming and kicking. To comfort him she gave him a little mechanical dancing monkey he had long admired. His tears were turned to joy. Pleasure swept upward as it had progressed downward till at the last Monsieur Balestrier was able to smile as he kissed Philip on both cheeks and bade him return to Quebec when he found Ontario unbearable as certainly he would.

The furniture was to be stored in Quebec till sent for; only their personal luggage, their livestock, consisting of Nero and Maggie, the goat, journeyed with the family and their two servants. It was a heartbreak for Marie to part with Gussie. She cried till her features were blurred and Gussie cried too, though she was pleased to be going on a journey with her Mamma and Papa. She would have liked to leave Nicholas behind, for she had as yet no love for him. She had a real affection for Nero and Maggie.

She remembered vaguely her sea voyage and, when she realized that they were going to travel by ship again, her mouth went down at the corners and she clung tightly to her nurse's skirt. But this was a fine steamer and its progress was made up the bright river in complete comfort and serenity. At Lachine they left the steamer and were installed on splendid "bateaux" drawn by the lively French-Canadian ponies. Gussie was enchanted. She gave a cry of delight when Patsy snatched her up exclaiming:—

"Look, yer honor, Miss! There is a pretty sight for ye!"

"Who are dose mens?" demanded Gussie in her limited English.

"Sure, 't is the Governor of the Northwest, they say, and him goin' back to his seat. Ah,. that's the life I'd like! Look at the fine clothes on him and the red Indians in war paint to escort him!"

All the party stood gazing at the Governor. A crowd had gathered and a cheer arose. Officers in uniform were with him and eight noble canoes manned by Indians were his escort. Their bronzed faces fierce with war paint, their gay bead-embroidered jackets, the feathers that swept from their jetty hair to their muscular shoulders, filled Adeline with delight. She grasped an arm of Philip and of Wilmott on her either side.

"Oh, what a letter I shall write home!" she cried. "I shall tell all this to my father in a way to astonish him."

In dignity the stately boats swept by. Three dozen paddles rose and dipped, as though guided by one arm. A British flag on every prow spread its crosses to the sun. The Indians sang as they paddled, in rich but mournful tones:—

"A la claire fontaine,
M'en allant promener,
J'ai trouvé l'eau si belle,
Que je m'y suis baigné.
Il y a longtemps que je t'aime,
Jamais je ne t'oublirai."

Gussie raised her voice and joined in the song which she had so often heard from Marie. She joined in, to her own satisfaction though no one heard a sound she uttered.

Through canals, along shores where orchards flourished, past wild rapids and peaceful slopes, now by barge, now by stagecoach, the party leisurely made their pleasant way. The sky arched high and turquoise blue, the land smiled its promise. There seemed no limit to the possibilities of this country. From the stagecoach they alighted at taverns with painted floors and French cooking. On they journeyed till they came to taverns with unpainted floors and a flow of hard spirits. Philip, Adeline, Gussie, Nicholas, Matilda his nurse, Patsy O'Flynn, Nero the Newfoundland dog, Maggie the little goat, Wilmott, who studied maps and deplored the way Philip scattered money about, all moved westward to their new home. Only Wilmott did not go as far as the Vaughans' but remained in the nearest village to inquire about the possibility of buying a small place for himself.

VII

Vaughanlands

DAVID VAUGHAN had acquired from the government, at a very moderate cost, several hundreds of acres of beautifully wooded fertile land. He had built a comfortable but unpretentious house with a wide verandah across the front, on which he and his family spent much of their time in the fine weather. He had now lived there for three years and he regarded them as his happiest years. He was one of those fortunate men who can look back on the greatest undertaking of their life and say it was well done, who can look forward to the future secure in the thought that they are settled exactly where they want to be and that no further change is to be considered. He loved and admired his wife. He was proud of his son. It was his most cherished wish to draw congenial people to the corner of the province where he had settled, and, with their help, establish the customs and traditions of England, to be enjoyed and cherished by their descendants. To these he wished to add the breadth and freedom of the New Land. He believed the combination to be the ideal one for comfort, tolerance, and content. He remembered Philip Whiteoak as a man who would fit admirably into this pattern of living. He had not met Philip's wife but he had heard that she was distinguished-looking and animated in her conversation. To him it seemed worth a real effort to persuade such desirable people to settle beside him.

As the trouble of a prolonged visit from the Whiteoaks would fall on Mrs. Vaughan she was less enthusiastic than he. She earnestly hoped they would not stay as long as he had suggested. However she prepared two bedrooms, one for the nurse and two infants, the other for their parents—Philip had forgotten to mention Patsy O'Flynn, the Newfoundland dog, and the goat—with a sense of cheerful anticipation. There was such an abundance of game and fish, almost at their own door, that the question of food was not too exacting. Later in the season, wild strawberries, raspberries, and blackberries would provide fruit. There was no better bread or butter than was made in her own house. She defied anyone to make as good cheese as she herself could. No, it was not the meals that hung over her, it was the thought of outsiders always denying their privacy and she felt hurt that her husband seemed not to mind that. As for her son, Robert, he was delighted. But what else could you expect of a boy of nineteen who sometimes found life a little too quiet in the country?

It was a lovely evening in the first week of June when Adeline and Philip first saw the scene where the rest of their lives would be spent. David Vaughan had sent a carriage and a pair of strong gray horses to meet the stagecoach. Also a light farm wagon for their luggage. The horses had spent the preceding night in the stable of an inn. They were fresh and well-groomed when they started out on the return journey. The Whiteoaks also had spent the night in the town and rose refreshed. But the unpaved road was rough. It was well for them that the floods of the spring were past, for at that time parts of the road had been washed away. Now it was rough but passable. The air was exquisite, the scenery charming. Between the trees they had glimpses of the lake which to them looked like a sea, sparkling at morning in endless bright ripples; still and of a hazy blue, in the afternoon; flaming beneath fiery clouds at sunset. Partridge and grouse were caring for their nestlings in the deep woods, small birds darted through the bright air. Above the thud of the horses' hoofs and the jingle of harness their song was heard.

The Vaughans came out to the verandah to greet them. David Vaughan and Philip had not met since Philip's marriage. They shook hands warmly, then each presented the other to his wife, the ladies to each other. Mrs. Vaughan and Adeline looked with a good deal of curiosity into each other's eyes. Mrs. Vaughan was determined to like Adeline but she had a misgiving when she looked into her eyes, even though Adeline's smile was sweet with blandishment. "I don't believe I shall like her," Alice Vaughan thought, "but what beautiful teeth and skin she has!"

Adeline saw a wife in Alice Vaughan, a woman whose thoughts never ranged beyond husband and children. She was handsome, in the early forties. Her prematurely gray hair framed a square face with even features and large gray eyes. Her complexion was clear and she had a good color in her cheeks. She wore a black silk dress but no crinoline. Her only ornament was a large cameo brooch. On her smoothly arranged hair was a small white lace cap. After a moment's hesitant scrutiny she took both Adeline's hands in hers and kissed her.

"Welcome to your new home," she said.

"How sweet of you to say that!" cried Adeline, and the fervor of her kiss was disconcerting.

"It is to be your home, you know," put in Colonel Vaughan, "till you have built a house for yourselves."

David Vaughan turned with tender eagerness to the children. Gussie looked tired-out, even though her little face was sunburned to an unnatural rosiness, but Nicholas, sitting on his nurse's arm, was superb. From under his white bonnet a dark curl hung over his fine brown eyes. His face expressed complete well-being.

"What dear, dear children!" said Mrs. Vaughan. "What a lovely baby! Do you think he will come to me?"

"He is a most gregarious rascal," said Philip. "He has made friends all the way from Quebec."

Young Robert Vaughan had stood by quietly watching the interchange of greetings. He resembled his father, who looked the man of letters rather than the soldier. Robert was slenderly made. He had reflective blue eyes and a mass of fine fair hair which he wore rather long. He had spent the first ten years of his life in India, then had been sent to school in England. He had not joined his parents in Canada till the summer before. He was to enter the university in Montreal in the autumn. He had not yet settled down to life in Canada. He felt scarcely acquainted with his parents. Two such extreme transplantings in his short life had had the effect of throwing his spirit back upon itself. He was defensive; he loved no one; the look in his eyes was so impersonal as to repel any intimacy. Yet he was gentle and made haste to help his mother with the guests.

After these had freshened themselves in their room they joined the Vaughans in the cool vine-shaded dining room for supper. Above the table hung a branch of cedar, the scent of which was supposed to repel the house flies which were so difficult to keep out. Pigeon pie and a fine ham were on the table and a bowl of large lettuce leaves. There was a cottage cheese and later came jam, made from wild strawberries, and a caraway-seed cake.

It was hard to believe that Philip and Adeline were at the end of a long journey. He looked as well-groomed as when he had promenaded the terrace at Quebec. She, finding her dress crumpled, had retained a long silk cape of tartan. She also wore black silk mittens which accented the whiteness of her fingers, ringless except for her wedding ring. Her jewels were safe in a traveling case upstairs. Her hair was brushed to Chinese sleekness on her shapely head. As the black mittens accented the whiteness of her fingers, her fine black brows and lashes increased the brightness of her eyes. She looked hungrily over the table.

"I declare," she said, "I have not had a decent meal since I left Quebec. I'm starving!"

"You have come to a land of plenty," said David Vaughan. He turned to Philip. "Do you like shooting?"

"Nothing better."

"Well, you need scarcely leave your door to pick up a brace of these." He indicated the pigeon pie which he now began to serve.

"And the fishing?"

David Vaughan laid down the fork and stared at him. "Believe it or not," he said, "the sea salmon come right up through the lake and into our river. I caught a whopper right here on my own property less than a month ago."

"Well, well, do you hear that, Adeline?"

"I do; we shall not starve, at any rate. How delicious this pie is!"

"Will you have some of the lettuce?" asked Mrs. Vaughan. "We pride ourselves on it. We are the only people who grow it. We supply the neighborhood."

"What about the neighborhood?" asked Philip. "Pretty congenial, from what you wrote, Vaughan."

"A very respectable community. You'll like them and they'll like you. I can tell you everyone is excited by your coming and will be still more so after meeting you." His eyes rested admiringly on Adeline.

"I left good friends in Quebec," she said.

"Too damn French!" said Philip.

"That's what I felt," said David Vaughan. "My aim is to keep this little settlement purely British. Indeed if I had my way, only the English, Scottish, and Welsh should be allowed to settle in any part of Canada."

"No Irish?" asked Adeline.

Before he could reply, Philip broke in—"I warn you, my wife is straight from the Ould Sod."

"I should welcome just one Irish lady," said Vaughan, "to be Queen of us all."

"How flowery the old boy is," thought Robert. "I could not have said that. But she liked it." He fixed his shy, impersonal gaze on Adeline, who was smiling at his father.

David Vaughan was giving the history of the principal families of the neighborhood. He would forget to eat till his wife reminded him. When, after the meal, they returned to the verandah, he brought out a map of the district which he had himself made, showing the course of the small rivers, the residences of the families he had described, the roads and forest. A thousand acres of richly timbered land, adjacent to his own property, was for sale and this he counseled Philip to buy. Nowhere would he find a better opportunity for establishing himself in a superior position in the Province. Nowhere would he find better land, better sport, within such easy reach of railway and town. Nowhere would he find more hospitable, kinder-hearted or better bred people. Nowhere would he and his family be more welcome.

As he and Philip bent over the map spread on the table before them, the red light of the setting sun illumined their features. Adeline, in her bright tartan mantle, sat on one side with Mrs. Vaughan. Young Robert, perched on the verandah railing, only half-heard what the men were saying but strained his ears to hear Adeline's voice, to him so exotic in its inflections. His shy, cool gaze studied the lines of her shoulder as she leant on the arm of her chair, the beauty of her sleek auburn head. He wondered if she was conscious of his presence. She seemed not to be, yet, when the cry of a whippoorwill broke with melancholy strangeness on the air, she turned quickly to him.

"What is it?" she asked.

"A whippoorwill. There are hundreds about here."

"I've never before heard one! It's lovely but it's sad."

"This one is just the right distance away. They can be too noisy."

Again and again and again came the bird's cry. Then after a moment's silence it flew nearer and, in mournful haste, repeated the three notes as though it were a tragic message. Sunset had faded and a sombre dusk emanated as though palpably from the massive trees. The house stood in a grassy hollow.

In their room, Philip remarked to Adeline:—

"I shall not make the mistake of building our house in a hollow. Fifty years from now this place will be buried in greenery. If I cannot find a rise to build on I shall at least be out in the open."

"Is there an 'out in the open,' " she wondered, peering through the window. "Trees trees there are trees everywhere. How many varieties did Colonel Vaughan say there are?"

"I forget. But what I mean is, I shall make a large clearing for our house and it must be on the highest point on our land."

"I don't like the thought of a large clearing. I like trees about. I like a park."

"You shall have a park with deer in it."

"How lovely! Where does the land lie? Am I looking out toward it?"

"Yes. I think so."

She drew a deep breath. "Just fancy! I am breathing the air from our land! Over there is our land—the very spot our foundations will rise from! Will the house be stone?"

"That depends on what material is to be had. For myself, I like a nice mellow brick. It looks warm-colored among the trees. It has a cozy, hospitable look."

"I rather like the white wooden houses they have in Quebec villages."

"Too flimsy."

"They say not."

"I don't like the looks of them. Don't you want a nice mellow brick?"

"If there is nothing better."

"What could be better?" he asked severely.

"I don't know."

"Then why raise objections?"

"I wasn't."

"You said you wanted wood."

"I said I like wood."

"But you don't object to brick?"

"Not in the least. . . . Philip"—she came and sat on his knee—"I have not seen you alone all day. I can't believe we are actually here."

He pressed her close to his broad chest. "What a time we shall have, my sweet! We're going to be happier than we've ever been and that's saying a good deal, isn't it? You look pale, Adeline."

She relaxed against him. "Oh, how tired I am!" she exclaimed. "Yet I am too excited for sleep. My body relaxes but my brain refuses."

He found her eyelids with his lips. "There, close your eyes. Now I command you. Keep them closed while I kiss each ten times."

But, as he spoke, he raised his head and listened. There came the rumble of wagon wheels and the loud barking of dogs.

"They have arrived!" he exclaimed.

She started up. "Nero and Maggie!" she cried. "And I forgot to tell the Vaughans about them! Did you?"

"By Jove, no! Still, they are expecting the wagon with our boxes. I shall explain about the dog and the goat to-morrow. I wish you had left the damn goat in Quebec. Gussie does not need her milk now."

"Leave Maggie behind! And she wearing the dear little bell my own mother tied to her neck! Why, 't would bring bad luck to us! What is one small goat anyhow? Surely there is room for her in this great place!"

The rumbling of wagon wheels ceased but now came the snarls and yells of a dog fight. Men were shouting at them.

"Their dogs are killing Nero!" she cried. "Oh, Philip, run! Quick! Quick! Save Nero!"

"He can take care of himself." But Philip hurried from the room. A small lamp still burned in the hall. Downstairs he found David

Vaughan with a lighted lantern. They went together to the stable.

Adeline stood by the window listening to the dreadful noise of the fight. Then silence fell. She began to undress. The silence was too deep. She wished Philip would return but she dreaded what he might have to report.

It was some time before he came.

"Well," he said, "it was more sound and fury than bloodshed. But Vaughan's bulldog and collie gave our Nero the worst of it. He has a torn ear and a bite on his forehead."

"Oh, the brutes!" she cried. "And was he able to do them no harm?"

"He had his teeth into the collie's paw and there was blood on the bulldog but I'm afraid it was Nero's."

"I do hope Mr. Vaughan will keep his dogs tied up."

"We can scarcely expect that. I must say he was very decent about it. He gave me a box stall for Nero for the present."

"And how is Maggie?"

"Right as a trivet. Little bell tinkling and all."

Adeline began to cry. "This dog fight was the last straw," she declared. "I shall not sleep to-night. Feel my heart."

He laid his hand on her chemise beneath the right breast. "My God," she cried, "it's not there!" In exasperation she snatched his hand and put it in the right place.

"It beats no faster than usual," he said. "And you obviously are panting to quicken it. Come, my dear, you are quite all right."

"I shan't sleep to-night!"

But in thirty minutes by the grandfather clock in the hall she was in County Meath with her brothers, though her head was pillowed on Philip's shoulder.

VIII

The Land

THIS morning in June was perfect. It seemed that no exquisite detail had been forgotten to ensure that perfection. The turquoise sky arched above the woods, cloudless. The trees themselves stood grand and strong, not crowded as though in struggle for existence, but free to thrust out their roots, to extend their branches in pride. Through their rich foliage the sun poured down upon the dark loam and drew from it such a carpet of moss, fern, and wild flower that where was one to step without crushing something fragile and sweet?

There was enough breeze to sway the branches so that in turn light shade and warm sunbeam fell on this variegated growth. The wild grapevine draped the trunk of an elm which towered so tall, before it sent out a branch, that it seemed to know nothing of what clung so lovingly to its base. A stump became the throne of a pale convolvulus that tossed up a fresh bloom each hour. There were patches of daintily formed moss into which one's feet sank as into living plush. Then wintergreen spread its glossy mat. Trailing arbutus sent down a delicate root, sent up a waxen bell and pressed on, as though in haste to claim the land for its own. Butterflies flew not by one or two but in bright throngs, sometimes hanging like flowers on a branch, then moving swiftly away, stirred by some subtle but inexorable impulse. They rose above the treetops, beat their tiny wings against the azure of the sky, then sank, drawn down by the same invisible guide till they hung on the branch of the maple. The birds at this hour were mostly unseen, living their enthralling life, from the routine of which they never deviated, among the rich green foliage. But their song was heard in every part of the wood, from the clear pipe of the wild canary, the studied cadence of the oriole, to the deep note of the wood pigeon. As they flew from bough to bough the leaves fluttered and sometimes a pointed wing or a bright breast was revealed. And in their burrows mole, ground hog, fox, and rabbit reared their young, in complete certainty that theirs was the most important mission of all.

Philip and Adeline were standing on their own land. Philip had a small hamper containing their lunch strapped to his shoulder. Two weeks had passed since their arrival. During that time they had inspected the property, made the necessary visits to government offices, paid the sum demanded, been given the deed with impressive red seals, and now could say—"The land is ours."

"It is a paradise," cried Adeline, turning her head from side to side, "a perfect paradise, and it is ours!"

It was the first time they had visited the place alone. Each previous time one of the Vaughans or a government agent had come with them. Always there had been boundaries or business of some sort to discuss. But now they were alone. There was no need to talk to the Vaughans, pleasant as they were. They could stand gazing in rapt attention at each new vista that opened up. They could explore like eager children, running here and there, shouting to each other to "Look! Look!" How Adeline deplored her long skirts and remembered her girlhood in Ireland when she would tuck them up and leave the agile legs free. Once, when she was wrestling with one of her brothers, he had torn the skirt clean off her and she had risen in her pantalettes. Oh, the bliss of it! She had leaped and run, higher and faster than any of them. She had been caught and given a whipping but she now recalled the incident with a grin.

"We might be Adam and Eve," said Philip. "We might be the only two people on earth. Upon my soul you'd think the land knew we owned it—it's so smiling!"

"Philip, my angel, you are a poet!"

"No . . . but I do feel . . . well, I can't explain . . . I know it sounds ridiculous."

"It isn't ridiculous. It's true! Everything has a different air this morning."

"Now you're going to laugh."

"At what? Not at you being poetical, I promise."

"What I'm thinking is—we've got the key of all this . . . not just the land, you know. But everything."

"Yes. I understand. It's like being born again."

"I say, Adeline—we've come to the ravine from a different angle. Look!"

They stood, shoulder to shoulder, looking down into the green dusk where the stream narrowed and was half-hidden in wild honeysuckle and purple iris. Spotted lilies grew there and a pair of blue herons rose, their legs stiff. But Philip and Adeline could not descend the ravine because of the undergrowth. They could only glimpse the river, palely foaming about the great stones that had once rolled down the mossy steep into it.

"Our house must be near the ravine," she said. "I want to be able to walk across a velvety lawn, open a gate, a low broad gate, and make a path down to the stream's edge."

"We will built a rustic bridge," he said, "across the stream. A path on the far side would lead us back to Vaughanlands, I think."

"You are so good at directions! Now Vaughanlands seems to me in the opposite one."

He took out the compass which was attached to his watch chain, and consulted it.

"I'm right!" he exclaimed triumphantly. "The Vaughans' house is straight over there. A bridge across the stream and we should have a short cut to it."

"Shall we ever get all this undergrowth cleared? Good heavens, if one of the children wanders away we shall never find him!"

"We are fortunate in its being a good hard-bush—I believe that's the proper expression. There's a great deal of maple, oak, white ash, hickory and so forth. A few strong axes swinging, a few days' work, and your forest will look like a park."

"How much you know!" she cried, admiringly.

"Well, Vaughan has told me a good deal in the past fortnight."

She tugged at his arm. "Come, let's choose the site for the house!"

"I have a spot in mind. If only I can find it! Vaughan approves of it too. It must be quite near. There's a sort of natural clearing and a spring."

"Oh, if there's anything I love, it's a spring! I shall plant water-cress about it and mint and honeysuckle!"

"It is comparatively near the road, too. We must be near the road . . . Hello—here's the devil entering our Eden!"

They could see the tall thin figure of a man but he had drawn much nearer before they recognized him as Wilmott. He had remained at a hotel in the town to make inquiries for a suitable habitation for himself. Philip had been to see him when he visited the government offices and had told him of his purchase of a thousand acres. Wilmott had promised to come out to inspect it. He had cast aside the clothes of convention and now wore brown breeches tucked into top boots, a shirt open at the throat, and a broad-brimmed hat. He was a little self-conscious and asked, after greetings had been exchanged:—

"How do you think I look?"

"Like the devil," said Philip.

Wilmott was astonished. "Well, I thought I should dress appropriately."

"You're not going to be a lumberjack, are you?"

"No. But I shall have rough work to do and I must save the clothes I brought with me. It will be some time before I can afford to buy new ones."

"I think you look charming," said Adeline, "except for the side whiskers. They are incongruous."

He gave her an intent look. "Do you really dislike them?" he asked in a low tone. Philip had moved ahead.

She looked at him boldly. "Yes. I do."

"They'll come off to-night!"

"How did you find us?" demanded Philip over his shoulder.

"I engaged a man to drive me out. We stopped to ask the way of a man with a horse and buggy down the road a bit. He turned out to be your Patsy O'Flynn. I don't know what was so funny about it but seeing him as he had looked in Galway and on board ship and in Quebec, and then seeing him sitting in a buggy by a rail fence, was just too much for me. I laughed and laughed. He must have thought I was just as funny for he laughed and laughed too."

Philip and Adeline had never seen Wilmott like this. He seemed hilarious.

"I love the freedom of this country!" he exclaimed. "You are not going to get rid of me, you know. On the way here I discovered a little log house. The man who lives in it wants to move farther north. He wants to get away from so much civilization! Well, the long and short of it is, I'm going to buy his property—a highly superior log cabin and fifty acres, part of which is swamp. It is on the edge of a river and a bigger, better river than yours, the man tells me."

Philip looked at him dubiously. He was afraid Wilmott had made a bad bargain. He liked him but was not sure that he wanted him for a neighbor. There was an uncertain quality in Wilmott. Also he had a way of assuming an intellectual intimacy with Adeline, as though they two looked on things from the same angle. But Philip liked him and his frank face lighted. He gave Wilmott a slap on the shoulder.

"Good man!" he said. "But I must bring Vaughan to see the log house before you pay the cash. He will know if it is worth it."

"Nothing shall dissuade me," said Wilmott. "It's the sort of place I've been dreaming of."

"What about the swamp?"

"The owner says it will grow onions."

"Onions! What would you do with them?"

"Sell them."

"My dear fellow, you're in for a tumble if you bank on making money from onions."

"The swamp is a haven for wild fowl. All varieties make their home there. Just come and see."

"You had better help us choose a site for our house. I have the axemen engaged but haven't yet decided where to put it."

"Are you sure you aren't lost?"

"Positive." Philip again consulted his compass. They moved on through the wood.

"I wish D'Arcy and Brent could see us," said Wilmott. "I had a letter from D'Arcy the other day. They are in New York. It's very amusing they say. Strange fashions—spittoons everywhere. Negroes in unbelievable clothes! They saw Fanny Kemble and think she overacts." He turned to Adeline. "Have you seen Fanny Kemble?"

"No. What I enjoyed most in London was *The Bohemian Girl.* I declare I shall never forget that evening. It was heavenly."

Philip shouted—"Here is the spot!"

He had pushed ahead and now awaited them in an open space. Perhaps in an earlier time some settler had chosen it as his dwelling, for great stumps showed where forest trees had been felled. But these were buried in the luxuriant foliage of the wild grape, or clothed in moss. The clearing had a friendly air. The sun poured into it and the trees which had been spared spread into extraordinary beauty. A tall young silver birch fluttered its satin leaves and its satin bark was flawless. As they drew near to it a flock of bluebirds rose from its midst, not in fright but rather in play, and flew skyward where their blueness soon was merged.

Adeline never had heard of the sentimental belief in the bluebird for happiness but she liked their looks, and cried:—

"Oh, the pretty things! They know the spot! We shall build here! I am so happy I could die."

It was the day of fainting. She tried to faint to demonstrate her emotion but could not. She staggered a little.

"What's the matter?" asked Philip.

"Can't you see I'm fainting?"

"Nonsense," he said, but he looked at her a little anxiously.

"Sit down here," begged Wilmott. He led her to a low moss-grown stump.

She sat down, closing her eyes. Wilmott snatched off his hat and began fanning her.

"She's not fainting," said Philip. "Look at the color in her lips."

She put her fingers over her lips and sighed. She felt a stirring beneath her. She sprang up. A large adder glided across the stump and into the grass. Adeline's shriek might have been heard to Vaughanlands. The two men stared in horror.

"A snake!" she screamed. "A poisonous snake! There—in the grass!"

They found sticks and ran after it, beating the grass.

She was composed on their return.

"Did you kill it?" she asked.

"Yes," answered Philip. "Want to see it?"

"I'd rather not."

"It was a yard long," said Wilmott, "and as thick as my arm."

"How horrible!"

"Never mind," said Philip. "We shall soon be rid of them. Vaughan told me there were a few about his place. When we have the undergrowth cleared there will be an end to them."

"This is a superb site for your house," said Wilmott. "That little rise is the perfect place. It should face south." He seemed to have forgotten Adeline's fright and paced up and down marking the size of the foundation.

Philip had gone off to the spring. He now returned carrying a tin mug of water. He looked anxiously at Adeline, as he gave her the drink.

"I'm surprised at your making such a fuss," he said, "after the snakes you've seen in India. The snakes here are harmless."

She meekly drank the icy spring water.

"I had never sat on one before." She shuddered.

Wilmott called out—"You need not worry about excavating. The soil is just right and the site well-drained. I should advise a basement for the kitchen and usual offices. It will be warm in winter and cool in summer. You must have a square hall, with drawing-room on one side and library and dining room on the other. A deep porch would look well."

"He'll be telling us next what to name the house," said Philip.

Adeline rose.

"How do you feel?" he asked.

"Better. But I was almost fainting before the snake came. Why was I?"

"I forget."

"Oh, yes—it was the bluebirds. They made me so happy."

"You should try to restrain your emotions."

"But they're all so fresh and strong."

"Bottle 'em up!"

"But they won't keep."

Wilmott called out—"Behind the main stairway you should have space for another good room. The house should be broad, substantial and hospitable-looking."

"I shall see to that," said Philip, testily.

"I recommend a third story. It makes the house more impressive, and if your family is large—"

"It's not going to be large."

"Still I should have the third story."

He came back to them. His thin face was alight.

"I am so hungry," said Adeline. "Let us have our sandwiches."

"Good," said Philip. "Will you join us, Wilmott?"

"Are you sure you have enough for three? However you need not worry about me. One will be plenty."

They sat down on the sun-warmed grass where one must crush tiny pink flowers, they grew so close. Philip unstrapped his lunch basket and took out sandwiches, small cakes, a leather-covered flask of wine and collapsible drinking cup.

"Do you remember our picnics in Quebec?" asked Wilmott.

"Oh, what fun we had!" exclaimed Adeline, her mouth full of chicken sandwich.

"With the Balestrier children all over the place!" said Philip. "If I can't bring up my children to behave better I'll eat my hat."

"How is the charming little Augusta?" asked Wilmott.

"Being utterly spoilt by Mrs. Vaughan," answered Philip. "However she is forgetting French and learning to speak English."

"Tell her I shall bring her a present. A doll—to take the place of the one stolen on board ship. Does she still miss her ayah?"

"No. She has forgotten her."

There was a moment's silence as their minds flew back to the funeral at sea. Then Wilmott said:—

"The mosquitoes are a pest here. I suffer tortures at night from the itching of old bites and the hideous buzzing as new bites are inflicted."

"I am writing home," said Philip, "for mosquito netting. We shall cover our beds with it when our house is built. The Vaughans seem quite reconciled to being eaten alive."

"As a matter of fact," said Adeline, "the mosquitoes pass by the Vaughans to feast on Philip."

Philip picked up the flask of wine. "We have only one drinking cup," he remarked. "I was going to give it to Adeline and myself drink from the flask. But she and I can use the one cup."

"Give me the tin mug," said Wilmott.

"Wherever did you find it, Philip?"

"By the spring. And there were footprints about. Vaughan tells me that there is a log hut on the property and that an old Scotsman, called Fiddling Jock, has taken up his abode there. Vaughan says he's harmless."

"How large is the hut?" asked Wilmott. "I might have lived there."

Philip opened his eyes till they were a little prominent. "What about land?" he asked.

"True," returned Wilmott. "I must have land."

"Couldn't we sell him fifty acres?" asked Adeline, in a stage aside.

"Out of the heart of the property? Never."

"Oh, I am quite satisfied with the place I have chosen. I shall live on berries and fish and wild fowl and read all the books I have been wanting to read."

"Where will you get them?"

"I have brought them with me."

The Whiteoaks stared. "I knew you had brought some books," said Adeline, "for you lent me several, but I didn't know you had enough to keep you going."

"There is quite a respectable library in the town. Also D'Arcy is picking up some in New York. Quite rare ones but worth the price."

For the hundredth time the Whiteoaks wondered about Wilmott's financial status. At times he talked quite largely, at others as though he were a pauper. Now he asked:—

"What of the neighborhood? Are there any interesting or intelligent people?"

"A good many," said Philip. "David Vaughan to begin with. He and his wife gave a dinner party for us the other evening and we met the neighbors. A quite respectable and well-informed circle. There is a Mr. Lacey who has a son in the Navy; Mr. Pink, the clergyman; Dr. Ramsey, a rather cantankerous fellow but a man of character and, I believe, very capable; and half a dozen other families. We discussed the future of the Province. Their sincere hope is to keep it free of foreigners. They want to build up the population slowly but solidly out of sturdy British material. They want both freedom and integrity in the land. And I've pledged myself to this project. Vaughan contends that the United States is going to pay bitterly for opening its gates to old Europe. Well, after all, these people from Eastern and Southern Europe would as soon as not stick a knife into your back. Their religion is superstition. They'd do you in for a few pounds. Torture and cruelty are in their blood. I've lived a good many years in India and I've seen enough of treachery. Let's go slow and sure. Let's keep British."

"*And* Irish," added Adeline.

"I'm with you," said Wilmott. "Here's to the building of your house and this Province!" He raised the tin mug.

When they had drunk the toast Philip produced a leather cigar case and offered a cigar to Wilmott.

"This will keep off the mosquitoes."

"Thanks. I haven't smoked a cigar since the last one you gave me."

Philip and Adeline were embarrassed. Wilmott was using his poverty-stricken tone. Perhaps he was conscious of this, for he added as he took the tip off his cigar:—

"I'm no smoker."

"Well, I am," said Philip, "and I can tell you that it irritates me not to be allowed to smoke in the house. Mrs. Vaughan won't have it."

"Doesn't he smoke?"

"He has a pipe on the verandah after breakfast and at bedtime."

Wilmott stared about him, with a look both reflective and wondering. He said—"I suppose these forests go on and on, right to the Arctic."

"Yes. It gives one—a feeling."

"For the grandeur of it, you mean?"

"Yes. And the stability. There ought to be enough timber for all time."

"Not if the people go on hacking it down and burning it—just to get rid of it."

Adeline rose and shook out her skirt. She said—"I want to walk about."

"I'll stay here," said Wilmott. "You two go. I shall smoke and conjure up a suitable name for your house."

"He's too damned officious," said Philip, when they were alone. "He's planned our house to his satisfaction. Now he's going to name it. Whatever name he chooses I'll not have it!"

"Oh, Phil, don't be silly!" She gave a skip of joy. She held up her heavy skirt and petticoat and danced across the flowery grass.

"Here will be our kitchen," she chanted. "With a big fireplace and a brick floor! Here will be the pantries and the larder! Here the servants' quarters! A nice wee room for Patsy O'Flynn!"

Tucking up his coat tails and placing his hands on his hips, Philip danced to meet her.

"Here, Madam, is my wine cellar," he declared, "well stocked, maturing at leisure!"

She clasped him in her arms and laid her face against his shoulder.

"Let's live to be old—old," she said. "So we may enjoy it—together—for years and years and years."

"I promise."

"And you must promise to let me die first."

"Very well, dear. I promise."

"What shall we name the place? If we don't do it soon, it's just as you say, Wilmott will do it for us."

"I should like a name that has associations for me at home."

"But I don't want an English name."

He stared, a little truculently.

"I should like," she said, "a name which has associations for me. What about Bally—"

He interrupted her. "I'm dashed if I can stomach an Irish name."

She glared at him.

Wilmott's tall figure was approaching. He was almost on the run. "I have it!" he cried.

"Have what?" asked Philip.

"A name for your place."

They looked at him defensively.

"The name of your military station in India," he went on. "You met there. You were married there. You will probably never be quite as happy again as you were then. It is a pretty name. It is striking. It is easy to remember. It is—"

"Jalna," said Adeline, musingly.

"No," said Philip. He looked defiantly at Wilmott.

"Don't you like the name?"

"I like it well enough."

"Do you like it, Mrs. Whiteoak?" Wilmott looked eagerly into

Adeline's eyes. The pupils were reflecting the green of the forest. They looked mysterious.

"You took the word out of my mouth," she said. "I was thinking—Jalna—Jalna—as hard as I could—when you called out."

Philip's face lighted. "Were you really? I confess that I like it—now I hear you say it. Jalna . . . yes, it's pretty good. It's a souvenir of my regiment. A seal on the past."

"And a good omen for the future," she added. "I'm glad I thought of it."

Wilmott stood irresolute.

"It's a damned good name," said Philip. "It's extraordinary you should think of it just before Wilmott did."

"It came in a flash. *Jalna,* I said to myself! Then Mr. Wilmott came running with it in his mouth. But I said it first."

IX

The Foundation

THE woodsmen's blows resounded on the trunks of the trees. With axe and with long-handled billhook they cut away the saplings and the undergrowth. Then they attacked the trees. Now the axes were whetted to extraordinary sharpness. The man swung the axe and brought it down in a deft, slanting stroke on the proud bole. Then he struck upward, meeting the first incision, and a clean chip sprang out. So, down and up, down and up, till the bole was cut halfway through. Next he attacked it from the other side. The blows rang. The sweat ran down the man's face. The tree gave a little tremor, as though of surprise. The tremor ran through all its boughs, even to the smallest twig. At the next stroke an agitation swept among its leaves. As though in a fury he struck. Then the beech fell. At first without haste, then in a panic it flung to the ground, moaning, cracking, swinging its boughs in a storm of green leaves.

The woodsmen were orderly, making no chaos of trunks and severed branches. The great stumps and long-reaching roots were dug up. The brush heaps grew. The trees which were left to ornament the grounds spread their branches in proud security. The bright axe had passed them by. You could have driven a carriage and pair between them. The grounds took on the aspect of a park. But later, fields would stretch about the park, they would be ploughed and sown, orchards planted.

Adeline saw Philip in a new light. He who had always been fastidious in his dress, a bit of a dandy in fact, would return to

Vaughanlands with muddy boots, with clothes wrinkled and hands scratched by thorns. He who had even sent his best shirts to England to be laundered because they could not be done to his satisfaction in India now appeared with crumpled linen and seemed not to care, even to rejoice in his condition. He had taken an axe into his hands but he was chagrined by his own efforts as compared to the performance of these practised, tobacco-chewing woodsmen. But he spent his days in watching their progress, in lending a hand where he could. He was bitten by black flies and mosquitoes. He grew deeply tanned. All his exercise and polo playing in India had not toughened him as this life was doing. But in the evening he again presented himself as the dashing Captain of Hussars, agreeable to the neighborhood, properly attentive to Mrs. Vaughan. Before going to bed he would remove himself to the verandah and there smoke a last cigar.

A competent architect was recommended by David Vaughan. Simplicity in design was the order of the neighborhood, but the Whiteoaks wanted their house to be the most impressive. Not pretentious but one worth looking at, with good gables and large chimneys. It was a thrilling moment when the first sod was turned for the foundation. A sharp spade was placed in Adeline's hands by the foreman. The sod already had been marked out and loosened. She rubbed her palms together, took a grip on the handle, placed her foot on the spade, gave an arch look at the assembled workmen and drove it deep into the loam. She bent, she heaved, the sod resisted.

"It's pretty tough, I'm afraid," said the foreman. "I'll loosen it some more."

"No," said Adeline, her color bright.

"Put your back into it," adjured Philip.

She did. The sod released its hold, came up. She held it triumphantly on the spade, then turned it over. The house had its first foothold on the land.

Philip admired the way these men worked. They worked with might and good heart, in fierce heat, in enervating humidity. Only during the electrical storm or the downpour of rain did they crowd into the wooden shelter they had made themselves. The Newfoundland dog, Nero, came each morning to the scene of the building with Philip. He so greatly felt the heat that Philip one day put him between his knees and clipped his fur to the shoulders so that he looked like an immense poodle.

Wilmott kept his promise and shaved his whiskers. When he appeared before Adeline clean-shaven she scarcely knew him. He had been interesting, dignified. Now the contour of his face was visible she found him with a hungry, haunted look that was almost romantic. The bones in his face were fine. The hollows of his cheeks showed odd planes of light.

"How you have changed!" she exclaimed.

"It is well not to look always the same," he answered laconically. "I suppose I look even less attractive. Handsome looks are not my strong point."

"Who wants handsome looks in a man!"

"You do."

"I? Philip would be the same to me if he had a snub nose and no chin."

"Now you are talking nonsense, Mrs. Whiteoak."

"How rigid you are! Surely you might call me Adeline."

"It wouldn't be the thing at all."

"Not in this wilderness?"

"This is already a close conventional community."

"What about your log house and swamp?"

"That's my own corner. . . . In it I have always called you Adeline."

"Please don't say *Adelyne*. I am accustomed to *Adeleen.*"

"I suppose that is why I pronounce it *Adelyne.*"

"How cantankerous you are!" she exclaimed. "I declare I think it's a good thing you are not married."

He reddened a little.

"But perhaps you are," she smiled.

"I am not," he answered stiffly, "and I thank God for it."

"You would be a more amiable man if you were."

"Should I? I doubt it."

She gave her happy smile. "I'm glad you aren't," she said. "Because I should dislike your wife. You are the sort of man who would choose a woman I'd dislike."

"I'd have chosen you—if I'd had the chance."

They were sitting on a pile of freshly cut, sappy logs, within sight and sound of the workmen. But his words created a separate space for them, an isolation as of a portrait of two, in a picture frame. They sat listening to the sound of the axe, the thud of spade, their nostrils drew in the resinous scent of the logs but they were no longer a part of the scene. Their eyes looked straight ahead and, if they had been, in fact, figures in a portrait, it would have been said that the eyes followed you everywhere.

Nero was lying at Adeline's feet. She put a hand on his crown and grasping a handful of thick curly hair rocked his head gently. He suffered the indignity of the caress with inviolable majesty.

"You say that," she murmured, "because of this place. It makes one more emotional."

He turned his eyes steadily on her but she saw his lips tremble. He asked:—

"Do you doubt my sincerity?"

"You can't deny that you sometimes put things—oddly."

"Well, there's nothing odd about that. Most men would say it."

"And you've seen me in real tempers!"

"I am not saying you're perfect," he replied testily. "I am saying—" He broke off.

"It's very sweet of you, Mr. Wilmott—after seeing me at my worst for over a year."

"Now, you're talking nonsense."

"It's better to talk nonsense."

"You mean in order to cover up what I said? Don't worry. I'm not going to plague you. I just had an irrational wish to let you know."

Adeline's lips curved. She looked at him almost tenderly.

"You are laughing at me!" exclaimed Wilmott hotly. "You are going to make me sorry I told you."

"I was just smiling to see you so—impulsive. I like you all the better for it."

"If you think Philip wouldn't mind my calling you by your Christian name—it would give me great pleasure."

"I'll ask him."

"No, don't . . . I'd rather not."

Philip was coming toward them, striding in riding breeches

across the broken ground where each day flowers opened, fern fronds uncurled, only to be crushed. He said as he drew near:—

"I have to go to inspect some brick with the architect. I don't know how long I shall be. Will you take Mrs. Whiteoak back, Wilmott?"

"Goodness, why don't we call each other by our Christian names?" exclaimed Adeline. "Surely we needn't go on Misses and Mistering in the wilds!"

"All right," agreed Philip. "I'm willing. James, will you take Adeline back to Vaughanlands?"

"She hasn't seen my estate yet," said Wilmott. "It's palatial. I should like to show it her first."

"Splendid. You'll admire what he has done, Adeline. Now I must be off." He strode back to where the architect stood waiting.

Adeline and Wilmott clambered into the dusty buggy lent by the Vaughans. The gray mare was tied to a post where the main entrance was to be. She was now so in the habit of waiting that she had ambled into the ditch. It was a miracle that the buggy was not overturned.

"This nag is as quiet as a sheep," said Wilmot, taking the reins. "I wish I owned it."

"What an admission!"

"I want to be lazy and worthless for the rest of my life."

"You can't be worthless—not while Philip and I are your friends, James."

"It's handsome of you to say that," and he added stiffly—"Adeline."

The horse jogged along the sunny road that lay deep in fine white dust. Yet the road led between dense woods and seemed no more than a pale ribbon dividing a wilderness. For all that, they met heavy wagons loaded with material for the building of Jalna, a ragged, barefoot girl driving a cow, an old cart drawn by a mule and filled with an Indian family and their effects. Raspberries glowed redly in the tangle of growth at the road's edge. Wild lupine, chicory and gentian made patches of celestial blue. There was a constant movement among the trees as birds fluttered or squirrels and chipmunks leaped from bough to bough. Sometimes a field appeared, heavy with tall grain. It seemed a country in which fulfillment pressed forward to meet promise.

Philip had been forced to admit that Wilmott had got a bargain in his log house and the fifty acres that went with it. They had gone over the place together carefully. Wilmott had paid the money and moved in at once but had not wished Adeline to see it till it was, to his mind, presentable. Now on the bank of a full-flowing river it stood out in its little clearing, strong and weather-proof. Wilmott was proud of it. There was a dignified swagger in his movements as he assisted Adeline to dismount from the high step of the buggy, then led the way along a grass path to the door. The voice of the river came to them and the sibilant whispering of reeds on its edge. An old punt was tied to a mossy stake.

"How lovely!" exclaimed Adeline. "I had no idea it would be so lovely. Why didn't you tell me?"

"I wanted to surprise you," he answered, not doubting her sincerity, for he himself thought the spot perfection. He unlocked the door which opened stubbornly, and showed her inside the dwelling. It had only one room with a lean-to at the back. Evidently he had hoped she would come to-day or was amazingly precise in his habits. Nothing was scattered about, in the way Philip scattered his belongings. The floor was bare and was still moist from scrubbing. A hooked rug, showing a picture of a ship, lay in front of the small stove. The furniture had been made by the former owner—a table, two chairs, a bunk spread with a patch-work quilt. Red curtains hung at the one window. In a cupboard on the wall a patently new tea set of blue china spoke of England. Along one wall Wilmott had himself built bookshelves which were filled with books old and new, the leather and gold of their backs shining in a shaft of sunlight which fell on them as though directed. There was something touching in it all and the poor man living alone! Adeline said, in a tremulous voice, as though she had never seen anything to equal it:—

"And you have done it all by yourself!"

"Yes."

"I don't see how you managed it. It's lovely."

"Oh, 't will do."

"It's so tidy!"

"You should see it sometimes."

"And the sweet tea set! When did you buy it?"

"Two days ago." He went to the cupboard, took out the cream jug and handed it to her. "You like the design?" he asked.

She saw a shepherd and shepherdess reclining under a tree by a river—in the background a castle. She touched the jug to her cheek.

"What smooth china! Shall I ever drink tea from it, I wonder."

"I'll make it now," he said. "That is, if you will stay."

"I'd like nothing better. Do let me help."

He hesitated. "What of the conventions? Would people talk?"

"Because I drank tea with you? Let them! My dear James, I've come here to spend the rest of my days. People had better begin their gossip at once. I'll give 'em food for it!" She moved with elastic step and swaying skirt across the room.

He returned the jug to its place. Then he turned to her impulsively. "I shall light the fire, then," he said.

The fire was already laid. He touched a match to it and it flared up brightly. He took the tin kettle and went to the spring for water. Through the window she watched his tall figure, so conventional in its movements. "I wonder what you have in that head of yours," she mused. "But I like you. Yes, I like you very much, James Wilmott."

She ran her eyes over his books. Philosophy, essays, history, dry stuff for the most part, but there were a few volumes of poetry, a few works of fiction. She took out a copy of Tennyson's poems. It had passages marked. She read:—

Give us long rest or death, dark death or dreamful ease.

Wilmott came in with the kettle, from which clear drops dripped.

"I'm reading," she said.

"What?" he asked, stopping to look over her shoulder. "Oh, that," he said, impassively, and went to set the kettle over the flame.

"It doesn't seem at all like you."

"Why?"

"It—seems too indolent."

"Am I so energetic?"

"No. But you are purposeful, I think. This is more like you:—

"I built my soul a lordly pleasure-house,
Wherein at ease for aye to dwell . . .

You should have marked that one."

"My God!" he ejaculated. "That isn't me! I wish it were. My soul is houseless."

"I am not subtle," she said, replacing the book. "I'm going to take off my hat." She removed the ridiculous little hat she wore, that had two small ribbons fluttering at the back. A sudden intimacy clouded the room.

Wilmott looked about him puzzled, as though he had forgotten where he had left things.

"Let me make the tea," she said.

"No. I could not bear that."

Adeline laughed. "Not bear to see me make tea?"

He gave a rather grim smile. "No. It would be too beautiful. Such things aren't for me."

He brewed the tea deftly enough, set out the new dishes, a square of honey in the comb, then invited her to sit down. All the while he talked. He told her of the farmer's wife who baked his bread and sold him honey. He had bought a cow, two pigs, and some poultry. Philip was on the lookout for a good team of horses for him. Oats and barley had been sown by his predecessor. He would learn farming. With what income remained to him he would get on very well. "In short," he said, cutting a square of honey for her, "I've never been so consciously happy in my life."

Adeline took a large mouthful of bread and honey. Her eyes glowed. "Neither have I," she said.

Wilmott was amused. "I'll wager you have never known an hour's real unhappiness."

"What about when I told my mother good-bye? What about when I saw my mother and father on the pier and couldn't go back to them? What about the voyage and Huneefa? All that since you've known me!"

"You must confirm what I have always thought."

"What?"

"That you are the happiest creature I have ever known."

"I don't go about blazoning my sorrows," she said, trying to look haughty as she helped herself to more honey.

"Do I?" He had reddened a little. Adeline regarded him speculatively. "Well, you said a moment ago that you are consciously happy. Perhaps you are sometimes consciously unhappy. I'm not afraid of life. I never expect the worst."

"I am going to tell you about myself," he said. "I never intended to but—I'm going to."

She leant forward eagerly. "Oh, do!"

"I must beg you to keep it secret."

"Never shall I breathe it to the face of clay!"

"Very well." He rose, took the teapot to the stove and added water to it from the kettle. With it still in his hand he turned to her abruptly.

"I *am* married," he said.

She stared unbelievingly. "Oh, surely not," she said. "Surely not."

He gave a short laugh. "I don't think I am mistaken. I'm not only a husband but a father."

"Of all things! Then you lied to me, for you told me you were single."

"Yes. I lied to you."

"Yet you seem to me the perfect bachelor."

"Many a time I was called the perfect husband."

"Ah, well," she said, with her Irish inflections intensified, "whatever you were, you'd be good at it!" She mused a moment and then added—"Lover and all."

"*And* liar!"

She looked him in the eyes. "Are you going to tell me why you lied?" she asked.

"Yes." He came and sat down.

"What I mean is, why you hid the fact of your marriage."

"Yes, of course . . . I was running away."

"Leaving her?"

"Yes."

"And the child?"

"Yes."

"Boy or girl?"

"Girl of fourteen."

"Then you were married a long while!"

"Fifteen years. I was twenty-five." He added, with sudden force—"Fifteen years of misery!"

"Surely not the whole fifteen!"

"We weren't married six months till I knew I had made a mistake. The remaining years were spent in realizing it more and more."

"Couldn't you do anything about it?"

"Nothing. I was rooted. Hopelessly. You can't imagine how I was rooted, because you've never lived that sort of life."

As his hand rested on the table she laid hers on it for an instant. "Please tell me about it," she said.

Through the open door came the voice of the river, talking among its reeds. The cow Wilmott had bought lowed at the gate.

"She wants to be milked," he said.

"Can you do it?"

"I have a young Indian helping me."

"Oh, I do love this little place!" exclaimed Adeline. "I don't want to think you're unhappy here."

"I have told you how happy I am. But things won't be right with me till you know all the truth."

"You're a dangerous kind of man," she said.

"You mean it isn't safe to tell the truth?"

"I can bear it, but not all women can. Perhaps your wife couldn't."

"She never knew anything about me. Not really. She knew I held a responsible position in a large shipping house. I had married too young but I kept my nose to the grindstone. I was good at figures. They thought well of me in the business. Our friends—that is, my wife's—said I was such a good husband and father. It was no wonder. I had a good training. She never let me alone. Tidiness, order, meticulous living, that was her aim from morning to night. That and the acquiring of possessions. No sooner had we got one thing than her heart went out to another. Glass, silver, carpets, curtains, clothes—and all to be kept in the most perfect order. No dogs about the place. The two maids—we had risen to two when I left—constantly scouring and cleaning. But if only she could have done it peaceably. She did nothing peaceably. She talked without ceasing. She would talk for hours about some trivial social triumph or defeat, or the misdoings of a maid. If she was silent it was because she was in a cold fury and that I could not stand. I would either quarrel with her to get her out of it or just succumb and be meek. You see, she was the stronger character."

"And the little girl?" asked Adeline, trying to fit Wilmott into this new picture.

"She's not a little girl," he returned testily. "She's a big lump of a girl, with no affection and small intelligence. Her mother is convinced that Hettie inherits my musical ability. She took music lessons and was always pounding out the same piece, always with the very same mistakes. My wife was eternally talking but Hettie rarely spoke. She just sat and stared at me."

"Faith, it was a queer life for you!" said Adeline.

Wilmott sat smiling gently at her. "You could not imagine it," he said.

"And then what happened?"

"I applied myself more assiduously to my work. I was promoted. I made more money but managed to keep the fact secret. I began to talk to her of the East and how I longed to go there. I would interrupt her discourse on a friend's *soirée* to talk of Bombay and Kashmir. All the while I was planning to come to the West. She could not understand my sudden talkativeness. My talk bored her excessively. Hettie would just sit staring. Hettie was always sucking lozenges flavored with cloves. When I think of her I smell cloves."

"Ah, you should have been a bachelor!" said Adeline.

"Would that have made me immune to the scent of cloves?" he asked tartly.

"I mean, you weren't fitted for the intimacies of family life. Not the way my father is. Smells don't affect him or whether a woman is silent or talks. He has the knack of marriage."

"Upon my word," exclaimed Wilmott, "one might think you sympathized with my wife."

"A good beating was what she needed. It would have brought out the good in her. Was she plain or pretty?"

"Pretty," he returned glumly.

"Did she keep her looks?"

"She did."

"And Hettie? Was she pretty?"

"As pretty as a suet pudding."

"Whom did she resemble then?"

"My wife's father. He was always taking snuff. It was always scattered over his waistcoat."

"There you go again—noticing small things! Maybe you have a talent for writing."

Wilmott flushed. "I have faint hopes in that direction."

"Don't let 'em be faint!" said Adeline. "Let 'em be fierce! I don't believe in faint hopes. It wasn't faint hopes that got me Philip."

The mention of Philip's name put a damper on Wilmott's confidence. He could feel Philip's presence in the room. He said stiffly:—

"I should not be telling you all this."

"And why not? What else is friendship for?"

"You despise me."

"Could I despise my friend? You are my only friend in all this country, James Wilmott." She spoke fondly, cherishing his friendship and his ambition. Then she added quickly—"But is that your real name?"

He nodded.

"Are you sure you're not lying again?" She smiled at him coaxingly, as though to worm the truth out of him.

"I deserve that," he said. "But this time I am telling you the truth. Perhaps I should have changed my name, as I ran away from her."

"You ran away! Good for you! Ah, I'm glad you left her—the nagging woman! How did you leave her?"

He did not answer for a moment. His thoughts had flown backward. Then he said composedly:—

"I knew for five years that I was going to do it. But I made up my mind that I would not leave her badly off. I can tell you, I did not spare myself. I never was anything but tired and tense—in all that five years. . . . At last I had my affairs as I wanted them.

Henrietta would own the house, have a respectable income. I made over everything into her name. Then I wrote her a letter telling her that I was going to the East to spend the rest of my life and that she would never hear from me again. I got leave from the office to go for a week to Paris. I bought a ticket to Paris. Then I went to Liverpool, took a boat for Ireland, and you know the rest . . . You don't think she can trace me, do you?"

"Never. She'll never trace you. But—I wish you had changed your name."

"Somehow I could not think of myself except as James Wilmott." He got up and paced the room. "If you knew the pleasure I've had in this new life! In being free and *alone!* Sometimes I deliberately leave the place in complete disorder—just to prove to myself that I'm free. I'm like a prisoner released. I no longer have to concentrate. As I sit fishing in my river my mind is a delicious blank—for hours at a time. My past begins to seem like a dream."

"We all are going to be happy here," said Adeline. "I love this country. Come and show me your cow. And the young Indian who is working for you. I must see him—and the pigs—and the great fish you caught."

X

The Walls

As THE summer sped on, the walls of the house rose from the foundation in solid strength. Philip, acting on the advice of David Vaughan, had offered wages which had attracted good masons and carpenters. The best quality of brick had been ordered, built on a foundation of stone. The brick was of a fine red that would mellow to the color of a dark dahlia. The basement was paved with bricks and contained the large kitchen, two servants' bedrooms, pantries, coal and wine cellars. Not a house in the neighborhood had a wine cellar and Philip affirmed that this was to be well-stocked. He had studied the catalogues of dealers and had already placed a respectable order with the most reliable firm. Not that he was a hard drinker. He had never drunk himself under the table as some of his ancestors had done, in a day when it was quite the thing for a gentleman to do. Philip, in fact, was careful of his health and had no wish to become gouty and irascible as his grandfather had been.

While the walls were rising from the foundation, an army of axemen were clearing the land. Noble timber was being swept away to make room for fields of grain. As there was no space in which to preserve all this timber or use for it if it were preserved, much of it was to be burned. It lay awaiting this end which would be accomplished in the autumn when danger of forest fires was past. The great green branches were struck from the trunks and mounded in piles by themselves, birds' nests flying in all directions, leaves crushed, the vines which had draped themselves in profligate luxuriance along the boughs, torn up by the roots and going down to disaster with the rest. Honeysuckle and wild grapes with clinging tendrils wilted and sank in the heat. As for the great trunks of the trees, their wounds bled resin, filling the air with pungent odor, while woodpeckers ran up and down them glutting themselves on the myriad insects that had made their home in the bark. Rabbits and groundhogs hid in the mounded boughs and at the noon hour the workmen amused themselves by discovering these and killing them. Some made catapults and became expert at shooting birds and squirrels, though if caught by Adeline in this pastime they tasted the sting of her anger. So, building up, tearing down, killing for the lust of killing, the days passed in bright succession.

The red plumes of the sumach turned to brown, the clusters of chokeberries ripened to blackness but still hung secure from birds because of their bitter flavor. Mushrooms sprang up in hordes on the cleared ground: meaty meadow mushrooms of a delicate brownish pink beneath; pretty parasol mushrooms with fringed edges; the destroying angel, set in its snow-white cup, and in the woods mushrooms of crimson and purple, pretty as flowers. Of the meadow mushrooms many a good dish was made for the table at Vaughanlands. Adeline never before had had such an appetite.

In early September young Robert Vaughan and Adeline set out together along the path which that summer had been made from Vaughanlands to the new estate. It led across a level field, red with the stubble of a fine crop of barley, through a wood of oaks and pines, then down steeply into the ravine where the stream which, in those days, almost merited the name of river, ran swiftly over shimmering sand and flat stones. In one place it narrowed between its banks and here a temporary bridge of logs had been thrown across. The pungent smell from their resin-oozing wood mingled with the cool damp earthy smell from the ravine. Adeline never set her foot on this path without a sense of adventure. She had pride in realizing that this path, now well-cleared of undergrowth and showing a decided depression where feet had many times trodden it, was the print of her own and Philip's passage. It had been virgin, untouched, but she and Philip had, as it were, made it a link between their old life and the new. She had trodden it in all sorts of weather and often alone. Now on this September day she thought she had never seen it so inviting. The season of mosquitoes was past, the air was of almost palpable sweetness and full of renewed bird song, for now the young could fly. The stream made a steady murmuring.

As they crossed the bridge of logs young Vaughan took her arm to guide her. Adeline was well able to cross the logs unaided and had done so many a time when they were slippery with rain. But now she leant against Robert's shoulder as though timidly and her fingers clasped his.

"We shall have a rustic bridge here, later on," she said.

He pressed her arm a little. "Then you won't need my help," he said.

"Now I'm very glad of it."

"If you knew what it has been to me," he said, flushing, "to have you here. Before you came I never knew what to do with myself. You know, I'm not really acquainted with my parents yet. The truth is I feel that I know you better than I do them."

"Ah, I'm easy to get on with."

"It's not that. But I feel you understand me and you are the only one who does."

"You're very sweet, Bobby."

It was a real irritation to Robert's parents to hear Adeline call him Bobby. They tried to intimate their disapproval by pronouncing his name very distinctly when they addressed him. But Adeline was oblivious of this or took, as they thought, pleasure in opposing them. The two began to mount the opposite side of the ravine.

"My mother is rather upset this morning," said the boy.

"I hope it's nothing I've done—or Philip or the children—or our dog or our goat."

"No—nothing of that sort. It's about a cousin of mine, Daisy Vaughan. She's coming to visit us and Mother wishes she wouldn't, just now."

"Then why doesn't she write and tell her not to?" asked Adeline.

"She can't very well, as Father thinks we should have Daisy. She is his only brother's child and an orphan. She's been staying with relatives on her mother's side, in Montreal. She's had a falling-out with them and written a pathetic letter to Father and he's inviting her to spend some months with us."

"I declare," said Adeline, "this is a nuisance! The house is full enough already, what with me and mine. No wonder your mother is vexed."

"Oh, she'll manage. Mother always does."

"Do you know this Daisy?"

"Yes, I've been to her aunt's house in Montreal. There were daughters in the house. I don't think she got on very well with them."

"Is she forward, then—or pert? If she is, I'll take her down."

"She's almost as old as you. About twenty-five. Quite dashing, too, but not at all interesting to me. In fact, the thought of her coming bores me excessively. I hate the thought that college will soon open and I must go." He looked into her eyes, his sensitive boy's face troubled.

"Don't worry, Bobby. We're friends and always shall be."

"I am not thinking of the future," he said. "It's the present that interests me. You make light of my feelings. You don't care tuppence, really."

"I care a great deal. I am a stranger here. You have helped to make me happy."

"You are lucky to be able to settle down so quickly. I don't belong anywhere."

Adeline opened her brown eyes wide at him. "Why, Bobby, what a way to talk! When you've had more experience of life you'll not worry about belonging places."

He answered gloomily—"That's the trouble. I have no experience. You are only interested in men who have had experience. Your stiff-necked friend, Wilmott, for example."

"What do you know about him?" she asked sharply.

"Oh, nothing—except that he looks unutterable things . . . I can't tolerate him."

They had, somewhat breathless from talking while they climbed, reached the top of the steep. The walls of the house rose before them, roofless, with gaping windows and scantling floors. Great stacks of brick and mounds of gravel flanked it. Piles of sweet-scented lumber lay ready. But the workmen, their lunch eaten, were having their noon-hour relaxation. They lay on the ground or sprawling on the lumber, with the exception of two French Canadians. These were lumbermen who had been attracted by the high wages Philip offered. As though they had not had exercise enough in their work they now were dancing with great vivacity and energy. They leaped, stamped, twirled, with intricate steps, snapping their fingers, their teeth flashing. One was middle-aged, with a red handkerchief tied about a thin corded neck, the other young, handsome but no more agile, indeed not so much so. The music for the dance was supplied by an old man seated on the great stump of a pine tree. He was Fiddling Jock. He had expected to be turned out but the Whiteoaks had been taken by his oddity and allowed him to stay on. Philip had given him shingles to mend his leaky roof and new glass to fill the broken windows. No one knew when the cottage had been built, probably by some settler who long ago had died or found the place too lonely. Adeline had christened it Fiddler's Hut. Now she sang out:—

"Splendid, Jock! Ah, but that's a fine tune! Play up! Make 'em dance!"

The old fellow nodded violently. With a flourish of his bow he increased the tempo of the music till the feet of the two dancers seemed possessed of a mad spirit. Robert Vaughan was, as usual, amused and a little embarrassed by her familiarity with the men. He would not have had her different but he resented the fact that her unconventionality gave rise to criticism in the neighborhood. "Damn their strait-lacedness!" he thought. "She is perfect." But still she made him feel embarrassed.

The Frenchmen sat down breathless. The old Scot reached for a tin mug of tea and took a swig of it. The mug was held to no visible mouth, for the lower part of his face was hidden by an enormous growth of grizzled beard. He wore a gray jacket and a kilt of Scotch tartan so faded that to which clan it belonged was no longer discernible. His bare knees were thin and hairy. He looked as durable and tough as a tree growing on a stony hillside but there was an appealing, lonely look in his wide-open blue eyes.

Adeline clapped her hands. She exclaimed:—

"You should give them an Irish tune, Jock. If you played an Irish jig for them on Irish pipes they'd not be hopping about in that feeble fashion."

"There's nae chunes sae fu' o' sperrit as the Scottish chunes," he answered stoutly. "And as for dancin', I'll warrant no Irishman livin' could beat yon Frenchies."

"Ah, you should see them dance in Galway," she said. "And their whistling as clear as a pipe!"

"We have two Irishmen here," said Jock, "and they have no more dance in them than clods."

"They're from Belfast. That's the reason." She turned to the French Canadians—*"Bon! Vous êtes très agiles. Je vous admire beaucoup."*

"Merci, Madame," they said in one voice.

"Wad ye be givin' a pairty when ye move into your fine hoose?" asked Jock.

"Indeed we shall."

"I'd like fine tae play ma fiddle for it. D'ye think I micht? I'll learn an Irish jig for the occasion if ye'll allow me."

"I engage you on the spot."

"It will cost ye naething, mind. I'd like to mak' a return for a' ye've done for me."

As they went toward the walls of the house Robert exclaimed—"You can't have that fellow play at your party! It would be the talk of the countryside."

"But he plays at all the weddings and christenings, doesn't he?"

"Not of your sort."

"I'm just an immigrant," she declared. "I want to be like the other immigrants."

"Captain Whiteoak will never agree."

"We shall see."

They mounted the temporary steps and went in at the doorless door.

But Robert continued to look gloomy. He said—"Women exert too much influence on us men."

A dimple darted into Adeline's cheek and away again.

"If she's the right sort of woman it's good for you, isn't it?"

"The right sort of woman could do anything with me."

"Then we must be on the watch for her. But don't you ever let her do things to you till I have inspected her . . . Come along, Bobby, let's see the house!" She took his hand and led him in. "Isn't it enchanting?"

They had inspected it the day before but the beams put into place since then, the rows of bricks added, the mortar just setting into hardness, were of enthralling interest. The walls had no more to support than the ethereal arch of the sky. But they stood solid, waiting, as though in a kind of benevolent eagerness to shoulder their expected burden.

"Isn't it enchanting?" she repeated. "Oh, the things that will happen here! It's enough to frighten one, isn't it, Bobby, to think of the things that are crowding in on us?" She bent her brows to a dark line. "Wouldn't it have been strange if, when the architect brought us the sketches for the house, he could have brought a sketch of all that lay before us here?"

"Perhaps you will not spend all the rest of your days here. You may want to move. Perhaps you will want to go to another part of the country or even back to the Old Land. There are many who do."

"Never! Not Philip and me! We've come here to stay. Canada will have our bones. Jalna will be our home." Her eyes filled with tears. "Do you know, Bobby, that is the first time I have called the place *Jalna*, naturally and easily. Now the name belongs to it just as Philip and I do."

Young Vaughan was watching a figure bent double behind a newly rising partition. He pressed her arm and whispered:—

"There's a half-breed fellow in there. I think he's stealing something. Let's watch him."

They crept forward in time to see the youth filling his pockets with nails and screws from a box of carpenter supplies. As he saw himself observed he straightened his body and looked at them coolly. He was very thin, very dark, with chiseled features of surprising beauty. They were of the aquiline Indian type, though less pronounced, but he had a warm color in his cheeks and his hair, instead of being coarse and straight, was fine and hung in wavy locks about his thin cheeks. His clothes were ragged. He was about Robert's age.

"Well now," said Adeline, "that's a fine trick you're at!"

"I work for Mr. Wilmott," he answered gently. "I'm building a poultry house for him and I ran short of nails. I thought maybe the carpenters wouldn't mind me taking a few."

"It's a good thing for you they didn't catch you at it," said Robert.

"They were for Mr. Wilmott," he returned, keeping his eyes on Adeline's face.

She went forward eagerly. "Take all you want!" she exclaimed. "There are all sizes and shapes here. Come, let's see what you have."

Hesitatingly he drew some specimens from his pockets.

" 'T is not half enough! Come, here is a bit of sacking. Fill it up. Would you like some of these nice hinges and hooks? And here's a funny-looking thing but it might be useful."

The young half-breed knelt eagerly beside her, and began snatching all that caught his eye.

"My goodness," exclaimed Robert, "you mustn't do that! The carpenters know just what supplies they have and need them."

"We can buy more," said Adeline. "Besides there are tons of nails here. No one could miss what we've taken."

The half-breed deftly knotted the four corners of the sacking and slipped away. Before he left he gave Adeline a smile of gratitude.

"It will be a wonder to me," said Robert Vaughan, "if anything movable is left on this place after two days. Every thief in the neighborhood will be here."

"But the Indians are honest. Your father told me so."

"The half-breeds aren't."

"Tell me about that boy."

"I don't know much except that his name is Titus Sharrow. They call him Tite. He's no good. I don't see why Mr. Wilmott employs him. I am told that he sleeps in the house."

"How does he come to be a half-breed? Are his parents living?"

"I don't think so. I believe he's really a quarter French. His mother's father was a French Canadian. It's a shame, the way they took up with the Indian women."

"The boy is charming."

"I call that a funny adjective to use about a half-breed thief."

"He wasn't stealing."

"Do you think Mr. Wilmott sent him for the nails, then?"

"I daresay," she answered a little huffily, as though Wilmott's honor were in question, or her friendship for him.

"Well, here comes Captain Whiteoak! Let's tell him all about it."

"For pity's sake, no! Don't breathe a word of it, please."

Philip strode up. "Adeline, I have a dozen things to ask you," he exclaimed, and they entered on a long and fascinating discussion of building problems.

Two weeks passed and the niece, Daisy Vaughan, arrived. She was a visitor unwanted by all. David Vaughan had not seen his niece since she was in her teens. The slight reports he had had of her were not endearing. Her coming would disarrange his wife's housekeeping still further and, heaven knew, the Whiteoaks had disarranged it enough for any woman's endurance. But he had family loyalty. Daisy was his only brother's only child. She had written him a pathetic letter. He could do no less than offer her hospitality. Mrs. Vaughan would not have dreamed of opposing him but she felt injured. This sense of well-bred and restrained injury encircled her silvery head like a dim halo. Adeline was all on her side. "Dear Mrs. Vaughan," she would say, "this is the last straw for you, I know. Philip and I and our tribe were quite enough but, with your husband's relations trooping in, 't will be the end of you. Once the roof is on our house I promise you we shall decamp."

"Don't speak of it," said Mrs. Vaughan. "I shall manage."

Robert was certain that Daisy would always be on hand when he wanted to talk to Adeline. If they two walked together, Daisy would be present. She was a pushing, unnecessary girl and he hated the thought of her.

Aside from the feeling that her coming would make rather a crowd in the house, Philip was not averse to it. Daisy was a pretty name. She would be sprightly, probably amusing—in truth he was so happily absorbed in the building of his house that events outside it affected him little. He stood somewhat behind the others, his hands in his pockets, while they put the best face on their welcome. Robert had driven the long way to meet her.

She wasn't petite and she wasn't pretty. She wasn't at all like a daisy. But, by Jove, Philip thought, she had self-confidence and she displayed originality in her dress. You could see that, even though it was travel-worn. She kissed her aunt and uncle and was introduced to the Whiteoaks.

"Are you very tired, my dear?" asked Mrs. Vaughan, herself looking very tired.

"Not at all," answered Daisy, "though it was monstrous hot and dusty traveling. The friends I was traveling with from Montreal were half-dead but I seem to be made of India rubber."

As she spoke she untied the wide ribbon of her bonnet from beneath the brim of which her face looked out with an eagerness that seemed to express determination to take in at one glance everything that was to be seen.

"She is like no Vaughan that ever was," thought her uncle.

"I do hope she is not a minx," thought Mrs. Vaughan.

"Egad, what a small waist," was Philip's inward comment.

"Ugly, but dangerous." Adeline was taking her in. "A grinning hussy. Let her keep away from me!" She said: "You are not in the least like a daisy. Your parents should not have named you till they'd had a better look at you."

Daisy looked sidewise at her. "Can you think of a flower name that would suit me better? They were set on a flower name."

"In Ireland," said Adeline, "there's a wild flower the peasants call Trollopin' Bet."

Philip caught Adeline's fingers in his hand and pressed them sharply. "Behave yourself!" he said. He gave a startled look at Daisy.

Adeline jerked away her hand like a child who says— "I will do as I please!"

"You can't offend me," laughed Daisy. "I'm made of India rubber, as I told you."

"I don't understand," said Mr. Vaughan. "What did Adeline say?"

"She said I should have been named for that red-haired Queen Elizabeth," answered Daisy. She took off her bonnet and disclosed luxuriant dark hair, dressed elegantly.

The scornful emphasis on the word *red-haired* had brought the color to Adeline's cheeks. She sought for words to fling at the newcomer which would not affront her host and hostess.

"If 't is my head—" she began.

"Good God!" interrupted Philip. "Nicholas is going to fall downstairs!"

He sprang up the steps, three at a time, to catch the baby who, on hands and knees, had crept to the top to see what was going on.

Philip ran down with him in his arms and held him up for the visitor's inspection.

"What do you think of this," he demanded, "at nine months!"

"The angel!" exclaimed Daisy Vaughan.

Nicholas knew not what shyness was. He sat on his father's arm, his hair rising in a curly crest, and beamed at the visitor. He had a look of unutterable well-being. When she held out her hands to him he went to her with great good-humor and examined her face with interest.

It was a short face with high cheekbones, narrow eyes, and a turned-up nose. The mouth was large and full of fine teeth. When the under lip met the upper, which it did not often do, it caused the chin to recede a little though not enough to be disfiguring. She was thin but not bony. Her waist was indeed incredibly small. To this part of her Adeline bent a look of extreme exasperation, for she had recently made certain that she herself was to have another child. The sight of that waist and the thought of what lay before herself was enough to put her out of temper.

"I know nothing of babies," said Daisy, "but to me this one seems the most beautiful I have seen. Is he your only child?" She raised her eyes to Philip's face.

"We have a little daughter," he answered. "She's up there somewhere with her nurse."

"How lovely! How old is she?"

"I'm not quite sure. How old is Gussie, Adeline?"

"I'm damned if I know," returned Adeline, bitterly. "But I know I had her."

She took care to lower her voice so as not to be heard by Mrs. Vaughan, who now exclaimed:—

"Gussie is the dearest child and so intelligent! Will you let me take you to your room now, my dear, then you must have something to eat."

David Vaughan went to the dining room to fetch a decanter of sherry. Robert followed his mother and Daisy up the stairs, carrying Daisy's dressing case. The Whiteoaks were alone in the hall. Philip had again taken Nicholas into his own arms. He said with a stern look at Adeline:—

"You seem determined to disgrace yourself. You must know that the Vaughans aren't used to such talk."

She wound a lock of her red hair on her finger. "They will be used to it before I leave," she said.

"You may have to leave sooner than you are prepared for, if you go on like this."

"I am prepared for anything!" she answered hotly.

"Where would you plan to go from here," he returned, "with the roof not yet on our house?"

"I could stay with Mr. Wilmott." She gave him a roguish look.

He laughed. "I believe Wilmott could manage you."

"You little know him," she returned.

"That's a funny remark," he said.

"Why?"

"It sounds as though you had a peculiar knowledge of him."

"I'm a better judge of character than you."

"You only jump at conclusions, Adeline. You have taken a dislike to this Daisy Vaughan for no reason whatever. For my part, I think she is an interesting creature."

"Of course you do! Just because she made eyes at you."

Philip looked not ill-pleased. "I didn't see her make eyes," he said.

"Oh, Philip, what a liar you are!" she exclaimed.

Nicholas leaned from his father's arms to embrace Adeline. Their heads were close together. David Vaughan returned with the sherry. "I hope the ladies won't remain too long upstairs," he said. "What a nice family group! I think Nicholas has come on well, since his dresses are shortened. He appears freer in his movements."

"He gets into more mischief," said Philip.

Nicholas took his mother's finger into his mouth and bit on it. She suffered the pain because his new tooth must come through.

XI

The Roof

It was wonderful to see the roof begin to spread above the walls. It was music to hear the tap-tap of the carpenters' hammers as they made secure the shingles, one overlapping the other. The shingles were new and clean and sweet-smelling. Up the slopes of the gables they climbed, and down they crowded to the eaves. Above all rose the five tall chimneys never yet darkened by smoke, awaiting the first fire. Now the house had a meaning, a promise. It rose against the brilliant autumn foliage as something new and tough-fibred to be reckoned with in the landscape. The house was windowless, doorless, in some places floorless, the partitions were incomplete but, with the roof bending above it, it spoke for the first time. Adeline and Philip would stand with linked fingers, gazing up at it in admiration. For generations their families had lived in old houses, heavy with traditions of their forebears. Jalna was hers and Philip's and theirs only.

Robert had gone off to his university. It had been as he had foretold. Daisy had interfered sadly with his enjoyment of his last days at home. Her thin supple figure edged itself into every crevice of companionship. She had something to say on every subject and though she tried, almost too assiduously, to make what she said agreeable, a jarring note, and edged word, often crept in. Adeline declared there was malice in everything she said and did. Philip persisted that she was an interesting creature and went out of his way to be pleasant to her, to make up for Adeline's coolness, he said, but Adeline said it was because Daisy flattered him. If she had been a fragile little thing, Adeline could better have endured her but she was lithe and strong and she imitated everything that Adeline did. If Adeline walked swiftly across the temporary bridge of logs that spanned the stream, Daisy ran across it. She screamed in fright as she ran but she did run. If Adeline penetrated the woods to gather the great glossy blackberries, Daisy pressed just ahead snatching at the best ones. Adeline had a horror of snakes but Daisy showed a morbid liking for them. She would pick up a small one by its tail, to the admiration of the workingmen. When they carried home the pretty red vines of the poison ivy, it was Adeline who suffered for it. Daisy was immune.

A spacious barn was being erected at some distance from the house. Later on Philip would have stables built but at present the underpart of the barn was to serve as shelter for horses and cattle. Adeline and Daisy strolled over to inspect it one afternoon in Indian summer. The framework of the barn stood as a lofty skeleton against the background of dark green spruces, balsams and pines, with here and there a group of maples like a conflagration of color. Piles of lumber lay about filling the air with the sweet smell of their resin. Great chips and wedges of pine were scattered on the ground, showing a pinkness almost equal to that color in the sea shell. Slabs of bark were scattered too, and strands of moss and crushed fern leaves. But hardly did anything die here before a fresh growth pushed up to take its place, or erase its memory, if there had been eyes to notice it. Birds were migrating and now a cloud of swallows had settled on the framework of the barn to rest. It was Sunday and no workmen were about. There was a primeval stillness that was broken only by the myriad twitterings from the swallows' throats. They sat on the scaffolding not in hundreds but in thousands. They perched wing to wing as close as they could sit. Their forked tails made a fringe beneath their perch. They changed the skeleton edifice from the color of freshly hewn wood to bands of darkness. Only a few darted overhead as guides and watchers. When these saw the two young women draw near they made some word or sign, for a slight stir took place among the swallows but they showed no real alarm. There they were, guardians of land and fruit and flower, benign toward man, capable to hold down any insect pest that ever rose, powerful to protect every kind of crop and harvest. Insects were their food. All these thousands of sharp beaks, bright eyes and swift wings, were alive for the destruction of insects.

Adeline snatched up a wedge of pine and threw it up among the birds. Daisy's predatory laugh rang out and she also began to throw chips at them. The birds bent their heads, looking down in surprise. Then they rose from every scaffold, scantling, and smallest perch. They rose in a body, forming themselves into a whirling cloud, making the sound of wind among the trees with their twitterings. They flew in all directions yet remained within their own system, and that moved southward.

"Don't go, don't go!" cried Adeline. She turned in anger to Daisy. "You should not have frightened them! 'T will bring bad luck to the barn. They had made it their resting place and now they are going."

"You threw first, Mrs. Whiteoak."

"I only tossed a wee stick among them to see if they would notice it."

"But you went on throwing. You didn't stop. You were quite violent."

"It was because you excited me. You should remember that I was a girl among a horde of brothers who were always ready to let fly a stick. But you—you were an only child—a little girl alone. You should be gentle."

"I am gentle, Mrs. Whiteoak."

"You were not then! You were showing all your teeth and laughing as you threw the sticks."

"Not one bird was struck."

"But they're going! They'll never come back! Look at them."

The swallows had risen high in the air. They looked no more than specks sinking and rising. They were like a floating sediment in the translucent bowl of the sky.

"It is natural for them to go to the South," said Daisy. "I wish I were."

Adeline raised her arched brows. "Then you aren't contented here?" she asked.

"What is there here for me?" asked Daisy.

"What do you want?" asked Adeline surprised.

"Experience. I'm not just a young girl."

"But you have been about a good deal, haven't you?"

"Always at other people's beck and call. You don't know what it is to be poor, Mrs. Whiteoak."

Adeline gave an ironic laugh. "Oh, no—I don't know what it is to be poor! Let me tell you, I never had two sovereigns to rub together till my great-aunt died and left me her money."

"How lucky you are! A fortune left you! And such a husband!"

"Aye, he's a good fellow," said Adeline curtly.

They had come to the barn and now stood gazing up into its towering framework. A ladder of scantlings was built against its base and up this Daisy began to climb. She climbed nimbly considering her voluminous skirts. At the top of the ladder she set out to walk along a beam while her fingers, just touching another, supported her.

"You are silly!" exclaimed Adeline. The girl was ready for any adventure, she thought.

"Oh, I love heights!" cried Daisy. "No height makes me dizzy. I revel in this."

"You should have been a tightrope walker."

"The view is lovely!" Daisy now walked with arms extended in precarious balance. "You look no more than a pigmy down there. Do come up."

"I daren't."

"Why not?"

"In the first place I have no desire and in the second I'm going to have a baby."

This announcement was more of a surprise to Daisy than Adeline had expected. It was almost a shock. She stiffened and stood still. Then she gave a cry, swayed and sank to the beam that supported her, crouching there in an attitude of terror. Her skirts stood about her like a balloon.

"I'm going to fall!" she cried. "Oh, Mrs. Whiteoak, save me, I'm going to fall!"

Adeline turned pale but she said sternly—"Come back the way you went. Surely you can do that! Just take hold of yourself and move carefully. You'll be all right." But the space from where Daisy clung, to the ground, seemed very far.

Daisy crouched shivering on the beam. "I daren't move," she said, in a tense voice. "Get help quickly! I'm going to fall!"

The thought of leaving Daisy in this predicament while she sought help made Adeline hesitate. At that moment Philip strolled out of the wood and came toward them. Adeline ran to him.

"That interesting creature, as you call her," she said, "has climbed to the top of the barn and is stuck there! She says she is going to fall."

"My God!" exclaimed Philip, looking up at Daisy. "She is likely to break her neck!" He called out—"Don't be frightened! I'll come and fetch you. Just keep calm and look upward."

He mounted the ladder and walked cautiously but steadily along the beam. A feeling of nausea came over Adeline. She closed her eyes for a space. When she opened them Philip had reached Daisy and was leading her back toward the ladder. When his feet were secure on it, Daisy collapsed against his shoulder.

"I cannot," she sobbed. "I cannot take another step!"

"You're quite safe," said Philip. "Just hang on to me. I'll carry you down."

Daisy did hang on to him and, as they reached the bottom, her cheek was against his tanned neck. She was sobbing.

"Oh, I'm so sorry," she said as he set her gently on her feet.

"You have need to be," said Adeline, "for you gave me a monstrous scare and risked Philip's life. You ought to be ashamed of yourself."

Philip was still supporting Daisy. "Don't scold her," he said. "Any girl is likely to do harebrained things. It's a good thing Miss Daisy's light. I should have had a time of it to carry you down, Adeline."

"I should have stayed up there till Doomsday before I'd have asked you to." She turned away. She looked up at the last of the swallows, now winging swiftly above the treetops.

"I was on my way to Wilmott's," said Philip. "Should you like to come with me? Do you feel able for a walk, Miss Daisy?" He had released her from his arm.

"I shall do whatever you say," she answered, in a new sweet voice.

"I think I shall go back," said Adeline, coldly.

"In that case, we'll all go back," said Philip.

"I am quite capable of returning by myself." But she was ready to be persuaded by him.

"Come along," he said, coaxingly.

They took the path which was now beaten by usage and led to where Wilmott lived, two miles away. Philip led the way, holding back branches when they intervened, striking with his stick at brambles that would have torn their skirts. High above, the cloud of swallows moved, as though leading them.

Daisy's misadventure and Philip's rescue of her had made a constraint among them. They spoke little and then only of what they saw. Sometimes the path was edged by bracken and sometimes by the purplish foliage of blackberries. Sometimes it was carpeted with pine needles, or the scarlet leaves of the soft maple, the first to fall. Mushrooms as large as dinner plates sprang up on it or scores of little ones marched like soldiers. An owl and her five young ones sat in a row on the limb of a beech tree. Philip raised his arm to point them out to his companions. The mother owl shot past him like a bolt, dealing him a blow that nearly felled him. The young ones stared down imperturbably.

Adeline flung her arms about Philip.

"Oh, are you hurt?" she cried. "Let me see!" Clasping his head in her hands she examined his scarlet cheek.

"It's all but bleeding," she said, his head still possessively in her hands.

"That's why I don't like this country," said Daisy. "You never know what will happen next. I always have the feeling that something wild is going to happen, and it depresses me."

"I thought you said you longed for experience," Adeline said, beginning to walk along the path again.

"I meant experience in myself—not to be buffeted about."

"I can tell you that owl gave me a clout," said Philip. "It's monstrous strange how having young makes the female wicked."

Adeline's eyes burned into his back and he remembered. He looked over his shoulder and gave her a wink. "I don't mean you," he said, in a low voice. He plucked a red maple leaf and stuck it in his hat, as though in salute to her.

They found Wilmott fishing from his flat-bottomed boat on the broad breast of the river. Equinoctial rains had swollen it but it lay tranquil, reflecting the bright color of the foliage at its brink. Wilmott sat, with an expression of bliss, his eyes fixed on the little red float that moved gently on the water.

"What a way to spend Sunday!" exclaimed Adeline.

Wilmott rose in his boat and drew in the line. "I look on this as necessary toil," he said. "I'm fishing for my supper. I suppose you have just returned from the afternoon church service."

"No need to be sarcastic," said Philip. "There was no service today. What have you caught?" Wilmott held up a pickerel.

"Go on with your fishing," said Adeline. "We'll watch you. It will be a nice rest after all we've been through."

"I must come over here and fish with you," said Philip. "But the fact is I have little time for anything save the building of my house. Just one thing after another happens."

"Yes, I know," said Wilmott. "It's the same here." He laid the fish on the bottom of the boat and picked up the oars. He dipped them lazily into the calmness of the water.

"Why, you're making a lovely little wharf," exclaimed Adeline.

"Yes," he answered, rowing gently toward her. "Tite and I work at it in our spare time."

"This is Mr. Wilmott, Daisy," said Adeline. "Miss Vaughan, James."

Wilmott steadied the boat with the oars and bowed gravely. Daisy returned his greeting and all stared down at the small landing stage on which tools lay.

"A nice saw," said Philip, picking it up. "And a new hammer."

"They belong to Tite," said Wilmott. "He has very good tools. A man he worked for couldn't pay him the cash, so he paid him with tools."

"What lots of nails!" said Daisy. "Did he pay him with nails too?"

"He found the nails," answered Wilmott. "Someone had dropped them on the road."

"I bought a supply of good tools," said Philip. "They have a way of disappearing, so I carve my initials on the handles." He turned the hammer over in his hand.

"Why, here is a clear P. W. on the saw!" cried Daisy.

Wilmott got out of the boat and tied it to the landing. He bent his head beside Philip's.

"Let's see," he said. Then he added—"I'll be hanged, if your initials aren't on the hammer!"

"That's the way with half-breeds," said Philip, easily. "Keep the tools. I have finished with them. You're quite welcome."

"Oh, no," returned Wilmott. "I shall return them when we have finished the work. I couldn't think of keeping them."

"As you like."

"Oh, what an enchanting little house!" cried Daisy. "Will you show it me?"

As they went in at Wilmott's invitation they saw Tite rapidly picking up things from here and there and carrying them into the kitchen. Before he disappeared he gave Adeline his gentle smile in which there was a touch of sadness.

Daisy was delighted with the place which Wilmott had indeed made homelike, if in rather an austere fashion. She exclaimed at everything but especially at the oddity of encountering so many books in a log house.

"I love reading," she said. "I wonder if you would lend me a book to read. Have you that new one of Bulwer-Lytton's?"

"I'm afraid not," said Wilmott. "But, if you can find anything to please you, do take it."

"Will you help me choose?" she asked Philip. "I should like something you can recommend."

"I'm no great reader," he answered, "but I'll do what I can."

She and Philip went to the bookshelves. Adeline turned to Wilmott.

"Are you still happy here?" she asked.

"I'm serenely and consciously happy every hour of the day and, I could almost add, of the night. This life just suits me. I could live a hundred years of it, without complaint. I lack only one thing."

"And what is that?"

"More frequent glimpses of you. Of course I have no right to say it but seeing you, talking to you, gives an added zest to everything I do."

Daisy had taken up an exercise book and was examining it.

"I am teaching my young Tite to read and write," explained Wilmott. "He is very intelligent."

"What lovely pothooks!" exclaimed Daisy. "Look, Captain Whiteoak, what lovely pothooks!"

"You must teach him to read my initials, Wilmott," said Philip.

"Wilmott!" repeated Daisy. "Why, I thought your friend's name was Wilton!"

"No—Wilmott."

"Now here is a coincidence," she cried. "Before I left Montreal I met a Mrs. Wilmott. Let me see, where did I meet her? Oh, yes, it was at a *soirée* given by the wife of a Montreal banker. This Mrs. Wilmott—I remarked the name because it is not a common one—this Mrs. Wilmott struck me as quite unusual. She seemed a woman with a purpose. She is out here from England—I think to meet her husband."

Wilmott had taken Tite's copybook into his hands. He bent his gaze on it in an absent-minded way. Adeline came and looked over his shoulder. She said, in an undertone:—

"I shall come over to-morrow morning—soon after breakfast."

"Names are amusing," Philip was saying. "I knew another Vaughan in the Army in India. He was no relation to your uncle, Miss Daisy, but he had the same name. He even looked like him. Did you ever notice that people who look alike have similar voices?"

"To-morrow morning," whispered Adeline, into the copybook, "and—don't worry."

XII

Henrietta

Anxious as Adeline was she drew in the reins and slackened the pace of the quiet bay horse so that she might look up the drive that led to Jalna. There was no gate as yet. The drive was no more than a rough track. Piles of lumber, heaps of brick and sand disfigured the ground before the house, but there stood the house with its roof firmly on, its five chimneys staunch and tall, waiting for her and Philip! There was a sagacious look about it, as though it were conscious that it had no drab destiny, but was to be the home of two people who were beloved by each other and who loved life. The builder promised that in early spring they should move in.

Adeline could scarcely endure the waiting for that day. She had now been five months at Vaughanlands. No people could have put themselves about with a better grace than the Vaughans. Still, two grownups, two children and their nurse, were a large addition to the work of the house. Domestic help was cheap enough but untrained and ignorant. All her life Adeline had been waited on. Work got done somehow and never had she troubled her head as to how. In the past months she had often seen Mrs. Vaughan tired-out. Yet, when she tried to help her she did everything wrong and experienced dreadful boredom into the bargain. It took all the nurse's time to care for the children and to wash and iron their little clothes. She saw to it that it took all her time. Adeline at last appealed to Patsy O'Flynn.

"For the love of God, Patsy-Joe, take hold and help with the housework! For if you can't make yourself useful I shall have to send you back to Ireland."

"Me make mesilf useful!
like to know who has! Ho
the babies and the goat a
me! 'T is yersilf has man
uselessness in me teeth a

"Very well, Patsy-Joe
and wash the glass and
that."

"Well, I'll do what I
inconvenient house I

He did turn in an
heard saying to the
wench. Curtsy and
misthress, or I'll be t
part. Wherever Patsy-Joe went

The horse's hoofs moved quietly in the
spite of early autumn rains, the land lay dry as tinder.
heavy dews at night could do no more than moisten the parched lips of the plants. But color was bright on every side. With careless flamboyance the trees ran the bold scale from bronze to fiery red. The fields showed the hot blue of chicory and yellow stubble, the fence corners, the crimson sumacs. The purple clusters of elderberries looked ready to drip from the trees in their overripeness. Ten thousand crickets filled the lazy air with their metallic music. How much, thought Adeline, they could do with two single notes! One note was grave and one was gay, and with the two they could do anything.

She had slept little last night. It was only by strong curbing of herself that she had remained in bed. She had felt that by springing up and pacing the floor she might find some means of saving Wilmott from discovery by his wife. The aghast look in his eyes had frightened her. What if he were gone when she arrived at his house? He had looked capable of anything at the moment when Daisy had told of the meeting with that woman. But Daisy and Philip had seemed to notice nothing. Wilmott was not a man you would suspect. Not that he seemed without mystery but he appeared to carry it in his heart and not as a physical covering. You wouldn't think of him as hiding from a woman, thought Adeline.

ust be protected. Her love for Philip
ll, unbridled something in her that would
, with a bold protective love.
as smooth as a blue glass plate and the rushes
n in their dryness, were too still for whispering.
nding stage shone out clean and white. His fishing
and the flat-bottomed boat was moored beside it.
was so still that Adeline had a sense of foreboding as
d at the door. There was no answer but she saw the win-
d move and had a glimpse of Tite's thin dark hand.
is Mrs. Whiteoak!" she called out.
he door opened and he stood there, in shirt and trousers but
arefoot. He said, in his soft voice:—

"Come in, Missis. My boss he want to see you. You wait here and I bring him. You go inside and shut the door."

She entered the house.

Tite's copybook was open on the table. He had been at work, the ink was still wet on his laborious pothooks. Her heart was warm with pity for Wilmott as she looked about the room where he had made himself so comfortable, so mentally at ease. It was very tidy. Try as he might he would never shake off the punctilious habits inflicted on him by that wife. He came quickly into the room alone and closed the door behind him. He looked pale and his eyes were heavy.

"You have not slept either," she said.

"I did not trouble to go to bed. But I'm sorry you should lie awake on my account. After all, we have jumped to a conclusion. There might conceivably be another Mrs. Wilmott—one who would be welcomed by her husband." He smiled grimly. "I must try to find out more particulars from Miss Vaughan. Yesterday my mind refused to work. I was as near to panic as I have ever been."

"I'm afraid you have reason for it," she said. "When I had Daisy to myself I brought up the matter again and found that the Mrs. Wilmott she met came from the very part of London you lived in. She was pretty, too—very neat in appearance, Daisy said, and precise in her speech, with a high-pitched voice and a little quirk at the corner of her mouth."

"My God," he exclaimed, "you'll have the girl suspicious!"

"I don't think so. Anyhow, we had to make certain. I think we can be certain, don't you?"

"My wife will never rest till she finds me!" he exclaimed. He looked wildly about the room.

"Don't look so desperate."

"I *am* desperate. I tell you, Adeline, I will not live with my wife again. I'll hang myself from one of these rafters first!"

"She must not find you."

"She will find me! You don't know her. I tell you she's indefatigable. Nothing will stop her."

"You tell me this," cried Adeline. "Yet you took passage to Canada without changing your name! You lived in Quebec under your own name! What did you expect?"

He spoke more calmly. "I thought she would abide by my decision."

"Was that her habit?"

"Don't be sarcastic, Adeline. I left her well provided for. She had the child. Why should she follow me?"

"Oh, listen to the man!" Adeline folded her arms to imprison her exasperation. "Oh, the innocence! It is no wonder she is seeking you, James. For what a blank you have left in her life! How can she be herself without you there to badger and to hector and harass? God help her, she is like a waterfall with nothing to fall over!"

"Well, she won't have me! I shall clear out. To think that she may walk in here at any moment! Did she mention a child?"

"Yes, she spoke of her daughter who had mumps on the voyage out."

Wilmott's face showed no fatherly concern at this news.

"Is the girl like her mother?" asked Adeline.

"No, but she is absolutely under her influence."

"Who wouldn't be!" exclaimed Adeline. "Who could live in the same house with such a woman and not be under her influence? You couldn't, James."

"I kept my secret hidden from her all those years," he said grimly. "My secret intention to leave her."

"You did well. What have you told Tite?"

"That I may be going away."

She swept to him and took his head between her hands. She looked compellingly into his eyes. "You shall not go!" she said.

He drew violently away from her. "Don't touch me! Don't touch me—I love you too well! I have to keep telling myself that Philip is my friend."

"We must take Philip into our confidence." Her hands had dropped to her sides as though they had not touched him. She looked at him calmly. "We must tell him all. He and I will go to the town and see if we can find out where your wife is. It's just as you say, she's had plenty of time to follow you here."

"What will Philip think of me?"

"He'll be on your side. You have impoverished yourself for her. You can't deliver over your body to her. What man would expect you to? Not Philip!"

"I wish it were not necessary to tell him."

"Tell him yourself. As man to man you'll make him understand."

"If anyone can do that, you can, Adeline."

She smiled. "Ah, I might do it too well."

"What do you mean by that?"

"I get carried away. I might make the situation too melodramatic. Philip might want to keep out of it. I'll send him to you. You shall tell him in your own dignified way."

"I still think it would be better for me to leave."

"There is no need for that," she declared. "I'll tell the woman you are dead."

Wilmott gave a sardonic laugh. "She'll never believe you," he said.

Adeline's eyes were blazing when she turned on him. "Not believe me!" she cried. "If I can't convince a flibbertygibbet like that, my name is not Adeline Court!" She took his hand, as though sealing a compact. Then she went to the door. "To think," she said, "that Henrietta may walk up this path at any moment!"

Then she showed her white teeth in a mischievous smile. "Leave Henrietta to me," she said.

Wilmott stood looking at the russet plaits of her hair beneath the little velvet hat, and the intimate grace of her nape as it melted into her shoulder. It was hard for him to believe in the existence of Henrietta.

"The first thing is to find Philip," she said finally, "and to send him here to you."

"My God, what an interview!"

He went with her to where the horse was tethered, and helped her to mount. "Everything will be all right," she called back to him as she rode away.

She was halfway to Jalna when she saw a carriage approaching. It was of the type hired out by livery stables and drawn by a pair of lean horses. She saw that a woman and a young girl were in the seat behind the driver.

Adeline's heart began to thud rapidly against her side. But she hastened forward. As she passed the dust-covered carriage she took a good look at the occupants.

The driver wore a shabby livery and weather-beaten top hat. He had a harassed, almost plaintive look. He was comforting himself by chewing tobacco, a trickle from which discolored his chin. Behind him, very upright on the uncomfortable seat, sat a smallish, fresh-colored woman. She was pretty and self-possessed, looking young to be the mother of the lumpish girl at her side. She gave Adeline a keen look, then leaned forward and poked the driver in the back.

"Stop the horses," she commanded.

Either from stupidity or self-will he continued on his way, his eyes fixed on the flies that buzzed above the heads of the horses, moving with them in a horrid halo.

Mrs. Wilmott poked him again but more fiercely.

"I shall certainly complain of you to your master," she declared. "You are the stupidest man I have ever seen. Stop the horses and try to attract that lady's attention!"

The driver gave her a lowering look over his shoulder. "Did you say *master?*" he growled. "We don't call no one master in this country. This here country is a free country. But if you want me to holler to the lady, I will."

He gave a loud bellow of—"Hi there, ma'am! You're wanted!"

His horses had not required any order to stop but now made as though to go into the ditch where they saw the long grass. He wrenched at the reins. "Whoa," he bellowed. "Stay on the road, can't you? It's bad enough to traipse all over the countryside without you pullin' the arms off me!" The horses, with hanging heads, settled down to wait.

Adeline had drawn bridle and was slowly approaching. Her color was high. She looked more composed than she felt. When she had stopped her horse beside the carriage she looked down inquiringly into the face of Mrs. Wilmott, who said:—

"I wonder if you can give me any information of the whereabouts of Mr. James Wilmott. I am told he bought a property in this locality."

"Yes," returned Adeline, in a deep quiet tone, "he did. A little log cabin it was, far up the river where the swamp is, and an acre or two of land. An Indian boy was with him."

"Oh!" Mrs. Wilmott's face showed a faint look of shock. "Really. A swamp, did you say? An Indian! How degrading!"

"It was not all swamp. He had a cow and a pig and a few fowls. He might have been worse off."

"Is he gone from there?"

"Yes. He's gone."

Mrs. Wilmott drew a deep breath, then between pale lips she said, in a tense tone—"I should like to speak to you privately." She looked at the slumping back of the driver. Then she said:—

"Just drive along the road a short distance while I converse with this lady. Hold the horses steady whilst my daughter and I get out of the carriage. Now be very careful. Steady the horses!"

"Remember I'm paid by the hour," he grumbled. "You'll have a pretty bill." He shifted his tobacco to the other cheek and looked vindictively over his shoulder at her.

"I shall certainly complain to your master," she declared. "You are disobliging and impudent."

"There's no master here!" He glared at her. "No masters, I tell ye! No masters!"

"Mind your manners, my man!"

"There's no manners here neither and no 'my man-ing.' It's a free country. Now are you goin' to get out or sit there complaining?"

Mrs. Wilmott alighted cautiously, followed by her daughter. The driver went a little distance down the road. Adeline dismounted and led the way to a grassy knoll. Her horse began at once to crop the dry herbage. She said: "We can talk quite privately here. Will you sit down?"

She invited Mrs. Wilmott to be seated as though in her own drawing-room. Mrs. Wilmott looked at her inquisitively, and at the same moment explained herself. Adeline's gaze was sympathetic.

"I am Mrs. Wilmott," she said. "I am here to seek my husband. You must think the circumstances very strange. They are indeed. My husband is a very strange man. He is a very peculiar man. I've had to come all the way from London, England, in search of him. My father, Mr. Peter Quinton, he is descended from Sir Ralph Quinton who was a great inventor and scientist of the sixteenth century—you may have heard of him—I mean of Sir Ralph, of course, not of my father. Not that I should say my father is not a man of some importance, for he has stood for his borough more than once and been not too badly defeated. But naturally, he is not as important as Sir Ralph. He said to me and much as I dislike repeating the private remarks of my family to a stranger, I shall repeat this to you, for you appear so exceedingly reliable and sympathetic —he said to me—that is, my father, not Sir Ralph, said to me—'Henrietta, a man who had no more consciousness of his responsibilities than to go to a distant country on a pleasure trip and remain away for a year and a half without writing a line home, is not worth seeking,' but I'm not of that opinion. A husband's place is with his wife, I insist. Don't you agree?"

"If it can be done," said Adeline, her sympathetic eyes on Mrs. Wilmott's face.

"That's just what I say. And I have left no stone unturned till I have tracked James down. You have met him, I gather."

"Yes. I have met him."

"And how were you impressed by him? Pray do not try to spare my feelings. If he lived here, as you say, in a swamp with a cow and a pig, he must have reached a very low ebb."

"He had."

"Dear me! It is mortifying to think of such a situation. And where did he go from here? I must ask you your name. Really I never have been so informal in my life. Anyone seeing me sitting in this dusty ditch would scarcely credit what my position in London is. My father, Mr. Peter Quinton, who, I think I mentioned, is—"

The young girl here distracted her mother's attention by the ferocity with which she was scratching mosquito bites on her plump legs.

"Hettie!" cried Mrs. Wilmott. "Stop it!"

"I can't," returned Hettie, in a hoarse whimpering voice. "They itch."

"What if they do! No lady would scratch her limbs under any circumstances."

"Can I go into the fence corner and scratch them?"

"No. I say no, Hettie."

"They itch."

"I say no. That is final." Mrs. Wilmott turned to Adeline. "I was about to ask you your name and where Mr. Wilmott went from here, but this child has me at my wit's end with her disabilities. Since we left England she has suffered in turn from train sickness, seasickness, mumps, dyspepsia, hives, ingrowing toenail, sties, and now it is bites."

"They itch," said Hettie.

"Of course they itch!" exclaimed Mrs. Wilmott, in complete exasperation. "What else are they for?"

"I hate midges."

"Well, hate them or not, you are to stop scratching." Again she turned her eyes questioningly to Adeline.

"I am Mrs. White," Adeline answered, swallowing the last syllable of the name. "My husband and I came over on the same ship with Mr. Wilmott. We saw a good deal of him."

"Oh, how fortunate that I should find you! How did my husband conduct himself on the voyage?"

"Very miserable," said Adeline.

"Did he speak of his family?"

"Never a word."

"Dear, dear! How unfeeling of him! Dear me! What a man! And he has left this place, you say?"

"Some time ago."

"Where did he go? Wherever it is I shall follow him."

"He left in the darkness of night, with no word to anyone, but 't is said he went to Mexico and died of a fever there. Now, I can give you the address of two Irish gentlemen who are staying in

New York and who can tell you much more about him than I can. If any two men on this continent can help you to discover what the true end of your husband was, these are the two."

"He died!" cried Mrs. Wilmott, on a note of frustration. "You say he died! Oh, surely not. He never had a day's illness in his life. He can't be dead."

" 'T is said he died in Mexico," said Adeline, plucking a handful of grass.

"Who says so?"

"The word came and went. I cannot remember who said it first."

"I must talk to these people. Who are they?"

"They'll be glad to talk to you for, when he left, he owed money to everyone in the neighborhood. I suppose you will pay his debts?"

"Never!" There were two sharp points in Mrs. Wilmott's eyes. "I am under no such obligation or ever could be."

"It is a strange country," said Adeline. "You never know what will be brought up against you."

"James was always talking about the East," said Mrs. Wilmott. "He appeared fascinated by the East. I can't imagine why he came here."

"I believe he thought he was bound for the East." Adeline laid the handful of grass in a little mound like a grave. "But he got on to the wrong ship."

"Dear, oh dear, oh dear! It's enough to make me say I am well rid of him."

"I think you are indeed," said Adeline. "A man like that is bound to do something desperate. It boils up in him for years and then it bursts forth."

"I thank heaven that my child bears no faintest resemblance to him. She is the image of my father."

"I don't like Grandpa," said Hettie.

Mrs. Wilmott almost screamed—"Hettie, how dare you say such a thing! Your dear Grandpapa who is so superior to other people in every way!"

"I don't like him."

Mrs. Wilmott turned to Adeline in despair.

"I don't know what has come over the child. Before we left home she was the most docile and respectful girl you could imagine. Now she will say quite shocking things."

"It's the traveling," said Adeline. "It ruins them. On the voyage out there was a young girl about your daughter's age, traveling with her mother. Well, what did this girl do, d'ye suppose? At the first port she eloped with my own young brother whom I was bringing out here! She ran off with him and left her widowed mother. The poor lady was carried to the dock on a stretcher, more dead than alive."

A slow smile spread over Hettie's face. There was a brightening of her eyes. But Mrs. Wilmott paled as the news of her husband's death had not made her pale. She looked with a kind of horror at Hettie. Then she said rather tremulously to Adeline:—

"What do you advise me to do?"

"I advise you to go straight to New York and make inquiries from the two gentlemen whose names I shall give you. Then, when you are satisfied of your husband's whereabouts or of his departure from this life, you can sail from there. I am told their sailing clippers are unequaled for comfort and their new steamships too."

"That is just what I shall do! And if I can locate Mr. Wilmott it will be due entirely to you."

"I never liked him either," put in Hettie.

Mrs. Wilmott looked meaningly at Adeline. Then she said—"Stop scratching your limbs, Hettie."

"They itch."

"You must control yourself."

"I hate the midges."

"You have said that far too often."

"Not so often as they have bitten me. Mamma, when can we go?"

"Very soon, Hettie." Mrs. Wilmott opened her reticule and took out a small memorandum tablet. She handed it to Adeline. "Will you be so kind as to write down the names and addresses of the gentlemen in New York." Their hands touched. A feeling of benevolence came over Adeline. She had the feeling of taking care of Mrs. Wilmott, guiding her in the way she should go. She wrote the names of D'Arcy and Brent in her bold handwriting and returned the tablet.

"Irishmen, you say," Mrs. Wilmott remarked.

"Yes."

"I have never liked the Irish."

"There you go," said Hettie.

"What do you mean, child?"

"Saying what you tell me not to say."

"Hettie, do you want to be punished?"

"How?"

"By a hard smack."

"Smack me on the midge bites and I'd like it."

Mrs. Wilmott rose. "I want you to believe, Mrs. White," she said, "that my daughter was not like this at home."

"That is what traveling does to them. My own daughter has not the manners she had."

"It is deplorable." Mrs. Wilmott held out her hand. "Well, good-bye," she said. "I cannot tell you how thankful I am that we met."

"Faith, so am I!" Adeline's benevolent clasp enfolded Mrs. Wilmott's small dry hand. "I should ask you to drink a dish of tea with me but my little girl has whooping cough"—this was indeed true—"and yours might contract it."

The very thought of such a contingency was upsetting to Mrs. Wilmott. Again she told, and this time in detail, all she had been through with Hettie since leaving home. Hettie interrupted her by saying—"The carriage is going."

The livery horses were indeed ambling dejectedly down the road, for the driver had fallen asleep and let the reins drop from his hand.

Mrs. Wilmott gave a cry and began to run after it.

"I'll fetch him for you!" exclaimed Adeline. She hastened to her horse and began to lead him back to the road.

However, the driver had been woken by Mrs. Wilmott's cries. He looked vindictively over his shoulder, again possessed himself of the reins, and the carriage was stopped.

Mrs. Wilmott's bonnet had fallen back on her nape but she still was dignified. On reaching the carriage she opened her reticule and took out her handkerchief which she waved in farewell. Hettie looked on in complete pessimism. She said:—

"I hope we don't find him."

"Really!" exclaimed Adeline.

"Yes. I never liked him."

Laughing, in sudden hilarity, Adeline mounted her horse. She trotted to where Mrs. Wilmott waited. Her face sobered. She said genially:—

"A pleasant journey to you, Mrs. Wilmott."

"Thank you and thank you again for your help. Dear, oh, dear, when I think of all that lies before me! When I think of all that lies behind! Mrs. White, I had other chances. Mr. Wilmott was not my only suitor. I shall say that and nothing more, except that my dear father was always against the alliance. 'You can do better, Henrietta,' he repeatedly said. 'James Wilmott never will be a man of consequence. There is a great lack in him.' But I was determined and this is what I get. Do hasten, Hettie! Was there ever such a slow girl! It will be night before we reach the town. When I consider the inconvenience, the expense I am put to, it is enough to turn my hair white." She lifted her skirt and cautiously climbed into the carriage. The driver took up his whip.

Hettie was approaching slowly, dragging her feet. Her mother urged and directed her every step. At last they were seated side by side.

"Say good-bye to Mrs. White, Hettie, and thank her prettily."

"Good-bye," said Hettie morosely.

"Good-bye, Hettie."

The driver chirruped to his horses. As they moved off he turned to look at Adeline. He contorted one side of his face into what seemed to be a wink of derision toward the occupants of the carriage. A cloud of dust rose and, in its midst, a white handkerchief fluttered.

XIII

Autumn Rain

Adeline did not go on to Jalna but returned to Wilmott's log house. She felt a strangeness in returning there. So much had happened since she had left. Again she knocked and again she saw Tite's dark hand draw aside the curtain. He opened the door at once.

"You want to see my boss?" he asked.

Wilmott now appeared.

"It's a pretty sort of life I lead," he exclaimed. "Like a criminal! And I suppose that, in a degree, I am. You may go, Tite."

When they were alone, Adeline said rather breathlessly—"I've seen her!"

"Not Henrietta?"

"Yes."

"My God!" He stared incredulously. "Is she here then?"

"She was. She's gone. I had no time to find Philip. When I reached the road I met her coming in a hired carriage."

"I tell you," he said, between his teeth, "I will never go back to that woman. But I am done for in this place! Where is she?"

"On her way back to the town. To-morrow she will go to New York in search of you. I told her it is said here that you went to Mexico and died of a fever. Ah, the lies I've uttered on your behalf!"

"And she believed you?" He cared nothing for the lies. He turned a look of concentrated anxiety on Adeline.

"Do I do things well or do I not? Of course, she believed me. I told her you had lived near here with a cow, a pig and an Indian.

You lived in a swamp, I said, and when you left you were in debt to all the neighborhood."

He could not restrain a look of consternation. "Good God, and that is my epitaph in England! Henrietta will tell everyone. She can't control that tongue of hers."

Adeline turned to him fiercely. "Follow her then and deny it! She'll be easy to find."

He made an excited turn about the room. "Don't be angry with me," he said. "Don't expect me to say the right thing at such a moment. Don't imagine that I'm not overflowing in gratitude to you. But I'm fairly dazed by it all. It's happened so quickly."

"You resent my blackening your character. Who cares for character! You are not seeking a situation! Oh, James Wilmott, the thing was to be rid of that woman! I could see meanness and cruelty sticking out all over her. What a time you must have had to please her!"

"I never pleased her—not after the first year. And I resent nothing you told her. I am grateful, with my whole soul. Just think—if it were not for you—she might have her feet on this land at this moment!" He just touched Adeline's shoulder with his thin hand. "There you stand—beautiful and strong—and my protector—not from Henrietta but from what she would make of my life!"

"Don't thank me. I loved getting the best of her. Faith, if ever she comes back, I stand ready for another bout!"

"If only we had some way of finding out if she really goes to New York and if she sails from there!"

"We have!" said Adeline triumphantly. "Thomas D'Arcy and Michael Brent will tell us."

"D'Arcy and Brent!" cried Wilmott, stiffening. "How could they know anything of the matter?"

"I gave her their address so she could find out all the truth about your trip to Mexico from them."

"You must have been mad!" shouted Wilmott. "What do they know of this affair?"

"Nothing. But I shall write posthaste and tell them to expect her. I know those two Irishmen. D'Arcy is a rip and Brent a regular playboy. They'll like nothing so well as to tell fairy tales to Henrietta for my sake."

"You place yourself in a strange light," said Wilmott. "What will they think of you?"

"There you go, wondering what people will think! I say people will think ill of you no matter what you do. It's human nature."

"I would not have taken a thousand pounds and had those two told this of me."

"Then I shall not write to them."

"Have you no reasoning power?"

"No. I have only instinct. Why?"

"Naturally they will have to know everything—now you have sent Henrietta to them."

"You need not care. You will never see them again."

"I possibly never shall. But will Messrs. D'Arcy and Brent refrain from telling this good story to their friends after dinner?"

"I will swear them to secrecy, James."

"Do you think they will remember to be secret when they have drunk well? No. All their friends will hear this story."

"You need not care. You are dead."

"I had better be," he returned bitterly.

They eyed each other coldly. Then Adeline exclaimed in exasperation—"What in the name of God did you expect? Did you expect me to meet Henrietta with a full-fledged plan in my head, with no weak spots in it? I think I have done very well but what thanks does one ever get for interfering between husband and wife?"

"She is no wife to me, nor has been for five years."

"Then why worry about her now that she is far away? I may add that Hettie doesn't want you back."

Wilmott stared. "Was Hettie there?" he asked incredulously.

"She was. And showed no desire for a reunion with her papa."

Wilmott exploded in bitter laughter. "What a family we are! And how unworthy of your interest in us!"

She gave him a piercing look. "If you still say *us* about yourself and those two, I wash my hands of you."

"I don't!" he exclaimed. "I announce myself free. I have never been so happy in my life as I have been here. I shall trust in a beneficent Providence and go on being happy."

"Just trust in me," she returned.

Wilmott turned to her, his features working, his eyes full of sudden tears. "If I am happy here," he said, "it is because you are near me."

Adeline gave a little laugh. "Come with me," she said, "to Jalna. I will not leave you alone."

He looked about him. "It doesn't seem too much for a man to ask to have this log house in peace and yet I cannot feel at all convinced that I shall."

"You shall not stay here alone to-day," she returned. "We'll go to Jalna and see the staircase. The men are just building it and Philip has found a woodcarver who is carving a beautiful newel post for it. The newel post is to be of walnut and done in a design of grapes and their leaves, with a grand bunch at the top. Shouldn't you like to see it, James?"

"I should like nothing better."

He got his hat. He no longer wore the woodsman's clothes he had affected when he first arrived but he had kept his word about taking off his whiskers. Adeline again remarked the improvement in his appearance.

"I declare," she said, "you look very distinguished, now that you have got rid of those whiskers."

"As a matter of fact they were quite small ones," he returned.

"All whiskers are too large. Don't you want one to say that you look distinguished?"

"Everything you say is so important to me that I am bound to criticize it."

"You are a character, James, as we say in Ireland, and sometimes I could find it in my heart to pity Henrietta."

They went through the intricate paths that led to Jalna, he leading her horse, she with the long skirt of her habit thrown across her arm. They found Colonel Vaughan with Philip. They clustered about the stairway, discussing the width of the treads, the curve of the banister, the design of the proposed newel post. Adeline declared that, for ease of mounting, the steps had never been equaled. She could run up and down them all day, she said, with a baby on either arm.

Colonel Vaughan invited Wilmott to join his other guests at dinner. Wilmott was invited to Vaughanlands less frequently than he might have been had Mrs. Vaughan liked him better. She had on several occasions heard him express views on religion and politics which were antagonistic to her. She had seen that her husband admired him. She felt that he was a dangerous companion for Robert. What she disliked still more about him was the admiration for Adeline which she had glimpsed alight in his eyes. She thought it was reckless of Adeline to visit his home alone and so make herself the subject of gossip. She thought it lax of Philip to allow her to do so. She said as much to Adeline that same afternoon before dinner.

"Dear Mrs. Vaughan," said Adeline smiling, a little dangerously, "please don't take me to task for something entirely innocent."

"I am not taking you to task, Mrs. Whiteoak. I am only warning you."

"Warning me of what?"

"That you will find yourself talked about."

"You mean that I am already talked about?"

"You must acknowledge that what you are doing is unconventional."

"Philip and I are unconventional people. We don't care a fig what gossips or busybodies say."

"But these people are not gossips or busybodies. They are nice people and your future neighbors, you must remember."

"Oh, Mrs. Vaughan, please don't take a chiding tone with me!" Adeline's cheeks were scarlet but she added more calmly—"While I am here with you I shall not go again alone to Mr. Wilmott's house. I hope that will satisfy everyone."

She went off to dress for dinner, feeling the constriction of a prolonged visit. She stopped at the children's door and opened it. Nicholas had just been given his bath and was sitting on his nurse's knee, wet and shining as a shell just lifted from the sea. His hair flew upward in moist waves from his forehead. His eyes had a look of infant hilarity and daring. He had thrown the great sponge to the floor and now, on Matilda's knee, reached for his slippery pink toes. She, with the prideful, fatuous smile of the nurse, looked up at Adeline as though to say—"You may have borne him but just now he is mine, mine."

Nicholas did not care whose he was. He took a large magnanimous view of life. His chief occupation was to destroy what was nearest.

"You angel!" cried Adeline. "Oh, Nurse, how he grows! Aren't his dimples enchanting?"

"They are indeed, ma'am," answered the nurse, as smugly as though she had put them in with her own finger.

Gussie came forward carrying a doll Wilmott had given her. It had a pink-and-white face and black curls all painted on its china head. It wore only a chemise.

"Look," said Gussie, holding up the doll.

"Oh, how pretty!" said Adeline, but her eyes returned at once to Nicholas.

"Look," said Gussie, drawing back the doll's chemise and displaying its body.

"It's a marvel," said Adeline, but she did not look.

Gussie laid the doll in the bath and pressed it firmly down. As it sank, an odd look came into her eyes. She remembered something. She turned to her mother.

"Huneefa," she said.

Adeline was startled, almost horrified. What did the child remember? Why had she said the ayah's name?

"There she goes, at her naughtiness!" exclaimed the nurse. "All day long I can't keep up to her. If it isn't one thing it's another. If you would punish her, ma'am, it might do some good."

Gussie began to cough from whooping cough, ending in that strange crowing noise. The cough shook her tiny frame. It was pathetic to see her supporting herself by grasping the arm of a chair. When the paroxysm had passed her face was crimson and her forehead moist with sweat. Adeline wiped it with her own handkerchief.

"Poor little Gussie," she murmured, bending over her. "How you do cough! This is what comes, Nurse, of her going to tea with the young Pinks."

"Well, ma'am, it was your own wish. I didn't like the idea myself. You can't be too careful—not with a baby in the house."

"Good heavens, how was I to know the little Pinks were taking whooping cough?"

"You never can tell what clergymen's children will be taking, ma'am."

A step came on the stair. There was a quick knock at the door.

"It is the doctor," said Nurse, enfolding Nicholas's nakedness in a huge bath towel.

Adeline opened the door and Dr. Ramsey came in. He was a young man of just under thirty, of bony frame but particularly healthy appearance. His high cheekbones and firmly cut lips gave him a look of endurance, even defiance. His manner was somewhat abrupt. After greeting Adeline he turned to his little patient.

"Hullo," he said. "Another bout of coughing, eh?"

Gussie gravely assented. She passed her hand across her forehead, putting back the curls that clung moistly there.

Dr. Ramsey sat down and took her on his knee. He laid his fingers on her tiny wrist but his eyes were on Adeline.

"I wish," he said, "we had some way of isolating her. I shall be very sorry if you develop whooping cough, Mrs. Whiteoak."

"There is little likelihood of that, since I did not take it when all five of my brothers had it at one time."

"I wish you had taken it then," he returned.

"Indeed then, I don't, for I should have missed the races in Dublin, to which my grandfather took me, and all my five brothers whooping away at home!"

"Better the miss of some races," he returned, "than the miscarriage of a child."

Adeline varied between having complete trust in Dr. Ramsey and disliking him. The dislike did not impair the trust but it tarnished it. She said:—

"All I worry about is my baby. He has never yet had a day's illness."

Dr. Ramsey turned to Nicholas, sprawling in supreme comfort in his nurse's lap.

"If he contracts this cough," he said, "it will take off some of that fine flesh of his."

"If only Miss Augusta would keep away from him," said the nurse, "but she won't."

"If only Mrs. Whiteoak would keep away from Augusta!" said Dr. Ramsey.

Philip found Adeline dressing in their room. Between Mrs. Vaughan's criticism of her visits to Wilmott's house and a certain irritation provoked by Dr. Ramsey, Adeline's mood was not an amenable one. Her head in the wardrobe, her voice came out to Philip on a note of dissatisfaction.

"I declare," she said. "I am sick and tired of considering other people's feelings. From morning to night I am put to it not to give offense. My clothes are all in a heap. My children are in a heap. You and I are in a heap."

"What's up?" asked Philip laconically, unbuttoning his waistcoat.

"It's all very well for you! You live unhampered. You are free as air. You are not chided for visiting your neighbor. You are not going to have a baby. You haven't seventeen crinolines hanging on one hook!"

"I have to sit with my head out of the window or up the chimney when I smoke a cigar," he returned mildly. "Was it about going to Wilmott's that Mrs. Vaughan spoke to you?"

She withdrew her head from the wardrobe and faced him with disheveled locks and flushed cheeks. "Yes. Who told you?"

"Vaughan. He thinks it is rather too unconventional of you and I expect he is right. I have given you a loose rein, Adeline, because I think it is the best way with you, and I believe Wilmott is a decent fellow. I told Vaughan I would speak to you."

"You needn't have troubled. I've told Mrs. Vaughan I shall not go to Wilmott's again while I am here. . . . Dr. Ramsey says it will go hard with me if I get whooping cough."

Philip looked aghast at the thought. "You are to keep away from those children. I command you."

"I am not worrying. It is just that I don't very much like Dr. Ramsey. I wish Dr. St. Charles were here. Do you think perhaps he would come and look after me if we asked him?"

"I'm afraid it is rather too far. For my part, I think Ramsey is a very capable fellow. What is that you are putting on?"

She had taken a green taffeta dress from the wardrobe. It was cut very low and to Philip seemed extreme in fashion for such an occasion. He told her so.

Adeline threw it on the floor and desired him to find her something hideous enough to grace the moment. He looked at his watch.

"We are going to be late for dinner," he said. "Your head is like a hayrick. If you want to appear with your head like a hayrick and your body overdressed, I shall try to endure it but, I promise you, I shall be ashamed."

She sat down gloomily, looking out of the window. "How sweet it is in County Meath at this time of the year," she said.

"Aye," he returned, "and it's nice in Warwickshire, too."

"Ah, you English have no heart for your country! You don't know the deep, dark, hungering love we Irish know for ours."

"And a very good thing, too. Else we should be where Ireland is."

"It is you English who have made us what we are!" she flared.

"We can do nothing with you and you well know it."

She laughed, a little comforted. She began to play a tune on the window sill. "How out of practice I am!" she exclaimed. "I can feel my fingers getting quite stiff and I used to be able to play 'The Maiden's Prayer' with only three mistakes."

Philip came behind her chair, put his hands beneath her arms and raised her to her feet.

"Now," he said, "you dress for dinner or I'll take a stick to you!"

She leant back against his shoulder and sighed. "I'm tired," she said. "If only you knew the day I've had!"

She did not wear the green dress to dinner but a much simpler dress of maize-colored India muslin, and had time only to twist her hair into a sleek knot. But she was able to show off a little with long yellow diamond earrings and a late yellow rose in her hair.

Wilmott was extraordinarily lively at table. He was always either more or less animated than those about him. His mood never quite fitted into the mood of the moment. When his eyes met Adeline's they would exchange a look of understanding. The image of Henrietta flashed between them. Mrs. Vaughan intercepted one of these glances and she had a disconcerting sense of being surrounded by intrigue. The behavior of her niece did not make her any happier. Daisy so obviously was straining to capture the attention of Dr. Ramsey. She had made up for the simplicity of her dress by an elaborate arrangement of her hair that hung in a glossy dark waterfall to her shoulders. Mrs. Vaughan had a dreadful suspicion that Daisy had rouge on her cheeks. She laughed too much, showing too many teeth. She leaned too far across the table to attract the young doctor's eye. He had just returned from a hunting trip and Philip was eager to hear its details. He planned next year, when he had his family installed at Jalna, to join the party. Daisy cried out to hear of the hazards endured by the hunters, and the magnificence of the quarry. Deer, a moose, and a bear, had been killed. Wilmot maintained that no man had a right to kill more than he could eat and he also maintained that, sitting in his own boat on his own river, he had as good sport as any man needed. Daisy took sides almost fiercely with the doctor and declared that, if she were a man, she would go to India and shoot tigers as Captain Whiteoak had. She had a mind to marry some big-game hunter and accompany him on his expeditions.

"You would very soon get enough of it, Miss Daisy," said Philip.

"It would depend entirely on the man," she returned. "With the right man, I would face any danger."

"You had better come with us on our hunting trip next year, as a preparation," said Dr. Ramsey.

"Ah, but would the right man be there to give me the moral support I need?"

"At any rate, Dr. Ramsey could attend to your physical injuries," said her uncle.

This turned the conversation to arduous journeys the doctor had had to make in his profession, to remote places in the depth of winter. When the ladies had left the room he was encouraged to enlarge on these. Colonel Vaughan again circulated the decanter of port.

"You would be surprised," said Ramsey, "to see what shift I can make when I am put to it. A few weeks ago I was visiting a patient, when a neighbor came in a great state of excitement to fetch me. Her husband had given his foot a great gash with an axe. Well, when I reached their little farm, there was the man looking pretty weak. It was a bad wound. I had nothing with me for sewing it up. There was no linen thread in the house. So I just went to the barn and pulled a few good white hairs from the tail of one of their nags and they did the trick. Not very sanitary, of course, but that gash healed as well as any I've seen."

He told other experiences which were shocking to Wilmott. He bolstered himself with the port. No one noticed that he walked rather unsteadily when they returned to the parlor, or that he had become very quiet. He went and sat beside Adeline. Rain was beginning to fall. They could hear it beating against the windows.

"I am glad to hear that rain," said Colonel Vaughan. "It is badly needed."

"I wish it had waited till I reached home," said Dr. Ramsey. "It will be an uncomfortable ride. My mare never fails to step in every hole and puddle. Just listen how it's coming down!" He turned to Wilmott. "Were you on horseback, sir?"

Wilmott looked bewildered. "Yes—yes," he began slowly. "I hope to buy a good horse. A team—yes—and in time—a saddle horse."

"I asked," returned Dr. Ramsey, irritably, "if you rode here."

"No—no—I never ride."

Philip, seated on the other side of the room on a sofa beside Daisy, knew that she wanted to be urged to play on the piano. He said to Mrs. Vaughan:

"I wish you could persuade your niece to play for us. She's adamant to my implorings."

"I think it would be very nice," said Mrs. Vaughan. "Do play something, Daisy."

"Oh, Aunt. I perform so horribly! Please don't insist."

"I don't wish to insist, Daisy, but I think it would be agreeable to everyone."

"Not to Dr. Ramsey, I'm sure. I am positive he hates the pianoforte."

"I don't know how I gave that impression," said the doctor. "I myself can play 'The Bluebells of Scotland' with one finger and take great pride in it."

"Oh, please do! I should so love to hear you."

"After your performance."

"Come, Miss Daisy," urged Philip, "don't be obstinate. It's not becoming in a young girl."

She rose, gracefully reluctant, and went to the instrument. It required some twirlings of the piano stool to make it of the height to suit her. Philip assisted in this and also in the finding of her music.

Adeline said in an undertone to Wilmott—"If the creature didn't pose so, I could tolerate her."

"I hate all women but you."

There was something uncontrolled in his voice that made Adeline turn to him quickly.

"What is the matter with you, James?"

"Nothing," he answered. "Except that I've had a little too much to drink."

Daisy was sailing brightly through a Strauss waltz, while Philip turned the pages for her.

"Oh, to waltz!" sighed Adeline. "What wouldn't I give to waltz?"

"Why not waltz then? I should like nothing better."

"In this room! On this carpet! Come, be sensible . . . I mean in a real ballroom and to a waltz played sensitively—languorously."

There was a murmur of approbation as the music ceased. Daisy refused to play another piece.

"My heart is set," she said, "on hearing Mrs. Whiteoak and Mr. Wilmott sing together from *The Bohemian Girl.* I know they do it excessively well because Captain Whiteoak has told me. Do command them to do it, Captain Whiteoak."

"It is impossible," said Philip, "for my wife to keep on the tune. But I'll engage to make her sing, if the company demands it."

"I demand it," said Dr. Ramsey.

"What about it, Wilmott?" asked Philip. "Do you think you can keep Adeline to the tune?"

Wilmott rose with sudden alacrity.

"Come," he said to Adeline, "we'll show them what a really finished performance is." He held out his hand to her.

She allowed herself to be led to the piano but she gave Wilmott a look askance. She was a little mistrustful of him. However he sat down before the keyboard with an air of confidence. He knew the accompaniment by heart. He played the opening chords. But his first vocal note was a kind of discordant groan. He looked up at her in astonishment.

"Is anything wrong?" asked Colonel Vaughan.

"No, no," said Adeline. She bent over Wilmott. "Are you going to shame us both," she whispered, "or are you going to sing?"

"Going to sing," he muttered.

Philip beat a tattoo with his heels. He would have liked to be a little rowdy, but was afraid of Mrs. Vaughan.

Wilmott struck the opening bars afresh. Then, abruptly he took his hands from the keys, crossed his arms on the music rack and laid his head on them. Mrs. Vaughan sprang up.

"Is Mr. Wilmott ill?" she asked.

"No," answered Adeline, "not really ill, just a little faint."

"I'll get my smelling salts." She hurried from the room.

Philip came and looked down into that part of his friend's face which was visible. Dr. Ramsey also bent over him.

"Are you aware what is wrong with him?" asked the doctor.

"Yes. I've been suspicious of him ever since dinner. We'd better get him out in the air before Mrs. Vaughan comes back."

Philip turned to Adeline. "You and Daisy must go to Mrs. Vaughan and tell her we've taken Wilmott outside. Hadn't you the wit to see that he was tipsy? You should not have attempted to sing with him."

She stood abashed for once. Then she murmured—"He's had such a day—the poor man!"

"You can tell me about that later."

He and Dr. Ramsey got Wilmott to his feet and steered him across the room. The two young women went to find Mrs. Vaughan. Colonel Vaughan followed the other men. The rain was beating in on the verandah. He said:—

"You can't take him out there."

"It will do him good," said the doctor.

They placed Wilmott in a rocking chair. It swayed with him so that his head rolled against his shoulder. Philip winked at the doctor.

"He looks pretty seedy, doesn't he?"

Dr. Ramsey nodded grimly. "He'll not go home to-night."

Wilmott opened his eyes and looked at them. "I'm afraid I can't sing," he said.

"We'll excuse you, old man," said Philip. He went to the Colonel. "Do you think you could put him up for the night?" he asked apologetically.

Colonel Vaughan replied coldly—"Certainly. He may have

Robert's room. We must keep this from my wife. Her feelings would be outraged."

"Upon my word," said Philip to Adeline, as they were getting ready for bed, "I shall be glad when we are in our own home. I like to be able to put a friend to bed when he needs it, without all this secrecy. Vaughan has thoroughly spoiled his wife. But why did that fool, Wilmott, choose this house, of all places, to get tight in?"

"He was so tired, poor man."

Philip turned his full blue eyes on her. "Tired of what? Sitting in a punt fishing? Or teaching young Tite to make pothooks?"

"Ah, he has worries you will never know."

"What worries?"

"I'm not at liberty to tell them."

"Now, look here, Madam," said Philip, "I don't want you to be made the confidante for Wilmott's past. If his past is such as to make him drink too much at the mere thought of it, let him keep it to himself or confide in another man."

"True," said Adeline mildly. "True." Then with a long-drawn breath she added—"I feel ailing to-night. D'ye think I am perhaps going to have a miscarriage?" She crept into the deep feather bed.

Philip's expression became one of concern but he said stoutly—"I think you are tired and a bit worried by Wilmott's behavior. What you need is a good night's rest." He drew the blankets snugly about her. "There now, isn't that cozy? I'll be beside you in a jiffy. Egad, listen to the rain! It's coming down in a torrent."

XIV

Winter Sport

THE rains were heavy in November. Often they were joined by winds, mostly from east and northeast. These swept the last of the leaves from the trees, leaving the conifers in dark possession of the woods. On the roads, wheels sank in the deep mud, carpenters were forced to wait for the material to work with but still the building of Jalna proceeded at a satisfactory speed. The workmen built themselves a log weather-proof shelter with bunks, and a stove was installed in the shed where they took their meals. They were healthy and, on the whole, jolly, for they had months of well-paid work ahead of them. Several of them played on mouth organs, one on a flute. Then there was Fiddling Jock who had more music in him than many a concert musician. There were the two French Canadians who could dance, and others had good voices for a song, so their evenings passed cheerfully and, on Saturday nights when they had had a good deal to drink, noisily. There were a few quite bloody fights among them.

The wind veered to the north, the wet weather turned to frosty brightness. There were snow flurries. Nero, the Newfoundland dog, grew a tremendously thick coat and bounded in riotous health over the estate which he considered to be his to guard. He knew all the carpenters, masons, and bricklayers. He was hail fellow with the woodcutters but, to a stranger looking for work, he was fierce and formidable. The foreman fed him many a heaping tin plate of potatoes and pork in addition to the regular meals he had at Vaughanlands, so that he grew rather more stout than he should have been. He also devoured the bones of wild fowl which the men threw him. Some canine Providence must have had him in mind for, though he occasionally was very sick, it was only for a few minutes. Neither did splinters of bone pierce his vitals. He was robust, he was good-tempered, he was as happy as a lark. He was bounding. He was rough.

Adeline had contracted whooping cough from Augusta and coughed with frightening violence up to Christmas time. Indeed the cough never really left her till the following spring. Dr. Ramsey dosed her with flaxseed tea. Mrs. Vaughan gave her large quantities of honey and rum. Mr. Pink, the rector, brought her a bottle of Radway's Ready Relief. Mrs. Lacey a bottle of Pine and Tar Syrup. Philip never went into the town without returning with some new tablets or lozenges for her relief. These multiple remedies had little effect on her except to spoil her appetite. She consequently grew thin and, because of this, would have shown her condition of pregnancy more but for the way she laced. By means of long French stays and a wide crinoline she continued to look graceful and even elegant. It is true that Mrs. Vaughan counseled her otherwise. She would injure the health of the infant, Mrs. Vaughan said, but she sympathized with Adeline's desire to conceal her state, especially with Robert coming home for his holidays. It would have been embarrassing indeed to have had a bulky Adeline about, with Robert and Daisy in the house. She was so kind to Adeline in these days that Adeline never forgot it.

The various cough medicines of which Gussie partook, along with her mother, had a worse effect on the little girl. She not only lost her appetite but could ill digest the little she did eat. Her eyes looked enormous with the dark rings about them, her lips had a bluish color except after a bout of coughing when her whole face would become almost purple. Nicholas on the other hand flourished like a weed. He weighed more than Gussie and, though he had not begun to walk, he crept everywhere with surprising strength and speed. He had a temper when things went wrong and would fill the house with his roars of rage. He slept like a top but woke at sunrise shouting and chuckling his pleasure in the new day. He was a pet with everyone and promised to be a spoilt and headstrong boy but he had great charm, and his smile could not be resisted by anyone in that house.

Oh, how cold it suddenly was! Clear and cold and sharp as a knife. The cold woods stood darkly waiting. The trees marched on to meet the great forests of the north, on and on till their march was ended and there were no more trees but only frozen lakes and ice-bound land. The night Robert returned from his university the weather moderated, the sky grew heavy. All night the snow fell. There was to be real Christmas weather.

With Robert's luggage carried to his room, with Robert tall and fair and smiling in the house, Mrs. Vaughan's heart sang. She felt that she really was to become acquainted with the son of whom she had seen so little. But Robert found it easier to be natural with Adeline than with his parents.

"Perhaps it is that they expect so much of me," he said when he had voiced this feeling to Adeline. "They expect me to be a loyal Canadian when I scarcely know the country. They expect me to be a noble character when I am really full of faults. They expect me to show my affection when I'm really confoundedly shy. But you expect no more of me than I can achieve." He gave her an eloquent look. "If you knew my thoughts as the train was bringing me home you would have been surprised."

She smiled. "Should I?"

"Yes. I was wondering what it was all about. Why was I cramming my head with book learning at the university? What fate had thrown you into my life . . . what would my life be . . . should I ever really belong anywhere . . . was I real . . . what do all our struggles mean? Now this house you are building—can you cling to it? Does it make you feel safe? I was wondering about these things."

"From season to season is enough for me," she said. "If I have my very own roof and those who belong to me under it—that is real."

"My friendship means nothing to you!" he exclaimed.

"I should love this place less if you were not my friend."

"I should hate it if you weren't here," he exclaimed hotly. "This country is just a great waste to me. Perhaps my son, if I have one, will love it, but I never shall. Look at the snow. It will cover everything for months. In Montreal it is worse."

Adeline touched his cheek with her fingers.

"Ah, Bobby," she said, "what a one you are for talking! Let us go out and make snowballs. I used to make them in Quebec with the Balestrier children."

"Am I a child too?" he asked mournfully.

"You are very sweet," she answered.

Mrs. Vaughan groaned as she saw the two pelting each other with snowballs. Adeline's recklessness frightened her. To handle snow and she with such a cough! To exert so in her condition was almost wicked. But she held the children up to the window to see their mother's wild behavior. As Philip appeared from the woods he was greeted by a snowball full on the breast and, when he entered the battle, it became fierce indeed. Nero bounded after the snowballs, he jumped up on the opponents, almost overthrowing them.

"Heaven help that unborn child," thought Mrs. Vaughan. She stroked back the crest of hair from Nicholas's forehead. "Just look at your mother!" she said.

He chuckled, wet his finger in his mouth, and drew it across the pane.

Mrs. Vaughan stroked Gussie's head. "Your mother is as wild as a deer," she said. "It is not good for the next little brother."

"No more little brothers, please," answered Gussie. She felt the cough rising in the pit of her stomach.

"When you are a little older, perhaps on your next birthday, Gussie, I am going to have a tea party for you. About six nice little children. The little Pink boys—" She felt the cough shaking Gussie's chest. Then it came.

By Christmas the land was frozen solid but not with the bitter coldness of Quebec. Wilmott's river formed a glassy pond just by his wharf. He and Tite cleared it of snow and swept it clean. They worked together in complete happiness. From the night of his intoxication, Wilmott had avoided the Vaughans. On that night he had taken a dislike to Mrs. Vaughan and to Dr. Ramsey. But he had settled down to life in the neighborhood. He went to the Pinks' and the Laceys' to play whist, to talk politics and religion. The

Reverend Heber Pink was a sturdy, florid-complexioned man of early middle age, with a wife rather like himself except that she was timid where he was hearty and sure of himself in all company. He was very hard-worked and was accustomed to expose himself in all weathers. He had three parishes, one with a good church in the village of Stead where the community about Jalna attended service, two in smaller villages, considerable distances apart and with small wooden churches which he was struggling to improve. He was argumentative but tolerant and he enjoyed his talks with Wilmott. But he liked Philip much better and was encouraging him to donate land and give substantial aid to the building of a new church. If this were done, Mr. Pink would be relieved of his two small churches.

Captain Lacey's young son had leave from his ship which was lying at Halifax, and was home for the holiday season. He was a high-spirited boy, not at all like Robert Vaughan, but the two youths became friendly at once. There was a festive feeling in the neighborhood. The building of Jalna had added a new interest to life. The house was talked of for miles about and people drove long distances to inspect it.

Wilmott had made up his mind to give a skating party. No one in the neighborhood had done such a thing before nor had he himself ever given a skating party. But it now became the one form of entertainment which appealed to him. To be sure, his house was very small but, if the day were not too cold, refreshments could be served out of doors. He had bought skates, not only for himself but for Tite, and the two had practised for days on the river with many bruises and sore muscles. The Pinks and the Laceys were competent skaters. So were others in the neighborhood, including the Busbys, a family who had lived in Canada for generations and had several young sons and daughters. Adeline never had had the opportunity to skate. Now she was determined to, though Mrs. Vaughan did her utmost to dissuade her and even braced herself to speak to Philip about it. He, surprisingly, seemed to think it would not hurt Adeline and was himself eager to skate. "If the unborn child is a cripple," thought Mrs. Vaughan, "the blame is on their heads. But I could weep when I think of the poor little thing."

Philip had had some practice in Quebec and chaffed Wilmott

because he had not taken advantage of his opportunities there. He bought skates for Adeline and for Daisy also, who was in a state of bliss because she not only could skate but could do the figure eight and the grapevine. She promised Philip to teach him to waltz on the ice.

Christmas Day passed in pleasant serenity. A tree was brought from the woods for the children and decorated with tinsel and candles. Large packages of presents came from Philip's sister in Devonshire and at least a dozen, very badly wrapped and in which many of the contents were broken, from Adeline's relatives in Ireland. She had bought Philip a dark green velvet smoking jacket and cap, and embroidered a design in gay silks on the cuffs and collar of the jacket and around the cap, from the top of which depended a gold tassel. He looked so perfectly beautiful when adorned in these that Adeline could have wept to see him. He was a little rueful to think he could not wear them at once, but must lay them away till he was under his own roof. He wore the rueful expression when displaying the gifts to Mrs. Vaughan, which somewhat embarrassed her but not to the extent of telling him to light a cigar that very moment.

On Christmas Day, Gussie wore her first pantalettes and in them appeared a little girl, no longer just a baby. They were of dainty whiteness beneath a blue silk frock with short sleeves and low-cut neck, and Adeline had herself made the lace which edged them. Gussie looked so adorable in these that Adeline could have wept to see her, also. She snatched her up and covered her face with kisses, then held her out for Philip's inspection, her little blue shoes dangling beneath the pantalettes.

"Did you ever see anything so enchanting and ridiculous?" she exclaimed.

Gussie looked faintly offended. She thought they were laughing at her. Nicholas, who was accustomed to being the centre of attraction, could not bear to see his sister so enthroned. He crept to Adeline's skirt and attempted to climb up it, ruffle by ruffle. Philip picked him up and set him on his broad shoulder.

"They are a pretty pair," he declared. "The little Balestriers cannot hold a candle to 'em."

"Neither can the little Pinks."

"Nor any other children I know."

"I wonder who our new baby will be like."

"I hope for another boy. But I wish the little beggar weren't coming."

"I hope he will be fair and the image of you."

"Yes. It is about time there was one like me. But he will probably be the image of your father, red hair and all."

"Heaven forbid!"

"I think I should like to call him Charles, after my father. He was a fine man and Charles goes well with Whiteoak."

"If you name him for your father he must be named for mine too."

"I don't see why."

"Do you want to push my poor father out of everything?" she flared.

"You said a moment ago that you hoped the child wouldn't look like him."

"That is different."

"Do you mean to say you would call your son Renny?"

"My father has more than one name. His name is Dennis Patrick Crawshay St. John Renny."

"Hmph. I can't say I like any of them."

"Not Dennis?"

"Dennis is not bad."

"My dear father," she said, in a mild tone, "was called Dennis all his life till he was twenty-three. Then the uncle he was named for offered him a thousand pounds if he would use one of his other names. So my father, who was willing to come for any name whatever when money was in question, cast aside Dennis and became Renny. But indeed there are members of the family who still call him Dennis, because they so hate him that they will not call him by their grandfather's name. Not that their grandfather was a man to boast of. He was—"

Philip was looking at his watch. "It is time to dress," he interrupted, "and if you want me to hook up your stays we had better begin."

The weather on the day of Wilmott's skating party was crystal-bright and cold. But there was no wind and the cold was exhilarating. A glittering snow powder was now and again sifted through the clear air which was devoid of all scent, but struck the nostrils impersonal and penetrating. Footprints of the wild creatures lay like little etchings on the glittering snow. It was as though the day had been especially ordered.

Wilmott and Tite worked hard all the morning clearing the ice of snow, sweeping it with brooms, not only on the pond but for some distance up the river. They had built benches for the ladies to rest on and over them they had laid red and gray blankets. A neighboring farmer's wife had come in to help with the refreshments. To grace the occasion, Wilmott had put on a red scarf, the long fringed ends of which dangled over his waistcoat.

The Pinks were the first to arrive and Wilmott was glad of this. They lent an air of comfort to a party. The Rector chaffed Wilmott about introducing new and frivolous ways to the community. Mrs. Pink laughed a little when her husband made a joke, smiled when Wilmott made one. She was thankful to say that her little boys were quite recovered from whooping cough.

The next to arrive were the Laceys. They brought with them their son, an only child like Robert Vaughan, but in this case the only child raised out of three, so he was trebly precious. The Laceys were the Pinks' most intimate friends. They quickly merged into a group so congenial that Wilmott felt a little out of it. He looked anxiously toward the road, for he could hear the jingle of sleigh bells. A large sleigh drawn by two rawboned, only half-broken-in horses precariously entered the gate. A lusty young fellow was driving them and with some trouble brought them to a halt. Another lusty young fellow jumped out of the sleigh and ran to their heads. Three buxom girls scrambled out. Young Lacey flew to their assistance but was in time only to assist their enormously stout mother.

The father of the family came last. He was Elihu Busby who had been the original owner of much of the land hereabout. He was in his early sixties but might well have passed for less than fifty. He was so straight as almost to lean backward. He had fought in the War of 1812 under General Sir Isaac Brock and had lost an arm in the battle of Queenston Heights. He was of mixed English, Irish, and Scottish extraction but had a faint contempt for each of these peoples which, in the case of the Scotch, amounted to dislike. But his strongest prejudice was against the Americans. He was descended from United Empire Loyalists who had left affluence behind them in New England and escaped to Canada in the early days of the Revolution. The persecutions they had suffered before they left rankled with amazing freshness in his mind, for he had drunk them in as a boy from his grandparents' relating. He was proud and egotistical but he had taken a fancy to Wilmott and enjoyed nothing more than to inform the newcomer on all affairs of the Province. His eldest daughter, Kate, also had taken a fancy to Wilmott but a much warmer one, and could scarcely wait for the moment when they would skate together. Busby himself was businesslike about the skating and, immediately after greeting his host, sat down at the edge of the river and commanded his eldest son, Isaac, to put his skates on him, which he could not do for himself because of his lost arm.

The Whiteoaks and Robert and Daisy Vaughan now joined the party. A little later it was completed by the appearance of Dr. Ramsey who tied his mare to a tree, blanketed it and stalked up to Wilmott, as though he were a patient who probably would never pay his bill.

"I can't stay long," he announced. "I have to go to Stead. I have a man there with his arm broken in three places."

"Amputate it," advised Busby, over his shoulder, "the way they did mine. Give him a gill of whiskey and amputate it."

Dr. Ramsey ignored this remark. He folded his arms and looked disapprovingly at Adeline.

"She has no business to be here," he said. "Just recovering from whooping cough and due to have a child in April! And look at the way she is laced!"

Wilmott thought this remark in bad taste. Dr. Ramsey's presence froze him. He said vaguely:—

"Oh, I expect all will be well."

Dr. Ramsey turned a pair of cold bright eyes on him.

"Why?" he asked.

"I don't know."

"It seldom is, I may tell you."

Elihu Busby was the first on the ice. He glided smoothly across the river and would have been graceful but for an angularity in his posture due to his lack of one arm. Nero, who had arrived with the Whiteoaks, had never before seen a person on skates. The sight filled him with a kind of savage hilarity. He rushed, sliding and slipping as he went, after Mr. Busby. Adeline shrieked Nero's name and Philip shouted it, but he sped on, woolly and inexorable. He leaped on Mr. Busby's shoulders and in an instant they were prone together.

"I expect he has broken his only arm," observed Dr. Ramsey grimly. He skated rapidly to Mr. Busby's aid.

When Nero saw a newcomer on skates he sprang to attention, with feet planted wide apart, ready to deal with him as he had dealt with Mr. Busby.

"Keep off, you brute!" shouted Dr. Ramsey.

But with a joyous bark Nero was on his chest. For an instant the doctor struck an extraordinary and grotesque figure which might have gained him fame as a fancy skater if he could have held it. But that was the last thing he desired to do. He was now in a kneeling posture, for he dared not rise to his feet. However his manner was far from supplicating as he swore and struck at Nero who circled about him in an abandon of barking.

Mr. Busby had not been at all hurt and, sitting on the ice, gave way to shouts of laughter.

Philip had on one skate but in his excitement could not fasten the clasp of the other. He kept on roaring "Nero!" which served only to stimulate Nero's pleasure in having two men down.

"Capture that dog!" Wilmott ordered Tite.

"Boss, I dare not," answered Tite.

"I say, capture him!"

With stealthy grace the boy crept across the ice toward the Newfoundland. It was like a play to those on the shore. Now that the Busbys were sure that their husband and father was not injured, they could enjoy the scene to the full. Nero did not notice Tite till he had caught him by the collar. Then he bounded with the boy's light figure clinging to him, he gamboled, dragging Tite after him while Mr. Busby continued to shake with laughter and Dr. Ramsey to curse.

Suddenly Patsy O'Flynn appeared, almost as broad as tall he was so bundled up against the cold, and stalked toward Nero. He took him by the collar and led him, with an air of swagger, from the river. There was a round of applause. Patsy exclaimed:—

"Sure, he's like meself—a lamb, if yez know how to handle him!"

Now all were brave to hurry to the two roughly used gentlemen. Now everyone was laughing, even the doctor. Wilmott had engaged the old Scotsman, Jock, to make music for the skating. He tuned up his fiddle and to a lively reel the ring of blades on the smooth ice was heard. Kate Busby had her wish and soon was sailing about with Wilmott. Truth to tell, she was his support rather than he hers, so good a skater was she. His arm linked within that of the good-natured girl, Wilmott wondered what life with such a companion would be. What sort of man would he be to-day, he wondered, if *he* had had such a companion. Daisy and Robert Vaughan were the most graceful couple on the ice. He wore a belted jacket with fur collar, very tight trousers, and a fur cap of a rather long yellowish fur, beneath which his fair face looked out as from a strange, prehistoric headdress. Daisy, in black skirt and scarlet jacket trimmed with gold braid, made the Busby girls feel shy and countrified, Mrs. Pink disapproving. She considered Daisy's movements entirely too free of restraint. But Daisy was really longing to skate with Dr. Ramsey. He had been watching young Lacey steer Adeline about with a good deal of anxiety. Now he himself approached her. He said:—

"If you must endanger yourself in skating, Mrs. Whiteoak, I must ask you to skate with me. I am the strongest skater and most sure-footed here."

Adeline laughed, though she surrendered herself to skate with him. "I'm glad you have told me," she said. "At any rate, I hope I shall be easier to manage than Nero was."

"You need not rub that in," he returned.

As they left the pond and moved slowly up the river, he began to lecture her on the care she should take of herself. She drew sharply away from him. She exclaimed:—

"Very well. If you are going to be disagreeable to me I shall skate by myself." She took a long, sweeping stroke for which she had not the skill, and would have fallen had not Wilmott, now skating with Mrs. Pink, glided forward and caught her. She clung to him, laughing into his face.

"For heaven's sake, take me away," she implored, "Dr. Ramsey is a tyrant! Mrs. Pink, would you mind changing partners? Dr. Ramsey and I have had a falling-out."

"I shall be quite glad to," said Mrs. Pink. "Mr. Wilmott is too fast for me."

"It's the speed of the imbecile," said the doctor, under his breath.

The poplar trees by the river's edge now began to cast long, blue shadows across the ice. The snow, piled high at its verge, lay like ruins of some marble tower that had fallen in its first white splendor. The reddening sun lowered toward the pines. Tite and the farmer's wife were carrying about hot broth and scones, baked on the bricks. On a table, covered by a cloth of red-and-white check, were a huge jug of coffee, cups and saucers, plates mounded with cinnamon drops and plum cake. Inside the house was a bowl of punch, to be served later.

Adeline hovered near the refreshments, anxious for Wilmott's sake that all should go well. Indeed all had gone well. The innovation had been a success. The company wore an air of unaffected jollity. Most of them were gathered about the table where the cake and coffee were, but a few of the younger ones were still on the ice. One of these was young Guy Lacey who was taking lessons in figure skating from Daisy Vaughan and, with a sailor's abandon, eating a slice of plum cake at the same time. Daisy could give him her wholehearted attention, for Dr. Ramsey had taken his leave. Not long before this the children's nurse had appeared, having pushed the white sleigh brought from Quebec all the long way from Vaughanlands with Augusta and Nicholas in it. They had been greeted with delight and instantly supplied with cinnamon drops. Now the younger Busby boy was propelling them, with somewhat reckless speed, over the ice. Nero, escaped from Patsy O'Flynn, bounded joyfully at the side of the sleigh, now and again uttering a deep-throated bark.

As the punch was being drunk and pronounced excellent, Wilmott said to Adeline:—

"I think everything has gone off fairly well, don't you?"

"Everything has been perfect," she declared, looking at the snow through the redness in her glass. "I don't know when I have had a better time. And look at Philip, as blithe as a schoolboy."

"He will catch his death of cold. He should not have taken off his cap in this temperature."

Philip held his mink cap in his hand and his light brown hair stood up in moist waves. His expression was one of staunch assurance that the system under which he lived was perfect, and a serene belief that the future would hold nothing which Adeline and he could not cope with.

"Put on your cap," she called out.

He pretended not to hear.

"Your cap!" she repeated. "You'll take cold."

"Tommyrot. I never take cold."

Lydia Busby firmly possessed herself of his cap and standing on tiptoe placed it on his head, herself blushing furiously at her own temerity.

"Too far back!" cried Adeline. "It looks like a baby's bonnet."

Philip instantly assumed an expression of infantile innocence. Lydia, blushing still more, drew the cap forward on his brow.

"Horrible," declared Wilmott. "He now resembles a dancing dervish with a mop of hair in his eyes."

Philip quickly changed his expression to one of barbarous ferocity.

"Oh, Captain Whiteoak, how you frighten me!" exclaimed Lydia. She snatched the cap from his head.

"Lydia," called out her mother. "That's enough."

"Try again, Miss Lydia, try again!" urged Philip.

This time she placed it jauntily to one side.

"Will that do?" she asked.

Philip winked at her.

"Perfect!" cried Mrs. Pink. "Perfect."

"Lydia," called out Mrs. Busby. "That is enough."

But now Adeline was looking toward the gate. Two men had alighted there from a hired cutter and were paying the driver. Her eyes widened. She stared, scarcely believing their evidence. Then, as the men approached, she turned to Wilmott.

"It's Thomas D'Arcy," she said, "and Michael Brent! Whatever are they doing here?"

Wilmott gave them a look of apprehension, almost panic. "I

won't see them!" he exclaimed. "Not after what has happened. Oh, Adeline, why did you tell them about me?"

She could not answer, for the Irishmen were upon them. She hastened forward. "Don't say a word about James Wilmott's wife," she warned them, giving each a hand. "How well you both look! And what wonderful new hats. You bought them in New York, I'll be bound."

"We did indeed," said D'Arcy. "You yourself are looking superb, if I may make bold to say so."

"What luck," said Brent, "that we should arrive in time for a skating party! We can skate too. Have you some skates to spare?"

"We have just come from Niagara Falls," interrupted D'Arcy. "Superb in wintertime. Really superb. We heard the jolly noises when we arrived here and we said at once—'This is Jalna!' You see, we remember the name. So we told the driver to put us down on the spot."

They shook hands with Wilmott.

"You here too!" said Brent, with a roguish look. "What good fortune!"

"This is my own home," Wilmott returned, rather stiffly. "You are very welcome."

"Then it's not Jalna! But our luggage has been put off at your gate! Never mind, we shall carry it to Jalna."

D'Arcy said, out of the side of his mouth, to Wilmott—"We got rid of her for you. She's off to Mexico. What a tartar! I don't blame you. I'd have done the same myself."

Wilmott, with a set face, stared straight ahead.

Philip now discovered the visitors. They were provided with refreshments and, after that, with Mr. Pink's and Wilmott's skates. Wilmott and Tite went to the gate where their luggage was and carried it into the house. Philip met them there and it was decided that Wilmott could give them his room for the night and himself sleep in Tite's bed. Tite should sleep on the floor.

While they were talking Captain Lacey joined them. He declared that, if Wilmott could put the two Irishmen up for the night, they would be welcome in his house after that, for his son was leaving the next day to join his ship and it would be a good thing for himself and his wife to have such lively company to cheer them up.

XV

In Wilmott's House

THE skating party was over and the farmer's wife had, more or less, tidied up after it. Fiddling Jock had finished the punch and gone back to his hut in the woods singing "Loch Lomond" at the top of his lungs. There was bright young moonlight. The wild things came out of their burrows and there were cries of terror as the stronger seized the weaker.

It was hot inside the house, for Wilmott had heaped up the logs. The two Irishmen, Philip, Adeline and Daisy, were gathered about the fire while the travelers poured out their adventures in the States. Adeline had tried to persuade Daisy to leave with the others but it had been impossible. Daisy was in a state of high exhilaration at being part of so unconventional a gathering. D'Arcy and Brent had racy tongues. It seemed that they had done everything there was to do in New York and Chicago. They were enthusiastic about life in America. Then the conversation turned to the voyage from Ireland on the *Alanna,* the stay in Quebec. There was so much to talk of yet, all the while, Wilmott and Adeline were thinking about Henrietta. Quite suddenly Daisy exclaimed:—

"Oh, to skate in the moonlight! I have always longed to do that above all things. May I go to the river all by myself, Mr. Wilmott? It would be so mysterious, so eerie, to skate in the moonlight."

"Miss Daisy is bored by us, D'Arcy," said Brent. "We talk too much about ourselves."

"On the contrary," said his friend, "she wishes to be alone to decide which of us she loves best."

Philip passed a large white handkerchief across his forehead. "You keep your house confoundedly hot, Wilmott. I believe I shall go skating with Miss Daisy and help her make a choice—if she'll allow me."

"Oh, heavenly!" cried Daisy. "I should adore that."

Brent asked—"Can you feel mysterious and eerie skating with Captain Whiteoak?"

"We shall drift over the ice like disembodied spirits," she returned.

Wilmott looked anxiously at Philip. "I'm afraid you are taking cold," he said, and laid his fingers on Philip's wrist as though he had been a doctor.

Philip looked down at their two hands and then, rather puzzled, into Wilmott's eyes. Wilmott had a feeling of anger against the three who knew his secret. He felt that Philip was the only true and honorable one of all those in the room.

When the door had closed behind Daisy and Philip, there was silence for a space. One of the two candles on the table was sputtering. Its flame hung low and sickly. But the moonlight strengthened, throwing the outline of the windowpanes sharply on the bare floor. Wilmott got up and snuffed the candle which now burned steadily but very small.

The three from Ireland had brought some essence of their country into the room. It felt foreign to Wilmott, and himself a stranger. The others waited for him to say something.

"Among you," he said, "you have placed me in a pretty position."

"I—I don't understand. What do you mean?" asked Brent, blankly.

"I am a man who first deserted his wife and daughter and then allowed them to be sent on a fool's errand."

"Why—" said Brent, "we thought you'd be pleased."

"After what Mrs. Whiteoak had told us," put in D'Arcy—then he too stared blankly and stopped.

"It's not what we've done," said Adeline. "It's the way we have done it."

"I can look nothing but a scoundrel to anyone." Wilmott spoke bitterly.

D'Arcy ran his hand through his hair. "Now look here," he said. "I'm no bachelor. I've been separated from my wife for years. I know how you feel. Sometimes you think it may have been your fault."

"You only had to meet Mrs. Wilmott," said Brent, "to realize who is to blame in this case. I'd run around the globe to escape that woman."

"She's a terror," added D'Arcy. "You can see that. It's self—self—self with her and never stop talking."

"No man could stand it." Brent spoke in a soothing tone.

D'Arcy raised his voice. "With my wife it was a violent temper. She'd fly off the handle for next to nothing and throw things at me or at the servants."

Wilmott sat hunched up. He drew back his lips and tapped his teeth with his fingernails.

"You don't wish I had let Henrietta come here, do you, James?" asked Adeline.

"No."

"You aren't sorry I got her out of the country?"

"How can I be?"

"Then what is wrong?"

"Everything."

"Don't imagine we did not treat her in a gentlemanlike way," said Brent. "We were most considerate."

"It was a lark to you!" exclaimed Wilmott.

"It was no lark at all," said Brent. "We took it very seriously. We were considerate but firm."

"You sent her on a fool's errand to a half-civilized country!"

"Mexico was civilized," said D'Arcy, "long before this part of the country. And I think that the lady really wanted to see it."

"The trouble with Wilmott is that he has too lively a conscience," put in Brent.

"No, it's not that," said Wilmott, "but what I did was a thing that should be kept secret in a man's own mind. When you bring it out into the light it looks much worse. It looks like a crime, which I suppose it really is."

"I understand"—D'Arcy spoke patiently—"that you gave your

wife practically all you have. You certainly are not living in luxury here. All you deny her is your presence."

To this Brent added—"And to judge from all she said, you didn't make her happy when you were with her."

"No—far from it."

Adeline's eyes were large and gentle as they rested on Wilmott, but it was to the others she spoke.

"What the poor man needs is a drink. He is tired after his party and all. Is there nothing but that little drop of punch in the house?"

The three looked at Wilmott as though he were an invalid. He felt hypnotized. D'Arcy rose and tiptoed to the cupboard. His shadow on the wall was enormous. He brought out a bottle more than half full of rum. He held it at arm's length and looked through it at the candle flame. They could hear Daisy laughing on the river.

"There are tumblers on the shelf," said Wilmott, as though he *were* an invalid.

"Will you have a taste of spirits, Mrs. Whiteoak?" asked D'Arcy.

"No, no, thank you. I shall finish the punch."

Wilmott took a drink and began to laugh. "It's all rather funny," he said. "It's as though we were in the cabin of the *Alanna* again. Only that outside there is a sea of snow."

"Thank God we are here and not there," said Adeline.

There was silence except for the soft flapping of a flame against a log. Then Brent spoke. "Wherever I go I find life amusing. I may be sad for a little but I am soon amused again."

"I am the same," said Wilmott.

D'Arcy refilled his glass. "I am never greatly amused or greatly sad. I am critical, analytical, and philosophic."

"I am the same," said Adeline.

When the skaters came in, Nero bounded after them. He stood in the middle of the room and shook himself, sending out a snow shower. Then he laid the side of his face on the floor and pushed it rapidly first in one direction, then in another.

"He is like an elephant in the room," said Wilmott. "When I get a dog it must be a small one I can tuck under my arm. Did I tell you that Tite has a pet raccoon?"

Philip and Daisy had cheeks like roses after the cold air. Their eyes were bright and they had some joke between them. Both refused anything to drink.

"I am starving," Daisy said, unwinding yards of pale blue crocheted scarf from about her neck. "I had nothing but a piece of plum cake and a cup of coffee."

"I'm enormously hungry also," said Philip. "Have you a cold game pie in your larder, Wilmott? And some bottles of stout?"

Nero lay down at Adeline's feet and began to lick the snow from his great paws.

"He's no less than a snowdrift beside you," exclaimed Wilmott. He sprang up and dragged Nero in front of the fire. Nero gave him a long, puzzled, mournful look, then returned to the licking of his paws.

Wilmott bent over Philip. "I have nothing in the house," he said, "but a side of bacon, some eggs from my own hens, some cold boiled potatoes and a jar of apple butter."

"A meal fit for a prince," said Philip. "Daisy and I shall cook it."

Adeline thought—"Miss Daisy when they went out to skate—Daisy when they come back. I wish she'd settle down to chasing only one man."

Daisy arranged her ringlets on her shoulders. "This is the happiest day of my life," she said. "If you knew how conventional it's been you would understand. But now I've left all that behind. I'm a pioneer! If I heard a wolf howling outside I'd not be afraid. I'd just take that gun and go out and shoot him."

A long-drawn howl sounded mournfully somewhere in the darkness. Daisy shrieked and threw herself into Philip's arms. Nero rose trembling.

The men stared at each other, waiting for the next howl. It came—nearer, louder. Adeline gave a hysterical laugh. Wilmott threw open the door into the kitchen. Tite stood there, slim and dark, his mouth open, shaping another howl.

"You young rapscallion!" said Adeline. "You ought to be flogged." But she laughed naturally now.

When the Irishmen understood, they were disappointed. It was hard to persuade them that Tite had given those realistic howls. "Do it again!" they cried, like boys. Wilmott looked sternly at Tite.

"No—no!" cried Daisy. "I can't bear it!" She made wide eyes from Philip's shoulder.

Brent took the gun from the wall. "Here, Miss Daisy," he said, "let us see you shoot him. Remember your boast." He put the gun into her hand.

With sudden swagger she grasped it. There was a loud explosion. The ball entered the wall above Tite's head. Philip gave Daisy an astonished look and took the gun from her. "That's enough from you, young woman," he said. "Behave yourself."

She stood with her breast heaving and her eyes defiant. "I'm not one to be challenged and not take it."

"Did the lady mean to kill me?" asked Tite.

Wilmott went into the kitchen and closed the door behind him. He said sternly:—

"Never do such a thing again. You have frightened those ladies terribly."

"But the Mees Daisy one wanted to hear a wolf howl and I can do it so well."

"You were listening at the door, Tite."

"Yes. I was wondering if you want something before I go to bed. Did the Mees Daisy one want to kill me?"

"No, no, she was overexcited."

"Boss," Tite spoke in a low voice, "do you think she is a harlot? She told me I had long eyelashes and a mouth like a pomegranate flower. Now I repeated this to my grandmother and she says Mees Daisy is a harlot. But since then she has tried to kill me, so perhaps she is reformed."

"Bring out the bacon, the eggs, and the cold potatoes," ordered Wilmott. "God knows what we shall have left to eat to-morrow."

"Another time," continued Tite stubbornly, "she said my neck was like a bronze statue's and I told my grandmother and my grandmother said again she is a harlot."

XVI

Progress of the Season

THERE were no more hospitable people in the neighborhood than the Laceys. Their house was not large but their hearts were. They liked gaiety and movement about them and the two Irishmen satisfied their liking in an extraordinary degree. They were almost always gay and they seldom were still. They settled down for a long visit with the Laceys. They had been traveling so long that they were glad of the change to this backwater. Their expenses had been heavy; they were glad to pay in the coin of good fellowship. Not that they did nothing to make themselves useful. When heavy snowfalls came in midwinter, they armed themselves with shovels and dug the Laceys out, with speed and efficiency. They went over icy roads to the town to shop for Mrs. Lacey and brought her presents of Scotch marmalade and German cheese and French wine. D'Arcy played chess with Captain Lacey and Brent read aloud from the works of Thackeray and Sir Walter Scott.

Wilmott's skating party had started the ball rolling and that winter saw more dancing, skating and charades, than the neighborhood had ever before known. On Sunday, unless a blizzard were blowing, everybody turned out to attend the church service in the village eight miles away. In rough weather this often was a hardship. Feet and legs would be numb with cold, faces half-frozen. But the Whiteoaks found the climate mild as compared to that of Quebec. Here zero weather was thought to be very cold indeed. *There* twenty below zero had been accepted as no more than winter's due.

Before long it was seen by all that Kate Busby had transferred her interest from Wilmott to Brent. Before long her interest amounted to attachment. It was said that Brent himself was smitten. By the time February had arrived it was obvious that he was smitten. At a St. Valentine's party given by the Pinks he proposed, and so novel was the manner of his proposal that the entire community was startled by it. Mrs. Pink's ingenuity and originality in entertaining her guests were endless. On this occasion a small gift or favor was laid by the plate of each. These were in the shape of hearts cut from red flannel. Beneath these were attached several other hearts, cut from white flannel and the whole held together by rosettes of red and white wool. In the case of the ladies, bright new needles were stuck in the white hearts, thus converting them into a needlebook. In the case of the gentlemen, a fine new goose feather was thrust through the rosette, only needing to be sharpened to the required point for a pen. And there was the penwiper!

On the spot and before he would eat a mouthful, Brent took out his penknife and sharpened the quill to a long graceful point. He then got possession of Kate's needlebook. After the meal he disappeared into another room and when he came back restored it to her—but how changed, how glorified! He had cut out a heart from a sheet of notepaper and fixed it among the white flannel hearts. On it he had written:—

To My Valentine

Dearest Kate
I ask no better fate
Than that the rest of my life should be with
you spent.
Your adoring
Michael Brent

His intentions were of the best. If Kate would not live in Ireland he would settle down to live in Ontario. The one obstacle to their marriage was religion. Elihu Busby would not give his consent to his daughter's union with a Catholic. Every man in that group of friends tried his hand at persuading him—they all liked Brent—but to no avail.

The weather was so severe in February that work on the building of Jalna all but ceased, though the sound of a lonely hammer or saw preserved the sense of continuity. The felling of trees still went on in full swing of axe. The noble growth of fifty years was felled, dismembered, and neatly piled in as many minutes. The men made great fires, partly to warm themselves by, partly to get rid of the wood. In heedless extravagance they heaped the finest oak, maple, and pine on the blaze; just as the deer hunters farther north would kill five deer where one would have sufficed and left the surplus carcasses to rot, just as the wild fowl were shot down in mad excess of need, and the singing birds for pleasure.

Adeline expected her child in April and her most cherished hope was to be established in her own home before the birth. In February, with the almost cessation of work, she saw this hope fade. Long ago the architect, the contractor, and the foreman had promised that the house would be ready by April the first. She had never doubted the fulfillment of that promise. When doubt and disappointment crowded in on her she was in despair. One might have thought, as Philip said, that her life and the life of the child depended on the removal. To which, with her head buried in the pillows of her bed, she replied that it was probably so. He said that, if anyone had reason to be worried, it was he. Sitting up, with blazing eyes, she demanded what he had to worry about. In terse language he told her. They forgot they were visiting and quarreled with the abandon of people who have been snowbound for a week and are frustrated in all their plans. They raised their voices and tried to talk each other down. Mrs. Vaughan in the room below, could hear them and was mortified for them. Daisy, just outside their door, was so fiercely on Philip's side that she could barely refrain from rushing in and taking part.

Mrs. Vaughan, in her restrained way, was almost as deeply disappointed in the delay as Adeline. The thought of having a birth in the house was terribly upsetting. It was so long since she herself had been confined that the complications of such an event seemed unbelievable. What, for instance, was she to do with Robert who at that time would be home from his university? Certainly he must be sent away somewhere and her pleasure in his vacation ruined. Then there was Daisy. There seemed no prospect of her visit ending for some months to come. In truth, Mrs. Vaughan felt fairly certain that nothing save marriage would remove Daisy from the family circle. She had settled herself far too comfortably into it. Her behavior had not shown the propriety which Mrs. Vaughan would have liked. Indeed she had more than once been driven to speak to Daisy because of the lack of delicacy she showed in her pursuit of Dr. Ramsey. He dropped in several times each week to see Adeline and, on his way in or out, Daisy was certain to waylay him. She was knitting an immense muffler for him and this had to be tried on. The doctor surrendered himself to this operation with a rather grim grace but he did surrender, and Mrs. Vaughan could not help thinking that in his heart he enjoyed it though what could be more futile than to attempt to make a *muffler* fit?

The thing that worried Mrs. Vaughan about Daisy was that she appeared to be not only after Dr. Ramsey alone. When the doctor was with Adeline, Daisy was certain to be with Philip, if he were in the house. In these days, Adeline felt a weariness on her and retired early to bed. Daisy always manoeuvred to sit up with Philip who did not care when he went to bed. She would go with him over the snowdrifts on snowshoes which she had been given at Christmas, to visit Jalna. When Adeline was present, Daisy was circumspection itself but when Adeline was not there, Daisy directed almost all her conversation to Philip, and laughed a good deal. Mrs. Vaughan had tried hard to love Daisy but had not succeeded. She was critical of Adeline but could not help loving her.

Even more than she loved their mother, Mrs. Vaughan loved the children. They grew more charming every day, she thought, yet they filled the house with their noise and the confusion of their living. Nicholas was developing a temper and when he was frustrated would make the echoes ring with his screams of rage.

Then when things were at their gloomiest, March came in like a lamb. It did not come in like an ordinary lamb but as a gay, sweetly gamboling lamb whose bleat was the gurgle of running water, whose eyes shone like summer stars, whose tail flicked all care aside. In short the weather was unseasonably warm. But now the work on Jalna boomed and buzzed. The workmen rose early and worked late. Things which it seemed never would happen took place in the twinkling of an eye. Plaster was slapped on. Window glass was puttied in. Doorknobs and locks were screwed into place. The spindles and rail of the banister miraculously appeared and, at the foot of the stairs, the carved newel post, smooth as satin with its clustering grapes and their leaves. The men sang as they worked. The hot sun beat down on the roof and blazed in at the new windows. Great clouds of migratory birds passed overhead. The earth was teeming with vitality. The melting of the snow had been so quickly accomplished that the stream had been fed beyond control. It raged through the ravine, sweeping away the bridge of logs and carrying it to the lake. Wilmott's river was in spate also. One night it came to his very door and he began to pack his books. He dared not to go to bed but remained watching. Every now and again he would open the door and, holding a lantern above his head, survey the threatening flood. But by sunrise it had a little subsided and by noon his books were again on their shelves.

It was a great day for Philip and Adeline when a van, drawn by four horses, stopped in front of the door of Jalna. Here was their furniture at last! Here were the painted leather bedstead they had brought from India, and the chest of drawers with its ornate brass trimmings, the cabinet and the packing case full of jade, ivory, and silver ornaments to grace it. Here were the rugs that had taken generations of work to make, the draperies with delicate embroidery; here were the very scents and sounds of India! Here were the delicate Chippendale chairs and tables given Philip by his sister, the Empire sofa they had brought from Quebec, the massive wardrobe they had bought in London! Here the Irish silver and linen given by Lady Honoria! Here the old life in the new!

March had only three more days to go, and still it was gentle. If only Adeline might have her own room in order—the rest of the house could wait—so that her child might be born in peace under her own roof! Day and night she strained toward this object. She could scarcely sleep for the planning in her head and the weariness of her body. The thought of time became palpable to her, as an antagonistic something with which she was running a race. Once, in the middle of the night, she pictured the unborn child as timekeeper in this race. She pictured him as a little gnome sitting cross-legged with a gold watch in his hand. At this fancy she burst out laughing.

"What's the matter?" exclaimed Philip starting up.

"I laughed—so that I should not cry."

"Nonsense. Why should you cry?"

"I'd better be dead than go through all I have to go through."

"Now, Adeline, behave yourself and think of all our mercies," he said, for something to say.

"Do you count yourself one of them?"

"Assuredly."

"Then you count one too many."

He raised himself on his elbow and looked down at her. Bright moonlight was shining through the window into his face. His sister, Augusta, had sent him an embroidered nightcap and it was perched jauntily on one side of his head.

"Oh, Philip, you look enchanting!" she exclaimed. She drew down his head and kissed him.

"Now you must settle yourself and go to sleep," he said, patting her shoulder.

She sighed. "I think I might if the window were open."

"You know very well the doctor has warned you most particularly against night air, since you had whooping cough."

"Oh, do let us have it open, just a tiny way!"

He got up grumbling a little and opened the window a few inches. Then he drew a chair between her and the window and spread her great, flounced petticoat across it.

"There," he said with satisfaction, "that will keep the draught off you."

"Oh, thank you, Phil," she said, breathing deeply. "How sweet the night air is! What a pity it should be so dangerous!" She snuggled down.

The petticoat did not keep the night air off Philip. He could feel it fanning his cheek in the most disagreeable way. But he did not like to change his position for fear of disturbing Adeline. He began to be miserable. He was not afraid of what the night air would do to him. He just did not like it.

Finally he solved the problem by pulling his nightcap right down over his eyes, down over his uppermost cheek, till he was sheltered but still could breathe.

April came in wild and windy. The wind, discovering the five tall new chimneys, blew down them, shrieked and roared through them, as though they were outlet enough for all its energy. The new doors slammed and banged; shavings of wood blew in all directions; workmen whistled at the top of their lungs; one of them was blown from the top of a ladder and might have been killed but was scarcely hurt. The furniture was uncrated and the canvas wrappings removed. Rugs were heaped in corners. The great painted bedstead, with its design of rich-colored flowers and fruit, through which the forms of birds and monkeys could be glimpsed, was set up in the principal bedroom. Fifty times a day Nero went upstairs and down, overseeing all.

With the furniture from Uncle Nicholas's house in Quebec had come the grand piano. It was delivered in a wagon by itself. When it arrived there was so much else to be done that it was decided to unload it and let it stand in its case, covered by tarpaulin, till men could be spared for the handling of such a load. The wagon was backed toward a convenient spot near the ravine. But the ground still was icy in the shade. The wagon wheels began to slip. The whole great weight began to move backward into the ravine, dragging the horses with it. Philip and Adeline looked on with dismay on his part, horror on hers. In another moment the plunging horses would be over the edge.

"Loose the traces!" Philip shouted.

Adeline shrieked—"Loose the traces!"

Two men sprang forward. Massive shapes strove together above the ravine. The driver leaped from his seat in time to save himself. The heavy draught horses moved forward lightly, free of their load which crashed inexorably to the stream. It broke off branches and young trees as it fell, then came to rest supported by two boulders, so that it was not actually in the water.

"By the Lord Harry," said Philip, "that was a close shave!"

"I'll bet that pianner is bust to bits," said a man with a red neckerchief. "Nobody'll never play on it no more."

All but the driver ran through the icy slush to look down at the piano. It had been made in France, crossed the ocean, stood for many years in the drawing-room of the house in the Rue St. Louis, traveled by barge, boat, and wagon to this place and now lay, dumb and disgraced at the bottom of the ravine.

"Can we get it up, do you think?" asked Adeline, still white from the shock.

"It'll take four horses to haul it up and it'll fall to pieces on the way," said the man who had spoken before.

"Certainly we shall raise it," said Philip comfortingly to Adeline. "You will play 'The Harp that Once thro' Tara's Halls,' on it yet." He turned to the man with the red neckerchief. "It was you who directed the driver. Otherwise the piano would not be where it is. Now you say it can't be raised whole. I don't want men like you working on my place. Ask the foreman for your money. You're discharged."

The man stared at him. "The foreman engaged me," he said. "It's for him to discharge me. Not you."

Philip took him by the red neckerchief. "I have a mind," he said, "to throw you down on top of the piano." He gave him a hearty push. "Now, go, and be quick about it." The man skulked off.

All the rest of the day Adeline felt shaken. Her knees trembled as she hastened to and from the bedroom she was preparing. They had chosen the room at the end of the hall behind the drawing-room as their own; cool in summer and warm in winter, far from the noise of the children. A servant had been engaged, the daughter of a farm laborer, who followed Adeline about, getting in her way rather than helping her. The girl could neither read nor write. Her incompetence and stupidity were a marvel to Adeline but she was good-natured and strong as an ox.

A married couple, the man a trained gardener and the woman a good cook, were on their way from Devon. They had been engaged by Philip's sister and it was hoped that they would be installed in the house before the time of Adeline's confinement, a fortnight or more hence. Their bedroom, comfortably furnished in the basement, awaited them. They were bringing with them a supply of kitchen utensils and garden tools such as they had been accustomed to. Adeline wished with all her heart that they were at Jalna, as she strove to bring some slight order out of the chaos which surrounded her. Everywhere she went the girl, Lizzie, followed her, tripping over the litter on the floor, dropping things, exclaiming at the wonders from India.

"Sakes alive!" she said, pointing to the painted bedstead. "Is that there to sleep in?"

"Yes. Draw the mattress toward you. It's not on straight."

"Land sakes, I'd have bad dreams if I slept in it."

"I dare say. Now help me to open this chest."

"What's them things all over it?"

"Dragons."

"They look heathenish."

"They are."

"Your furniture don't look like Christian furniture."

"It isn't. What have you dropped now?"

"It looks like a doll."

The small porcelain figure had been wrapped in a piece of Eastern embroidery which the girl had taken from the chest. Adeline snatched it up from the floor. She examined it anxiously. "Thank God," she exclaimed, "it isn't broken! If you had broken that, my girl, I'd have made an end of you." She held the porcelain figure tenderly in her hands. It was the goddess, Kuan Yin.

"Is it a doll?" asked Lizzie.

"It is a Chinese goddess. Oh, how beautiful and wise she is! How glad I am she wasn't broken! See her sweet hands and her little feet like flowers!"

"She looks comic," said Lizzie.

"I wish I could put you down in China for five years, Lizzie, and see what would happen to you."

Lizzie giggled. "Perhaps I'd come back looking like that there," she said.

Adeline set the goddess on the mantelpiece. "There I shall place her," she said, "to guard this room. She shall stay there always."

"It's sinful to worship images," said Lizzie. "My pa wouldn't let me work for folks that worship images."

"Well, when you next see him, you can tell him I say my prayers to this one. It will be fun to see what happens."

"I won't do that, ma'am. I want to stay here."

"Good for you, Lizzie! Now gather up some of the paper and shavings from the hall and lay a fire here. It's very cold."

"You don't look cold," observed Lizzie. "Your cheeks is red as if you had the fever." She crammed paper and shavings tightly into the grate.

"No, no, not that way, Lizzie!" Adeline was worn-out by the

girl's stupidity but she liked her. She wondered what the well-trained Devon servants would make of her.

Mrs. Pink came in later to see what she could do to help but her admiration for what was already unpacked, and her shock over the disaster to the piano, took most of her energy. Mr. Pink called for her and he too joined in the inspection and condolence. Still later Philip came, accompanied by Captain Lacey, Thomas D'Arcy, and Michael Brent. It was like a party. Philip tore down to the wine cellar where already a case of wine was installed and brought up a bottle of Madeira. Wine glasses were discovered. Wilmott appeared and at once said that he knew the proper method for rescuing the piano from the ravine and that if he had been there it never would have fallen. Adeline was suddenly gay and full of confidence. When she and Philip drove back to Vaughanlands, she felt strong and hopeful of having everything in order before the arrival of her child. It was disgraceful, Mrs. Vaughan thought, the way Adeline laced herself though, after all, who could blame her, considering how she was exposed to public view? Her condition might well pass unnoticed, so small was her waist, so voluminous her skirts.

When Adelinc woke in the dawn with a mild rain pattering on the roof and the song of a chickadee coming from the maple tree outside the window, she had a startled feeling as though someone had put a hand on her and roughly disturbed her. She lay very still, her heart beating quickly. She lay waiting, her wide-open eyes fixed on the window, pale in the early light.

Then she felt the touch again. It was a sharp pain that stabbed her very vitals. She was filled with apprehension. Was this the warning of her confinement? Was she to be caught here, be forced to have her child where she was determined not to have it? Sweat broke out on her forehead. She gave a little moan.

Then she felt better. Probably it was a false alarm. She had had others in her time. But she would take no risks. Let Philip oppose her as he might, she would sleep that night in her own house! She lay planning each step of the day. After a while she slept.

When she woke it was still gently raining. Though the unseasonable heat was gone, there was a feeling of spring in the air. She found that Philip had dressed. The house was very quiet. She had slept late. At breakfast there were only herself and Daisy. The men had gone out and Mrs. Vaughan was not well. She had come down, had a cup of tea and been forced to return to her bed. She was subject to severe headaches.

Daisy talked volubly. The subject which enthralled her at the moment was the love affair between Kate Busby and Michael Brent. In her opinion, Kate should defy her father and elope with her lover. She herself had counseled Kate to do this. Did not Adeline think she was right? After all what was there in life greater than sincere attachment?

Adeline was somewhat taciturn. She ate oatmeal porridge, cold ham and several sausages, with expedition. Then she went to Mrs. Vaughan's bedroom door and tapped.

"Come in." Mrs. Vaughan spoke in the tone of one who had prayed to be left alone.

Adeline came to the side of the bed. "It is a pity you are feeling so ill," she said.

"Oh, I shall be all right. You know I have these miserable times."

"Yes. 'T is a pity. I myself am not too well. I had a heavy pain at dawn."

Mrs. Vaughan was startled. "Do you mean—oh, surely your pains aren't coming on yet! You told me the third week in April!"

"Yes. That's when it's due. But I think I shall make haste and get under my own roof to-day."

"No, no, you must stay where you are. You must take things quietly. We can manage."

Suddenly Adeline knelt down and took Mrs. Vaughan into her strong arms and kissed her.

"You are so kind," she said. "How can I ever repay you!"

"Then you'll stay?" asked Mrs. Vaughan faintly.

"No. I have a fancy to have my child at Jalna."

"But those pains!"

"Oh, I warrant I shall hold out till the third week in April."

Mrs. Vaughan burst into tears of relief, mingled with real affection.

"I am very fond of you," she said, "much fonder than I am of Daisy."

Adeline gave a little laugh. "Who wouldn't be?" she said.

As she passed the children's room she heard them prattling at their play. They were all right. No need to worry about them. She went to her own room, found a portmanteau and began to pack it with toilet articles. To them she added two nightdresses, heavily trimmed with embroidery and stiff with tucks from collar to hem, and a red velvet peignoir. She felt a little giddy and sat back on her heels to collect herself. It took some time.

Was there anything else she should take? Yes, the silver flask of brandy they had on shipboard. She found it in Philip's top drawer. She shook it. It was quite half-full. Another pain struck her, tearing at her like a wild beast. She gave a cry, then pressed her hands over her mouth. She ground her teeth together. She would not give in. She would have her baby in her own bed.

The pain passed. She groped in the wardrobe for her bonnet and cloak. As she was putting them on she remembered that she had not ordered the horse and buggy to be brought to the door. She saw Patsy O'Flynn crossing the lawn and opened her window and called out to him:—

"Patsy-Joe, bring round the gray horse and buggy. If ever you moved quickly in your life move quickly now. Just throw the harness on to the beast and gallop back to the house."

"What's up, yer honor, Miss?"

"I'll tell you later. Hurry—hurry! Run!"

Patsy-Joe ran to the stable, swinging his arms like flails to propel himself. When he returned it was obvious that he had thrown the harness on the horse. He met Adeline with a wild look. His sandy whiskers stood out on either side of his thin face. He snatched the portmanteau from her hand and hurled it into the buggy.

"Run to the parlor," she said, "and fetch Boney! He must not be left."

Patsy-Joe flung himself into the house and flung out again, the bird cage swinging from his hand. Boney, hilarious at this sudden break in the boredom of his present life, hung head downward from the top of his cage, uttering cries of delight. In his travels he had learned the word "good-bye" and he now screamed it repeatedly though without any accent of affection or gratitude.

"Good-bye—good-bye—good-bye!" he screamed, and his mouth curved upward beneath his dark beak.

Tremblingly Adeline climbed into the buggy. The parrot's cries had made the old horse restive and he rolled his eyes and tried to move forward and backward simultaneously. Adeline caught up the reins. "My baby will be coming before long," she said.

"Be quate, will you?" cried Patsy-Joe to the horse, putting in the portmanteau and the bird cage. "D'ye want to put me lady on to the gravel, you brute?" He scrambled to the seat beside Adeline. "Och, Miss Adeline, yer honor, I can see by the look in yer eyes that you have great pain in you and no wonder, the way you have run up and down thim stairs and lugged great armfuls of linen about! 'T is himself will be vexed with you for lavin' Misthress Vaughan's house when naught is ready at Jalna." He looked anxiously into her face. "But don't worry. I'll get ye there in good time."

"You must not breathe a word of this to anyone till I tell you. I feel better now. Drive fast but be careful of the ruts." She took the cage on to her lap to steady it. Patsy had put up the buggy top so she was sheltered from the rain that fell like a silver veil from the dim gray sky.

Patsy set the portmanteau and the bird cage on the bed in Adeline's room. "Shall I unpack the bags fer ye, Miss?" he asked, bending over and peering into her face. She had dropped panting into a chair. Loud hammering resounded through the house. It beat cruelly on her nerves. She said "Tell them to stop the hammering, Patsy-Joe. Say that my head aches. Just that. Nothing more, mind. Then find Lizzie and send her to me. Tell her to come at once. Then drive to the Rectory and ask Mrs. Pink if she will come back with you. She'll understand."

"I will. I'll be back with her before you know it, Miss. Hadn't I better fetch the doctor or the midwife if himself is out? Sure you'll need all the help you can get."

"Not yet. I have things to do."

"But can ye wait?"

"Yes. Run along, Patsy."

"Hadn't I better fetch the masther?"

"No, no. Do just what I have told you."

He gave her a look of concentrated assurance of his capacity, so intense as to be comic. Then he tiptoed heavily from the room and clumped along the hall. In a moment the hammering ceased. She heard the sound of horses' hoofs and the rattle of the buggy. Now all was silent except for the quiet drip of rain from the roof. Adeline drew a long quivering breath of relief. She sat with arms outstretched in her lap, relaxing her nerves, resting.

Now she heard Lizzie coming up the basement stairs.

"I was just on my way here," she said, "when I met Mr. O'Flynn. He told me you are kind of sick. Shall I make you a cup of tea, ma'am?"

"Yes. I'd like a cup of tea. Build the fire up quickly and put on the big copper of water to heat."

"Do you want this floor scrubbed and the window cleaned right now, ma'am?"

"No. Yes—you had better clean the window. I'll find curtains and we'll hang them. We're preparing for a confinement, Lizzie." She smiled a little maliciously at the girl.

"Land's sakes alive!" Lizzie almost screamed. "I haven't had no experience with them. I'm not twenty yet. You can't expect me to know. I'd be scared to death."

"I don't expect anything of you except to do what you are told. The doctor will be here. There is plenty of time. Now—make the tea and put on the water to heat."

Lizzie clattered down the stairs, almost beside herself from excitement. Adeline felt strong and capable. She opened the linen chest and took out sheets and blankets. When Lizzie returned they made the bed together. Adeline chose two small rugs from the mound in the hall and laid them on the floor of the bedroom. Lizzie cleaned and polished the window and, as they had no curtain rings or rods, they tacked up as a curtain a piece of Indian embroidery. Adeline fortified herself with strong tea. All the while she talked cheerfully to Lizzie who gave her frequent looks of apprehension. Now the room looked really habitable. Adeline could have sung for joy to think she was in it—safe under her own roof.

At last Mrs. Pink appeared in the doorway.

"Oh, how nice—how very nice!" she exclaimed. Then added—"From what your man tells me, you're not feeling very well. Really I think you are running a great risk in working to the last minute."

"Would you want to have your baby in another person's house with a young lad just coming home from college?"

"No, indeed. I don't blame you. But this is much sooner than you expected, isn't it?"

"Yes. I'm afraid I've been overdoing it. Then there was the piano taking that tumble—I thought the horses were going over, too—it gave me quite a start."

"Dr. Ramsey was not at home but his housekeeper will send him here as soon as he returns."

More tea was made. Mrs. Pink busied herself unpacking the portmanteau, laying Adeline's toilet articles on the dressing table. The figure of Kuan Yin caught her eye. "How pretty!" she said. "It's Chinese, isn't it?"

"Yes. The goddess Kuan Yin. She has promised to look after me."

Adeline spoke with such an air of sincerity that Mrs. Pink was startled.

"Oh, Mrs. Whiteoak, you're joking, aren't you?"

"Well, I think there's a good deal in those Eastern religions."

"Still, I don't think Christians should countenance them, do you?"

"God has countenanced them for a good many centuries, hasn't He?"

"His ways are beyond our understanding, my husband says."

Adeline moved restlessly about the room, then turned sharply to Mrs. Pink. "I think Philip had better be sent for. It is well to be on the safe side."

Mrs. Pink hurried out. She sent one of the men to fetch Philip, then went down to the kitchen to see that Lizzie had preparations in progress. Adeline was alone when Philip came to her. He gave an astonished look about the room and at the freshly made bed where her nightdress and peignoir were laid out.

"What's this?" he demanded.

"I've moved in." She smiled up at him.

"The house is not ready and won't be for another ten days. You can't do it."

"I have done it. It's accomplished." She surveyed what she had done with satisfaction. "Oh, Philip, dear, you'd not want me to have my baby at Vaughanlands, would you?"

"It's not due till the end of the month."

She spoke in a small voice. "I think it is coming to-day. I have sent Patsy for the doctor."

"Good God!" he exclaimed, his blue eyes prominent.

"You wouldn't want me to be out of my own bed, would you, Philip? I've had a time of it to get everything ready, I can tell you. But doesn't it look nice?"

"Very nice," he answered grimly.

Mrs. Pink returned to ask Adeline how she was.

"Better. I shall be all right for hours, I expect. Should you like to go home to see your little boy?"

"If you think you can spare me." She turned to Philip. "My youngest has a gathering in his ear. I am keeping hearts of hot roast onions in it. I can't trust the servant to do it. The doctor will be here any moment, I'm sure, and I shall not be gone long."

Philip went to drive her to the Rectory. Adeline was alone but she did not mind. She was supremely happy. There, under her own roof, with the rain pattering lightly on it, she awaited her ordeal with more of pride than fear. She was in her own house. From now on she would do what she liked. Oh, how she loved the house! It spoke to her, as though in a deep reassuring voice. It resolved itself from the chaos of building and took shape as a home about her. Echoes of footsteps sounded through it, footsteps to come; unborn voices called out to her, not only the voice of the child to whom she was about to give birth but of her children's children. She would spend all her days here. She and the house would have many secrets together. The house would teem with life, with emotion. It would hold all together inside its walls, over which in time vines and their leaves would grow.

XVII

Springtime at Jalna

PHILIP said, and said it from the bottom of his heart, that he hoped and prayed Adeline would never have another child. To say nothing of her sufferings and the risk to her life, it was too hard on him. He felt a nervous wreck after this last. The doctor had been so long in coming that it looked as though the infant might be born without his assistance. The midwife had never arrived, being engaged in another confinement. It seemed for a time that Philip and Mrs. Pink would be Adeline's sole support. At the mere thought of such a contingency, a cold sweat broke out on him. Adeline had more than her share of endurance but, for some reason, her self-control deserted her and she cried out with every pain. Time and again she declared that she was dying. When Dr. Ramsey came at last she faced him with defiance and momentary calm. Before he did anything for her relief he told her his opinion of her actions of the morning. In half an hour the child was born.

Though Adeline had gone through so much, her recovery was quick. This was probably because of her great content. The weather too became sunny and warm. All about her, indoors and out, the work went forward. There was jubilation among the workmen at the news of the birth in the new house. To the best of their ability they did their work quietly. When the infant was ten days old, Philip carried him out to show him to them. He was a smaller, weaker child than Nicholas had been but he had pretty features, an exquisite skin, and his eyes were like forget-me-nots. The woodsmen, horny-handed and unkempt, crowded about him. They were pleased by the fineness of his long white robe and the little lace cap he wore. He looked up at them reflectively, placing the finger tips of one hand against those of the other.

Philip was delighted because he was the first of his children to show a resemblance to his own family. Adeline, with him on the pillow beside her, would study the small face and declare that, though his coloring was Philip's, his features never would be. There was some discussion over his name. Philip chose Charles, his own father's name. Adeline chose Dennis as the name least aggressively her father's. Certainly, she declared, she would never name him after their doctor, as she had Nicholas after her loved Dr. St. Charles. But they could not decide which of his names he should go by. Each disliked the choice of the other. "Charles is a stern name," she affirmed.

"Nonsense," said Philip. "It's as agreeable a name as there is. Dennis sounds like a comical Irish story."

"You just show your bad feeling when you say such a thing," she retorted. " 'T is a grand name!"

But the problem was settled by a book Wilmott sent her. It was *Ernest Maltravers,* by Lord Lytton. Adeline had not read halfway through the book before she cried—"His name shall be Ernest!"

Philip had to acknowledge that the name was a good one and Wilmott, when he came to see the infant, said that nothing could be more suitable and expressive of the tiny personality. So he was named, Ernest Charles Dennis, but continued to be called Baby, for some time.

Philip's heart glowed with pride when he sat by Adeline's bed and saw her propped on the pillows, the week-old infant snuggled in the curve of her arm, the two older children perched beside them. Adeline's pallor brought out the superb contours of the bones of her face which would, even in age, be arresting. Her hair, massed on the pillow, made a striking background. Her white arms curved about her children with maternal satisfaction.

The children had been brought from Vaughanlands by their nurse to inspect their baby brother for the first time. Augusta, now three years of age, sat decorously at the infant's feet, her hands crossed in her lap, her eyes fixed in wonder on his pink face. Nicholas however was more excited by the painting on the head of the bed. The brilliant flowers and fruit with their strange sensuous beauty filled him with delight. He bounced on his plump behind, his hands now clasped ecstatically beneath his chin, now stretched out to grasp them. He laughed and shouted.

"Dr. Ramsey says," remarked Adeline, "that I might have a child every year without harm, if only I would take care of myself."

"Not one more," said Philip, "unless Ramsey promises to sit on our doorstep for the last month. In any case, three is enough. We have a daughter to comfort our old age. We have two sons, so we are certain of an heir. Surely you don't want more!"

"No. Three is enough."

He folded his arms on his broad chest. "I have made up my mind to one thing, Adeline. This boy, Ernest, shall be christened in our own church. Of course, you know that Pink and I have talked a good deal of the desirability of a church in the neighborhood. You remember what we went through last winter in discomfort in those long drives to the service. Now I am willing to give the land for a church and we might, with a great deal of effort, raise a fund sufficient for a poor-looking edifice. But I want a substantial church to sit in on a Sunday and, if I am to be by far the largest subscriber, I say that I might as well build the place myself. Then I shall have it as I want it and no bickering."

"It would take a lot of money just to build one little church."

"Adeline, that church will provide for your spiritual needs for the rest of your life, and for these children after you. That is not a little thing, is it?"

"You have the Church in your blood," she said. "I haven't."

"But you would like to *own* a church, wouldn't you?"

"It would be heavenly. If I didn't like the clergyman I should just put him out."

"Oh, you couldn't do that! But—you would have a good deal of influence."

"But, if it were *my* church, I could," she said stubbornly.

"Once the church is consecrated it is under the jurisdiction of the bishop of the diocese."

The dimple flashed in her cheek. "I should attend to the bishop."

Their talk had been punctuated by Nicholas's shouts. Now he

became too noisy to ignore. He crept to the head of the bed to kiss the grinning face of a monkey that peered between bright blossoms. He knelt on his mother's hair.

"Young rascal!" exclaimed Philip, picking him up and setting him on his knee. He took out his great gold watch and held it to Nicholas's ear.

"Ga—ga—ga—ga!" shouted Nicholas, his eyes dancing like stars.

"You see," said Philip, "the time is as propitious as ever it will be for building a church. I have the men on the spot. I have the money to spare. Large amounts of material left over from the building of the house and barn can be utilized. The Rector has a book of excellent plans for churches in the Colonies where there are not great sums of money available. It will be an unpretentious building but, in time, as the community grows it can be added to. The Rector is most enthusiastic, as there are a good many of the poorer people who seldom have the opportunity of attending a service. You can imagine how they would welcome a church and a parish room where they could meet and be sociable."

"Ga—ga—ga!" shouted Nicholas. "Ga—ga!"

"My sister would be tremendously pleased. I am sure she would send a substantial donation. I should screw something out of the Dean also."

"If you think you will get anything out of my people, you're mistaken," said Adeline.

"I had no such thought," he returned.

"But my mother would embroider a beautiful altar cloth."

"That would be very nice."

"My grandfather might give a pair of silver candlesticks."

"I doubt if candles on the altar would be acceptable. The Rector is against ritualism."

"Ga—ga—ga—ga!" said Nicholas, violently shaking the watch, then biting on it.

Philip returned it to his pocket. He rose, took his elder son beneath the arms, and tossed him in the air. Nicholas's face became a mask of hysterical delight. He would not have minded if he had been tossed clear into the sky.

Adeline smiled lazily, her hand rhythmically patting the back of her last-born. Gussie was enraptured. She scrambled down from the bed and ran to her father and clasped him about the legs. If any hard feeling existed between them, it was now forgotten.

"Me too!" she shrieked. "Gussie too!"

Philip set Nicholas on the floor and snatched up Gussie. He tossed her up and caught her. Again and again. Higher and higher, till she almost touched the ceiling. At each upward flight she uttered a cry of mingled fright and joy. Her dark curls stood on end. Her dress of pale blue merino, cut low at the neck and with short sleeves, blew out like a little balloon. Her tiny kid-clad feet hung helpless beneath her white pantalettes.

Adeline lay laughing at them. Nicholas pouted a little. But Ernest kept his forget-me-not blue eyes fixed on space and the tips of his pink fingers just touching.

"Stop," said Adeline at last. "You will make her giddy."

He desisted but before he put her down he gave her a hearty kiss on the mouth.

"Little daughter!" he said. "Little daughter!"

When he had led the children away to their nurse Adeline lay still, savoring her happiness. She lay on her embroidered pillows, relaxed but not drowsy, her difficult undertaking of giving birth accomplished, a thousand pleasant things waiting to be done as soon as she had the strength to do them. Her mind traveled back over her past life and she felt that she really must have lived quite a long time to have experienced so much. There were the young, untrammeled, headstrong days in Ireland, full of the sound of boys' voices, the music of the hunting horn, the drift of fine rain against green leaves. There was her married life in India, the bold bright color of it, the passion of her love for Philip, her friendship with native princes. It began to seem strangely unreal. She thought of the voyage from India and remembered rising early one hot morning, having a glimpse of Philip stripped on deck while two sailors dashed buckets of cold water over him. She remembered the pleased look on the faces of the sailors. None had seen her looking on.

She thought she would have a lilac tree planted outside the window of this room. Lilac had such a lovely scent in springtime. Mrs. Pink had promised her a root of it, as well as other garden plants. She would have flowers all about the place and an orchard with fruit of all sorts. She would plant a peach tree and a grapevine and ask Captain Lacey to show her how to make peach brandy and grape wine.

Oh, how she wished she were able to unpack the chest of ivory and jade ornaments! And she was able—if only Dr. Ramsey would let her! Suddenly she grew restless. She tossed herself on the pillows. Was she to lie here forever, doing nothing? The infant was sunk in deep, almost prenatal slumber.

Half an hour later she was in her clothes, with the exception of her stays. But she had put on her linen chemise, her long, lace-edged drawers, her hand-knit silk stockings with clocks on the sides, her white flannel petticoat, her voluminous finely tucked cambric petticoat, her dark red skirt with flounces edged with ruby-colored velvet ribbon, her little sacque with lawn and lace undersleeves, her gaily embroidered Indian slippers. She felt oddly weak when she had finished dressing and did not attempt to arrange her hair. It hung to her waist in a rich russet mane. She opened the door and looked into the hall. Then she cast a backward glance at Ernest. At this moment there was no tenderness in it. He had been with her too much. She wanted to get away from him.

Though she felt a little giddy there was an exhilarating lightness in her body as she moved along the hall. In the dining room she saw the heavy cornices above the windows waiting for curtains to be hung. She saw the massive sideboard and dining table, the chairs from the house in the Rue St. Louis not arranged but standing just where they had been uncrated. She would have yellow velours curtains for this room, with heavy cords and tassels. Already richly embossed wallpaper from France had been ordered in Quebec. She stood for a moment, caressing the satin smoothness of the newel post, while her eyes roved speculatively from the library on her left to the drawing-room on her right. She smiled to think that Philip insisted on having a library, because there had been one in his home in England. They had brought few books with them but she was fond of reading. They would acquire a good collection in time. The light from the colored glass windows on either side of the front door cast bright patches of green, purple, and red over her. What lovely windows, she thought, and they had been her very own idea! By their brightness she saw that the sky had cleared. The sun was shining. She opened the door and stepped into the porch. She found herself face to face with Dr. Ramsey.

He reddened with anger. "Mrs. Whiteoak, how dare you!" he exclaimed, taking off his hat and throwing it on the floor of the porch.

She had known he had a temper but such an exhibition of it filled her with amusement. She clung to the door handle, laughing at him.

"How dare you!" he repeated. "I have given my permission for you to be up in your own room in two days and here you are in the porch! And alone! Let me tell you, you may bring on trouble that will keep you in bed for weeks."

"I'm as right as rain," she said, using the new slang of the period.

He looked down at his hat as though he had a mind to kick it. Then he said, still looking at it:—

"If you feel so capable of looking after yourself, you may do so at your next confinement."

"There is not going to be another," she answered, loftily.

He gave an ironic smile. "You tell me that—a passionate woman like you!" Now his eyes were on her.

"I have a husband who considers my health," she returned, still more loftily.

"Does he give you permission to ignore my orders?"

"I do what I like!"

"Well, you shall go back to bed now."

"I will not."

"You shall!"

"I defy you!"

He caught her by the arms and turned her round. His grip was like iron. For a moment she felt helpless, then she threw her weight against his shoulder and stretching up her hand took a handful of his rather long, wiry hair.

"Will you loose me!" she panted.

He gave a little excited laugh. With a sharp intake of breath, he bent his head and kissed her lips.

Both stood motionless a space. They heard a light step on the newly spread gravel of the drive. Dr. Ramsey picked up his hat and, still more flushed, turned to face Daisy Vaughan. She was astonished by the sight of Adeline.

"Why, Mrs. Whiteoak—you up!" she cried. "How lovely!"

"Yes, isn't it?"

"And how well you look! You have an enchanting color. Hasn't she, Dr. Ramsey?" She gave him an intent look.

"Quite," he returned stiffly.

There was a somewhat embarrassed silence but it was soon broken by Daisy's exclaiming:—

"What do you suppose has happened? Kate Busby has eloped with Mr. Brent! Her father is in a towering rage and says he will never forgive her. Do you think he ever will, Dr. Ramsey?"

"I haven't the faintest idea."

"I think an elopement is so romantic. Nothing would hinder me from marrying the man I loved. I would fly with him to the ends of the earth. Everyone seems to think Mr. Brent is a quite good match, even though his means are uncertain. What do you think of such infatuation, Dr. Ramsey? I'll wager you disapprove of it."

"I'm in no position to judge anyone's conduct," he returned.

Adeline's eyes were laughing at him. She leant against the stone wall of the porch, folding her arms. "Both parties are lucky," she said. "They'll make a nice pair."

"I'm so glad you think so," said Daisy. "But I wish there had been a wedding. Even though I shall never be a bride I should love to be a bridesmaid."

"You'll be a bride without doubt," said Adeline.

A faint cry came from her bedroom. She turned her eyes in that direction with something of the expression of a fine Persian cat, aloof yet attentive to the cry of its young.

"Oh, the darling baby!" cried Daisy, darting down the hall and throwing herself on her knees by the side of the bed. "Oh you darling, angelic little Ernest!" She clasped him to her breast. But she had nothing he wanted. He continued to cry.

He thrived in the weeks that followed and continued to be an object of great interest to all about, for he had set the seal of birth on the new house. Nicholas found himself of less consequence.

Frequently Gussie was set to minding Nicholas, amusing him while the baby slept. Though so young, she had a capable way with her and often he would do her bidding. But, when he set his will against hers, she had no power to control him. He would shout and scream in her face. He would pull her curls. He now weighed more than she and would push her aside to grasp a toy or reach his mother's knee. Gussie loved little Ernest. He was sweeter than her best doll. But she did not love Nicholas. There were times when she liked him very much but there were other times when she would have liked to get rid of him.

On a warm bright morning in May the nurse had set Nicholas in his perambulator on the grass. It was near the ravine where passing workmen might amuse him, or the flight of returning birds. They came in great numbers, in clouds, filling the air with their song. Always there was some living thing to watch at Jalna.

A farm hand led past a fine team of Percheron horses, just bought by Philip. They trotted by in gentleness and strength, moving obediently to the slight drawing of the rein. Nicholas ceased to play with his woolly lamb and leant forward to watch them as though appraisingly; his brilliant dark eyes looked out from under the frill of his pale blue silk bonnet. The great glossy flanks of the Percherons jogged up and down, the bright metal trimmings of the harness jingled. Nicholas saw how their cream-colored tails were caught in a knot with red ribbons. He turned over his lamb to see if its tail was the same, and finding it had nothing more than a little scut of wool, he pushed out his underlip in disapproval. Gussie, sitting on a little stool by his side, thought he was about to cry. She joggled the perambulator up and down with an experienced hand.

He turned his gaze somewhat resentfully on her. He did not want to be joggled. He wanted to get out and walk. He tried to unfasten the strap which held him.

"No, no," said Gussie. "Naughty."

She rose and held his two hands in hers. This infuriated him. He glared at her and struggled. She thought she would push the pram about to quiet him. The ground was level and smooth here so she managed very well. It was a great pleasure to her to push the pram, though their nurse had strictly forbidden it.

But Nicholas was thoroughly disgruntled. He could not forget how she had held his hands. He hurled his lamb overboard. He lay down on his back and kicked. With a great deal of effort she moved the pram to where the resurrected piano stood in its case at the edge of the ravine.

"Nice piano," she said. "Gussie will play on it." Then she added —"But not Nicholas."

He could not understand that there was a piano in the big box but he did understand that he was going to be denied something she was to have. He turned over and struggled to his knees, still encircled by the restraining strap. She did not see what he had done, for her head was bent in Herculean efforts. The ground had become rougher.

Nicholas leant over the back of the pram and gripped Gussie's hat by the crown. He dragged it forward over her eyes, badly pulling her hair that was caught in the elastic. She gave a cry of pain and rage but continued to push the pram with all her might.

Only the day before the piano had, with much shouting and cracking of whip, been dragged up from the brink of the river. Every carpenter, plasterer, woodsman and farm hand had left his task to share the excitement. All the neighborhood had gathered to see the four horses strain and stamp, in their efforts to raise the piano. Once the ropes had slipped and it had all but plunged back again but, at last, it stood safe on the top. To-day it was to be carried into the drawing-room.

All that she had borne from Nicholas now crowded upon Gussie. Whatever she had, he wanted. Whatever she did, he interfered. He was the centre of everything. Mamma, Papa, Nurse, Lizzie—everyone liked him best. Even Patsy O'Flynn had put her down from his shoulder this morning to elevate Nicholas to that eminence. Little Ernest was nice. She could do with him but Nicholas she could not abide. The long sharp slope, up which the piano had been dragged, lay before her. It had been scraped to comparative smoothness by the weight of the piano. Gussie put all her strength into a last push to the pram. She let it go.

Down the slope it hurtled, Nicholas still clinging to the back of the seat. His expression changed from surprise to joyful devil-may-careness. A wheel striking a stone caused a bump that threw him into the air. He landed in the pram again but in a different position. Gussie could no longer see his face.

Now the perambulator reached the river's edge. It overturned, with Nicholas beneath it. He did not move. The front wheels were above the water. Suddenly Gussie was frightened. She felt alone in an immense world. She looked down the steep. The piano had been at the bottom. Now it was at the top. The pram had been at the top, now it was at the bottom. Nicholas had been noisy, now he was silent. Things changed too much. Gussie was afraid.

She trotted in the direction from whence came the sound of an axe and voices of the two French Canadians singing. Their singing reminded her of something long past, something that was pleasant and soothing. She stood concealed, watching the swing of the axes and the way the muscles rose in lumps on their brown arms.

Gussie gave a little skip of pleasure. For an instant the forest was blotted out and she saw the kitchen of the house in the Rue St. Louis and felt Marie's arms about her, rocking her, heard Marie's voice singing.

> *"'Alouette, Alouette, gentile Alouette,*
> *Je te plumerait . . .'"*

She discovered tiny pink flowers starring the young grass at her feet and bent to put her face down to theirs. She heard the nurse's voice calling.

"Augusta! Augusta!" There was a frantic note in the voice.

Then Nurse saw her and ran to her.

"Where is Baby?" she panted.

"Down there," said Gussie pointing to the bottom of the ravine.

"Merciful heaven!" She ran to the verge and peered over. Gussie followed her, watched her run frantically down the steep. Finger in mouth, she saw Nurse lift the pram, take Nicholas into her arms and examine him, then toil up again, her face crimson.

Nicholas had been no more hurt than the piano had been, Gussie decided, staring up into his face. He looked quiet and puzzled. His bonnet was down over one eye. Nurse set him on the ground, then again descended into the ravine and brought up the pram. She was completely winded. She took out the pillow and coverings and shook the earth from them. She plumped up the pillow and rearranged all. Every now and again she cast a fearful glance toward the house. When Nicholas had been embraced and tenderly kissed, Nurse bent over Gussie.

"How did it happen?" she demanded fiercely. "What did you do, you wicked girl?"

"I pushed the pram," answered Gussie, "and it went over. I was giving him a ride."

"It's a marvel you did not kill him." She took Gussie by the shoulders and shook her violently, then slapped first her hands, then her cheeks. "Take that!" she said. "And don't you dare tell Mamma or Papa about this. Now stop crying. You haven't got the half of what you deserve."

That afternoon the piano case was removed. The piano stood exposed to the sunlight, apparently none the worse for all it had been through. It remained to be seen what its tone would be. A platform on rollers had been constructed, on which it was drawn to the house, and a half-dozen men carried it with what were, to Gussie, rather frightening shoutings and strugglings. When at last it was safe in the drawing-room, the men stood about it admiring its rosewood case, the carvings of its legs, its silver candleholders, with almost as much pride as if it had been their own.

When the men were gone, Adeline and Philip, Daisy and Wilmott, were left.

"Now," exclaimed Daisy, "things really begin to look settled and homelike! I always say that the piano is the soul of the house. I do hope it is not too dreadfully out of tune."

"Please sit down and play something," said Philip. "Let's find out the worst at once."

Daisy arranged herself on the stool, after a number of twirlings of it up and down till it was of the desired height. Then she broke into a Strauss waltz.

"It's not bad," she declared, above the music. "Not bad at all. The tone is sweet."

Philip was delighted. He put an arm about Adeline's waist and, without considering whether or not she was in condition to waltz, whirled her away. "Hoop-la!" he cried. "Why, it's ages since we've danced together."

Supple and strong, Adeline skimmed the floor with him. Wilmott stood looking on a little gloomily, wishing he too had a partner. Then, seeing Gussie peeping round the door, he went to her, bowed deeply in the Frenchified manner he had picked up in Quebec, and said:—

"Will you do me the honor, Miss Whiteoak?"

She bowed gravely and, holding her by her hands, he led her round and round.

"We shall often have parties here," said Adeline across Philip's shoulder. "Surely we are the happiest people in the world!" She sank down on a sofa, happily flushed but a little tired after the waltz. Daisy turned round on the stool.

"I should so love to dance," she said. "If anyone would dance with me."

"Play us a tune, Wilmott!" said Philip, and raised Daisy to her feet.

Daisy's playing had been gay, facile, if somewhat incorrect. Wilmott's was slow, with a kind of precise sensuousness. Daisy's sinuous body expressed, almost brazenly, her pleasure in the rhythmic movement. The two had frequently danced together the past winter.

"I do so love dancing with you, Captain Whiteoak," she breathed. "I'm lost to all else in the world."

He gave a gay laugh, held her a little more firmly and whirled farther down the room. Augusta stood by Wilmott's side, thumping her small fists on the bass notes. He shook his head at her but she persisted.

"Gussie is spoiling everything," cried Daisy. "Do stop her, Mrs. Whiteoak!"

Adeline swooped down on Gussie, picked her up and set her on the sofa. Gussie's little pantaletted legs dangled helplessly.

"Is there no hope of our dancing together?" Wilmott asked of Adeline.

"When I have rested a little."

Wilmott played a polka which the dancers executed with spirit. Then he came and sat by Adeline's side. He said:—

"I don't think I want to dance with you to that girl's playing. She plays horribly."

Adeline stretched out her hand and took his. "You seem to be in an evil mood, James," she said. "I think Daisy performs beautifully on the piano. And how she dances!"

"I had rather die than dance with her," he said.

Philip came to them. "When you see the wallpaper on this room," he said, "and the really handsome curtains at the windows and the carpet on the floor, you will see a room of some elegance."

"It is certainly large," said Wilmott. "The floor space is twice that of my entire house."

"It is a divine room!" cried Daisy. "Picture it at night with all the candles blazing, dancers gliding over the floor, flowers in vases, an orchestra sweetly playing and outside the vastness of the forest! Oh, I envy you such a room! What do you suppose it feels like to be a pauper, Captain Whiteoak?"

"Very jolly, to judge by the look of you," returned Philip.

"Oh, how cruel! Just because I hide my misery beneath a smile, you think I don't care! Here I am—doomed to single blessedness! What man yearns to marry a girl without a penny?"

"In a primitive country," said Wilmott, "a female is judged by her brawn."

Daisy ran across the floor, holding out her arms.

"In that respect," she cried, "I am even worse off. Look at me! Skin and bone! Nothing more."

"Hoop-la!" exclaimed Philip, dancing toward her. "Strike up the music, Wilmott."

He swept Daisy into another waltz, the music for which he provided by an extraordinarily sweet whistling.

"I have something I want to tell you," said Wilmott, taking Gussie's tiny slippered foot into his hand. "But we never have an opportunity to talk nowadays."

"Once we are settled it will be different. Then I shall have oceans of leisure. What is it you were going to tell me?"

"I have begun to write a book."

Her face lighted. "Splendid! Is it a novel? Am I in it?"

"It is and I'm afraid you are. Try as I would, I could not keep you out."

"I should be furious if you had. When will you read to me what you have written?"

"I don't know. Perhaps never. I am very uncertain about it."

"Those two," observed Philip to Daisy, "seem disposed to converse forever."

"They are so intellectual. As for me, I have only two ideas."

"Do tell me what they are."

"To be loved—and to love!"

Wilmott rose and went to the piano. He began to play, gravely yet sensuously. Gussie slid down from the sofa and followed him. She strummed on the bass notes.

XVIII

Visitors from Ireland

As PHILIP looked about him, he was struck anew by all that had been accomplished since Adeline and he had come here. He was often struck by this but this particular evening he felt something approaching awe. Not much more than a year ago he had purchased a thousand acres of land—forest, with the exception of a small clearing. Now a substantial house stood in its midst. About it was a park with as fine trees as you would see anywhere. Beyond the park there were fields, cleared of stumps and planted with oats and barley. There were even vegetables—next year there would be a flower border for Adeline. A barn was completed and in the stable beneath it there were two teams of fine farm horses, two saddle horses, and a general-purpose mare who was used for the trap or for light work. He had not been in haste to buy a carriage and carriage horses. His taste in such was exacting.

He stood between the barn and the house which he could just see through the trees, the warm red of its walls deepened by the glow from the setting sun. Smoke rose from two of its chimneys, grayish blue against the blue of the sky. Even the Jersey cows, grazing near him and looking as though such as they had grazed and bred in this spot for generations, did not move Philip as did the sight of the smoke from his own chimneys against the sky. It was as though the smoke traced the word *home* there. Well, he had given his heart to this land. He wanted no other.

It seemed strange to him, when he thought of it, how he had been willing to leave the Army where he could have, with confidence, looked forward to advancement, how he had thrown all that aside for so primitive a life. As a youth he had wanted to enter the Army. It was a tradition of his family. Many a time he had rejoiced in the activities of military life. What had happened to him, then? It seemed that, from the time of his marriage, a strange element of unrest had come into his life. Not that Adeline had not enjoyed the pleasures of the military station, not that she had been a simple-minded country girl whose presence had drawn him from the old life. No, it had been something much deeper. It was as though Adeline had always been searching for truth and that when their lives were joined they had set out to search for it together. They had wanted reality, freedom from rules made long before their time, the opportunity to lead their lives in their own fashion. In Canada they had found that opportunity. Not once had he regretted what he had given up, nay—he rejoiced in what he had attained! He looked down at his heavy boots, his leather leggings, his corduroy breeches and jacket, and rejoiced that he looked and felt like a countryman. He went to the youngest of the cows who had lately had her first calf which still was with her, and put his hand on the cream-colored smoothness of her shoulder. She was friendly, not timid, and raised her eyes to his face, her mouth full of the tender grass. Her little calf was by her side, weak yet lively, making feeble jumpings. He would not have exchanged them for a regiment of cavalry. A deep serenity possessed him. From early morning to night he had congenial things to do. In truth he had so much to do that sometimes he felt overwhelmed. Still, there was plenty of time ahead of him. In time he and Adeline would make Jalna what they wanted it to be. There was no haste. He had plenty of money. He had confidence in the future. He had a comfortable belief in God—a not too personal God, with His eye always on your misdeeds, but ready to give you a hand in time of trouble and waiting at the last with magnanimous forgiveness for your sins—if they had not been heinous.

"Co-boss," he said to the young cow, having learned the word from the farm hands, "nice little co-boss." The calf bumped against his knees, its pink tongue protruding.

He saw Colonel Vaughan coming toward him across the field. He was carrying a basket. They exchanged greetings and the Colonel opened the basket.

"I have a little present for your wife," he said. "Some lettuces—ours are especially fine this year—also some cherries and a score of the marauders who planned to devour them."

The interior of the basket was as pretty as a picture, Philip thought. The two great heads of lettuce were as green as the youngest grass. Their leaves were folded over their hearts, layer upon layer, firm and cool with scarcely a wrinkle. Only the edges were crisply curled. Against this greenness the glossy crimson of the cherries shone. A partition divided the basket and in the other half lay the bodies of twenty small, bright-colored birds. They had throats as red as the cherries and crests on their little heads. Nothing could have been sleeker than their plumage.

"The rascals came in a cloud," said Colonel Vaughan, "and settled on the tree. It was a pretty sight but I had no time to waste in admiring it. I got my shotgun and fired it into the tree. I recharged it for the stragglers. They fell off the branches like fruit."

"By Jove, they're pretty! But what is Adeline to do with them?"

"Have them stuffed. There is quite a good taxidermist in the town. A glass case filled with them, nicely arranged on small branches, is as pretty an ornament for a room as you could wish. If you want more I can give you double the number. I am having a score stuffed for myself."

"Thanks very much. Adeline will be delighted."

But he was a little doubtful as he entered the drawing-room where Adeline was sitting at her embroidery frame, utilizing the last brightness from the west. She looked charming, he thought, in her dress of white cashmere with a cascade of lace down the front and at the elbow sleeves. He took twin cherries from the basket and hung them on one of her ears.

"There's an earring for you!"

She put up her hand to feel. "Cherries! Oh, do give me a handful! Are they from Vaughanlands?"

"Yes. And these too. Look."

She peered into the basket. Her face paled.

"Oh, how cruel! Who killed them?"

"Vaughan. But they were devouring his cherries. They would soon have finished them."

"It was cruel—cruel," she repeated. "Why did he send the birds here?"

"He brought them himself—for you—they're to be stuffed. You'll admire them when you see them in a nice glass case."

"Never! Take them out of my sight! Oh, the darlings! No—let me see them!" She took one from the basket and held it against her cheek. Tears ran from her eyes.

"Now Adeline, be sensible. You work yourself into a stew over nothing—or next to nothing. What of the partridges, the pheasants, the grouse that are shot?"

"That is sport. This is murder. Those birds are used as food. These—" She pressed the dead bird she held to her lips, then raised her eyes with an outraged expression to Philip's face. "These little birds are for beauty and song! What if they do eat the cherries?"

"What if there were no cherries left?"

"Who would care?" She kissed the breast of the bird. "Who would care?"

"Adeline, you have blood on your lips!" He took out his large linen handkerchief and wiped her lips. "Now, enough of this. Give me the bird. I shall find someone else who will enjoy having them."

She submitted, only exclaiming—"They shall not be put into a glass case! I shall bury them myself." She peered into the basket and again her tears overflowed.

Mrs. Coveyduck came into the room. She and her husband had arrived at Jalna some weeks before. They had been engaged in Devon by Philip's sister, as cook and gardener. No two could have been more satisfactory. Sam Coveyduck was short, thickset and florid. He thought of growing things from morning to night and it was a dying thing that would not grow for him. He had a deep, luscious voice with a strong Devon accent. His wife was short too but more slender. She had sleek brown hair, a nunlike face and a will like iron. She was a good cook. She adored order. She settled down to rule the young couple at Jalna, benignly yet firmly.

"Just look, Mrs. Coveyduck," cried Adeline, "at the dear little birds! What do you think of a gentleman who would kill dear little birds—just for fun?"

"It wasn't for fun," said Philip.

"It was for fun! Else why should he have galloped over here to show his spoils?"

"He didn't gallop," said Philip, "he walked. He thought you'd be pleased."

"I don't care *how* he came!" screamed Adeline. "He came, bringing his little victims, and that is enough! I always felt something wicked in him. Now I remember hearing how he shot down natives in India for just a little tiny uprising."

"Those natives had killed English civilians. One of them a woman. Anyhow, it wasn't this Vaughan but the other Vaughan."

"Ah, trust you to cover up your friend's misdeeds!"

"Trust you," returned Philip, glaring at her, "to think the worst of people."

"I can see as far through a stone wall as anyone. I know sport when I see it and I know cruelty when I see it. And this is cruelty."

"Eh, well," said Mrs. Coveyduck, soothingly, "I'll fetch 'ee a nice cup of tea to comfort 'ee. As for thicey birds, we'll have a proper funeral for they. I'll find a nice box and line it with leaves. Coveyduck shall dig the grave and the children shall strew flowers over top. Would you like the cherries stewed, or in a tart, ma'am?"

Neither Philip nor Adeline replied. Both would have preferred a tart but neither would, in the stress of the moment, admit it.

"Stewed, or in a tart?" repeated Mrs. Coveyduck, fixing them with eyes as blue as the sky.

"I have no preference," answered Philip, stiffly.

"Nor I," said Adeline.

"Then stewed—with Devonshire cream," said Mrs. Coveyduck, well knowing their preference. She took the basket and turned to go.

Emotion always made Adeline hungry. She turned a look of hate on Philip to think he had not said cherry tart.

He thrust his hands deep into his pockets and whistled between his teeth.

"This is no stable," she said, "nor you a groom."

"I want cherry tart," he returned.

Adeline smiled broadly at Mrs. Coveyduck. "The master demands cherry tart," she said.

It was on the very day when the little birds were buried that Adeline had a letter from her brother Conway, saying that he and Mary were in Montreal and would soon come to Jalna for a visit. They were in that town to look after the affairs of Mrs. Cameron who had died in the early spring, leaving Mary a modest but not inconsiderable fortune. Both were well and longing to see Philip, dear Adeline, and the children. Sholto had accompanied them.

Adeline was divided between delight and dismay. If only they had waited a little longer for their visit, delight would have been unalloyed. But the house was not yet in order. The walls of the drawing-room and library had been papered, the curtains hung. They were inviting but not yet complete. No pictures were on the walls, no ornaments arranged. As for the dining room, it was still in chaos, the furniture swathed, scaffolds erected for the paper-hangers. Meals were eaten in the library. There was as yet no furniture in the guest rooms.

Fortunately a private sale of household effects was advertised at no great distance. Philip went off to it, a little disgruntled because he had his hands so full at home. But it was always pleasant to spend money and he returned in great good humor having acquired two bedroom suites, one of walnut with much carving, the other of mahogany and of a good design. He also acquired complete toilet sets with enormous ewers, basins, soap dishes, slop bowls, chamber pots and toothbrush holders, tall enough for the toothbrushes of mastodons. Added to this were a large tin bath painted green, a wire stand for potted plants, a cuckoo clock, a stuffed deer's head, a huge volume of *British Poets*, and a dog kennel. Adeline had to leave her hanging of curtains to inspect these. She declared them all to be beautiful and, clasping the anthology of *British Poets* to her breast, flew with it to the library and placed it conspicuously on the book-shelves. She and Philip stood hand in hand admiring the effect.

Mrs. Coveyduck was without peer in the process of settling in. She never became confused or irritated. She went from attic to basement and never seemed to tire. Tranquilly and without fuss she had her own way. The young girl, Lizzie, under her guidance, was rapidly becoming an efficient housemaid. She thought Mrs. Coveyduck perfect and it was amusing to see her modeling herself in imitation.

Oh, the joy to Adeline and Philip to be in their own house! No longer was he obliged to put his head out of the window to smoke his cigar. Now, with his velvet smoking cap on his head, the gold tassel dangling jauntily over one eye, he could smoke where he chose. She would run from room to room, singing as she went. She could drop things wherever she chose, secure in the knowledge that Mrs. Coveyduck or Lizzie would pick them up. The children might cry at the top of their lungs, she had no need to worry. As for Nero, no longer was he an outcast. He so suffered from the summer's heat that Patsy O'Flynn clipped him to his shoulders again. He was here, there, and everywhere. Already the new front door was scored by his scratchings to be admitted.

The party from Montreal arrived on a hot, bright but windy day. Everything seemed in motion, from the waving of branches to the waving of Nero's tail.

"How heavenly to see you boys again!" cried Adeline, clasping her brothers to her in turn.

"Dear Sis," said Conway, submitting languidly, "it is heaven to be here after the discomforts we have endured. How well you look!"

He himself had not at all changed, nor had Sholto. There they stood, slim as wands, their pale red hair worn too long, their long pale faces with the pointed chins and supercilious nostrils reminding Philip as always of the faces on playing cards—looking little older than when they had run away from the ship. But Mary had changed—from a colorless child to a fashionable young woman though, on close inspection, she looked a little overshadowed by the clothes which she had bought in Paris. Though she had all the money, Conway had firmly impressed on her that he had done her a great favor in marrying her. Her adoring eyes followed him wherever he went and, when he was absent from her, she waited in dejection for his return. She often bored him and he preferred the more congenial company of his brother.

"What a dear little house!" he exclaimed. "And all so fresh and clean! And what a wilderness surrounding it!"

"Heavens! Look at the dog!" Sholto simulated terror. "Or is he a lion? What a creature!"

"He comes from Newfoundland and he's more lamb than lion," answered Adeline, patting Nero.

"What sweet babies!" Mary ran to inspect the children. "There's nothing I want so much as a baby but I don't seem able to have one."

Conway winked at Adeline. "There is nothing on earth I want less," he said, arranging his silk cravat.

"What perfect repair everything is in!" remarked Sholto, staring about him.

"Child," said Adeline, "the house is barely built. It's as fresh as a daisy."

He looked at her blankly. He could not imagine a new house.

"How is dear Mamma?" she asked.

"Looking lovely," answered Conway. "You remember that she lost a front tooth? Well, she has had a beautiful new one put in its place. It is a miracle. A new discovery. You should see it."

"She says she is coming over here just to show it you," said Sholto. "Both she and Dada are coming."

"Really!" Philip could not help looking a little aghast. "You say they are coming to Jalna?"

"Yes. Dada doesn't believe half of what Sis writes of the place. He's coming to see with his own eyes."

"How is Dada?" asked Adeline pensively.

"Beastly as ever," returned Sholto emphatically. "He beat me till I was black and blue just two days before we sailed. I thought I should have had to remain at home."

"It served you right," said his brother.

Mary asked—"Where are the two Irish gentlemen?"

"Mr. D'Arcy returned to Ireland some months ago. Mr. Brent eloped with a Canadian girl. They have lately returned and been forgiven by her father."

"Had she money?" asked Mary.

"Her father is quite well off—as riches go in this country."

"How well is he off as riches go in Ireland?" asked Conway.

"Rolling in wealth. Now come and see your rooms. Then we shall have dinner."

She led them upstairs. They ran from room to room, examining them with the curiosity of children. Adeline herself felt like a child again. It was delightful having them with her.

They made quite a sensation in the neighborhood, with their odd looks, their clothes in the extreme of European fashion, their free-and-easy manners. The Laceys gave a lawn party for them but, as it turned out, they were not the centre of interest at it for Michael Brent and his bride, newly returned and forgiven by her father, were surrounded by a welcoming circle.

Brent disengaged himself as soon as he could and drew Adeline aside. He said:—

"I have good news for your gloomy friend."

"I have no gloomy friend," she returned. "I demand good spirits in any friend of mine. If, by chance, it is James Wilmott you refer to, you are mistaken. He would be the happiest man here, if—"

"There need be no if, from now on," interrupted Brent. "Do please capture him and let me relieve his mind."

Adeline found Wilmott in the midst of a group engaged in the sport of archery. He had just raised his bow to his shoulder and was looking intently at the target. She waited till the arrow pierced the bull's-eye and, amid applause, he gave way to another player before she spoke.

"Oh, James," she said, "can you leave this game and come with me? Michael Brent has just told me that he had good news for you. He is waiting near the summerhouse. Do excuse yourself and come."

"I have won the contest," said Wilmott. "I can come with you at once."

Adeline lingered a moment to watch Daisy Vaughan who, bow in hand, was about to play in a new round. She was the subject of much banter because she could not be made to understand how to hold her bow.

"But I never *could* hold a bow!" she cried.

"The thing is to *catch* your beau," laughed Kate Brent. "Once you've caught him it's very easy to hold him."

"What does she mean?" asked Daisy, innocently.

"Oh, Daisy, how slow you are!" cried Lydia Busby. "Don't you see? Bow and *beau*—b-e-a-u?"

"I declare," said Daisy, "I don't see any connection. I repeat that, if I had a dozen bows, I could not hold one of them."

There were peals of laughter.

Philip came to her side and put his arm about her, placing her hands correctly on the bow. She smiled helplessly up at him.

As Adeline and Wilmott turned away she asked:—

"What do you think of Daisy, James?"

"I think she's a hussy," he returned curtly.

"I thought so too, at the beginning. Then I thought she was just a silly girl. Now I don't know what to think. She calls herself my friend."

"She's no friend of yours. Nor of any woman's! Adeline, she is *man-mad*. The bachelors have not come up to the scratch. I think she has given up her ambition for Dr. Ramsey. Now I believe she is after Philip."

"She has always laid herself out to allure him. But I have been only amused by her tricks."

"Philip is the most attractive man in the place."

"But he's mine!"

"What does she care? Adeline, that girl told my boy, Tite, that he had enchanting eyelashes and a mouth like a pomegranate flower."

Adeline laughed delightedly. "Oh, James, to hear you say that!"

He replied with some heat—"Poetic phrases might not come so ill from my lips as you imagine."

She gave him an almost tender look. "I never should have laughed if they had been your own, but to hear you repeat them, as from Daisy to Tite, fills me with hilarity. How did Tite take it?"

"The young devil liked it. He has taken to looking at himself in my looking-glass—trying to see his eyelashes and making mouths."

"He's more French than Indian, by a long shot, Philip says."

They found Brent hiding in the lattice summerhouse. He called out softly:—

"Here I am. Come and hear the news, Wilmott."

They went in. Adeline seated herself by the side of Brent. Wilmott stood, as though defensively, in the doorway. Brent's ruddy face was wreathed in a smile of good-fellowship.

"I have seen your wife," he announced.

"Yes?" Wilmott spoke quietly.

"You know, Kate and I went to New York on our honeymoon. We had been there only a few days when Mrs. Wilmott discovered me, looking in at the window of a bookshop. She was coming out with a book she had bought. It was almost a year since I had seen her and my first thought was how well she was looking. Really like a different woman."

Wilmott just stared.

"She is not worrying over your whereabouts any longer. She is immersed—literally up to the neck—in the anti-slavery campaign!"

Wilmott's jaw dropped. He uttered an incoherent sound.

"You see," continued Brent, "she is by nature a woman with a mission. She is completely carried away by this. She never reached Mexico, for she made friends with people who warned her what a precarious and almost hopeless expedition it would be. These friends are anti-slavery enthusiasts. She became one. She traveled with them through the South. Now she is on a lecturing tour in the North, arousing feeling there. She is returning later to England to lecture."

"Lecture!" ejaculated Wilmott.

"Yes. Lecture. She pointed out a card in the window of the book-shop, advertising the one she was giving that night. She begged me to attend it. Fortunately Kate was a little indisposed, so I was able to go alone."

"And Mrs. Wilmott mounted a platform and lectured!" cried Adeline. "Eh, but I should have liked to hear her. Was there a crowd?"

"The hall was not very well filled but those who were there could not have been more enthusiastic. She roused them to a really vindictive anger. They would have marched forth and set fire to the house of any slave owner—if they could have found one."

"It puzzles me," said Wilmott, "how she could have kept to the one subject. Her tongue had a fashion of running away with her."

"It did run away with her!" exclaimed Brent. "That's just the point. Words literally poured from her. She submerged the audience with words. She gave us statistics and tortures in the same breath. For my part, if it hadn't been for Kate I was almost ready to join in the campaign. In a small clear penetrating voice—"

"Ah," said Wilmott gloomily. "I know that voice. It used to beat on my brain for hours after we had gone to bed and something had started her lecturing."

"Lecturing—ah, there you are! She's a born lecturer. In your day, she had an audience of only one. Now she has hundreds and it will not surprise me if, before this controversy is finished, she has thousands. After the lecture she was besieged by people who were interested. Then I escorted her to her hotel and we had a long talk. That is to say, I listened and she talked."

"Did she speak of me?" asked Wilmott.

"She did that. She said that your leaving her had been the greatest mercy of her life. She said that, with the exception of giving her Hetty, it was the one good thing you had ever done for her."

"She said not a word of my having crippled myself financially to leave her in security?"

"Not a word. She even spoke of your indolence, your lack of ambition. She said that, having dedicated herself to her great mission, she never wanted to hear of you again and that if you should, in time to come, seek her out and beg for forgiveness, she would cast you off."

"She did, did she, eh?" said Wilmott, with a savage grin.

Adeline sprang to her feet. She embraced Wilmott.

"Oh, James," she cried, "what glorious news for you!"

She then turned to Brent and embraced him.

"How splendid you have been!" she exclaimed. "Have you breathed a word of this to Kate?"

"Not a word—and never shall. As a matter of fact, dear Mrs. Whiteoak, there are so many little incidents in my own past which I must conceal from Kate that *this* from *Wilmott's* is imperceptible."

"Oh, you rogue!" said Adeline, kissing him.

No one could call Wilmott a rogue. He stood glowering at them.

"Aren't you delighted?" asked Brent.

"Yes. I am delighted. Did Mrs. Wilmott speak of my daughter?"

"Hetty! Ah, yes, Hetty! Her mother is very pleased with Hetty. That girl is transformed. She too has thrown herself into the work. She has grown tall and strong and serious. She was seated at a small table inside the door of the lecture hall. She was distributing pamphlets against slavery. Selling autographed copies of a booklet written by her mother, at fifty cents each. The proceeds to go to the Cause. I bought one for you. Here it is."

He unbuttoned his coat and took the booklet from his inner pocket. Wilmott accepted it gingerly.

"Thank you," he said. "Thank you, very much."

"You know," said Brent, "if ever this affair should leak out—as so help me God it never will through me—you can say quite simply that you and your wife separated because of her views on slavery. You can express a profound sympathy with the South."

"He could say nothing that would make him more unpopular here," said Adeline. "We're all against slavery."

"Then say," continued Brent, unabashed, "that she would never stay at home as a wife should but was always gallivanting over the country, lecturing. Say you parted by mutual agreement which I can certify you have."

"Thank you," said Wilmott, turning over the booklet in his hands.

"Splendid," Adeline agreed. "The very thing."

Kate Brent came seeking them.

"There are strawberries and cream!" she called. "Do come, everybody! The berries are monstrous big and the cream as thick as Michael's brogue."

"My treasure," said Brent. "I will follow you to the ends of the earth—if you offer me strawberries."

"Will you kindly give my excuses to Mrs. Lacey," said Wilmott. "I have to go home."

They could not dissuade him. Adeline lingered a moment. "It's ended better than we could have hoped for, hasn't it? And you think I did well in making Michael Brent our confidant, don't you?"

"I think you did superbly well. But, all the same—in spite of my relief—I feel that I cut a comic figure in all this."

"That is the trouble with you!" she cried. "You are always thinking of people's opinion. Now I never consider what people will think."

"It is a part of your charm that you don't. But I have no charm."

"James, you are one of the most charming men I know. And you ought to be one of the happiest."

"So I shall be. I promise you."

They parted and he followed the path through the luxuriant growth of July, to his own house.

Whenever he had been away, his first thought on returning was to wonder what Tite was doing. Now he found him by the river's edge, painting a wheelbarrow bright blue from a new pot of paint.

"Well, Tite," he said, "what are you up to?"

Tite made a graceful gesture with the paintbrush.

"Boss, my grandfather gave me this wheelbarrow because he is old and has no more use for it. But I do not like a red wheelbarrow, so—I paint it blue!"

"And a very good wheelbarrow it is. Tite, are you sure your grandfather gave it to you? You told me he was very poor."

"So he is, Boss. That is why he has nothing more than a wheelbarrow to leave me. He guesses he's soon going to die."

"And where did you get the pot of paint?"

"Boss, I found it floating on the river."

Wilmott sighed and went into the house. There was an ineffable sense of peace in it. He sat down by the table and took out Henrietta's booklet. He read it through. Then he laid it on the hearth and touched it with a lighted match. In an instant it was blazing. One word stood out from the printed page. *Slavery.*

A quiet smile lighted Wilmott's face.

"Well," he said, aloud, "she's set me free, thank God. I can begin again—in peace."

Tite put his head in at the door. "Boss," he said, "I want to say something."

Wilmott raised his head. "Yes, Tite?"

"Boss, the folks where the garden party is gave me a basket of strawberries. I've a dish of them ready for your tea. There's cream from our own cow."

"That sounds appetizing, Tite. I'm hungry. Bring the strawberries along."

Tite draped himself gracefully against the side of the door.

"Boss, the servant girl at the place they call Jalna gave me a slab of plum cake."

"She did! Well, that was handsome of her. Let's have tea."

Tite made a sudden leap forward, like a young animal galvanized by pleasure. He pulled off the red felt table cover and in its place laid a square of clean white linen. He began to place the dishes in orderly fashion. Wilmott put on the kettle. At first he had eaten his meals alone but he had grown so fond of Tite that he had enjoyed his company at table. The boy was slim, clean, well-behaved. Physically he was beautiful. Wilmott had ambitions for him. As they sat eating their strawberries and thick cream, Wilmott said:—

"I am going to teach you many things, Tite. History, geography, mathematics, English literature and even Latin."

"That is good, Boss," answered Tite, cutting the plum cake carefully in half. "I am always ready to learn."

XIX

The Bathing Party

"THESE croquet and archery parties are all very well," said Conway, "but I should like to see you give something more spirited in the way of entertainment. Now, where Mary and I were in the South of France, we went to some delightful parties on the seashore where the diversions were drinking champagne and bathing."

He raised his greenish eyes to his sister's face, from where he sat on the floor at her feet, his head resting against her knee. Sholto sat in an identical position with his head against her other knee. Mary sat in a straight-backed chair opposite, crocheting fine lace for a border on a cambric nightcap. She said:—

"Yes, indeed, dear Adeline, we had the most heavenly time you can imagine. Some of the bathing costumes were as pretty as pictures and when we were tired of the water we lay on the sands and sang."

"I can't picture it taking place here," said Adeline.

"It can take place quite simply," said Conway, "if only you will let me engineer it. First of all we must eliminate those oldsters who carp at the license the young take. You need only get together a congenial party, provide the refreshments, and I shall look after the rest."

"This lake is not the Mediterranean," said Adeline. "It's likely to be cold."

"In this torrid weather! No—it will be deliciously cool. Come along, Sis, say you will!"

"Do say you will," repeated Sholto, turning Adeline's rings about on her fingers.

"We have no bathing costumes."

"Conway and I have," said Mary. "The rest of you can easily buy or make them. Lydia Busby tells me she has a pattern for one. Do say yes!"

"There really is nothing to do," said Sholto. "We might as well be in Ireland."

"The moon is at the full," said Conway, "and would give us all the light we should need."

"You intend to stay after sunset, then?" asked Adeline.

"Assuredly," said Mary. "We'd die of the heat if we went before late afternoon. Oh, if only you knew the pleasure of such a party! The freedom from long skirts and tight shoes and—above all—convention!"

"I didn't know that convention had ever troubled any of you," returned Adeline.

"We feel it here," said Sholto. "We hate being hampered."

"Then go home," retorted his sister.

"What a beast you are, Sis," he returned, kissing her hand.

She took a handful of hair on each of their heads and gave it a tug. "Have your way, then. But there will be no champagne. A good claret cup must suffice. Make out your list, Conway. Get the pattern of the bathing costume, Mary. If we're to have the party before the dark of the moon, we must make haste."

They did make haste—the principal obstacle to overcome being lack of covering for their bodies. Those bidden to the party included Robert and Daisy Vaughan, the Brents, the three young Busbys, Dr. Ramsey and Wilmott. Including the five from Jalna there were to be fourteen at the bathing party. A sewing bee was held at Jalna where, with great speed and small consideration for the peculiarities of figure, costumes were produced. There was a singular likeness among them all. A bolt of dark blue flannel had been bought, along with several bolts of white braid, for the female costumes. The males were to wear their own white shirts but, for their nether parts, white flannel knee-length trousers were made. The cutting out of these, the sewing together of the two halves, produced such extraordinary results that shrieks of hysterical laughter resounded through the house. Mary laughed till she cried so that water had to be thrown on her and work was at a standstill for some time.

Finally Sholto, as the youngest and most innocent of the males, was made to dress in the first costume completed. His shirt of course fitted admirably but the trousers, reaching midway between knee and ankle, had such a comic effect that the work was once more held up by unrestrained laughter. Sholto capered about the room shamelessly, his pale red hair on end, his thin legs flashing. Whether the trousers should be lengthened or shortened, trimmed with braid or left plain, was the subject of excited talk. It was a blessing that neither Mrs. Vaughan nor Mrs. Lacey was present.

When Philip tried on his in the privacy of his bedroom, he found he could not sit down in them.

"Adeline," he shouted, "come here at once!"

She came expectantly.

"You may have the damned party without me," he said. "I can't sit down in these."

She walked round him, examining him critically.

"You don't need to sit down," she said. "They're for swimming in, not sitting in. You can swim, can't you?"

"Certainly, I can. But do you expect me to swim about continually while the rest of you sit on the shore drinking claret? Also, I doubt very much if I could swim in them. They are extraordinarily tight and a most evil shape."

"Faith, they are," said Adeline. "I shall give them to Wilmott and make you another pair. He's much thinner in the thigh."

Another pair was made of the very last of the flannel and, though from scarcity of material they had to be made rather shorter than the others, Philip did not object, for now he would be able both to swim and to sit down.

The heat was unusual. There had been nothing to equal it in the preceding summer. Toward the full of the moon it grew even more intense. It seemed almost too great an effort to set out for the bathing party. At four o'clock the shadows of trees made the road to the lake less glaring. But the leaves were as motionless as though carved from metal. The sky had the hard brightness of a gem. The Whiteoaks' new wagonette, drawn by a pair of spanking bays, bowled down the drive and through the gate, driven by Philip. He was a fine hand with the reins. The horses moved beautifully.

As well as their own party, there sat on the seats facing each other the two Vaughans and Wilmott. Hampers of food were disposed beneath the seats, as well as the boxes containing the bathing costumes. On the road they discovered the Brents in a shiny new buggy and the three Busbys in an old phaeton. Young Isaac Busby was determined to race his rawboned wild-looking horses against Philip's, in spite of the heat. Weather meant nothing to the Busbys.

"Come on—come on!" he shouted, cracking his whip. But Philip kept his horses at a gentle trot.

They could smell the freshness of the lake before they came upon it. A breeze rose from its faintly ruffled surface. All about it the forest crowded. It was like a guarded inland sea. Flocks of sandpipers moved trimly across the smooth beach. A cloud of kingfishers rose and cast their blueness upon the blue of the lake. A dozen ruby-throated hummingbirds hovered above a tangle of honeysuckle that grew near the beach. The road ended in a rough field and there the horses were unharnessed and tethered. Dr. Ramsey came last, riding his gray gelding and throwing a bundle on to the beach with the remark that no one was to bathe till thoroughly cooled off.

"Then I shall never bathe," cried Mary, "for I am sure I shall never be cool again."

"You should take great care of yourself, Mrs. Court," said the doctor. "You are very thin."

"I bathed twice a day in the Mediterranean," she said defiantly.

"That was very reckless of you." He came to her side with a professional air. "May I feel your pulse?" he asked.

Childishly she laid her thin wrist in his fingers.

"Just as I thought. You have a very quick pulse. You should not overexert."

"Do feel mine," said Adeline, "for I do believe it has stopped entirely."

"There is no use in my telling you to take care of yourself, Mrs. Whiteoak," he said, severely.

She gave a little grimace that made him smile in spite of himself. He colored, for he had hoped to make her forget, by his severity, how he once had given way to amatory impulse.

A thicket of wind-blown cedars grew where sand and soil met. Here Adeline, Mary, Daisy, Kate Brent, and her two sisters disrobed themselves and put on their bathing costumes. With the exception of Mary's, these were identical. Their full flannel skirts reached to the knees, the blouses had elbow-length sleeves, the skirts and sailor collars were edged with white braid. All wore long white cotton stockings.

Mary had kept her costume as a surprise. Now she appeared rather self-consciously out of the thicket, wearing a sky-blue bathing dress with bright red sash and scarf knotted beneath the sailor collar, and a little red silk cap. The others were enraptured, though the shortness of her skirt made Kate and her sisters gasp and filled Daisy Vaughan with envy.

"I do wonder if I could pin mine up a little," she said wistfully, to Adeline. "Are there any safety pins about?"

"Not one," said Adeline, firmly, "and you are showing quite enough leg."

"It does seem hard that Mrs. Court should display limbs that are so spindling while mine, which are neither like broomsticks nor too plump like the Busby girls', should be concealed."

"Girls are expected to be modest."

"At any rate, I shall let down my hair."

She unloosed the pins which restrained her ringlets and they fell luxuriantly about her shoulders. Placing her hands on her hips she caught up her skirt in her finger tips so that as she advanced with the other females out of their retreat she displayed as much leg as did Mary. The group made such a picture that the gentlemen, already assembled at the lake's rim, stared in admiration.

Conway's costume, like his wife's, was different. It was in red and white stripes running horizontally, and so much of his thin white person was exposed to view that only his youth and a faunlike quality in him preserved him from the appearance of immodesty. He flew to meet Mary who flew to meet him.

"My treasure," he exclaimed, "let us be first in the briny deep!"

"It isn't briny, you idiot," said Isaac Busby.

"Then I shall shed tears in it and make it briny."

The two, taking hands, skipped into the water.

Mary gave a cry as the chill of it touched her body. "Oh, how cold! How lovely and cold!"

"She could not do a worse thing," said Dr. Ramsey. He stalked judiciously to the lake's edge and took its temperature with his toes.

He had provided his own bathing costume which consisted of a gray flannel shirt and an old pair of breeches.

"Hoop-la!" cried Philip. "Let's make the plunge!"

He caught Daisy's hand in his and they ran laughing after Conway and Mary. In another moment all were disporting themselves in the grateful coolness of the lake. It was perfect.

Nero, who had run all the way from Jalna after the wagonette and was more dead than alive on arrival, now began to notice what was going on. He came from under the willows where he had lain, loudly panting, and advanced to the shore. From beneath his curly black thatch he observed many people apparently drowning.

As it was against his principles to allow people to drown, he uttered a loud bark of assurance, as though to shout—"Hold on! I'm coming!" and plunged into the water.

He had no especial gallantry toward the female sex. A man's life was to him as valuable as a woman's. Therefore as Dr. Ramsey happened to be nearest him he swam with all his strength to rescue him.

"Call your dog, Whiteoak!" the doctor shouted, warding off Nero with an upraised arm.

Nero took this gesture as one of supplication and made haste to grasp the doctor's shirt in his powerful jaws. He then began to drag him toward the shore.

Dr. Ramsey, in a fury, caught him a clout on the head but Nero's head was so protected by thick curly hair that it did not really hurt him and, if it had hurt him very badly, the result would have been the same. He would have tried only the harder to save the doctor.

"Nero!" shouted Philip, controlling his laughter. "Here, sir! Nero!" He swam toward Nero.

Dr. Ramsey continued to clout him. But, by the time Nero had got him to shore, his shirt was half off his back. Nero then swam toward Daisy.

"Help!" she shrieked. "Oh, Captain Whiteoak, save me from Nero!"

Philip now had the great fellow by the collar. He dragged him to the shore and discovering a stout stick of wood threw it far out for him to retrieve. Nero gave not another glance to drowning human beings but concentrated all his lifesaving proclivities on the stick. Again and again he brought it safely to shore till at length, quite tired-out, he retired with it beneath the willows.

There was now an exquisite coolness abroad. It was exhilarating to swim or merely to bob up and down in the bright water. Little waves were beginning to rise and there was a faint line of foam on the beach. When they came out of the lake to lie on the warm sand they had a feeling of something new and strange in their relations. The old conventions seemed cast aside and they lay relaxed in child-like abandon. Brent put his head on Kate's arm, while she wound his closely curling hair about her fingers. If ever she had had a fancy for Wilmott, it was forgotten now. She was utterly satisfied with her husband.

Young Vaughan had managed to draw Adeline a little to one side.

"I wish we two were the only ones on the beach," he said, his blue eyes drinking in the lithe beauty of her form.

"We shall have to come together for a bathe one day."

"Would you really? But you're not in earnest. Your eyes are smiling."

"What harm would there be in it?"

"None. But people are so abominable." He took a handful of sand and let it trickle through his fingers. "May I call you Adeline? Surely I have as much right as that man Wilmott."

"He's an old friend. I've known him for ages."

"You only met him on board ship."

"That seems ages ago. But—call me Adeline if you like." She scarcely heard what Robert said. She was looking across the sand at Daisy and Philip. There was an intangible something in their attitudes, a look in their eyes, that arrested her. Daisy was suddenly different. She was no longer the irresponsible girl, given to poses and extravagances, but a deliberate woman, filled with almost uncontrollable passion for a man. Her eyes devoured Philip. She was a huntress who, having made many experiments in the chase, now drew her bowstring taut, having discovered the coveted prey. That Philip was married meant little to her. She hungered for experience rather than permanence in the field of her emotions. Adeline could see how conscious Philip was of the unleashing of something wild in Daisy. Her heart gave a leap of anger, then she turned to Robert with a smile.

"I'd love to have you call me Adeline," she said.

"Thank you—Adeline . . . Of course, I've called you that a thousand times in secret. I seem always to be thinking of you."

"You're a dear boy, Bobby." Again her eyes moved toward Daisy and Philip. They were motionless, gazing at the rose-stained blueness of the lake. A single cloud hung like a crimson banner. The color was reflected on their faces which seemed flushed by their own turbulent thoughts. Again Adeline's heart gave a leap of anger—anger too at herself for being so blind. Her first thoughts about Daisy had been right. She was dangerous. Yet she had been foolish enough to laugh at Daisy—to pity her for her ineffective poses. Curiously, at this moment Daisy looked beautiful.

Generous Kate Brent put the thought into words.

"Doesn't Daisy look beautiful!" she exclaimed.

Everyone looked at Daisy who, with an enigmatic smile, continued to gaze at the lake.

"What a lucky dog you are, Philip!" said Conway. "Here I am completely under the dominance of my wife—not daring to glance at another woman."

"You two must learn to be tolerant, as Adeline and I are," returned Philip.

"Pray do not believe a word that Conway says," said Mary. "It is quite the other way about."

"Mary is right," put in Sholto. "It was only yesterday that he slapped her and pulled her hair. I can vouch for it because I was present."

Conway leaped up. "Now you're for it!" he said.

With an exclamation of terror, Sholto fled along the beach, Conway in pursuit. Their pale red hair flew backward from their pale brows.

"Will he hurt him?" asked Kate, anxiously.

"He will not kill him," returned Adeline, "but we are an untamed family. You never can tell what we shall do when we're roused."

"Conway is not really angry," said Mary.

Moved by irresistible curiosity for everything that Conway did, she rose and followed the youths who were now out of sight.

The three did not return till the picnic meal was ready to sit down to. The clothes of the bathers had been completely dried by the warm sand and the sun. They had regained appetites which the heat of the preceding days had taken away.

The young Busbys had gathered driftwood for a fire, and its bright blaze rose crackling from the beach. It was now past sunset and a deep velvet darkness was resting in the shadows. A kettle was boiled. Tea was made. The tempting dishes prepared by Mrs. Coveyduck were arranged on the cloth. The mysterious light, the unconventional costumes, the excellent wine produced by Philip, the relief from enervating heat made the atmosphere gay, with an almost Gallic liveliness. This was partly due to the constant reference by Conway and Mary to life in the South of France. French interjections made the two seem foreign, and Sholto imitated all they did. It was surprising how the behavior of these three, the youngest present with the exception of the youngest Busby who was almost speechless from shyness, affected the behavior of the more sedate. No one had ever seen Dr. Ramsey in such spirits. With his arm about the plump waist of Lydia Busby, he waved his glass aloft and recited some of the more amorous poems of Robert Burns. Wilmott obviously had taken too much wine. Adeline was in wild spirits. Together she and Wilmott sang "I Dreamt That I Dwelt in Marble Halls." There were tears in Wilmott's eyes as they recalled the night in Quebec when they had heard Jenny Lind sing. Life seemed strange and full of beautiful and violent possibilities. The moon rose out of the lake.

"Let's bathe again!" exclaimed Conway, suddenly. He stood slim and white at the water's rim.

"In the dark?" cried Lydia Busby. "Oh, surely not!"

"We did in the South of France," said Mary. "It was lovely. Far nicer than in daylight because the glare was gone."

"It's a grand idea," said Isaac Busby. "I shall be first in!" He ran into the water and plunged.

"It's glorious," he shouted. "Come on, everybody!"

They threw themselves into this new pleasure with the abandon of children. Adeline freed herself from Robert Vaughan and, taking

Wilmott's hand, led him across the rippling sand till the water reached their breasts. She smiled into his eyes.

"Do you feel better now, James?" she asked.

"Better? There is nothing wrong with me."

"Duck down, James. Let the water go over your head."

"Adeline, you don't understand me in the least. When I am at my happiest, you think I am tipsy or ill. But I do feel a little confused in the head and perhaps a ducking would help me." He looked submissively into her eyes. "Shall we do it now?"

"Yes. Take a deep breath first and hold it."

Down they went under the water. A singing, prehistoric world was theirs for a moment. A world where they had strange adventures, holding fast each other's hands. Then they came up and rediscovered the moon and their companions.

"I'm divinely happy," said Wilmott. "I really haven't a care in the world, since I know that Henrietta is satisfied and is no longer seeking me. I was wrong in saying you don't understand me. You are the only one who understands me. I have told you that I am writing a book. I should like to read the first chapters to you. I want your opinion of it."

"Oh, James, how lovely! Will you bring the manuscript tomorrow morning?"

"Yes. I think you will find it quite moving. Shall we go under again?"

"Yes, let's go under."

Again they disappeared and again rose out of the lake. The voices and laughter of the others came to them softly.

Lydia Busby looked lovelier in her bathing costume in the moonlight than anyone had dreamed it possible for her to look. The curves of her arms and neck were bewitching. There was an almost seductive sweetness in her smile, a new consciousness of her own charm. Hitherto she had seemed but a tomboy.

The fire had died down. Someone went to the shore and rebuilt it so that its flames rose bright. Suddenly, moved by a common impulse, all gathered round it, posturing and gesticulating in extravagant fashion. Dr. Ramsey picked up an empty bottle and waved it while he quoted Burns. At this moment Elihu Busby appeared from among the willows and stalked across the sand. Before he raised his voice to speak they realized that his sense of decorum was outraged. He flourished the stump of his right arm.

"I never thought," he said, "that I'd live to see the day my children would take part in such a scene."

" 'My heart's in the Highlands,' " chanted the doctor,

> *"my heart is not here;*
> *My heart's in the Highlands a-chasing the deer."*

"You ought to be ashamed of yourself, Dr. Ramsey—you who should be an example to the others."

"I have nothing to be ashamed of. I was invited to a party and I came. I am only making myself agreeable."

"If strangers choose to come here and bring outlandish habits from the Old World, we can't prevent 'em, but we can refuse to take part in 'em."

Again the doctor quoted Burns. "What does old Bobby say?" he declaimed. "He says:—

> *"The social, friendly, honest man,*
> *Whate'er he be,*
> *'Tis he fulfils great Nature's plan,*
> *And none but he."*

Elihu Busby turned from him to his eldest son.

"I'm sick at heart, Isaac," he said, "to think that you would allow your sisters to take part in such a dissipated scene—hopping about like grasshoppers, half-naked and streaming with water."

Lydia and her younger sister began to cry.

Young Isaac said—"Father, we meant no harm and you and Mother knew we were coming on a picnic."

"Would you have behaved in this fashion if your mother and I had been here? This picnic will be the talk of the countryside if it gets out. So far we have been a moral community."

Dr. Ramsey laid down the bottle and folded his arms. Again he quoted Burns.

> *"Morality, thou deadly bane,*
> *Thy tens o' thousands thou hast slain!"*

Elihu Busby ignored him. He said to his daughters:—

"Get into your clothes, girls. As for you, Kate, you are married now, and if your husband chooses to allow you to remain I can't force you to leave but, if I had known what his tastes are, I might not so soon have forgiven you your marriage to him."

Now Kate also began to cry.

"Really, sir," said Brent, with his disarming smile, "this has been a most innocent affair. I only wish you had been here from the first to see for yourself. But, if Kate's sisters are leaving, she and I will leave too. Come, Kate, gather up your things."

Weeping, Kate and her sisters fled to the shelter of the cedars.

With dignity and a little truculence, Philip came to Elihu Busby's side.

"I take it hardly," he said, "that you should come here and criticize my way of entertaining myself and my friends." Busby liked Philip and admired him. With some softening in his manner he said:—

"I don't contend, Captain Whiteoak, that anything disgraceful took place at this picnic. What I do say is that so much license is not good. In time it will lead to disgraceful things. If you drink wine and dance about a fire like pagans, what will your grandchildren do when they set out to have a good time? They'll probably get drunk on gin and dance naked. Manners and morals are never at a standstill. Either they rise or they decline. Like Empires."

"Then your ambition is," said Philip, smiling, "to have your grandchildren enjoy a picnic thus. The young ladies, after dipping a lily-white toe in the lake, will sit in a circle with their knitting while the most devil-may-care of the young men will read aloud from the works of Mr. Longfellow."

Dr. Ramsey had overheard. He sprang up. "Yes," he said, striking an angular attitude:—

"Lives of great men all remind us
We can make our lives sublime,
And, departing, leave behind us
Footprints on the sands of time."

So declaiming he planted a naked foot firmly on the moist sand. He then lifted it and carefully examined the imprint. "Picture the joy of the wanderer, ninety years hence, when he comes upon this! He'll immediately set about making his life sublime also." He stamped on the footprints. "Bah," he exclaimed, "I wouldn't give one line of old Bobby's for everything Mr. Longfellow has written or ever will write!"

Elihu Busby turned to Philip.

"Is Dr. Ramsey drunk?" he asked.

"No, no, not in the least."

"He waved that bottle about as though he were."

"That bottle, Mr. Busby, contained nothing but mineral water."

"All that is the matter with me," said the doctor, "is that I am relaxing. I work too hard. There should be three doctors in this neighborhood instead of one. Yet can you say, Elihu Busby, that I ever have neglected a patient?"

"Indeed I cannot," said Busby, heartily. "More than a few of us would be dead if it weren't for your devotion."

"Thank you," said the doctor, only a little mollified.

The three sisters now appeared from the cedar thicket, fully dressed and carrying their bathing costumes in a basket. Kate had recovered her spirits and walked with the assurance of a married woman, to her husband's side. He greeted her with a sly wink. Lydia, too, was now composed but her color was high and her eyes downcast till she passed Dr. Ramsey. Then she raised them and a look was exchanged, so warm, so full of tenderness that each was surprised and bewildered. The youngest sister, Abigail, was still weeping. But she was only sixteen. Their brother joined them and their father, with a commanding gesture, marched them away. Exhortations to the horses came out of the darkness beyond the willows. Then came the sound of wheels. Five of the party had departed. Nero, who had been exploring farther along the shore, had not become aware of Elihu Busby's presence till he was leaving. To make up for this laxness he followed his buggy for some distance, uttering loud threatening barks. After this demonstration of his watchfulness he padded back across the beach and asked Adeline for something to eat. She went to where the hampers stood and proceeded to pile high a plate for him.

Sholto raised his young voice loudly. "Who was the old gaffer?" he asked.

"The Busby girls' father, you ass," returned his brother.

"We should have ducked him in the lake for a spoil-sport."

"Hold your tongue," said Philip, laconically, "or I shall duck you."

"I wish you would duck me, Philip," cried Mary. "I'm longing for another dip."

The words had scarcely been spoken when Conway and Sholto seized her and carried her into the lake. With their pale hair flying in the moonlight the three resembled a mermaid captured by two mermen, and being carried off by them to their ocean cave. So thought Wilmott and he said so to Dr. Ramsey. They had separated themselves from the others in a new-found congeniality and were strolling along the beach.

"The lady whose appearance most struck me," said the doctor, "was Lydia Busby. To tell you the truth, I am pretty badly smitten. And this with a girl whom I have known for years and scarcely noticed, except for her healthy good looks. It is quite extraordinary what propinquity and a moonlit night will suddenly discover."

"Yes, yes," agreed Wilmott absently, his eyes on their two shadows on the beach. "Miss Lydia is a lovely girl."

"I admire her more than I admire Mrs. Whiteoak," went on Dr. Ramsey. "Certainly Mrs. Whiteoak has a very arresting face—" he fell silent a moment in thought, then continued, after a deep breath—"but she isn't the sort of woman I should care to marry—even if I had the chance." He laughed.

"Of course not. You would require quite a different sort of companion. . . . Do you know, I was surprised to hear you quote poetry this evening. I had not guessed that you have literary tastes."

The doctor laughed. "Oh, I don't show my real self on all occasions. I am a reserved man. But I read a good deal when I can find the time."

"You have an excellent memory."

"It's a pernicious memory. I never forget anything."

"I, on the contrary, find great pleasure in forgetting. I'm piling up new experience. And—at the same time—" he looked out across the still lake and spoke softly—"at the same time, I'm writing a book."

Dr. Ramsey looked impressed. "Now that is just what I should expect of you!" he exclaimed.

Wilmott was pleased. "Is it?"

"Yes. And I make a guess that it is a work of the imagination."

"You are right."

"Are you getting on well with it?"

"I have the first five chapters written."

"Can you tell me something about it?"

Wilmott launched forth. They strode on. A lovely freshness was rising from the lake. Dew was falling on the shore. Whippoorwills called and called again from the near-by woods. A loon uttered its wild laugh.

Robert Vaughan felt himself to be unwanted by Daisy and Philip who talked in a low tone. He was angry at Daisy, ashamed of what he considered her shameless overtures to Philip. Himself she ignored. He would have liked to order her home but instead sprang up and left them. Adeline was still among the willows with Nero. Robert felt alone, unwanted by anyone—not by the three disporting themselves in the lake, not by the two striding in the opposite direction, not by Philip and Daisy, in the intimacy of the firelight, not by Adeline, feeding her dog among the willows.

There was just moonlight enough for her to see what was in the hamper. She heaped a dish with slices of ham and pieces of bread but instead of setting this before Nero she fed him from her fingers. This suited him well because he already had had a good deal to eat and food tasted better when Adeline fed him. He loved her with a deep, warm, dark devotion. She was barely conscious that his lips touched her fingers. Her eyes were fixed on Daisy with an expression so cold, so hard, so almost blank that an observer might well have wondered if they could be the luminous and changeful eyes with which she generally looked out on the world.

Philip sat in the glow of the fire, motionless but with an enigmatic smile. His shirt open at the neck revealed his white chest, his uprolled sleeves his rounded yet muscular arms. Daisy sat close to him, almost leaning against him. She thought Adeline had gone along the beach with Wilmott and the doctor. Daisy, with her narrow slant eyes, her short face, her turn-up nose, had a kind of savage primitive beauty. Her mouth was upthrust toward Philip as though in preparation for a kiss.

"Is the girl mad or just a fool?" thought Adeline. "She might be sure someone would see her. Why doesn't that brute, Philip, push her away? By heaven, if he kisses her I will kill him!"

Suddenly, as though in uncontrolled passion, Daisy threw herself across Philip's thighs and, twining her arms about him, drew his head down to hers. Adeline could hear her speaking but not what she said.

Philip took hold of Daisy and lifted her upright but he kept his hands on her. Now he was speaking. The fire was between them and the lake. The bathers could be heard splashing and romping toward the shore. Daisy sat tense, turning a look of hate on them. They ran toward the fire. Mary huddled up to it.

"Oh, how cold it has got!" she cried.

"Cold!" laughed Conway. "It is just heavenly cool."

"Well, I am cold."

Sholto peered into Daisy's face.

"How odd you look, Miss Vaughan! Are you angry?"

"Angry!" she repeated, in a high voice. "I never was happier in all my life. I'm in the seventh heaven of content. Please stop staring at me."

"Oh, how cold it has got!" cried Mary, spreading her hands to the fire.

"Have a drink of lemonade," said Conway, callously.

"What have you been saying to my brother-in-law, Miss Vaughan?" asked Sholto, still peering into Daisy's face.

She struck at him. "You are an odious boy," she said.

Dr. Ramsey and Wilmott now returned from their ramble. They had been happy in each other's company but, when the doctor saw Mary shivering by the fire, he came to her frowning.

"I warned you, Mrs. Court," he said sternly. "Yet you have bathed three times. Now, I am afraid, you have really taken a chill." He laid his fingers on her pulse.

Mary looked ready to sink.

"She could not have taken a chill," exclaimed Conway. "She only wants to be fussed over!"

"See this long mane of wet hair down her back," said the doctor, collecting it in his hand like seaweed.

Conway brought a cloak and threw it carelessly about her shoulders.

"Where is Adeline?" he asked.

She came out from among the willows followed by Nero. She looked calm yet brilliant. Her white teeth flashed in her face as she came smiling toward the others.

"Where have you been?" asked Philip, suspiciously.

"Among the willows," she returned gaily, "feeding Nero. Ah, what a day it's been! What a success! Don't you all agree? But the moon is sinking. I think we ought to collect our things and return home or we shall be lost on the way."

All agreed that this was so and, with a sense of haste and yet regret, they collected their belongings and smothered the fire. With its dying, the bathing party was over. They had a time of it to capture the horses in the near-by field who had broken from their tether and were grazing at will. Out of the darkness appeared Tite. He had been waiting a long while with Wilmott's horse. Wilmott had only lately acquired it, was proud yet half-apologetic for it.

"What do you think of my mare?" he asked of the doctor.

Dr. Ramsey screwed up his eyes to examine its dark bulk. He broke into a laugh.

"What a back!" he exclaimed. "Certainly you can't fall out of that hollow!"

"She answers my purpose very well," answered Wilmott stiffly.

"I'm sure she does. I've known her for years. She's perfectly reliable. You did well to acquire her."

But Wilmott was offended. He climbed into the saddle. His feelings were hurt for his mare. He had pictured himself as cutting rather a fine figure on her.

"Good night!" he called out to the others and, without waiting for their company, rode away.

Tite trotted along the soft, sandy soil of the road beside him.

"You need not have brought the mare, Tite," said Wilmott. "I could very well have returned with the party to Jalna and from there walked home."

"I wanted to come, Boss," said Tite. "I wanted to see what a bathing party was like."

"And what did you think of it, Tite?"

"Well, Boss, I only wash to be clean and, when I see folks wash themselves again and again, I am surprised. I am surprised to see white folks do a war dance round the fire like Indian folks did in the old time. It made me want to do a war whoop."

"It is well for you that you restrained yourself, Tite."

"Boss," went on Tite, "it surprised me to see the ladies undressing among the trees."

"Gad," exclaimed Wilmott, "you came early to the party!"

"It made me laugh," went on Tite happily, "to see that one which my grandmother calls the harlot lay herself across Captain Whiteoak's knees and draw him down to her. I was sorry you were not there to see, Boss."

"If you do not come to a bad end, Tite," said Wilmott grimly, "it will be a wonder. Remember, you are not to talk of this to anyone—not even your grandmother!"

"Very well, Boss. But it is a pity I cannot tell my grandmother, for she does enjoy a good laugh."

XX

The Gallop in the Forest

MARY looked wan and blue about the lips when she reached Jalna. Adeline made her go to bed while she herself descended to the kitchen to prepare a hot drink for her. Her brothers followed her. They were as curious as monkeys and ran here and there carrying lighted candles in their hands and peering into every cupboard and corner. They went down the brick passage, past the rooms where the Coveyducks and Lizzie slept, to where they knew was the wine cellar. Philip had had it well stocked. He prided himself on his knowledge of wines and their qualities. When he entertained his friends he was able to give them the best.

Adeline heard the boys whispering outside the door of the wine cellar. A low fire was smouldering on the hearth and she put on a saucepan of milk to heat. She went on tiptoe to the arched doorway of the passage and listened. Sholto was saying:—

"I saw tools in the scullery. If I had a screwdriver I could easily take off the padlock. It would be fun to find what Philip has in there."

"Wait till they're in bed. We'll come down again and explore."

"No, you won't, you young ruffians!" said Adeline. "Come along out of there and, if I have to complain of you to Philip, you'll be sorry."

They came unrepentant, candle in hand. They looked strange and beautiful in the dim passage, with the flickering light in their faces. As they passed the Coveyducks' door, Conway gave it a thump with his candlestick. A groan came from within.

"Up with you!" he called out. "The house is on fire."

"How dare you!" said Adeline. "What a mischief you are! 'T is nothing, Coveyduck! Go to sleep again. I have but come down for a drink of milk."

"The milk is boiling over," observed Sholto.

"Snatch it off, you ninny!" said his sister.

Coveyduck sank to slumber again.

Adeline put a pinch of cinnamon in the milk and carried it up the two flights of stairs, the boys following her. Mary drank it gratefully. Sometimes she missed her mother's petting. She now put her thin arms about Adeline and kissed her.

"Good night," said Adeline, kissing her in return. "Sleep tight."

"It was a lovely bathing party."

"It was indeed."

"When may we have another?"

"When I can get the taste of this one out of my mouth." She turned abruptly and hastened from the room and down the stairs.

She set her candlestick on the dressing table and looked toward the bed. Philip was not there. He had driven the wagonette to the stable and probably was lingering to talk to the groom. She could not trust her self-control in the exchange of a word with Philip that night. She undressed in haste and put on her long, heavily embroidered nightdress. Her thick hair was still moist and when she lay down she spread it over the pillow away from her. She left the candle burning for Philip. It lighted the room but dimly yet, in an odd way, brought out the coloring of the bedstead and hangings more richly than a brighter light might have done. Boney, perched on his stand, glowed like a green and vermilion flower. Adeline composed her features, facing the candlelight. Her heart beat heavily in a primitive, wild anger at Daisy Vaughan.

The candle was burning low when Philip came. Between her lashes she saw him cast a look at it as though wondering if it would hold out for his undressing. He had left the front door wide open for the sake of coolness. The cool night air filled the hall and overflowed into their bedroom, meeting the air from the window. He too undressed quickly and lay down beside her. Before he had blown out the candle he had given her a long look, being suspicious of her sleeping. Now he laid his hand on her side and snuggled his head into the pillow.

As though galvanized, she sprang away from him.

"Don't put a hand on me!" she exclaimed.

"Now, what's up?" he asked.

She threw herself on her other side, her long damp hair streaming behind her.

"Very well," he said, "if you're going to be like that." He rolled over, turning his back on her.

"Like what?" she asked between her teeth.

"Hoity-toity." Again he snuggled into the pillow, breathing deeply as though consciously content.

Did he feel as innocent as he sounded? No—a thousand times no! She longed to turn and face him, grasp him by the shoulders and pour out on him all that rankled in her mind. Ah, it was lucky for him that he had put Daisy away from him! Lucky for him that he had a wife of character!

It was not Philip but Daisy who filled her heart with rage. Daisy was not only designing. She was unscrupulous. She was *bad*. There was nothing she would not do to take your man away from you, if she wanted him. The desire in Daisy's face as she drew Philip's down toward hers had filled Adeline with a horrid fear of the temptress. How could a man be held responsible for what he did, with such a woman about? After all, he was but flesh and blood.

Yet, as Adeline lay awake hour after hour, she was not so much apprehending what Daisy might do, as considering the punishment for what she had done. The grandfather clock in the hall struck one, two, and three. Still she had not slept. She resigned herself to a sleepless night. She relaxed and drew the sweet night smells into her nostrils. She was glad that Dr. Ramsey considered the night air of summer harmless. Yet she doubted if he would have approved of quite so much as now swept into the room.

The house seemed singularly alive to-night. It stood, in the hushed indrawn beauty of the night, hunched against the darkness, as though feeling in every stone the sting of the first unhappiness it had sheltered. They had been so happy here! Their very embraces had had in them an earthy pride that had risen out of the virgin land. The cycle of the days was not long enough for the expression of their content. "Think of the time when we shall see our own grain cut!" they had said. "What a Christmas we shall have! The house will be hung with pine and spruce boughs. . . . What will it be like to watch the spring coming to Jalna?"

She felt as though a catastrophe had fallen on the house. She saw the house as old, crumbling, weighed down by the sorrows that had been enacted there, sunk beneath the great creeper that would cover it.

She opened her eyes to reassure herself and saw a paleness where the window was. Morning was on the way. She must remember to water the little Virginia creeper Mrs. Vaughan had given her. It had been planted beside the porch and thriven well till the dry, hot days came. Suddenly she put out her hand toward Philip. It touched his back between the shoulders. He was breathing deeply. Drowsiness stole over her.

When she woke it was past nine o'clock. Mrs. Coveyduck was standing beside the bed with her morning tea on a tray. Already she had taken a comfortable motherly attitude toward Adeline.

"Bless my soul," she said, "what a way to treat your beautiful hair, ma'am! It looks as though you had dragged it through a hedge. You must let me give it a good brushing for 'ee. Come, drink this warm tea and tell me what I shall give 'ee for breakfast."

"Bacon and eggs," answered Adeline promptly. "Is it a fine morning? I want to ride."

"Aye, 't is as luvely a day as you could see in a whole zummer-time. But surely you will want to rest after such a late party on the beach."

"No, no, I am not tired."

She sat up, while Mrs. Coveyduck arranged the tray, with its pot of tea and two slices of thin bread and butter, in front of her.

"Coveyduck told me, ma'am, that you were down in the kitchen heating milk when you came home. You should have called me to get it for 'ee. He had no right to let me sleep like a gert log while you waited on yourself. But he has no sense except to make things grow."

"I told him not to wake you."

"Aye, but there's times to obey an order and times not to obey 'em. Now drink your tea and I'll give the bird his seeds."

She filled Boney's seed cup from the canister of parrot seed that stood on the mantelpiece. Boney looked on with interest and when she had finished he flew to the top of his cage, scrambled over it in great haste and went in at the door. He thrust his dark beak into the seed cup.

All the while Mrs. Coveyduck brushed Adeline's hair he talked in a cooing voice to her.

"Dilkoosha—dilkoosha—mera lal," he said, wriggling his body on the perch.

"What does he say, ma'am?" asked Mrs. Coveyduck.

"He calls me Pearl of the Harem."

"Does he now? Well, well, 't is a clever bird and no mistake."

"Mrs. Coveyduck, I want you to tell Patsy O'Flynn to go to Vaughanlands and give my compliments to Miss Vaughan and ask her if she will do Captain and Mrs. Whiteoak the honor of riding with them this morning."

"Yes, ma'am, I'll send him off at once."

Adeline wore her riding habit and hat to breakfast. She was alone, for Philip was always early about the estate and the others still slept. She could hear Gussie and Nicholas prattling at play under the young silver-birch tree. She heard Ernest crying with the intonation of hunger. Thank goodness, she was not still nursing this baby! Once again the milk from Maggie, the little goat, was succoring an infant Whiteoak. She heard the nurse going to the basement for Ernest's bottle. Adeline ate heartily.

Almost as soon as Patsy returned with the news that Miss Vaughan would be delighted to ride with Captain and Mrs. Whiteoak, Daisy herself appeared.

Really, thought Adeline, she was shameless! Adeline regarded her appraisingly as she sat before the door on Robert's own saddle horse, a charming young mare named Pixie. Daisy was dressed with great care. Her hair, caught at the nape, hung in three long curls that reached the saddle. And, oh, those little curls in front of the ears! Adeline could gladly have pulled them off. And her tasseled boots and her gauntleted gloves! And the false smile on her face! Adeline could gladly have killed her.

But she gave her a cheerful good-morning and, Patsy assisting her, mounted her own horse. He was a pale chestnut, graceful and of perfect motion, Philip's present to her on her birthday.

"How well you are looking, dear Mrs. Whiteoak!" cried Daisy. "I have never seen you look better. And what a sweet horse! Oh, I envy you the way you ride! You make me quite ashamed. And there are the pet children!" She threw kisses to them. "Good morning, Nicholas! Good morning, Gussie! What eyes they have! And where is Captain Whiteoak?"

"He is where they are building the church. He may join us there. But I hope you won't be too disappointed if we take our ride without him."

"Not at all. There is nothing I enjoy more than a tête-à-tête with you."

Somewhere there had been a storm. It had cleared the air and there was a pleasant freshness abroad. Axemen were still at work uprooting stumps, leveling the ground, while carpenters were doing the last jobs to house and barns. Still, there was now a finish about the place. It was surprising how much Coveyduck had already accomplished in the way of lawn and flower border. Every day he sang the praises of the power of the virgin soil.

Side by side the two horses trotted, past the new herd of Jersey cattle, past the pigs and ducks in the farmyard. They followed the cart track through the estate to the road where the church was being built. Philip had given this road for public use and already many a vehicle had passed along it but still it was rough and the forest pressed close to it.

Now they saw the walls of the church rising solid on a tree-crowned knoll. Loud hammering filled the air. The forest birds liked the noise of the hammers and sang their loudest to its accompaniment. The river circled below the graveyard where there was, as yet, no grave. They could see Mr. Pink in shirt sleeves working among the men. But there was no sign of Philip. Daisy could not quite conceal her disappointment when he was not to be found. She looked suspiciously at Adeline.

"Are you sure," she asked, "that he said he would ride with us?"

"Well, I think he did," returned Adeline with a little laugh. "But we are happy enough without him, aren't we? Let's gallop!"

The horses broke into a gallop, their hoofs thudding on the sandy soil. Trees arched overhead with boughs almost touching. The morning sunshine sifted golden through their greenness. When they drew rein, the sound of hammering was far behind. Daisy's color was high.

"Please let us not gallop again," she said. "The ground is too rough. It makes me nervous."

"Very well," answered Adeline affably, "we'll not gallop. We'll go at a nice walk. Let us follow this path that branches off. I've never been here before."

They turned into the path which was too narrow for them to ride abreast. Adeline led the way, her anger seething within her. At last in a grassy opening she drew rein, wheeled and faced Daisy.

"Now," she said, "you are to answer for the way you tried to seduce my husband last night."

For a moment Daisy was stunned. She could not take in the words. Then they sank into her, and the look on Adeline's face. She turned her horse sharply and made as though to gallop back.

"Stop!" exclaimed Adeline, and brought the weight of her riding crop across Daisy's back.

Daisy turned her mare and faced Adeline.

"You devil!" she said.

"If I am a devil," said Adeline, "it is you who have roused it in me! The men of my family would take their riding crop to a man who would play loose with their women. What did you do? You fairly wound yourself around my Philip's body! You threw yourself across his knees last night by the lake! What do you think I am? Blind? Or a creature of no spirit? Let me tell you—I have been watching you. Ah, my eye has been on you. Take that!" she shouted, brandishing her riding crop.

If Adeline had expected Daisy to fly in terror, she was mistaken. Daisy was indeed terrified but she was furious also. There was a snakelike quality in her sinuous body, crouched on the saddle, in her short, slant-eyed face with the lips drawn back from the teeth. She raised her own riding crop in menace as she avoided Adeline's blow.

"Don't you dare to strike me again!" she cried.

"I'll flog you as you deserve," exclaimed Adeline. But her horse was nervous. He struggled against the bit and danced here and there. She could not reach Daisy.

"What do you know of love?" Daisy cried out. "You're wrapped up in yourself. You're too proud to love Philip as he deserves. I'm not proud. I've always wanted him! I'm going to have him. He loves me. What you saw last night, that wasn't the half. We're lovers, I tell you!"

"Lies! Lies! There's no word of truth in you! But now you *shall* have your lesson."

Now she rode close to Daisy and again and again she struck her with the crop. At each blow Daisy gave a cry of rage, for she was scarcely conscious of pain. She struck at Adeline but the blow descended on the horse. In a convulsion of surprise he reared himself on his hind legs. Daisy's mare, as though in emulation, reared also. And there for a short space they faced each other immobile, like two riders cut from bronze, the green forest standing in its denseness about them, the lustrous blue sky arching above. It was a pity that there was no spectator of this scene or that none of the four participants was conscious of its beauty.

Then suddenly Adeline's horse began to plunge. He wheeled and galloped violently in the direction whence they had come and, as though in a concerted plan, the mare flew along the path into the forest. There was soon a wide space between them.

Adeline let him gallop but she spoke soothingly to him and bent forward to pat him.

"It was not I who hit you, Prince. It wasn't I, old man. It was that villain, Daisy. We've always known in our hearts she was bad. But I flogged her! Lord, how I laid it on!"

Her cheeks blazing, her eyes ashine, she galloped home.

It was now high noon and very warm. She went to her room and changed into a cool flowing dress. She went to the dining room and busied herself in arranging rows of delicate glass goblets in a French cabinet. The room was now papered; rugs were laid on the floor; the long curtains, of a golden yellow with heavy cords and tassels, hung from the ornate cornices. The portraits of herself and Philip were side by side, above the silver-laden sideboard. It was a handsome room, she thought. She would not be ashamed to entertain here.

She busied herself, humming a little tune. But one part of her mind she kept locked.

The Laceys came to dinner and it was not till they were leaving and the shadow of the young birch lay at length on the grass that Robert Vaughan drove up to the door. His face was pale.

"What has happened?" he demanded, as though all were aware of something unusual.

"Happened?" answered Philip. "What do you mean?"

"Is Mrs. Whiteoak safe?"

"She is."

"Well, my cousin isn't! Pixie has come home without her!"

Philip turned in astonishment to Adeline.

"You were riding with Daisy, weren't you?"

"Yes . . . We had words . . . a quarrel . . . and we separated. I came home alone."

"Oh," cried Mrs. Lacey. "I'm afraid the poor girl has had an accident! Oh, dear—oh, dear!"

"We must organize a search party at once," said Captain Lacey. He turned almost accusingly to Adeline. "Where was Miss Vaughan when you parted from her, Mrs. Whiteoak?"

Adeline knit her brow. "I don't know. It was quite a long way off. On the cart track leading from the church. Then along a narrow path to a clearing. We separated there."

"You must come and show us," said Philip.

Mary asked—"Do you think there are wolves about?"

"Not a wolf," answered Captain Lacey, but he spoke uneasily.

"I'll bring Nero," cried Sholto. "We shall need something in the way of a bloodhound."

"What I am afraid of is that she has been thrown and injured. How was her horse behaving when you parted from her, Mrs. Whiteoak?"

"She was a little restive."

Robert found the opportunity of saying to Adeline:—

"I have quarreled with Daisy too. I thought her behavior last night was detestable. But now I feel frightened."

"Nothing has happened to her."

"But how can you know?"

"Something tells me."

While Adeline and Philip were changing into their riding clothes, he exclaimed—"This is a pretty kettle of fish! If anything has happened to that girl, you will be blamed. You need not have said that you quarreled."

"I am of a frank nature," she returned.

"There is no need to disclose everything."

"I did not disclose the cause of our quarrel."

There was complete silence for a space. Then Philip said—"I don't want to be told what it was about."

"No. Because you already know."

He stared, his blue eyes prominent. "I know?"

"Of course, you know. We quarreled about you."

"Well, all I can say is, you were damn silly women."

"We were. But that is our nature, and our misfortune. She was lucky that I did no more than take my riding crop to her back."

Philip stood transfixed. "Good God!" he exclaimed.

Adeline laughed. "Oh, she struck back at me! She was not at all crushed. She rode off in a rage. She is probably playing a game of being lost in the forest, just to frighten me."

"A risky game. Adeline, you may be sorry for this."

She flung out—"Sorry for punishing a base female who has tried to seduce my husband! No—if a thousand wolves, bears or wild-cats, tear her to bits, I shall not be sorry! In any case I did not lose her. She lost herself. And she will be found. I'm certain of that."

They joined the others who were mounted for the search. All the laborers from the estate, the farm hands from the neighborhood, the men and boys from the village, armed with guns or lanterns, riding or on foot, were gathered by nightfall to help in the recovery of Daisy.

Adeline led them to the spot where the two horses had risen on their hind legs to face each other like symbolic beasts on a coat-of-arms. A good deal of speculation was caused by the scattered and uneven hoofprints. What had the two ladies been doing? She herself was surprised by the hoofprints. What had passed now seemed like a dream.

It was easy to follow Pixie's hoofprints to where she had turned homeward. They ran on smoothly for about three miles, following the path, then abruptly wheeled. The ground was trodden a little as though she had stood for a space. But there was no trace of Daisy. Adeline returned to Jalna with her brothers for escort. All night, in moonlight and after the moon sank, the search went on. Guns were fired; the men shouted; the beams of lanterns penetrated dark thickets where the foot of man had not yet trodden. A thousand birds were startled from their sleep. A thousand wild creatures trembled in their burrows. But there was no trace of Daisy.

When the searchers returned the next morning, worn-out, a fresh party was formed. It was headed by Colonel Vaughan and, though Philip had been out all night, he returned to the search. Men came from a distance. The whole countryside was aroused. Daisy's tragic case laid a shadow across every hearth.

At the end of the fourth day, Philip came in to the library where Adeline was embroidering an altar cloth for the new church. He looked tired out. He threw himself into a chair opposite her and remarked:—

"You look nice and cool."

"I am," she returned, putting her needle into the heart of a lily. But her hand trembled.

"It is well," he observed severely, "to be able to detach yourself so completely from what is going on about you."

"If you mean that I should be rending my garments in anguish over Daisy, I don't see any sense in it. She will be found."

"I wish you'd go out and find her, if you're so damned sure. Egad, I'm tired enough!"

"She'll come back." Adeline spoke doggedly.

"How can you know?"

"I feel it." Never must she let go that feeling!

"You have never before pretended to any occult power."

"It isn't occult. It's just a feeling."

"Well, I wish the rest of us felt that way. We are getting discouraged. The farmers are neglecting their crops. David Vaughan has offered a hundred pounds' reward for her discovery."

"That ought to help."

"Your attitude," he said, rising, "is odious."

"So is Daisy," she returned imperturbably.

The next day Wilmott came to see Adeline. He looked pale and anxious. Adeline was wheeling the perambulator up and down in front of the house with her two sons in it. After greeting her and admiring the babies, Wilmott fell into step with her and exclaimed:—

"I am worried almost to death."

She turned to him in dismay. "Have you heard from Henrietta?"

"No, no, not that. But bad enough."

"What then, James?"

"It's about Tite. He has disappeared."

"Since when?"

"Since the morning Miss Vaughan was lost. He set out that morning to spend two days with his relations. He has not come back. I grew so anxious yesterday that I rode to where the Indians live. I found his grandmother and she told me very vaguely that he had gone to an Indian Reserve to visit some cousins. He had left no message. That wasn't like Tite. It is now five days since he left. My God, I'm afraid something terrible has happened."

"But Indians are vague as to time, aren't they?"

"Not Tite. He has a cool, clear-cut mind. What is tormenting me is the thought—the suspicion—well, I may as well tell you . . . Daisy Vaughan was attracted by him. She let him see that she was attracted. He repeated things she had said to him. To be sure he is only a boy. But he is of mixed blood—savage blood! What if he discovered her that morning in the woods?"

Thoughts of rape and murder flashed like horrid lightning through Adeline's mind. Her heart trembled. Still she said as sturdily as before:—

"Daisy will be found alive. I'm sure of it."

She was right. Two days later Philip came to her, almost running in his excitement.

"She is found!" he cried, his blue eyes bright in his relief. "Daisy Vaughan is safe at her uncle's!"

"I told you!" she cried, her voice very young and clear. "I told you! Who found her?"

"That half-breed boy of Wilmott's. Young Tite. He'd been visiting his people and he was on his way back. He found her in a shelter some Indians had once built of boughs when they were hunting. She'd lived on berries all the while."

"Have you seen her?"

"No. Robert Vaughan just galloped over to tell us. There'll be great rejoicing. Come, and he'll tell us all about it."

"Is she well?"

"Quite uninjured but pretty bedraggled, poor girl. Oh, Adeline, when I think of your part in this, I'm thankful, I can tell you!"

"So am I!" she cried. Bursting into tears, she flung herself into his arms. "Oh, Philip, let this be a lesson to you!"

XXI

The Reward

Adeline and Philip found Robert Vaughan sitting on the porch. He did not look as elated as she had expected. But he smiled as he rose and came to shake hands.

"I could not go indoors," he said. "My boots were so muddy. Well, what do you think of the news? We're thankful, you may be sure. My mother especially. She has worried herself ill."

"I know," said Adeline, "and so have I. Even though I felt from the first that Daisy would be found."

"It's a miracle she survived," said Philip. "Now sit down and tell us all about it. Is she pretty weak?"

"No, she's not particularly weak," answered Robert, guardedly. "But she's very thin. Her riding habit is fairly torn to ribbons by brambles."

They sat down on the oak bench and Adeline's eyes searched Robert's face. She wished she had him alone. She said—"Now begin at the very beginning and tell all—when did you get the first word of her?"

"My father was dozing in his armchair on the verandah. He was done out, for he'd been away from home for the last two days and had almost no sleep or rest. He's not a young man, you know. Well, he heard a step and he gave a great start because he was always hoping Daisy would walk in, in just that way. But it was Mr. Wilmott's half-breed boy, Tite, and he came right up to father and said, 'Boss, I've found your lost girl.' "

"What a moment!" exclaimed Adeline. "Ah, I wish I'd been there!"

"My father could scarcely believe Tite at first but he was soon convinced. Tite had been visiting in the Reserve and on the way home he heard a voice crying, in a sort of wigwam of boughs and saplings that Indians had made a long while ago. He went in and there was Daisy lying on the ground weeping. She'd given up all hope."

"Poor girl," said Philip, in a tone not too heartfelt, for Adeline's eyes were on him. "Poor girl."

"Yes, indeed," agreed Adeline. "Poor girl."

Robert went on in the same curiously guarded tone:—

"Well, Tite's story was that having his gun with him he at once set out to find some food for her. He shot a grouse, built a fire and roasted it. Daisy was ravenous. When she had eaten and slept for a little he supported her as far as a certain clearing he knew and left her there while he came home for help."

"And she hadn't heard our shouting or the reports of our guns!" exclaimed Philip.

"She says she heard nothing."

"She must have wandered a long way."

"Yes, she had wandered a long way."

"That boy, Tite, must know the forest well."

"He knows it like the palm of his hand. Well, to make a long story short, I went back with Tite while my father set about spreading the word to the other searchers that Daisy was found. When we reached the clearing there she was, sitting waiting for us in rags and tatters, with her hair down her back and her face dirty. We put her on the horse behind me and brought her home. My mother almost fainted at the sight of her. Mother had got the big tin bath full of hot water, and fresh clothes ready for her. I came straight over here."

Adeline laid a gentle hand on Robert's arm. "You must be tired and hungry," she said. "Philip, dear, would you ask Mrs. Coveyduck to bring us some of the hot scones she's just made—and a pot of chocolate. My limbs are trembling so from excitement that I fear they'd fail me. Otherwise I'd never ask you to run my errands, Philip. You know I'm not the sort of wife to do that, am I?"

"Listen to her!" said Philip, giving Robert a wink. He went in search of Mrs. Coveyduck.

"Now," said Adeline, her face close to Robert's, "tell me what you think about it all."

He turned his face away.

"You don't believe this story, do you, Robert?"

"Not a word of it," he answered, his face sombre.

"But you believe that Tite found Daisy."

"Yes, I believe he found her."

"But not just to-day?"

"I tell you," he cried fiercely, "I hated to have her on the horse with me! I hated her arms about me!"

"She couldn't have helped but hear the guns and the shouting, could she?"

"Don't ask me."

"Why don't you believe Tite's story, Robert?"

"Because it was false. The story she poured out to me when I met her was false. Every tree in the forest shouted that she was false—false as hell!" He wrung his fingers together. "And when I saw my mother embracing her, weeping over her—my father shaken and aged by this week of misery—I could have killed her!"

"She can't help what she is, Robert," said Adeline, taking his hand. "I don't feel angry at her now. If it isn't one man, it's another—with her. How did she greet your mother?"

"Oh, I don't know! I came away."

Philip returned through the hall. He said:—

"Mrs. Coveyduck is delighted. The chocolate is preparing. The scones smell delicious. What about that reward of a hundred pounds which your father offered for Miss Daisy's discovery, Robert?"

"Oh, Tite had heard of that and claimed it in the first breath!"

"What a windfall for Tite!" exclaimed Philip, laughing. "He will probably leave Wilmott and set himself up as chief of his tribe."

As they spoke of him, they saw Wilmott hastening along the drive. His face was alight. "Have you heard the news?" he cried. Then, seeing Robert, added, "But of course you have. What a relief! I was with the searching party when Colonel Vaughan appeared. We had given up hope of finding Miss Vaughan alive." He sat down beside the others. He fanned himself with his hat. Then he turned to Robert. "There must be great rejoicing at Vaughanlands."

"Yes," answered Robert, with a smile that had more of pain than happiness in it. "But my mother is feeling quite ill."

"I am sorry to hear that." Wilmott's face was alight with sympathy.

"Faith," exclaimed Adeline, "we all have been under a cloud! But now it's lifted." Her eyes smiled into Robert's. "Now we must put all unhappy things out of our minds. We have a great deal to be thankful for."

"Listen to her!" said Philip. "She sounds like a preacher. She really is a bit of a devil but she has these pious spells. I am always afraid of what she may say at such times."

"You all know," said Adeline, still smiling, "that Daisy and I quarreled. Shall I tell you what I did to her?"

"No," answered Philip. "No one wants to know. Here comes the chocolate. While we drink it, Robert must tell us more of what happened this morning." He placed a small table and Mrs. Coveyduck beamingly set down a laden tray.

An hour later Robert returned to Vaughanlands. Philip hastened with relief to his workmen. Adeline and Wilmott were left alone. He said, with a somewhat remote expression on his thin face:—

"Now that this excitement is over perhaps you will be a little interested in my manuscript."

Her eyebrows flew up. "Is it possible, James, that you have been able to do any writing in this past week?"

"I had a considerable amount written at the time of the bathing party. I had intended reading it to you the next day, then—this fantastic thing happened. Perhaps you are no longer interested."

"I am indeed. Please bring the manuscript to-morrow morning. I promise you we shall be quite undisturbed. I am pining to hear it read."

"If it bores you, you must stop me."

"Nothing you write could bore me. . . . James, do you think Tite will get the reward?"

He flushed a little. "I imagine he will."

"Do you think he deserves it?"

"Well, it is certain that he found Miss Vaughan."

"Do you feel anything mysterious in his finding her?"

"Yes."

"What did Tite say when he came back?"

"Simply that he had found her and wanted the reward."

"It has been a strange affair," she said.

"Very strange."

"I was terribly frightened, James."

"I know."

There was a silence, then she said:—

"James, it's a fine thing to live with a forest all about you, you writing a beautiful book and fishing in your river, Philip building a church and raising crops! As for me—" she laid her hand on her heart—"here I am in the midst—as happy as a queen with my own roof over my head and my babies all about me!"

Wilmott's smile was curiously both tender and grim.

"You deserve to be," he said.

The next day he brought the manuscript and seated in the cool shade of the drawing-room he read aloud to her. While she listened, her gaze was intent on his face across which many expressions flitted, but through them all showed a certain battered wistfulness and an inviolate dignity. In repose, Wilmott looked singularly undefeated and even cold. As Adeline listened to the unfolding of the tale she recognized herself in the heroine and, for all his attempts at disguise, Wilmott in the hero. But this only increased her enjoyment. With her elbow on the arm of her chair and her chin in her palm she drank in every word and pronounced it a masterpiece. She could scarcely bear to wait for the ending. She begged him to waste no more time but to concentrate with all his might in completing the romance. It would be a great success. It would rival *The Mysteries of Udolpho*.

When Wilmott returned home he found Tite cleaning a fine salmon for their evening meal. The bright scales flew from the sharpness of his knife like sparks from an anvil. His slim brown torso was bare but he wore an old straw hat. He looked up smiling. He held up the fish for Wilmott's inspection.

"Boss," he said, "it is a fine fish."

"Yes, Tite, it's a fine one, and especially as the fishing has been poor of late. That is a good knife you have."

Tite turned the knife over in his hand and gazed reflectively at it. "Boss, it is a present from my cousin on the Reserve."

"Your relations are very kind to you."

"Yes. My cousin is descended from a great chief. He is all Indian but I am part French."

"I know. Tite, do you feel yourself different from the pure Indians?"

"Boss, if pure means good, I am as pure as they are." He sat back on his bare heels and looked up at Wilmott. "But that Mees Daisy says I have an Indian mouth and French eyes. Do you think I have?"

Wilmott exclaimed, in sudden anger—"If you mention Miss Daisy's name once more to me, Tite, I will throw you out, neck and crop!"

"Very well, Boss. But I have something I want to show you." He took off his hat and out of its crown brought a paper packet. He opened it and showed it to be made up of clean bank notes.

"The reward!" ejaculated Wilmott. "Is it all there?"

"Yes, Boss. But we had better take it into the house and count it." He held the bank notes to his nose and sniffed them. "I like the smell of money, Boss, but it smells better when it has been about more."

"Mr. Vaughan should not have handed over such a sum to a boy like you. He should have given it to some responsible person to keep for you. But, of course, I shall do that."

"Mr. Vaughan said he would keep it for me but I said I wanted it all—right away. He seemed to want to get rid of me."

"Well, wash your hands and we'll go in and count the notes."

Tite obediently laid the fish in a basket and washed his hands at the river's edge. In the house Wilmott sat down by the table in the kitchen and counted the money.

"One hundred pounds," he declared. "It is a lot of money for you to have earned so easily, Tite."

"Boss, it was not so easy. I searched the bush for a long while before I found her. You see, I do not say her name, Boss, as you told me not to. I wonder if my grandmother will still think she is a harlot when she hears of the good fortune she has brought me."

"We shall not discuss that."

Wilmott looked reflectively at Tite. What a change had taken place in the boy during this year of their close association. He could write a good clear hand. He could read any book Wilmott gave him and reading absorbed him completely. Every day his vocabulary was enlarged. He was studying history, geography, mathematics, and Latin. He was worthy of a good education, Wilmott thought. He said:—

"Your future is now assured, Tite. This reward, added to what I can do for you, will put you through college. You may be able to enter a profession if you work hard. What do you think you would like to be? Have you thought of it?"

Tite drew up a chair and faced Wilmott across the table.

"I want to be just what you are, Boss," he said.

Wilmott gave a bark of laughter. "That's no ambition at all," he said.

"It is enough for me, Boss," Tite returned. "Just to live here alone with you and fish in the river and grow a few things on the land and read books in the evenings, is all I want."

Wilmott was touched. "It suits me, too," he said, "better than any other life I can imagine. You've been a good boy, Tite, and I'm very fond of you."

"And I am very fond of you, also, Boss. Like mine, your eyelashes are long and your neck like bronze column. But I cannot say that your mouth—"

"What did I tell you, Tite?" said Wilmott. "If you think you will please me by applying to me the foolish things that girl said of you, you are much mistaken."

"Of course I am, Boss. I am sure she is a harlot."

"Now," said Wilmott, ignoring the last remark, "I am going to deposit this money in the bank for you, to be drawn on as needed. Do you agree?"

"Oh, yes, Boss. But could we keep back a pound or two to buy us a few treats, such as candied fruit and bull's-eyes?"

"I shall buy those for you," said Wilmott.

"But I should like to buy them with my own money, Boss. You see, the wages you pay me are not very high and I give something to my grandmother. Now that I come to think of it, I give all my wages to my family."

"Balderdash!" said Wilmott, but he flung him a pound note. "Take it," he said testily, "and do what you like with it."

"Mille remerciments," said Tite, smiling. "You see I can speak a little French, on occasion, Boss."

XXII

The Church

A WEEK later, Daisy Vaughan left her uncle's house and returned to Montreal. It was understood that the nervous and physical strain she had been under had made a complete change necessary. The Whiteoaks did not see her before her departure but those who did declared that she looked not in the least ill or dejected. Indeed Kate Brent said that Daisy had never looked better or been more talkative. It had been as good as a play to hear her description of the days she had been lost in the forest. She had had encounters with wild animals which had been seen by no other in that vicinity for a generation. But she seemed willing to return to Montreal. She could no longer endure, she said, to remain in such a backwater.

Colonel Vaughan accompanied his niece on the journey. Her visit had been an expensive one for him. Besides providing for her for a year, which included the buying of some quite expensive clothes, there had been considerable cost connected with the searching party, to say nothing of the large reward paid to Tite. Now there was the expense of the journey.

After Daisy's return to Montreal she corresponded regularly with Lydia Busby for some time. She wrote of the gaiety of that town, the *soirées,* the balls. She filled Lydia with a mad desire to do something of the sort. At last came the news of Daisy's engagement to a South American artist who had been painting in the Laurentians; and finally invitations to her wedding. She and her husband were to leave at once for Paris where they would for some years make their home.

But though these letters caused much disturbance in the breasts of the young Busbys, so that their father was put to it to keep them in order, they made little impression at Jalna. There, with the harvest to be garnered, the winter quarters for the growing number of livestock to be got ready, the house to be prepared for an impending visit from Adeline's parents, the building of the church to be sufficiently completed for consecration and the christening of Ernest, little interest was left over for the doings of the outer world. Adeline and Philip consigned Daisy to the past.

In truth, Philip could have very well done without this visit from his parents-in-law. He was somewhat tired of the three Courts who were still at Jalna. However it had been arranged that they were to return to Ireland with the older members of the family. Otherwise Philip feared they might have remained throughout the winter, for they had already expressed a desire to indulge in skating and snowshoeing.

Philip's face, in those days, expressed a serenity that might well have roused the envy of men of a later day. He was up almost at dawn. At night he was no more than healthily tired and was still so full of interest in all he had to do that he could scarcely bear to go to his bed. When he saw his heavy wagons, drawn by his ponderous farm horses, roll into the barn with their weight of barley, wheat or oats, his heart swelled with pride. It was not that he had much land under cultivation as yet but that what was cultivated had borne so well. Then there were his cattle, his pigs and his sheep, all flourishing and with good shelter and plenty of fodder for the coming winter. Above all, there was Adeline, the picture of glowing health and so happy in the new life! There were his children growing each day in strength and intelligence. Gussie already knew her letters, was learning to sew and could say by heart and without a mistake several poems suitable to her age. Nicholas, not yet two, might have passed for three, so upright, so full-chested, so stirring was he. His mop of curls now touched his shoulders and the combing out of their tangles caused him to fill the house with his cries of rage and pain. Ernest was an angel with his downy fair head, his forget-me-not blue eyes, and his smile that was even sweeter because it was toothless.

Nero worshiped all three children with a dark, stubborn, masterful worship. He would endure all three sprawling on his back at once but, if Nicholas went too near the edge of the ravine, he would draw him back by his dress, for somewhere in Nero's mind there remained a picture of Nicholas shooting downward to the river in the perambulator.

One morning in September, when goldenrod and Michaelmas daisies blazed in bloom about the new church, Adeline and Philip were standing together inside its doors, admiring the effect of the long strip of crimson carpet that extended from where they stood, up the chancel steps to the altar. Every day they came to the church. They had followed each step in its progress. They had a peculiar sense of achievement in it quite different from their feeling about Jalna. Jalna had beauty and some elegance. But here was a plain building with shiny, varnished pews, gray plaster walls and no stained-glass windows to mellow its light. Yet here was to be their spiritual home. Here was the link between them and the unknown forces of creation. Here their children would be baptized, their children married. Here, when their time came, would be read their own burial service. But this last was so distant, so misty in the mysterious future, that the thought of it gave them no pain.

The crimson carpet had put the final touch to the building, as a church. It was of excellent quality and had been expensive. But both felt that it was well worth the cost. The fact was, it made the church look holy. It was a glowing pathway from entrance to altar. When the foot touched it, calmness and peace stole upward into the soul. The money for it had been sent by Philip's sister, Augusta. This evening Adeline would sit down at her writing bureau and tell them just how imposing it looked.

The Dean had put his hand into his pocket and paid for the organ. It was not a pipe organ. No one would have expected that, but it was of a reliable make and guaranteed to have a sweet tone. It stood to one side of the chancel, the pulpit towering above it. Wilmott had agreed to be organist and was expected that very morning to try it. As for the pulpit, Adeline had paid for that. From the first she had wanted a substantial pulpit. "I don't like to see the preacher popping up like a jack-in-the-box out of a little pulpit," she had declared. "What he says will go down better if he mounts three steps to say it and is surrounded by massive carving. The same man who carved our newel post can do it and I'll foot the bill." There were a few who thought the pulpit was a little too ornate for the church but on the whole it was much admired.

Adeline took Philip by the hand. "Let us go," she said, "and sit in our own pew and see what it feels like."

She led him to the pew they had chosen, directly in front of the pulpit, and they seated themselves decorously but smilingly. The pulpit rose portentously before them, as though already overflowing with sabbatical wisdom.

"Confess now," said Adeline, "I could not have done better in the way of a pulpit."

"My one objection to it is that I am afraid Pink will feel himself so impressive in it that he will preach too long. He is already inclined that way."

"Then I shall go to sleep and snore."

They heard a step behind them and turning saw Wilmott coming down the aisle. He was carrying a large music book.

"Here I am!" he said. "Have you waited long?"

They had forgotten he was coming but agreed they had been waiting for some time.

"I have been to the Rectory," said Wilmott, "and Mrs. Pink has given me a hymnbook. I'm rather sorry I promised to play this organ. I don't feel capable of playing church music properly. But I seem to be the only one willing to attempt it."

"Kate Brent could have," said Adeline, "but she is now a Catholic. Anyhow I like to see a man at the organ."

"Play the Wedding March," said Philip. "Let's hear something lively."

"I have not the music." Wilmott seated himself at the organ, opened it and placed the hymnbook on the rack. He remarked—"I admire the red satin behind the fretwork. It's a pretty organ."

"Yes," agreed Philip. "My brother-in-law donated it and my sister the carpet."

"I know," said Wilmott. "You are a generous family. Even if I had the money, the community would go churchless a long while before I should build one."

"That's not stinginess, James," said Adeline. "It's prejudice."

"Yes. I'm not sure religion is good for people."

"What could take its place?" asked Philip. "I'll wager you have nothing to offer."

"Life itself is good."

"Come now, Wilmott, be sensible. A man can't live by material things alone."

"Then let him gaze at the stars."

"The stars aren't comfortable on a stormy night. Religion is."

"You had better not let Mr. Pink hear you say such things," put in Adeline, "or he'll not allow you to play the organ."

"He has heard me on many occasions."

"And doesn't mind?"

"Not a whit. He is a bland, dyed-in-the-wool Christian and he is convinced that everyone will eventually come round to his way of thinking."

"And so will you," said Philip. "So will you."

"Perhaps." Wilmott pressed the pedals, touched the keys. He began to play a new hymn that only recently had been translated from the Latin. But Philip and Adeline knew the first verse and sang it through.

"O come, O come, Emmanuel,
And ransom captive Israel.
That mourns in lonely exile here,
Until the Son of God appear.
Rejoice! Rejoice! Emmanuel
Shall come to thee, O Israel."

Neither Philip nor Adeline considered how extraordinary were these words coming from the green heart of a Canadian woods. They sang them with gusto and at the end Philip exclaimed:—

"It is a capital organ."

"I don't see how you can tell," said Wilmott drily, "singing as you were at the top of your voices."

"Oh, James, you are a cross old thing!" cried Adeline, going to his side.

"Well, you seem to have a service in full swing," came a voice from the door.

It was Dr. Ramsey. He entered and, after inspecting the new

acquisitions, said—"Congratulate me. Lydia Busby and I are to be married."

Adeline clapped her hands. "Splendid! I've seen it coming. Oh, I am glad!"

"A delightful girl," said Philip. "I congratulate you most sincerely."

Wilmott came forward and added his more guarded felicitations.

"It will be the first ceremony in the church," said the doctor. "We want to be married without delay."

"No," said Philip. "My son's christening is to be the first."

"And we cannot have him christened," added Adeline, "till my parents arrive from Ireland."

Dr. Ramsey regarded the Whiteoaks truculently. "Do you mean to say that my marriage must be postponed to give way to your child's christening?"

"I am sorry," said Philip. "But I'm afraid that is so."

"Then you consider that you own this church?" exclaimed Dr. Ramsey, his color mounting.

"Well, not exactly," said Philip.

"I suppose," said the doctor, "that Lydia and I can be married somewhere else. There is a church at Stead."

"No need to get huffy," said Philip.

"I'm not huffy. I'm simply astonished that I should be asked to postpone my wedding ceremony for the baptism of an infant."

Adeline folded her arms across her breast and faced the doctor.

"I should think," she said, "that as you brought the infant into the world, you would show a little consideration for him."

Dr. Ramsey had nothing to say in reply to this.

Adeline continued—"And, if I know Lydia Busby, she will want time for her preparations and not to be rushed to the altar as though there were need for urgency."

Again Dr. Ramsey could think of nothing to say.

As they stood staring at each other they little thought that her unborn son was to marry his unborn daughter and that these two were to become the parents of a future master of Jalna.

The embarrassing situation was pushed aside by the entrance of Conway, Sholto, and Mary, from the vestry. Sholto at once mounted the pulpit and, with a sanctimonious expression, intoned:—

"In the beginning God created the Courts."

"Come down out of that, you young rascal," said Philip.

But Sholto continued—"And God saw that the Courts were good. And later on God created the Whiteoaks. And the son of the Whiteoaks looked on the daughter of the Courts and he perceived that, though ill-favored, she was lusty, and he took her to wed."

Now Mr. Pink also entered from the vestry. He came up behind Sholto and lifted him bodily from the pulpit and deposited him on the floor.

"It is well for you, my boy," he said, "that the church is not yet consecrated but, as it is, I must severely censure you for making light of the Holy Scriptures."

"I was just telling him to stop it," said Philip.

Adeline exclaimed, to cover her brother's delinquency:—

"Oh, Mr. Pink, you should have come sooner and heard Philip and me singing a hymn!"

Coming to her aid Wilmott added—"The organ has an excellent tone, sir. Should you like to hear me play on it?"

In the vestry a carpenter began loudly to saw and, in the vestibule, another to hammer. Peace was restored.

XXIII

A Variety of Scenes

ADELINE'S parents arrived three weeks later. They were just in time for the ceremony of consecrating the new church. After the service the Bishop spent the night at Jalna. There had been a large dinner party and the neighborhood was happily excited. It was agreed that the church was handsome, the Bishop affable, and that Mr. Court and Lady Honoria were the most perfectly bred, good-humored and likable people imaginable.

This praise included Adeline's brother, Esmond Court, who had accompanied his parents without any previous warning. It seemed that they had had no time to write because Lady Honoria had decided only at the last moment to bring him. As Conway, who was not nearly so attractive, had picked up a quite well-off Canadian girl, Lady Honoria saw no reason why Esmond should not do even better for himself. He was the opposite of his two brothers already at Jalna, being dark and handsome, with a resemblance to Adeline. He made himself very agreeable to Philip but Philip could not help feeling that six of his wife's relations in the house at one time was rather a lot.

Some days after his arrival, Renny Court took to his bed with an attack of lumbago. He might have been the first sufferer from that ailment, so loud were his complaints and so convinced was he that it would be the end of him. He constantly demanded applications from without and doses from within so that the house was in a ferment of attendance on him. However, when he at last threw off the attack, his cure was complete. He first appeared downstairs supported on either side by Lady Honoria and Adeline. They progressed along the hall to the dining room with him leaning heavily on them, while he now and again uttered ejaculations of pain. The rest of the family followed with expressions of commiseration. But once he was seated at table with the roast quail on toast in front of him, with a glass of excellent claret by his plate, he was himself again. He was delighted by everything. If he had said things in disparagement of Canada, he now took them back. Jalna was a marvel of achievement. When he was sufficiently recovered to inspect the estate with Philip, he could not say too much in praise of its shipshapeness. There was nothing he liked so much to see as a place in good order and Philip was forced to admit that any suggestions he had to make were excellent.

As for Lady Honoria, the visit was one long happiness to her. To see her daughter so well established, where she had feared to find her in a wilderness, was a joy. To be reunited to her younger sons, even though they gave her so much worry, was a satisfaction. Above all, her grandchildren were a delight to her. Gussie was so intelligent, already so womanly in her ways, that she was a pleasing companion. To be sure, she had a temper but what Court had not? She and Nicholas did a good deal of hair-pulling. But what a darling he was! And Ernest was an enchanting baby. He seemed to know that he was to be the centre of attraction in the next party.

Lady Honoria herself seemed rejuvenated by the acquisition of the new tooth, a miracle of dentistry. She looked more like a sister to Adeline than a mother. In the exhilarating October weather, with the countryside aflame in scarlet and gold, she inspected the flower border and kitchen garden in the making. The little goat, on whose neck she had tied the bell, seemed to remember her for it followed her everywhere. She would collect the most brilliant of the autumn leaves to take back to Ireland with her. She herself originated a design of them for a mantel drape she was embroidering for Adeline. As for the church, Lady Honoria was never tired of doing things for its embellishment. Before she left home, she had embroidered an Easter altar cloth in a design of lilies, and also a beautiful stole for Mr. Pink. Now, out of her own slender purse, she had ordered a crimson cushion and four crimson hassocks for the Whiteoak pew.

Sometimes she and little Augusta would go to church together and wander happily about it. Gussie was so good you could trust her anywhere. When the little girl grew up and even when she was an old woman, she could remember this companionship between herself and her grandmother and could recall Lady Honoria's lovely smile quite clearly.

Jalna was teeming with vitality and Esmond Court had added a large share of it. He had a talent for bringing out the liveliness of others. He was pleased with himself and the world from morning to night, unless he were crossed, when he would display a most violent temper. But it was soon over. Philip had an exhibition of this in a fencing contest between Esmond and Mr. Court. Both were expert fencers and were giving an exhibition of their skill in the library. Suddenly something went wrong. It was a question of rules. An argument broke out. The faces of the fencers became masks of fury. Each set about demonstrating his own point of view. The foils flashed. It seemed for a moment that one or the other would be pierced to the vitals. Lady Honoria and Adeline shrieked. Mary turned faint. Recklessly Conway and Sholto flung themselves between the fencers. To Philip's astonishment the storm subsided as suddenly as it had arisen. With Sholto still clinging to him, Esmond apologized to his father and was forgiven but he was still trembling with anger, while Renny Court's hard features showed a triumphant grin.

"Oh, Dada," cried Adeline, "you were by far the most to blame! You nearly ran Esmond through!"

He made a grimace of annoyance. "Always against me, aren't you, Adeline? If my son cut me piecemeal you'd declare I was to blame!"

"Well, well," said his wife. "It's all over and do put those nasty swords away, children."

In these days almost all of Adeline's time was given to preparation for the christening. It turned out that Lydia Busby was quite willing to wait till that event was past, before marrying. On his part, Dr. Ramsey was anxious to hasten the event, so that he might join the shooting party Philip was organizing for his father-in-law. Renny Court was eager to make such an expedition for the sake of seeing the Northern wilds and such deer, elk, moose, bears, wildcats, or apes as might inhabit them. As his visit drew on he became less complimentary about the country.

Lady Honoria had a friendship of many years with Lord Elgin, now Governor-General of Canada. His duties had brought him to Kingston and, having received a letter from Lady Honoria, he was willing to extend his journey westward in order to renew their friendship and to act as godfather to her grandson. He arrived at Jalna on the day before the christening, a handsome gentleman of strong will who had a liberal and emphatic interest in the country. A few years before he had been the centre of a storm, when he had, as the English Canadians thought, favored the French. In Montreal he had been attacked with stones and his carriage badly broken and battered. But he had come through the trouble victorious and was now the most popular man in the entire country. He seemed not at all tired by his journey and he and Lady Honoria made lively conversation, talking of mutual friends. All was easy and natural. Even the weather, when the morning of the christening came, was perfect, a summer-like warmth blessing the autumn brilliance of the woods. Carriages conveyed the party from house to church where windows and doors stood open and Wilmott, in his best broadcloth, was already seated at the organ.

The church was half-filled with invited guests, for the Whiteoaks by this time had a large acquaintance. To be sure, the church was small and it did not take a crowd to fill it. Soon the vacant pews were overflowing with the country folk who had come from far and near to have a glimpse of Lord Elgin. Never had there been such a christening in those parts. The centre of it all lay dozing in his mother's arms, his long, tucked, embroidered and lace-trimmed robe almost touching the floor. His cape, his bonnet, were a marvel of elegance and intricacy. His two pink hands, with fingers extended like starfish, lay helpless as though washed up on the expanse of satin. In addition to Lord Elgin, Colonel Vaughan and Captain Lacey were godfathers and Mrs. Vaughan his godmother. Surely no godmother ever looked more benign than she, in her lavender silk with her prematurely white hair in full waves beneath her flowered bonnet! Adeline placed the infant in her arms and she stood, flanked by the three godfathers, facing Mr. Pink across the font.

This font, which was her gift to the church, was a handsome one and Ernest was the first child to be marked with the sign of the cross from its blessed brim. Adeline and Philip, with her parents and brothers, stood in a group near by. Lady Honoria held Gussie by the hand and Gussie's other hand held Nicholas. The two were dressed alike, in short-sleeved low-necked frocks with pale blue shoulder knots and fringed blue sashes. As a matter of truth they looked so lovely that even the presence of Lord Elgin was overshadowed by them.

Mr. Pink's sonorous voice now came:—

"Dearly beloved, forasmuch as all men are conceived and born in sin; and that our Saviour Christ saith, none can enter into the Kingdom of God, except he be regenerate and born anew of water and of The Holy Ghost . . ." The service proceeded, the congregation taking their part, according to the ancient form. At last Mr. Pink, turning to the godparents, asked the prescribed and searching questions regarding the spiritual convictions of Ernest Whiteoak. Mr. Pink asked of the godparents:—

"Dost thou, in the name of this child, renounce the devil and all his works, the vain pomp and glory of the world, with all covetous desires of the same, and the carnal desires of the flesh, so that thou wilt not follow, nor be led by them?"

And they responded: "I renounce them all."

Still Ernest slept.

But when the moment came when Mr. Pink took him into his own arms and, saying his name in full tones, sprinkled him liberally with water from the font, Ernest opened wide his forget-me-not eyes and uttered a loud cry of protest and alarm. When Nicholas saw his little brother so treated, he thrust out his underlip, tears rolled down his cheeks, and he sobbed. Seeing Nicholas weep, Gussie also broke into tears.

Nero, who was patiently waiting in the porch, could not endure the sound of the children's crying. He pushed open the door with his strong muzzle and put his head into the church. He looked about him with a lowering expression till he saw the white-robed figure at the font with the baby in its arms. Nero advanced into the church, fixing Mr. Pink with his eye and lifting his lip.

"For heaven's sake, take that brute out!" muttered Philip to Sholto, who sprang forward, grasped Nero by the collar, and dragged him back to the porch. A titter ran through the church. Lady Honoria comforted the children.

Ernest Whiteoak, having renounced the devil and his works and recovered from the shock of baptism, looked about him and smiled. He placed the finger tips of one tiny hand upon the finger tips of the other and regarded the assemblage magnanimously. Wilmott pressed down the loud pedal and all joined their voices to the organ accompaniment. They sang:—

" 'T is done! that new and heavenly birth
Which re-creates the sons of earth,
Has cleansed from guilt of Adam's sin
A soul which Jesus died to win."

The hymn swelled onward and upward into the Doxology.

There were white flowers on the altar, and the silver candlesticks presented by Lady Honoria. All the red and gold and green leaves, with bits of blue sky showing between, gave the windows an aspect even richer than that of stained glass. The congregation moved happily down the aisles, the little Pink boys in plaid dresses being barely restrained from capering by their mother's hand. The church overflowed into the graveyard where as yet there was but a single grave, that of a young bird which Lady Honoria and Gussie had found and buried there. The church bell, presented by Elihu Busby, pealed forth in rejoicing.

At Jalna, the doors between library and dining room were thrown open and long tables were loaded with refreshment. The infant's health was drunk in punch made from Lady Honoria's own receipt.

Another and more substantial meal was partaken of by a more intimate party before Lord Elgin left. In addition to the family there were the Pinks and the churchwardens and their wives. Elihu Busby could not restrain himself from being critical of the policy of the Governor-General toward French Canada.

"It is no wonder," he said, "that the English Canadians showed resentment and threw stones at Your Lordship's carriage!"

Lord Elgin laughed tolerantly. "Well, I have got even with them," he said. "For I have never yet had that battered vehicle repaired but drive everywhere in it so that the world may see how badly they behaved."

"I can't agree," said Busby, "in your coddling of the French. Make 'em English by force, I say."

"No, no," returned Lord Elgin. "I encourage them to use their native ability for the Empire, while assuring them of protection. Who will venture to say that the last hand which waves the British flag on American ground may not be that of a French Canadian?"

Before he left, he disclosed the fact that he was soon to go to India to act as Viceroy. Renny Court exclaimed:—

"Congratulations, sir! Who would not prefer India to this wilderness? Yet here my daughter and son-in-law came of their own free will and already I see the moss collecting on them. Philip's sword has become a ploughshare and as for Adeline—why, that girl was a beauty once and look at her now! A rough-handed, red-faced country wench!"

"If," said Lord Elgin, "I meet anyone half so delightful in India, I shall be content."

The guests were gone. It was afternoon of the following day. Philip and Adeline were strolling hand in hand across the lawn in the tranquil sunlight of declining Indian summer. They had talked over the events of the day, agreeing that all had passed off well and that Lord Elgin was a man of merit. Now they wanted only to be happy in each other's company, to look with satisfaction on the home they had built. It stood solid among its trees with an air of being ready for what might come.

"And look," cried Adeline, "the little Virginia creeper! It has turned bright scarlet just as though it were a grown-up vine!"

And so it had. Its tiny tendrils clung almost fiercely to the bricks as though it were in some way responsible for the staunchness of the house, and every leaf was crimson.

Then Philip exclaimed—"See the pigeons, Adeline! They are going south! Gad, what a horde of them!"

A number were flying overhead and these increased till they hung like a swift-moving cloud. The cloud was gray-blue but the wings in it made flashes of fire. Their strength reached from house to church and it was four hours and almost dark before they had passed. Then darkness closed about the house, the candles were lighted and extinguished. With her head on Philip's shoulder, Adeline slept.